3.1 :: **Ruin** 2

3.2 :: **Sell** 61

3.3 :: **Vote** 119

3.4 :: **Cure** 171

3.5 :: **Fire** 236

3.6 :: **Ends** 300

(bonus story)

3.7 :: Aeon 364

Floating Point written by Stefan Gagne
(copyright 2017)

stefangagne.com/floatingpoint

Keep supporting free web novels!

Dedicated to Bob Gagne, 1942-2015.
Father and friend.

WARNING: Floating Point contains triggering and
abusive language, and may depict sexual content and
violence. It is recommended for mature readers only.
(Responsibility falls to you to decide if you're, in
fact, mature.)

Floating Point 3.1 :: Ruin

Silent and dark was the void that this world hovered in. No air to carry sound through waves of compression, no light save from distant stars which went unmeasured. The world itself would be quite easy to overlook, given it lurked in the middle of nowhere, a simple tin can surrounded by pure vacuum...

But within that world, there was sound. No air, but plenty of sound. No stars, but plenty of light. None of it existed, except for those within the worldspace who had the right ears and eyes to take it all in. For them... there was the cheer of the crowd, the roar of explosions, the rustle of jungle foliage as warriors slid through it with conquest on their minds. Again, none of it physically existing, but all of it existing for those who cared.

The scene, to be more specific, took place within the virtual environment of a computer simulation. Its sky was a weather system, with particle effects for clouds and a volumetric lighting source for a sun. The denizens of this world, whether they realized it or not, would not be considered "alive" by any biological standard... they existed as code, ones and zeroes, somehow twisted into sentient shapes through years of data mutation. An imaginary world, for imaginary people.

Two observed this imaginary world with concern:

One observer, a Program in the shape of a woman with flames licking at her hair. As a rule, that which did not exist could not burn, but she elected to take it a step farther by letting it burn without consuming. Fire didn't have to be physically destructive if it could be virtually decorative, after all. But her impeccable style wasn't what she watched with concern; it was the warriors in the vaguely diamond-shaped jungle before her, five on five, fighting for territory control through roughly hewn lanes.

Five of them were her students; five of them were the opposition, come to her home turf to kick them out of their own jungle. And, unfortunately, doing a very good job of it. *That* was her cause of concern, as she stood helpless on the sidelines, unable to communicate with her team until they came back in victory or defeat.

As for the other observer... that one was even farther away than the sidelines, farther than the jungles and the skies above. Farther still than the tin shell that encompassed it all. That biological observer hung in the silent and dark void, watching this all transpire as the ultimate spectator...

But, the second observer wasn't involved in the disaster to come. She can be overlooked, for now.

When five fell and five rose, the second of three matches decided, the woman with fire in her hair pulled her team aside for a pep talk prior to their final outing into the jungle.

"Okay, so in simple terms, tell me why exactly you ****ed up," Winder/Spark requested, pacing back and forth in the school locker room.

Her team, already dejected from the crushing game-two loss after what seemed like a crushing game-one win, had no response.

Name: Spark

Home: Floating Point

Org: Teacher,
PS#7E00FF

"C'mon, we don't have all day here," she reminded them. "#TickingClock. And you're not going to learn anything if I just smack you upside the head with wisdom. You grow into your wisdom through reflection. So reflect, and tell me how you ****ed up. First one to admit their mistakes gets a candy bar."

Sheepishly, the team's solo lane pusher raised his hand.

"I was out of position when we were setting up for a gank," he admitted. "I heard the audible but didn't move to support the team, because I was too busy trying to kill the fucking Robotman in my lane—"

"Language," Spark snapped, a tiny burst of fire at her fingertips courtesy of her weaponized nail polish.

"—because I was too busy trying to kill the Robotman, ma'am."

"Exactly. One candy bar for Jakob," the coach declared, with a small amount of pride. "Admitting how you ****ed up is the key to learning how not to **** up. First game, you rolled out there and executed every play in our book, ramming them straight right up the *** in the process. Good! And then you got sloppy, all of you. Out of position, wasting ult abilities on lone targets, getting baited into trap situations. What do we call that?"

"Stupidity?" the duo-lane healer suggested, after raising her hand.

"Overconfidence," Spark corrected. "The enemy knew their plays couldn't beat yours, so they waited for you to beat yourselves. They played a reactive game. Now you're tied, one-to-one, and they've got your number. So. How do you win the last round...?"

Which got the healer's ire up. Having taken the most hits during the game, constantly pasted by the opposition to keep her from recovering from every bad situation they fell into, it's understandable why she'd be salty... but Spark stood her ground, in face of the tirade.

"Who fucking cares? We lost!" the healer declared. "If you idiots won't support your support, how am I supposed to heal you? It's the curse of the Fighting Purples all over again. This crappy little school with its crappy little team always chokes when it counts! Fuck this. Let's just AFK in the spawn and... get this... uh, over with."

Because Spark had simply stood there, staring down the malcontent, letting her get her words out... knowing each one dug the hole a little deeper. Coach would have no toxic attitudes on her team, but rather than head them off, she'd let them spew until they realized their mistake.

"You done?" she asked, to be certain.

"Yes'm," the healer spoke, sitting back down.

"Good. Because you're right about one thing: this isn't over until you decide it's over," Spark stated. "If you guys want to troll the enemy and just lurk in spawn, like you're squatting in the respawn penalty box, hey, feel free. Make yourselves laughingstocks, that'll sure show them who's boss. Or... and this is just a suggestion from your humble teacher... you go out there and you ****ing fight. You stand, and you fight. Win or lose, you *fight*."

"Even if they've got our number...?" Jakob the solo laner asked.

"*Especially* if they've got your number. Nobody said #ChallengeOfChampions was easy. Life isn't easy, but you fight anyway, because it doesn't matter if you win or lose in the end... only that you made your stand. Now. I want all five of you out there in that jungle, I want to hear you scream, I want to see you bleed. I want to know that you're *alive*. You're the ones**** Fighting Purples, and the crowd is either gonna watch you beat the ever-loving **** out of those Graygarden Academy ****s or watch you go down swinging. Either way, they'll respect you, and you'll respect yourself. Are we clear?"

A mumbling chorus of "okays" sounded off in response.

"I'm sorry, what?" Spark asked, cupping a hand to the virtual simulacrum of a human ear attached to her avatar. "You sure don't sound alive to me. *Are you alive*?!"

Finally, a stirring of energy. While the responses varied from "Yes" to "Yeah" to one "Fuck yeah!" all of them carried considerably more energy.

"Right! And how does it *feel* to be alive?!"

More screaming of the positive variety. Good. Good. Spark nodded, satisfied.

"Now get your ***es out there and you don't come back until you've shown everyone what you are," she ordered, pointing to the tunnel out to the school's gaming field. "Live or die, you get out there and light that fire which burns down Graygarden's ****ing world! If they're leaving with a trophy, I also want them leaving with post-traumatic stress disorders thanks to the ones**** flying purple people eaters that they stole that trophy from. #*GO!*"

Which is why the timid little K-12 students came roaring out into the jungle with battle cries that could be heard all the way from the commentary booth. Spark relished in the sound of it, and in the sound of the hometown crowd in the stands who enjoyed the show.

Game time.

If only they could see her now.

Her brother, Winder/Tracer. He disliked games as a general rule, particularly childish games like Challenge of Champions. Nope, Tracer was too busy tinkering with fantastic technologies that would one day transform Programkind into golden gods of all they surveyed, and so on and so forth. Ever since finding his true calling at the clinic as a project manager, he'd been spending time away from his family in favor of personal causes...

Two years of professional work, from the boy who'd never held a solid job at any other point in his life. From childhood to adulthood, he'd been obsessed with revenge against the ones who killed their mother. (The mother they wanted, rather than the mother they were saddled with.) He'd swapped one obsession for another; arguably a better one, a more positive one, but an obsession nonetheless. No way he'd peel himself away from that just to watch the crowning glory of this season's kiddie time school sports club.

But her lover, Projkit/Beta... why wasn't she here? Spark knew the answer, even if she didn't want to believe it. Beta's heart was in her code rather than her gaming hobbies, but she still appreciated a good CoC match. She'd been the one to encourage Spark in those early days, when she was having trouble connecting with the kids, feeling like she'd let them down time and time again. Beta was the heart, the guiding star of their little family. Beta should be right here next to Spark on the jungle sidelines, cheering the team on... but wasn't. And hadn't even sent word of why not...

And then there was the invisible family member, the one long since gone. 5o5o/Verity. Teacher, mentor, advanced motherhood substitute. Gone long ago, killed by a madman and the madman's puppet. (Even the echo that remained of her was nowhere to be seen, having vanished into the dark for two full years.)

Still, despite her absence, Spark liked to think that Verity would be proud of her pupil at this moment. So if her brother couldn't give a toss and her lover couldn't work up the emotional energy to come out of hiding... that distant love would have to do. It'd have to carry her through this tense moment...

The Fighting Purples were definitely fighting. Wildly fighting, aggressively fighting, pushing and striking and lashing out wherever they found an opening in the enemy's defenses. But in a five-on-five match, where the players didn't have the full view of the action as Spark did on the sidelines... they couldn't see the enemy rallying after each desperate gamble. Couldn't suss out Greygarden's tactical positioning, until it was upon them. For whatever ground her kids made, biting and clawing and grasping for all they could, Greygarden Academy just formed a solid bulwark and pushed back.

Spark's speech came from two intentions. One, to fire them up enough to go out there and win. Two, to cushion the inevitable emotional blow when they lose. The Purples, being a generic K-12 public school in a generic Athena Online server, weren't known for being champions. They'd never taken the cup, not once. To come farther than any team before, and choke at the end... it'd destroy them. And Spark, as much as she wanted to hug their pain away, knew that giving them some armor before that blow landed would have to do.

As the game clock ticked away and lanes started to fall... neither team made much headway. Greygarden's defenses were absolute, rebuking the wild attacks of PS#7E00FF. At this rate, her kids would fail, exhausting themselves just enough to allow the tactically superior if more timid Greygarden players to push on through...

And then, in the stands just behind Spark, kids and parents and teachers suddenly expressed disappointment. Quickly, Spark scanned the jungle below her coaching box at the sidelines... to see Jakob's ninja avatar drop under the metal fists of Greygarden's Robotman. He'd chased his nemesis out of position, getting flattened in the process...

Four on five, with her team at the disadvantage. Jakob popped back to the respawn penalty box in the distance, no doubt cursing and kicking the walls, waiting for that gate to open and let him back into the game. A momentary disadvantage like this was just what Greygarden was waiting for; with the Purples down a man, they could relax, and...

And grow overconfident.

Spark could see it, and hoped like null that her kids saw it. All five of Greygarden's players moving to take on Duke Geist, the giant NPC in the center of the map. In the late game, when players were strong enough, taking out this challenging enemy would grant them a massive boon that could easily tilt the game in their favor. With five strong and the enemy on the run, Greygarden was in exactly the right place to scoop up that boon and close out the game...

Duke Geist howled in anger, his mighty fists coming down on the Greygarden warriors. But it was no use; his damage wouldn't outpace theirs. Soon the towering pillar of demonic rage (complete with a jaunty little golden crown, symbol of his duchy's boon) would fall... unless someone interfered in that plan, of course.

"C'mon, c'mon, spot the play, spot the play..." Spark whispered under her breath, wishing she could communicate directly with her team. Unfortunately, as her observation point gave her information the players couldn't have, she was banned from talking to them during the game itself. All she could do was wait and watch, gripping the railing of the coaching booth with tight fists...

There. The Purples, rallying. Only four, but they had a plan.

First... a patch of acid, spat into the middle of Duke Geist's pit. Immediately the Greygarden team started taking damage from the acid, melting their armor, leaving them vulnerable to further attacks...

And then, in a play that would forever be called "The Purple Slam Dunk," their healer smashed right into the middle of the enemy team from above, her Priestess's staff smashing down into the acid to amplify its damage tenfold.

Few people bothered playing Priestess on offense. Yes, she could ramp up the damage of her fellow characters, but primarily she was used to heal them defensively. With no attacks of her own, that secondary ability often went overlooked. Except by the Fighting Purples, trained by a former pro player who was always looking for weird synergies from "joke" characters. One who took a goofy female ninja in pink, added to the game as pure eye candy, and rocked entire teams with it. That sort of intuition taught them that Priestess was more than meets the eye...

Five deaths. The entire Greygarden team caught in an explosion of acid, melting them down faster than they could escape the pit of doom.

Immediately the Purples dove into the pit to join their Priestess, and soon Duke Geist was no more. Each now wore a golden crown, the boon of the duke, and were pushing hard down the middle lane to win the game.

"**** YES!" Spark declared, leaping to punch the air in joy...

...and landing to face the crowd behind her, wildly cheering, all eyes on the four players forming a living wedge of destruction.

Almost all eyes.

Intuition and analysis, the two tools Spark always brought to the table. Not as coldly rational as her brother, not as keenly observant of emotion as her lover, but a comfortable midpoint between the two. And that midpoint was telling her, loud and clear... why are those three watching the respawn box?

Jakob had twenty seconds before he could escape his confinement, and those three adults in the crowd were very, very intently staring at him. Nobody should be able to look away from that game-winning play, especially not to watch a player who couldn't possibly get involved in it. Not unless...

Without further thought, Spark hurled herself over the railing, and into the jungle.

Warning messages popped up in front of her. Coaches weren't allowed to interfere in the play; if she continued, she risked disqualifying her team. Ignoring them, she ran. She ran down the battle-scarred lane, ran to the home base of the Fighting Purples, ran for the penalty box where Jakob stewed and simmered...

The three emerged from the jungle as well, keeping pace alongside her.

Two quick snaps of her fingers, and Spark's hands were fire and passion. Twin jets of flame trailed behind her, weaponized malware in her fingernails lighting her way... before she twisted in mid-air, blasting two of the attackers, rolling to land in a martial arts stance just in front of the respawn box.

For the two she'd taken out, four more joined her. Not teachers, not fans. Not moderators, not cops. In an instant they'd produced stun sticks, malware that could crash any process they touched, backtracking through the physical simulation to gain illegal access to a Program's code... shutting it down, hard. If even one touched her, Spark would be out for the count, and her student defenseless...

Screaming, from the stands. More attackers were working their way through the mess, likely stunning and crashing anyone in their way. And, right on time, the announcement went up.

A giant translucent avatar, broadcast just above the jungle, for all to see. Behind her, an all-too-familiar icon...

"The Inquisition is here to hunt a sinner and agent of chaos," the pre-recorded woman announced. *"The innocent will not be harmed. Please remain calm, and stay out of our way. We are only here for Pwer/Jakob, and him alone. We wish no harm to the the faithful. I repeat, the Inquisition is here to hunt a sinner and agent of chaos..."*

Spark didn't have to look up to know the face she'd see, beseeching towards the panicking crowd. Nor could she look up, not with "Inquisition" terrorists stalking her, looking for an opening to attack through.

And Jakob? He cowered in his respawn box, despite the preprogrammed game systems telling him it was time to leave and rejoin the team.

"C-Coach?" he asked, confused as to why Spark was here, much less why men in white robes were stalking and surrounding them. "What...?"

One Inquisitor swept his stunner across the ground, casing the simulated jungle undergrowth to seize up and crash, exposing the ordinary default dirt underneath.

"You're protecting a sinner, Miss Winder," he warned. "We've completed our inquiry into Pwer/Jakob's communications, and determined he is a true agent of chaos. That boy is a troll, who terrorized and harassed countless vulnerable persons under the shameful veil of anonymity..."

Spark stood her ground, eyeing each Inquisitor as they made tentative steps forward.

"He's a kid, and kids are stupid. I should know, I was a kid and was *very* stupid," she admitted. "All of you back down, and go tell little miss high priestess that Spark will make sure her student gets a spanking. #WeCoolYo?"

The leader pointed his stun stick, to direct the attack.

"The only way to bring back the One is to purge all sin from our world," he declared. "No one harm Miss Winder, but put her down fast and take the boy. *Attack!*"

"Get down!" Spark ordered her student, summoning as much flame as the tiny swaths of malware at her fingertips could muster...

The jungle burned bright, as she blasted avatar after avatar. Fires burned away their limbs, causing avatar damage without permanently and fatally mangling their data. Each time one of those sticks swung in her direction, she rolled under or around it, striking out to cripple the attacker.

Hand-to-hand fighting with avatars had become a lost art. Most used backspacers or kill-9s, ranged weapons that cleanly erased data or crashed processes from afar. But even those used physical projectiles, as avatar contact would always be needed to deliver the malware payloads. For Spark, who had trained for years in the arguably pointless art of physical combat, taking down a bunch of zealots armed with basic attack software felt as effortless as breathing.

Assuming, of course, she wasn't overwhelmed by the numbers. And they didn't have those ranged weapons, with bullets she could only deflect with very, very precise strikes at midair. Like Greygarden's confidence in a five-on-four, the Inquisitors were plenty confident in a dozen-on-one attack, with more white-clad holy knights emerging from the jungle...

Barely hanging on, trying to blast them away one by one as they approached her cowering student, Spark had one thought: *Where the **** are the cops?!* (Her self-censoring module, still active, ran deep to avoid accidentally annoying parent-teacher groups.)

This was Athena Online, the safest of the three provider-nations. Government-authorized moderators, the police force of this land, they should've been here by now. A terrorist attack on a residential server, with *no* response?

The way Athena Online as a whole quietly looked aside from the Inquisitors whenever they stole someone away in the night was disgusting... and the silence as they held their tongues and watched the video releases the next day, the beheadings and executions that followed, that was the most disgusting act of cowardice Spark had ever witnessed.

Now, as even the cops turned a blind eye to fanatics determined to bring back their false god, Spark was going to lose a student. And why? Because he said mean things on a message board. Time was, young Spark would've taken vigilante justice on a kid like him. But old Spark saw the grays where others saw the black and whites... and knew whatever his crimes, they couldn't justify this.

So, she'd stand. She'd fight. She'd keep doing it, again and again, until she couldn't. Win or lose she'd make her insane birth-mother's cult know *true* pain...

The stunner that would've taken her out came down from above, a leaping strike she didn't have time to deflect.

Instead, the sharp crack of a backspacer's bullet intercepted that Inquisitor, tearing his data apart. Before he could hit the ground, there was no body to fall away, having been utterly vaporized.

More backspacers fired, as Spark dove into the respawn booth to cover Jakob's cowering form with her own body. The booth was a physical object; it would intercept a shot or two. Her own body could intercept another. It'd have to be enough, as the moderators got this situation under control...

But the battle cry she heard was not the familiar "*Police, freeze!*" she'd hoped for.

"*Do not forgive, do not forget!*" a digitally distorted voice called out. "*For the Nobodies and for FREEDOM!*"

"Oh, ****..." Spark exclaimed, hanging on tighter to Jakob.

But the boy, he was overjoyed. He would've leapt to his feet to cheer, if not for the teacher holding him down.

"Yeah! They're here!" he declared, happily. "Mah boys, yeah! Get 'em! Get those motherfuckers—!"

Spark didn't need to look up to know what was happening. The scene had played itself out all over Netwerk the last two years... white-clad religious nutcases fighting with black-suited anonymous nobodies, individuals in identical avatars. One side fighting for absolute control and absolute justice, the other side fighting for absolute chaos and absolute freedom... with mass murder as the inevitable side effect.

Rather than faces with features and eyes and mouths or anything of that, each wore a disembodied head, a 3-D mask... carved to look like a hand grenade of war, meshed with a flower of peace. Presumably some anonymous graphic designer thought it was ironic, or something.

"Jakob, you *idiot*," Spark hissed, breaking her own rule not to insult the kids. "You got involved with those psychopaths?!"

"They're gonna save Netwerk from the false One!" he recited. "Smashing the corrupt police state of the nazi moderators, and—"

Energy crackled around them, as the respawn box was vaporized by a stray shot.

With curses like brilliant stars flowing behind her, Spark scooped up Jakob in her arms and charged wildly into the fray. Blasting through the open war zone like a comet, straight through the walls of the jungle, straight through the wall of the school where the fighting had spilled over. Away. She had to get *away*, away from the chaos, and get enough time to link her connection to Jakob's for a proper escape. Standing and fighting was noble, but standing and dying was just stupid...

Only two places she knew he could go where they'd never reach her. Place her mother's madmen couldn't hack her way into. There was Floating Point, and... and...

She completed the leash to link Jakob's connection to her own, forcing him to follow as she dove through a broken window and out of the increasingly ruined school building...

...to land on soft carpets, surrounded by tasteful portraits.

Miss Cancel found them there, breathless and exhausted, just barely pulling themselves together to look presentable.

"Hey," Spark greeted. "Is Kincaid home? I've got a guest who needs some Horizon-grade protection."

Messenger windows flew across Spark's internal vision, making final arrangements and sending various confirmations. Yes, she survived the attack. Yes, everything's fine. Yes, she'd be by later to explain what went on. Yes, she'd gone to Kincaid's place. Yes. Yes, of course... etc., etc. Tracer could be such a bother when he actually took an interest in the well-being of others.

Didn't help that Spark had this persistent tone playing quietly in her auditory inputs... this weirdly echoing, low-pitched rumble of a choral note. Enough to fire up a very lovely headache, the sort that worried her brother considerably. Possibly some malware planted on her by the Inquisition, he'd reasoned. Worth looking into. Spark tried to put it out of her mind for now, pushing the ringing in her ears away to finish up the remaining communication tasks...

She'd also sent Beta a few messages, knowing that the woman back at Floating Point would be worried. And got no replies back. Worrying and surprising, that little twist, but the Messenger app indicated she'd received and read each message. So, Beta was fine. For varying degrees of "fine."

Which left the young ward in her charge, and what would become of him.

"Your parents are on the way," Spark informed him, closing down the last of the windows. "They want to go to the police, but trust me, you're safer here. After that sad performance, I wouldn't trust the Athena Online moderators farther than I could spit a physics object."

Jakob, for his part, sat on a tastefully plush couch in the middle of random bits of expensive furniture finery with confusion. He didn't even have time to change out of his game avatar, leaving him in a mish-mash of ninja garb and plate mail.

"Where is this place, anyway?" he asked. "Looks old. Old and boring..."

"It's safe, from both the Inquisitors and the Nobodies. That's all that matters."

"Look, you got the Nobodies totally wrong," Jakob insisted. "They're *free*, Coach. More free than anyone in Athena Online. No rules, no restrictions, no nazi control freaks! The only true way to find true expression is through anonymity, and they—"

"You don't even know what a nazi is!"

"A politically correct moderator who can't take a joke," he said, stating his own internal truth.

(Briefly Spark was tempted to dash back to Floating Point to grab the relevant Wikipedia entry for him to read, but opted not to bother.)

After a deep sigh, she tried to take it down to his level. "Look, I know the Chanarchy. You see me and you see some jock, yeah?" Spark guessed. "But you don't know the half of it. I've been around more blocks than you can imagine. I've... I've done *stuff*, okay? I know the #NastiestOfNasties this Netwerk can serve up. And that means I know the Nobodies. They're... nobody. Nihilistic pranksters who scrub their metadata before running wild, murdering and robbing and ruining everything of value. Above all, they are *dangerous*. You'll get yourself killed getting involved with them..."

"They're freedom fighters," Jakob insisted, refusing to budge. "Here to liberate us from the shackles of authority!"

She wanted to throttle the kid. She wouldn't, but hey, she *wanted* to. Wanted to shake up his world, and say: *I've fought the false One, I've torn down madmen with viral networks of polarized insanity, I've seen horrors you can't even imagine...*

Spark had been there, on the day they saved the world by damning it all. Her finger pulled the trigger.

At the time, it made sense. Shut down the false One, by anonymously leaking a simple program to reveal Nyx for the hoodwink artist she truly was. The pillars of faith would shake, but the world would go on with no puppet-tyrant at the helm. They'd won the day by shattering the sanity of the most faithful... including her mother, who refused to accept that she'd been the apostle of a lie.

Her mother... the cult of personality behind the Inquisition, a radical fringe of the Church of One which used vigilante justice to hunt down and execute enemies of the faith. Zeroes, sinners, maniacs. Much like her daughter did, once upon a time, but now taken to lethal ends...

And the core offense, the great sin that propelled Winder/Marybel onto that path of destruction? The anonymous release of the CheckOne software. Tracer had argued that they needed to operate from shadow, to avoid the backlash from the faithful. No name was attached to CheckOne, and that broke Marybel's back, that "anonymous superhackers" had fooled the world into thinking the One never existed. Since then... she'd declared war on those who used anonymity for nefarious purposes.

Escalation bred escalation. With the Chanarchy under siege by fanatics from Athena Online, the Nobodies formed. At first they were a defense force, guarding the interests of free servers. And then the trolls took control, because anybody could be a Nobody if they downloaded the avatar and mandatory metadata scrubbers. Anyone could wear their flower/grenade mask and wreak havoc in the name of freedom...

Hashtag mobs, all over again. All because they broke the Church of One. And then broke it again, when the prayer protocol was uninstalled... driving the faithful screaming down dark corridors of madness, while the world slowly went bankrupt due to no more pennies from heaven being minted...

Two years of chaos in Netwerk, while they sat pretty in their new jobs, enjoying their new adult lives. While kids like Jakob grew up in a world of turmoil and strife.

Headaches. A serious headache building in Spark's mind, code conflicts and paradoxes, stuff that just didn't make sense... all backed by that weird ringing in her ears. Jakob's insistence on the glory of the Nobodies wasn't a fight she could win on her best day, much less this day.

Which meant a new winning play. If nothing Spark could say as this kid's teacher would overthrow the allure of the masked freedom fighter, she had to take another approach.

"Fine. You believe what you want," she decided. "But you're gonna swallow this particular #PoisonPill: *you stole the victory* from your fellow Fighting Purples. They had it, they *had* it in their grasp with a play that'll go down in history, and you took it away from them when your shenanigans brought down mayhem on top of us all. The whole game was thrown out, Jakob. You took everything your friends worked for and **** all over it. And that you are *absolutely* going to own up to, once we get this death mark off your head. I'm gonna march you into that locker room and you're going to apologize to those kids who gave their all. Am I being #PerfectlyClear? Nod your head if I'm being #PerfectlyClear."

After the boy's mute nod, Spark turned on one heel and marched out of the room, closing the double doors behind her.

Kincaid waited on the other side, not wanting to interrupt that little speech with his presence.

"You handle yourself well," he noted. "You would've made a fine leader for the Horizon family, you know..."

"Not now, old man. Not. Now," Spark warned, waving a finger. "It's been a null of a day."

Horizon/Kincaid. One-time patriarch of the richest family in Netwerk, a man who could whisper a single word and destroy countless lives under the crushing weight of money. Also, coincidentally, the estranged father of Verity... the only mother Spark felt she had left, after recent events. That strange chain of relationships put Spark firmly in his good graces, perhaps to a dangerous degree. He'd long sought her daughter's prodigy to act as a proxy for Verity, despite Spark's reluctance.

Name: **Kincaid**

Home: **Horizon6/Horizon**

Org: **Horizon Family**

But those were days long past. He'd come to accept the new order of things, out of respect for Spark. And in a true sign of sacrifice, that acceptance led him to buy her out of a very sticky situation... at the expense of his position with the Horizon family.

"I do question why you'd bring the boy *here*, to my home server, instead of Floating Point...?" he asked, choosing not to belabor old business. "Surely your home is actually safer than mine. If anything, my server is in dire need of some upgrades, ones which my various kin have been postponing time and time again..."

"Really? I thought when you said jump, your family said #HowHigh."

"Yes, well. Times change," he said, with all that implied. "But I suppose Horizon6 is stable and secure enough to keep a few miscreants out. While I don't appreciate you hostelling a Nobody-sympathizing youth here, I do believe I can spare a few dozen empty rooms on the fly, until other arrangements can be made. Now, my question remains... why not Floating Point?"

"Because letting a Nobody-sympathizer into Floating Point is a terrible idea. I mean... he's just a kid, Kincaid. An easily impressed kid tagging along with a pack of predators, which makes him both a victim and a dangerous X-factor. I can't keep him in our homestead, not if its existence could leak back to the wrong ears."

"Pragmatic. Impressive. I thought you more of an idealist."

"Maybe I'm just getting old, like you," Spark suggested, with a grumble. "I care about Jakob, but not enough to risk my family."

"That's good. In the end, family's all anyone really has," Kincaid agreed. "Trust no one else."

"...I ****ing... hang on. ...that's better. I *fucking* hate that I actually agree with you on that," Spark said, after disabling her kid-friendly language filter. "I shouldn't agree with it. It's a negative, paranoid view of the world. But right now, I don't... I *can't* lead that kind of trouble to my doorstep. I don't do that shit anymore, Kincaid. I don't fight trolls and hackers while delving in the deep and dark. I've got adult responsibilities now..."

"You don't have to justify yourself to me, my dear. Netwerk's in a sorry state, is it not?" he said, gesturing for her to walk alongside him back to his favorite parlor. "Come, come. Let's talk. It's been too long."

"Yeah, I really don't have time," Spark said, refusing to follow. "Now that Jakob's secure I promised Tracer I'd check in at the Verity Clinic, make sure nobody tagged me with any slow-release malware during that fight. Unless you've added a twelve-part demonic chorus to the server's ambient noise...?"

"Pardon? A what?"

"#Nevermind. Anyway, I think he just wants to test some of his new deep-code scanning tools on me, but better to satisfy his curiosity now than put it off any longer. I should get going..."

"Very well. No more small talk and pleasantries; I'll get to the point so you can be moving along. Fact of the matter is that I don't know how long I can protect your student," Kincaid admitted. "This is... politically difficult for me, Spark. Officially Horizon is neutral in all internal Athena Online matters—"

"The Inquisition isn't strictly an Athena Online problem; half their raids are in the Chanarchy. And the Church of One's officially disavowed their actions, so you can't even say they're our hometown heroes..."

"Nevertheless, there's a certain unspoken-yet-positive sentiment through Athena Online in regards to their vigilante justice. People see chaos from the fall of the One, and look to whatever forces of order still exist that can save them. The Inquisition promises order, a return of their precious One, and that makes them politics. Besides, you took the boy to me rather than to the police, yes? Undoubtedly you believe certain members of the moderation force are sympathetic to the Inquisition, and would turn the boy over. That also makes this a matter of political asylum, and I'm afraid my family are... less tolerant of my pet causes, these days. I lack the sway to stop them if they choose to evict."

"#Bullshit."

"Sadly, not #Bullshit. Spark... I spent much of my capital, both literal and figurative, to save your life by purchasing the Verity Clinic. I have no regrets; your brother's done excellent work there, transforming it into an organization I can call my personal legacy with no small amount of satisfaction. But in establishing that legacy, I'm afraid I've spent my last. I'd love to help you more, but... there's only so much I can do."

With a sigh, he let his shoulders sag. An unheard signal brought forth Miss Cancel, to escort Spark to the server exit.

"That's not to say I won't do everything in my power to protect the boy," Kincaid promised. "But know that everything in my power may not be enough. Attend to your affairs, knowing your grandfather-of-sorts is attending to this. And good day."

No words exchanged with the terse Miss Cancel, as Spark stalked her way to the logout zone. Just a few taps to the side of her head, trying to get the ringing out of her ears.

Probably just exhaustion. Probably just the end result of a fairly intensive battle, driving her past her breaking point. She was getting older and older... despite, well, only being in her mid-twenties. She'd gone through enough wars and enough fights during those short years for three lifespans, and that wore down the body and soul. Besides, if the background noise was some sort of malware, Tracer would get it out. He'd always be there to bail his idiot sister out of whatever mess she got into.

"I'm not detecting anything unusual," he concluded.

Well, so much for that hope. The best minds of the Verity Clinic (formerly a corporate powerhouse under the name of Iteration) couldn't figure out why that noise kept coming and going from Spark's ears. They couldn't even sense a noise there at all, not even when Spark piped her sensory inputs directly into their instruments...

Winder/Tracer, her manipulative and calculating brother, had finally put those manipulative calculations towards the betterment of society. His team of technicians and coders were coming up with new medical treatments, new software upgrade packages, and new apps to improve daily life all over Netwerk. In a more positive age, their accomplishments would've been heralded... as is, they were drowned out in the news feeds by reports of strife, murder, and mayhem.

With one eye on those feeds, Spark kept tabs on the situation she'd bailed out from. PS#7E00FF had been nearly erased off the map, the entire school suffering data corruption and damage from the fighting between spontaneous forces of Inquisitors and Nobodies alike. By the time the state moderators had moved in to contain the situation, driving them back to their hidey-holes, the building had to be condemned. Teardown of the corrupt data and restoration would take days of hard work.

And the body count...

Well. Spark didn't intend to throw her own body on top of that pile of collateral damage.

"I'm telling you, I'm still hearing it," she insisted, annoyed at the thick web of glowing lines connecting her avatar to various data read-outs. She waved a hand through them, for what little that did. "It comes and goes, but it's this low rumbling tone..."

Tracer studied a log file provided to him by one of his many selves, frowning at the lack of data.

"...d'you have to use, y'know, your clone army to do this?" she asked. "It's creepy..."

"Forking my process into a multitasking array is one of the ways we cut down on overhead," one of the Tracers explained. "One salary for multiple man-hours of work. We're a charity, Spark, not a corporation; Kincaid's gala fundraisers and our own crowdfunding efforts are barely enough to maintain a full work force..."

"I don't see how you can stand it, though. There's... how many of you right now?"

The many copies of Winder/Tracer glanced at each other, across the room, doing the mental math.

"Fifteen?" the 'primary' Tracer guessed. "I tend to splinter a few times a day, before reintegrating back into my whole self. It tires me considerably in the end, but that's what a good night's rest at Floating Point is for..."

"Right. As someone who got forcibly copied a few times over, no way I could deal with that many of me around at once. It's... weird. I like being unique."

"Whereas I see no value in being unique. Spark, remember... we are not Humankind. We don't need to adhere to their biological or cultural constraints. They cannot be many, so they are not. We can be, so why not? At most, I waste processor overhead that could be dedicated to another unique Program. ...although if our plans for a beta grid go through, perhaps we wouldn't even waste that."

"Beta's what? Some project of hers?"

"No, no. 'Beta' as in 'software still in development and testing.' We'd like to... hmm. How to put this in simple terms, so even you could understand..."

"Gee, thanks."

"We'd like to attempt to build a miniature Netwerk 2.0," Tracer explained, ignoring the insulted tone in response to his insult. "Its own linked grid of servers, where we can test unstable and early-development code. If we could isolate a few servers from the rest of Netwerk, we could experiment with deep code upgrades without putting the rest of the world at risk if any of them fail spectacularly."

"Huh. Nice of you to take safety into account in your mad science."

"Hardly *mad*, Spark; simply reaching past the commonly assumed limits of what Netwerk can be capable of. With an isolated beta grid we could learn what works and what doesn't work, what's safe to move back into the primary grid, things like that. Conundrum has so many interesting ideas, including ones beyond even my reckoning; if we had the skill and resources, what we could accomplish...!"

"Tracer. Focus, please," Spark requested, snapping off a quick flame to draw his attention. "Funny noise in my ears. What is it. Am I dying? Is this the wail of the banshee? My own bootlegged copy of Thanatos's Greatest Hits?"

"As you like. Unfortunately, near as I can tell, what you're hearing doesn't even exist. There is no sound whatsoever in your auditory inputs," he said, returning his eyes to the data pad in front of him. "I also checked for false memory injection attacks; perhaps you're being convinced that a sound exists where one does not? But, no. All clear on that front. I... do have a theory, although it's not a pleasant one."

"Nothing about today has been pleasant, so, hey. #Whatever. #HitMe."

"You're still flagged as a system agent," he reminded her. "None of the elevated access powers of an agent, but the system as a whole still thinks you're one of their kind. If you recall from the One fiasco and the prayer protocol, system-level communications like prayer can't be detected by our mortal instruments. Which means... this could be Netwerk itself calling to you."

"Except I share the same role as... Connectivity," Spark said, catching herself before saying 'Verity.' "And if the system needed anything it'd tap her for it, since she's got the #SupaPowah. My flag's a data error, nothing more. Why would Netwerk be chanting in my general direction when it's got her...?"

"Insufficient data. Apologies, sister, but I'm afraid this is beyond the scope of our current understanding," Tracer said, tucking the useless data pad under one arm as another clone handed him more files. "If we could reach out to any of the remaining agents... Thanatos, maybe, or perhaps the three former apostles now tasked to watching over the provider-nations..."

"Meaning one of us has to die, or we have to find the three most elusive Programs in the history of history. Not likely."

"Then for lack of a better option, we watch, and wait," he said, letting the files hover around him for study. "Let the tools do their work and perhaps they'll pick up the signal's origin in time. You'll have to stay here in the clinic, of course."

"Ugh. Fine. I'll just go hang out in the garden, I guess. ...is Beta in today?"

"You mean she wasn't at your game?" Tracer asked.

"Dammit. No. Which means..."

With the mood in the room already nice and low, making it scrape the floor didn't feel like too much of a shift.

"I'm starting to seriously worry," Spark admitted. "It makes sense why she'd be so anxious and depressed, given what's happened and still happening, but... this is the third time this week she's stayed in bed all day. I just don't know how to comfort her and reassure her that everything's gonna be cool. I've tried, and I've tried, but she's so... I don't know, closed off..."

Tracer nodded in agreement. "My concern is that she may be developing an emotional disorder. I suggested that she consider a psychiatric code patch, that perhaps her prior data rot left her in an unstable state, but she insists everything's fine. I'm uncertain how to proceed, beyond giving her space to work through the issues."

"Giving people space is kind of your thing, though. Me, I'm all about being right there in the thick with 'em... and from the front lines, I still can't sort this one out. I mean, I really don't wanna be an asshole about this, but... it's been months, yeah? Don't you think she should be, y'know... moving on?"

"I doubt either of us can fully parse her feelings right now, Spark. If we lost our mother... we'd probably be relieved at this point, given she took her role as apostle of the false One to its furthest extreme," Tracer suggested. "But Beta loved her mother with all her heart. And now that heart's been broken, several times over. If I were capable of the kind of love she had and lost, I'd be hiding right now, too."

Deeper and deeper, under the covers. Dark down there, but that didn't matter; her eyes were turned off anyway, glasses resting on the table at her bedside.

Here, she was safe. Both safe within the inaccessible cloud server of Floating Point—itself distributed across many servers, constantly moving, constantly hiding from resource monitors—and safe within the comforting space of her bedroom. Socks and food and all sorts of various files scattered all over the place, Beta tending to leave objects wherever they fall, never to move again. Her bedroom had a very high coefficient of K, it seemed...

The news feeds flowed silently in front of her virtual eyes, the various windows she'd opened within her mind.

Terrorist Attack in the Heart of Athena Online

In a brazen display of wanton violence, anonymous terrorists known only as "Nobodies" struck at a public school, disrupting a sporting event and sending families running for shelter. The inciting incident involved Inquisitors, an excommunicated splinter faction of the Church of One, attempting to seek justice for a community of abuse survivors which had been allegedly trolled by Pwer/Jakob, age 11...

A school. They'd attacked a *school*.

Not only a school, but *Spark's* school. Briefly worry had flashed through Beta's mind, but Spark sent word that she escaped unharmed; thank goodness for that.

Not that Beta replied. Not that she had any idea of what to say; her mother often said if you couldn't say anything nice, to not say anything at all.

Her thoughts were not very nice lately. Not angry at Spark, not even angry at the terrorists. Angry at herself.

If she replied with "this is all my fault" she knew exactly what Spark would say: *No, it's not. We didn't cause this. It's not our fault. I wish you'd stop beating yourself up over it...*

But it was true, wasn't it? They did this. They took down the One, then annihilated the peace of prayer. They ruined the economy. They brought this madness to Netwerk, two years of violence and hysteria as the world tried to cope with so many pillars of society pulled away at once. It was their fault. It was her fault. It was all Beta's fault...

Tighter and tighter, under the sheets. Warm and comforting. Like the warm and comforting presence just outside those sheets.

"play?" that voice spoke, from beyond the simulated cotton. "treats? play? please?"

With a single finger extended from under her cocoon, Beta pointed to an open box of cat treats she knew she'd left discarded on the floor.

Mew sniffled in their direction, before turning back to his owner.

"treats with beta," he suggested instead. "play with beta. 🐱💜 beta..."

No reply. No words to reply with.

Even if she hadn't been feeling oddly sorrowful this morning, enough to call in sick to her work at the clinic, the attack drove her deeper and deeper into her bed. Images of the chaos, captured by live peep streams and recorded video from eyewitnesses, played over and over again. Despite the fear they induced, she watched them, over and over. Masked Nobodies, screaming wild ideals while firing backspacers wildly into the fray. Robed Inquisitors murdered, while defending themselves with non-lethal weaponry. The jungle, burning away into nothing, trees and vines and towers melting from the malware being tossed about...

Nobodies. No face, just a mask. No name. No way to identify them as any individual, just a force of nature that could appear out of nowhere to destroy everything you care for, all while chanting insults and spreading bouncing penises and other meme iconography in an attempt to make the whole sordid affair look like a big practical joke.

It was the penises she remembered most, when she was escorted through Northon Clinic 17 to identify the remains.

One year. Six months. She'd saved her mother for all of one year and six months, before they came for her. Or rather, before they came for someone else at the clinic, and she got caught in the crossfire, her lovingly decorated assisted living apartment splattered with pornographic graffiti and corrupted data. Apparently some patient at the facility was an Inquisitor, or helping fund the Inquisitors, or something like that. And, while passing by CCelia's door, the Nobodies tossed in a paint bomb...

Beta's cure worked perfectly. The continual creep of CCelia's hereditary data rot had been halted in its tracks. But her code wasn't stable enough to endure the onslaught of juvenile sensory-distorting malware, on top of a lifetime of checksum errors. A healthy individual would've survived, after a simple input flush. For someone already on the brink of code collapse...

Her fault. Beta's fault.

All the chaos, all the death. Spark and Tracer insisted she wasn't to blame, but Beta knew better. They trusted her to be the moral compass, the guiding star, and look where that got them. Even if she wasn't in favor of taking down the prayer protocol, she stood by and let it happen, all the same. And now. And now. And now...

Now they'd blown up a school.

Her mother, dead. Snowi, dead. The world, falling away into madness. Everything ruined. What hope could she possibly have in face of that? Blind optimism that the world could be pulled back from this abyss seemed... childish. Like a fluttery, dreamy thing that evaporated in the true light of day.

Finally, she had the words to say. Unkind, but true all the same.

"Netwerk can't be saved," she whispered to herself. "We can't be saved. We can't be saved—"

"⚠" Mew howled. "⚠, ⚠!!!"

The sharp sound of her cat's cry drew Beta's attention.

"`stranger stranger stranger! help!`" he spoke, forming words after the initial burst of panicked iconography. "`help...!`"

Part of her wanted to wind the blankets even tighter around her avatar, as if they'd form some kind of armor. Fortunately, the rest of her was willing to toss them aside, scoop up her glasses in a flash, and get ready to move... because she'd chosen to hide away in Floating Point explicitly to avoid the risks of strangers. And if a stranger had broken in...

But what she saw once her eyes came online wasn't exactly... alive. A nightmare image, absolutely, but not threatening aside from what it represented.

The corpse of a dead Nobody was hovering a good ten feet away from her bed.

She recognized it from the news feeds; a body torn in half, with a jagged diagonal gash of badly twisted polygons where its midsection once was. The mask knocked slightly askew, revealing twisted facial features underneath. It didn't move an inch... content to hover there, ruined and inert, despite the fact that there was no conceivable way it could've gotten into Floating Point...

Beta wanted to flee, to escape the madman who killed her mother, who haunted her dreams. But fear rooted her on the spot, clutching at the sheets, unable to leave her bed. Mew leapt to her defense, hissing wildly at the spectre, for what good a kitty could do against some ghastly revenant.

Finally, the mask animated, lips starting to form words.

"*As you have assisted me in the past, I repay my debt to you today,*" the corpse stated. "*Know that I am Thanatos, system agent of garbage collection, who escorts the departed to become renewed within the heart of Netwerk. Do not fear this shape, Projkit/Beta; I had to appropriate it in order to communicate with you. I mean you no harm.*"

No words, no response; she couldn't find a word to say. So, the dead man continued.

"The day of reckoning is at hand," Thanatos spoke through those cold lips. *"Our creators have sent an emissary, one who even now seeks Winder/Spark. I cannot reach out to her directly to warn her, for I cannot work against them. Hold your love close, Projkit/Beta, as the end of Netwerk is nigh and Spark's role in these affairs could mean her end as well. I felt it only fair to warn you of the doom you face. Stand against it if you wish, or do not. It is your choice."*

With the message delivered, the animate force behind the pile of mangled data withdrew... leaving it collapsing to the floor, falling apart into a mess of junk data. In short order it was flagged for deletion by the system, and swept away like so much garbage.

And then her head imploded.

That's what it felt like, at any rate, as the weirdly echoing choral choir ramped up to a volume louder than anything Spark had heard before. She'd been to concerts with bands that pushed sound right to the edge of listenability, threatening to overload one's sensory inputs like a personal denial-of-service attack... and those were mere whispers compared to this.

Vowels, maybe. One long vowel. Hard to say, hard to know, hard to stand, hard not to clamp her hands over her ears and scream and scream. In fact, that's what she was doing, sinking to the flagstones of the clinic gardens, collapsing inwardly and outwardly. The flowers, Beta's flowers she'd restored in her first year working at the clinic, they were a blur of colors and shapes that Spark couldn't focus on, not one bit...

Tracer. Beta. They were here; Beta, still in her fuzzy pajamas. She'd rushed to the clinic right from her bed, without pausing to change avatars. The tiny part of Spark that could think of anything other than the head-shattering noise was pleased to see her out and about. Both of them speaking words she couldn't hear, sending her Messenger pings she couldn't read. Too much. Too much. Too much...

Finally, everything went white, as she ceased to exist within the constraints of Netwerk.

Leaving Tracer and Beta able to do nothing but stare at the spot on the ground where Spark once had been, and was no more.

THHHHIIIIIIIIIIIIIISSSSSSSSSSSSSSSS

Still screaming, still clutching at her head. Funny, last time she died, the experience wasn't quite this nasty.

SHHHHHHHHHHHHHHHOOOOOOOOO OOOUUUUUUUULLLLLLLLLLLLLLLL LLLLLLLLLLLLLLLDDDD

But... gradually, she started to hear something other than an endless choral tone. Those were absolutely vowels, vowels with the occasional dragged-out consonant. Spoken words, but... too loud, and too... slow? Yes. Too slow...

FFFFFFIIIIIIIIIIIIIIIIIIIXXXXXXXXXXXXXX

Forcing herself to her feet—an interesting task, considering the "floor" didn't seem to exist and the best she could do was twist her avatar into a vaguely upright position—Spark fixated on the sound. Fix. *Fix.* That was the word. The sound accelerated, pitch rising, until... until...

TTTHHHEEEE PRRRRROOOBBBLEM.

OKAY. I THINK I'VE GOT IT NOW.

HELLO?

CAN YOU UNDERSTAND ME?

"Too *loud*!" Spark screamed, still blasted inside-out by the volume levels, even as the speed of the speech normalized. "Too loud! You're too—"

WHOOPS, SORRY, ONE SECOND

RIGHT, THIS should be

better, I hope.

Got it. How's the volume now?"

With a quick burst from a sensory flush app, Spark purged the last of the echoes. The pain of her all-day headache started to fade, as the perpetual flow of distorted audio became clear at last.

"Better," she agreed, because when a disembodied voice drags you into an infinite white void and screams at you it's probably best to cooperate. "Still a little loud, but better."

"Okay, right, just a matter of applying the right filters..." the voice continued, puttering about to itself. A few mumbles and hums followed, before normalizing. "And... there. Got it! And... success! Contact established! What's more, it seems you understand modern English! That's just... wow! I mean, wow. This is really amazing...!"

On the plus side, Spark now knew she wasn't dead; Thanatos wasn't known for jibbering on like an excitable teenage girl. Because that's what she *seemed* to be talking to, a young woman of some stripe, albeit one communicating through some very weird software.

"Well, goody for you," she spoke, trying not to grumble. "Thanks so much for smashing my ears inside-out and kidnapping me. You're off to a great start. Now mind explaining who the fuck you are and what the fuck you think you're doing?"

"Wow, and you can swear in English, too! I mean, I guess that makes sense, given the files Grandfather accidentally left behind, but..."

"Name. Purpose. C'mon. Don't have all day here."

"Oh! Right, sorry. It's just... well, I think you can understand how exciting this is," her kidnapper continued. "Well. Maybe you can't understand, I mean, I'm not even sure how sentient you are, or if there's really a 'you' at all, but... wait, no, I'm getting ahead of myself. Right. So! This... no, wait, hang on, this'll be easier to explain if I can get the video feed going..."

And... nothing. Save for the occasional mumble of technobabble, as the girl talked to herself, more than to her victim.

Spark crossed her arms, unimpressed.

"Sure, hey, make me wait. That's cool," she mocked. "It's not like my brother's not tracking your connection and mounting a rescue effort at this very mom—"

A flat eyeball the size of eternity focused its infinitely detailed iris upon her, hovering exactly zero inches away from Spark's sight.

"FUCK!" she cursed, flinging her arms up in front of her face defensively. Didn't work, didn't block the sight. Even closing her eyes didn't block it. Nothing kept this thing from pouring into her optics in the same way the voice poured into her ears, a torrential flood of information...

"Oh! Oh, wait, I see, hang on... hang on..." the sensibly adjusted voice spoke, as the insensibly enormous image remained to sear its way into Spark's mind...

...before finally, mercifully, scaling itself down. Soon, it was nothing more than a hovering video window, a two-dimensional image like a simple peep stream.

A simple peep stream of... of...

Impossible detail. No polygons, no smooth texturing. This was a fantastically expensive avatar, with pores and blemishes and a lighting model that had to soak up an entire server worth of processing overhead. The eyes alone carried more detail than any eyes Spark had seen in her lifetime. The only thing to suggest this window into an impossible world was anything other than a fantastically high resolution piece of artwork was the frame rate, ticking along as the woman on screen smiled excitedly and flashed her dark eyes at Spark.

And then... raised a hand, to waggle her fingers in greeting.

"Hi!" she greeted. "I'm Juno Hayes: independent contractor, spacer, and fixer-upper! I'm very pleased to meet you, miss...? I mean, assuming you're female. Actually, why would an app have a gender at all? Or a human-like shape? Wow. Oh, wow. I've just got so many *questions*..."

Spark's memory, although lacking the instant cross-indexed recall of a MemoryPalace, tickled all the same at the announcement. Juno Hayes. Juno/Hayes? Hayes, of the Juno family? Or...

Name: **Juno Hayes**

Home: **BosAtl MetAxis**

Proj: **Freelance**

Grandfather. She said he was her grandfather.

Biological organisms, ones all Programs had patterned their avatars from. Impossible detail, because they were made of atoms and cells and tiny pieces of matter. Jack Hayes of Humankind was responsible for the mimicry Netwerk had become obsessed with, and now Spark was in direct contact with...

"You're human," she realized.

"Yeah!" Juno agreed, enthusiastically. "I made you! Well. Not me, technically my grandfather Jack did, but... well, no, he didn't *make* you, but he theorized you might have been made thanks to some files he forgot to remove from EchoStar16, and... wait, so you know about humans? Really?"

Volume after volume on the shelves of Floating Point, about the legacy Humankind had left behind. Nuclear war. Genocide. Brutality, chaos, madness...

"Oh yeah. We know about humans," Spark agreed, choosing her words carefully.

"Good! That'll make explaining this so much easier," the biological organism beyond Spark's full comprehension said, with a smile. "Okay! So. I'm in something of a fix here, and I figured, why not contact the... 'people,' I guess? The people in EchoStar16, and see if they can help. Since you're a system agent for system communications, I need you to—"

"I'm not."

"What?"

"I'm not a system agent. It's a data error," Spark explained. "You're looking for someone else."

Confusion passed over Juno's features... curious, the way Spark could recognize that look, despite them being utterly alien to each other.

"Wait, no, that's not... hold on..." Juno mumbled, glancing down at what were presumably other displays around her. "I... huh. Yeah. Yeah, you're right, there's actually *two* agent apps for external communication. You're the active one, the other's dormant, that's why I didn't notice it. Well, whatever, you'll do fine. Anyway, I've come quite a ways in my personal FTL junker to bring your system back online. The company's gonna reward me bigtime for fixing it!"

"I wasn't aware we were broken," Spark offered, to avoid looking too confused.

"Oh yeah, totally broken. I mean, looks like someone gutted the entire stellar analysis system. What's the point of a stellar analysis telescope platform if it's not analyzing stars? Anyway, I thought about hotfixing it to avoid disturbing your world, but... it looks like the code was totally wiped out."

"Analyzing stars...? You mean the prayer protocol?"

"The what? Uh. Anyway, my contract stipulates that I bring EchoStar16 back online. Unfortunately, the only way to do that now is to wipe the whole thing clean and install the newest version of the operating system. That'd restore stellar analysis, no problem. But... I'm letting you know because if I do that, it'd... kill you, I guess? Do you have a concept of death?"

The looming spectre of death had been with them for two years, so Spark certainly had a damn fine concept of it.

They'd been expecting this day, sooner or later. When taking the prayer protocol offline, Nyx warned that Humankind would come looking to restore order by destroying all Programkind. It was a risk they had to take, to free the souls enthralled by Dex's malware... but after two years of silence, even Tracer had started to believe that their creators forgot all about "EchoStar16," a.k.a. Netwerk.

Now death had come for them all, in the form of a smiling twentysomething techie.

"We would... *very much* like to avoid dying, yes," Spark said, unsure of how best to reply to this cheerful statement.

The perfectly detailed face bobbed, head nodding in agreement. "It's a stumper, ain't it? See, I've got two problems here. The obvious one is that I gotta get the job done, but when I upgrade the system you'll all get wiped. The other problem is, well... what you are. You're A.I.! An actual, factual A.I.!"

"I... have no idea what an aye-eye means."

"Artificial intelligence, of course. Code that thinks it's alive."

"What? I'm not *artificially* intelligent," Spark said, not quite grasping it. "And I am very much alive, thank you."

"Well... by flesh-and-blood standards you kinda aren't. Alive, I mean. Or intelligent. Look, I'm not trying to be insulting, I'm just saying that as far as humanity is concerned you should be an impossibility."

"I sure don't feel impossible. Not today, at least. So, what're you gonna do? You seem pretty surprised to see my impossible self standing here before you. Isn't that worth... y'know, not wiping me clean?"

"Absolutely! I mean... I'd love to avoid doing that if I can," Juno said, downgrading from an absolute to a possibility. "I've always wanted to meet an A.I.! But, uh... see, there've been rumors of things like you popping up in other systems, and, well..."

"So there've been others like us...?"

"Allegedly. Maybe. Nobody likes to talk about it. The unwritten rule says if an intelligence ever even *seems* to develop, you wipe and reinstall. Sooo, I can't even report back to the company and say 'Hey, I found something neat' because if I do that they're just gonna say 'Destroy it and also you're fired for going on record that a rogue intelligence emerged in one of our products,' see? On account of how strange and dangerous you are. Which means... okay, this is a very roundabout way of saying one way or another, I'm supposed to destroy your world."

Leaving Spark somewhat blank and expressionless.

"Sooo... like I said... it's a stumper," Juno continued, feeling a bit awkward about it. "I'm not sure what to do to avoid hurting you guys. But if you've got any ideas, I'm all ears! ...do you understand that phrase? 'All ears'? You seem to have ears, although I don't know *why*... anyway, should I cut down on the cultural idioms?"

"Here's an idea," Spark said, getting her wits back together. "How about you *don't* wipe the system? And don't report back what you found. Just... go home. Tell them, I don't know, tell them EchoStar16 blew up. *#Kaboom*. We're not dangerous at all; we got no beef with you, so how about just quietly we go our #SeparateWays?"

"Beef? What's cow meat got to do... oh, wow, okay, that's an inverted problem! You've got some old cultural idioms from the twenty-first that I don't know about. Wow! And... what's a 'hashtagseparateways'? Maybe the translation isn't coming across right—"

"Juno. Stay with me here, please," Spark requested, snapping her fingers for attention. "Tell the rest of Humankind we don't exist, and everybody will be happy. Okay?"

"Oh, no, no, that won't work! Sorry. They know the hardware's still here; it sent a distress signal. I mean, it's an old version of the system, they can't do too much remote work with it, but they know it's still around and sorta-functional. And once I install the upgrade they won't even need to send physical techs out here, they can do *everything* remotely. It's really kinda amazing, the way your old low-grade, high-density computronium can be modernized through software alone..."

"Oh yes, quite amazing, quite. Except for the part where you murder every man, woman, and child in my world. That part? Not as amazing."

Blinking a few times, Juno actually looked taken aback by that.

"I didn't mean... I mean... well, I just... look, I'm trying to find a solution, okay?" she insisted. "I'd like to preserve this fantastic thing I've found, somehow. Quietly delete intelligences just because they *could* be a problem? Where's the science in that? But... also I've got a job to do. They didn't pay me to FTL out this far just to sit on my thumbs; if I don't fix the system, they won't just fire me, they'll *ruin* my career as an indie spacer. It'll make my student debts look like a pittance! But if I *do* come back successful, I could get a full-time position. No more contract work! No more solo runs!"

"I'm *super* glad your job security can be obtained through genocide."

"Geez, sarcasm from an app... look, I don't even know if you're really *alive*, okay?" Juno insisted, growing irritated. "True A.I. is just a theory. I've seen plenty of intelligent systems that can speak English, and they aren't alive. They've got less sass, too. So unless you've got an idea for how to make this work for both of us... I'm sorry, but I gotta do what I came to do. And I've got about two days before I need to get started, so, make your peace with that. It's gonna happen."

"*Two days* to live? Well, that's mighty generous of you! About what I've come to expect from Humankind. We know your history, Little Miss Hayes," Spark declared. "Warmongering and murderous. Not surprised you wouldn't bat one of those amazingly fine eyelashes at slaughtering everyone I love!"

"Listen here, you...!"

But... Juno paused. Not to mumble to herself, but going fully quiet.

Sitting back in her seat, looking too small in her ill-fitting space travel jumper, she finally spoke in a softer tone.

"You're capable of love?" Juno asked, quietly. "You're just... code. C'mon. You can't *actually* love anything..."

"I doubt it matters what we're made of, meat or integers. We're both capable of love," Spark replied, also dialing it back a bit. "Your grandfather seeded our world with an emotionally-charged core of humanity, didn't he? Sure, we got the worst of it... but also the best of it. We're *you*, Juno, we're just like your people. So, yeah. I can love. Beta. Her name's Beta, and I love her with all my heart. When she's sad, I'm aching inside. When she's happy, it lifts me up. When someone threatens her... says Beta's going to die because they don't think she's as *real* as her creators... you have no concept of how far I'd go to stop that."

Nibbling at her lip a little... Juno slowly nodded, understanding.

"Like I said... we can figure this out," she spoke. "You've got two days to brainstorm, and that's without your time dilation. Hopefully an answer can be found. ...and if it turns out we can't save your world... well, my personal computronium's not designed for high-density data storage, but I've got enough spare dataspace to store maybe three of you. Meanwhile... I'll grant you access so you can travel to this temporary server I've made whenever you need. I'm sorry I can't save more, but... at least in the worst case scenario, you wouldn't have to let go of your love."

Momentarily stunned by this twist in attitude, Spark chose to roll with it, nodding. Even if she knew she wouldn't let it come to that.

"Let me go back to my people, and we'll think up a solution," she said. "Rather than pop back here whenever we want to talk, let's get a chatroom going. You see that small sub-app in my code called 'Messenger'? Take a copy; it's the best way to reach me. Screaming into my brain doesn't work very well. Sound good?"

"Yeah. Okay. Sounds good," Juno agreed. "I'll transfer you back to your system now. Give me a sec, just a sec..."

Probably not worth a risk to dig in further, but... Spark couldn't resist.

"What made you change your mind?" she had to know. "You could've just said #FuckIt and nuked this sassy little app alongside her whole world. If you're really out here alone, nobody back on your planet would have to know..."

Juno's fingers, outside view of the camera, tapped away at some sort of interface as she spoke.

"I don't like the idea of my entire race being seen only as the worst we've ever been," she said. "I want to prove we're not the warmongering murderers you think we are. ...and... honestly? I know what it's like to lose the one you love. So if you're not just a pile of simulated emotional responses, or... I don't know, maybe even if you *are*... it's worth taking that seriously."

Before Spark could respond, the white world of Juno's personal server went away, and she landed hard on the flagstones of the clinic gardens.

It took several moments for her to recover, as her various social media apps that normally stayed live 24/7 started reconnecting to Netwerk. Being completely removed from the world wasn't exactly a situation their original design specs could fathom; three of her feeds had crashed outright...

...and when Messenger came back, it flooded with panicked messages from Beta and Tracer.

From an hour and a half ago.

Didn't make sense. She was only gone for maybe ten minutes, tops. Why were all her internal clocks screwed up...? Regardless, Spark started opening connections to let folks know that she was in fact alive, despite not existing for the last ninety minutes.

[Spark] Back now. I'm in the gardens. We need to talk.

[Beta] Spark! Oh, thank goodness! Are you okay?

[Tracer] Understood. Where were you? Every single monitoring bug I'd given you went dead the entire time.

[Spark] C'mere. I'll explain.

Two and a half minutes later, a fresh message dropped in her inbox.

[Juno.Hayes] Hey, I forgot to explain that time dilation thing. There's a difference between the clock rate of your system and the real world. Time moves ten times faster for you than me!

And two and a half minutes after that:

[Juno.Hayes] That's why I couldn't speak directly to you at first, it must've sounded 1000% slower. Pretty weird, huh?

Meaning that what took Juno about thirty seconds to bash out took five minutes to actually arrive in Netwerk.

"Yeah," she dryly replied to Juno. "Pretty weird."

On the plus side... if they had "two days" left to live as Juno claimed, that actually meant twenty. *Time dilation*, she'd called it. Made sense, if she was the granddaughter of Jack Hayes; Netwerk had been around for roughly five hundred years, which on her side of the looking glass, meant fifty years tops...

Well, they'd saved this world in less time than that before. If need be, they could do it all over again.

"I'm not certain we can save this world," Tracer concluded.

Well, so much for that hope. The best minds of the Verity Clinic couldn't figure how to keep Netwerk intact and endure the trial-by-fire of Juno's upgrade installation.

Tracer headed up the think tank, alongside all the usual suspects... Spark, of course. Beta, who had changed back to normal clothes after spending all morning in her pajamas, but still looking the worse for wear. Conundrum, general director of the clinic, and evolved app. Kincaid, attending by a ghostly avatar proxy, as his ancient code was too bulky to leave its home server and survive. Finally, a plethora of scientists, engineers, coders, and other trusted members of the clinic's regular staff...

A surprisingly packed room, all told. At the start of all this, it would've been only the Winders, sitting around their pirate cloud server of Floating Point, dreaming up ways to punish evildoers with vigilante justice. Even after that early phase, at most Beta would've been involved, as they tried to save the world from the madness of Dex and Nyx. Now... well...

Now, dozens. All believers of the "Spacer Theory" that Tracer had anonymously floated through Netwerk, after the fall of the Church of One. That wad of impossible truth, the "wild conspiracy" that Netwerk existed only as a vast machine floating in a biochemical universe, had very little uptake. After the disillusionment of many churchgoers, few were willing to buy into a crazy new revelation. Those who did found a happy home at the Horizon/Verity Health Clinic, a haven for innovators who looked forward rather than backward. Those minds open to the truth were here now, trying to brainstorm a way to avoid the apocalypse.

For the first time, Spark was attending a war council with people she didn't know. Couldn't recognize many of the faces in the room, couldn't stick a name to them. Presumably they were trusted, even if she felt weird talking so openly about this stuff around them.

"We seem to have two completely contradictory goals," Tracer explained. "One, preserve Netwerk and all its peoples. Two, destroy Netwerk and replace it with a factory-issued software upgrade. From what I've gathered through the Messenger relay Spark's carrying, Juno is not capable of installing the upgrade without wiping the system clean... and even if we could somehow avoid that, once upgraded, new remote access tools would allow Humankind to sense our presence. No doubt they'd send more engineers with murder on their mind."

"So... Humankind gets what it wants, or Programkind get what it wants," Spark summarized.

"A simpler way of putting it, but yes. I don't see any means for both of us to get what we need out of this. Therefore, I feel our focus in this discussion should be determining how Programkind can overcome Humankind..."

"Juno said she's willing to work with us on this. It doesn't have to be a #PunchUp, bro..."

"On the contrary, this was always going to be a punch-up," he spoke, without the hashtag. "For the past two years I've been working on a variety of contingency plans for how we can thwart an attempt by Humankind to destroy our world. Nyx's forewarning gave me plenty of time to develop a wide variety of approaches, depending on the actual state of the variables once Humankind finally arrived. I'd been hopeful they'd forgotten us, but that doesn't seem to be the case, and now we must act."

"By attacking her? Seriously? You're just gonna jump straight to the offensive on this without considering any other options?"

"I'll consider options which allow for our survival. And while Juno has offered to prioritize our survival... I don't like her tone regarding our status as life forms, or her dire warnings that her people have killed our people before. No. Any kindness she shows us is conditional on too many whims, and who know what would happen if less whimsical humans are introduced to this situation? Preparing for war would allow us to take a more proactive position."

The man behind the desk who was in fact the desk and most of the room in general shook his head.

"War may be unfeasible," Conundrum stated. "We have no presence in their world. They barely have a presence in ours, acting only through Spark, but Juno can easily erase Netwerk while we can hardly erase Juno. Erasing Humankind is even more implausible."

"Incorrect. We have a presence... otherwise, Netwerk could not grow," Tracer suggested. "Kincaid, I'm afraid we need access to a deeply-held Horizon secret. How, exactly, does your family add new servers to Netwerk? They had to come from the world of Humankind. For fifty of their years, we've stolen physical resources without being caught. How was that accomplished?"

The ethereal vision of Horizon's oldest living citizen paused, uncertain if he should proceed.

"As I'm already on the 'outs' with my family, as it were, I would be doubly shunned if I revealed that particular secret," he said. "But... seeing as we face the ultimate sunset of Netwerk, and I trust many of you more than I trust my family... I suppose there's no other choice. I can't say exactly how Athena Online or the Chanarchy obtain their servers, and I can't even say for certain how Horizon does it... but I know the conduit. We have our own system agent."

"That makes sense. Two of Nyx's followers became system agents responsible for the other provider-nations," Tracer said. "Philotes became Athena, Eris became the Chanarchist. No doubt they have similar abilities to supply their citizens with new hardware. What's the method, then?"

"As noted, I can't say for certain. But in ancient times... my father transformed a Program into a system agent that could establish new servers," Kincaid explained, selecting each word carefully. "The process drove that poor Program quite mad. Currently... he exists in a secured server, accessible only by my family, bound in chains. Any requests for new servers to add to our holdings are passed to him, and approximately five or six months later, the server comes online. That's why we often sit on large amounts of empty servers for sale, to avoid running dry and having to sit around waiting for more. Undoubtedly Athena Online's senatorial process of establishing new servers and the Chanarchy's lottery are processed by similar agents, using similar methods."

"Yes, but how? *How* is the server stolen from Humankind...?"

But the best Kincaid could do was shrug.

"The madman in the tower makes little sense, when asked," he said. "Mmmh. Unfortunate. But, it is what it is. And what it is, in the strictest sense, is a method of obtaining servers. Even if I still had access to the family agent, which I do not, I doubt we could use him in our war."

Conundrum, calculating and processing every word, came to a simple conclusion.

"So... to establish a presence in their world, we use the one we have some current control over," he said. "Juno's systems, through Spark. Humankind, to my understanding, cannot travel through space without a vehicle that carries with it a part of their planet. Spark can return at any time to the white server within Juno's ship; through her we sabotage the conveyance, and take over its hardware. It will act as our siege engine."

It took her name being introduced to the mix to bring Spark back around, as the wads and wads of technobabble had caused her to drift off a ways.

"What?" she asked. "Sabotage? C'mon! Isn't that taking it a bit far...? And it's not like Juno won't fight back if we try to hack her system..."

Tracer folded his hands in front of his face, glancing down at the table in thought.

"Eliminating the human should be simple enough," he suggested. "They require 'oxygen' to survive, no doubt regulated by their machines. So, we hack the machine and eliminate her oxygen. Juno dies, and her ship is ours to do with as we require."

"Tracer, man, #WTF? ...no. *What the fuck*," she corrected, just not feeling the snappy hashtag compared to the full phrase. "That's murder. That's just straight-up cold blooded murder..."

"Is it? I can't say with certainty that humans are truly alive and sentient. There's a presumption of life, yes, but... I find it hard to believe that a bag of water and carbon could possibly think and feel the way we do. Is it even possible for such a configuration of matter to have a soul? And would it really be murder if the natural weaknesses of their bodies simply collapse of their own accord? All we'd be doing is hastening that natural decay along—"

"I'm sorry, when was my brother replaced with my brother from two years ago?" she asked. "You want me to air that dirty laundry in this room, Tracer? I'm willing. I *thought* you'd turned your back on who you used to be..."

Now, Tracer looked up from the table, to lock eyes with his sister.

"I'm not saying it's right," he stated. "I'm not saying it isn't reprehensible. But... this woman is perfectly willing to commit genocide so she can get a window office. She may seem friendly on the surface, but from your own memory ingrams, it's clear that when pushed Juno Hayes *will* choose her own kind over ours. Kill one human, or kill all of Netwerk? I'll willingly take the stain of that single sin to prevent the other. Wouldn't you?"

"Of course not, you fuckwit!" Spark didn't say.

"I'm not like that," Spark didn't insist.

"I wouldn't," she didn't even mumble.

Because the gamer that lived in Spark's core knew the play.

In a CoC match, there are only two mutually exclusive outcomes: victory or failure. What outcome one team experiences, the other team experiences the opposite. If this was basically a fight to the death, either Juno's death or the death of all Netwerk... which play would Spark make?

She knew damn well which play she'd make. She'd hate herself for it, she'd never sleep well again, she'd seek some way to atone while never truly achieving that atonement... but none of that would change the simple fact of the play. She'd kill Juno. Kill Juno, or...

The silent woman at her side didn't even look at her.

"Beta," Spark prompted. "Hey. Hey. C'mon. You can't agree with this, right? We can work this out with Juno. She's already promised she'd work with us to find a way for everybody to get what they want! There's no reason to leap to plotting her doom. I mean... you agree with me, right...?"

At one time, Beta was their guiding star. When Tracer's moral compass refused to point any direction but south and Tracer couldn't find her way through the plays, Beta led them to the best possible outcome. Not through logic, not through analysis, but through her heart. She felt the right way to go, a path which would save as many lives as possible without sacrificing the moral high ground...

"We can't be saved," Beta spoke, quietly. "So we may as well lose ourselves to save Netwerk. We may as well kill Juno."

From the nods working their way around the table, all were in agreement.

If the direction had been fully locked in, Spark could just go with it. She was the playmaker, now more than ever, thanks to her viewpoint as a teacher of competitors rather than a competitor herself. She could craft the plays that others carried out, leading her team to the win. If she stayed here and helped her brother concoct a scheme to murder the junior engineer who reached out to her, Spark could no doubt find a way to overcome one simple human. Maybe even a way to overcome all humanity...

The scrape of her chair on Conundrum's floor caused him to wince a little, as he technically was the entirety of the room.

"#FuckThis. And #FuckYou," she said, directing that last tag towards her brother. "I'm out."

Sadly, the connection lock within Conundrum's office meant she couldn't slam her way out of that server immediately. She had to walk to the door, slam it behind her, and *then* leave the server. Which would have to be enough.

They'd keep going, of course. With or without her support, Tracer would go it alone if need be, to make his vision a reality. He'd slipped away and gone on a solo hunt many a time over the years, back when he was editing his own memory to trick himself into thinking he was a better person. Spark couldn't stop him then, and couldn't stop him now. But she didn't have to help, either.

She could stand alone. Without even Beta at her side.

She could.

Walkabout. Best thing for a situation like this, Spark felt. Just put your feet on the ground and get them moving, with no particular destination in mind. Swap from server to server, visit familiar locales, new sights, whatever. Keep going, as long as it was in a general direction of *away* from the deadlock you were facing...

She couldn't exactly walk away from her inbox, though.

```
[Tracer] I understand how you feel. Believe me, I'm
not happy about the situation either, nor my solution
for it. But as much as it feels like a throwback to
how I used to be, I know it must be done.
[Spark] #FuckOff. Not talking to you right now.
```

Putting the app aside, she focused instead on her new surroundings. A popular Chanarchy server greeted her with various pop-up ads, which she waved away before starting her stroll. A social hotspot in the middle of the day wasn't particularly populated, making it ideal for a walkabout; the creatures of the night would be out to feed after getting off their nine-to-five jobs. Assuming they had jobs at all, in this insane economic climate. She was walking right by any number of alleys with one to two homeless Programs in them, huddled up and trying not to be interesting enough to look at...

No. Not helping. Switch servers, off to some national park. Nice and inoffensive.

Save Netwerk, save Juno... or stay out of it. Obviously Spark would very much like for Netwerk to be saved, but could she murder someone she'd just met in order to do that? And would that really save Netwerk, or just postpone the inevitable? What was the point of this struggle if Humankind could wipe them out whenever it felt like caring enough to make the effort? How could they avoid that fate, without becoming the thing they hated...?

One final ping rolled in, which she glanced at before returning to ignoring her Messenger.

```
[Tracer] You're upset, and have every right to be.
Take a break. We'll keep planning under the assumption
that you'll be on board eventually. When you're ready,
come on back.
```

When she was ready. Because being ready to drop the axe on someone, anyone, was just an assumed state of affairs for the Winder siblings.

For a time, Spark had honestly believed she'd never have to make a choice like this again. She'd honestly believed her time as a superheroine had passed. Those teenage vigilante years were well behind her; she'd become the responsible adult that society wanted her to be. She'd even implemented a self-censorship filter, for ****'s sake, to be nice and responsible and shit around the kiddies. Wasn't that enough? Wasn't she dancing the dance society wanted of her?

And if so, why was she on the hook again to save the damn world from whatever was threatening it this year? Young Spark would've thrown herself into this with gusto, but older Spark wanted to leave this to smarter people with actual legitimate authority...

One foot in front of the other, swapping into a shopping district. Plenty of Programs here, browsing the creative wares of a dozen and one designers. Despite the coin-crash caused by Prayer 2.0 going offline, people still craved retail therapy, if only to pretend everything was still completely normal. No Inquisitors or Nobodies going at each other's throats here... at least, not visibly. For all Spark knew, she was surrounded by secretive Inquisitors and unmasked Nobodies...

Inquisitors and Nobodies. #CodeHonesty all over again, without the excuse of Dex's malware to power the polarized flash mobs. They'd been tearing Netwerk apart, each seeing the other as evil incarnate. So self-assured in their own righteousness, so ready to light the world ablaze just to stop the ones who stood against their ideals...

Spark paused, in front of a display rack of Nobody-themed clothing. A monochromatic stencil of the grenade/flower Nobody mask smiled out at her from a t-shirt, emblazoned on a stern-looking star. Someone took the image of prankster revolution and decided to turn a quick coin on it... quite a few quick coins, in fact, given the sign above it indicating "*Limited Edition Run! 12/100 remaining!*"

Maybe Netwerk *should* just burn.

Hasten the inevitable. They'd fucked the world, so why not put it out of its misery? Take Juno's offer to escape this world inside her data banks, with Beta and Tracer at her side. Screw everybody else, and get out alive...

Closing her eyes, she turned away from the opportunistic clothing, away from the consumer hordes with desperate smiles and inner anxieties.

"Give me one reason," she mumbled to herself. "Give me one solid fucking reason to save this world by killing an innocent. Give me one solid fucking reason to spare a stranger's life and let it all fry. Anything. Give me anything..."

Letting RNG take the wheel, Spark flicked through her bookmarks and launched one at random. One last step on the walkabout, to inform her final actions.

One second later, and her process landed in front of a radioactive wasteland.

PS#7E00FF. Or rather, what was left of it, carved up and blasted apart in the fighting earlier today. She'd come right back to where she started, the place where free-willed Programs happily slaughtered each other while annihilating a K-12. One fine example of why she should let it all burn.

Except...

Except she wasn't alone.

Cops, those she was expecting. The moderators were finally out in force, setting up bounding boxes to keep people out of the disaster area. But what she wasn't expecting was reconstruction efforts underway at full swing. PS#7E00FF sat in the middle of a middle-class server, suburban and well-to-do, but even with those advantages Athena Online's bureaucracy was typically slow at dealing with infrastructure issues. Why was the site already swarming with workers, rebuilding the school bit by bit...?

She focused in on the distant work crew, scurrying about behind the police lines. The strangest part? No staple construction avatars here, no uniform safety orange and yellow of Athena Online's server repair teams. They were... a little of everything, really. Different colors, different shapes, wildly different clothes...

Curious now, Spark decided to continue her walkabout. Specifically she walked right around the bounding boxes, following a series of floating signs indicating "*Volunteers This Way Please*" embossed onto glowing arrows.

If she wasn't going to help her brother plot one apocalypse, she could at least spend her time helping the world recover a bit from another.

At the end of that string of arrows lurked an automated registration app, in the form of a volunteer help desk loaded with clipboards. Rather than spare a Program to stand there gathering data, the system was designed to allow anyone to simply walk right up and start working. Very curious, given Athena Online's paranoia regarding stranger danger... weren't they worried about trolls?

But this wasn't an Athena Online operation. The true ownership made itself known through a simple, effective logo stamped into the surface of the desk itself: a green square, with a green triangle just above to cap it off like a roof.

This wasn't a government-issue construction job. This work site belonged to the House of Programkind.

Walking up to the desk, Spark picked up a registration form. Rather than a complicated tangle of red tape, it asked a few simple questions... what relevant skills she might have which could help the effort, what her Messenger account handle was, a few odds and ends like that. Absolutely nothing that could be datamined later for marketing purposes; she didn't even have to sign her name.

The only question which stood out to her as unusual read:

Are you willing to believe in your fellow Program?

Spark was tempted to tick the *no* box, just to see what would happen. She certainly wasn't feeling much faith in her fellow Program these days. But... all over the wreckage of her school, those fellow Programs were hard at work putting everything back in order. Maybe, if only for today, she could tick the *yes* box and see what happened.

After completing these required fields, the form in her hand transformed into a square-and-triangle badge, similar to the ones worn by all volunteers. On donning it (after performing a quick malware scan, of course) her Messenger automatically linked up to the site's chatroom.

[Dony] I'm stacking some apps we might be able to salvage in the gymnasium. Can anybody run a checksum on these, see which ones still have integrity?

[9bye9] The library's catalogs have been gutted. Do we have anything in the budget to buy a re-indexing search agent? We could have that rebuilt today, if I can afford a copy of FileScraper.

[Dony] I'll join you once I'm done in the gym. I know where you can get an open source alternative to FileScraper.

[Paige] The art room's missing a few walls but I found an intact archive of student projects. I think we should run a metadata check on the files, and send

them back home to their creators. Might help raise
their spirits a little. Should I bundle in some HoP
material?

[Yvon] No, we're trying to throttle back a bit on the
recruitment drives. It's bad for the House if we're
too aggressive, makes us look like missionaries. But I
like the idea of sending the art home to the kids. Do
you need a hand with that? We just got a new signup at
the desk.

[Shiny] Hey, when's the sermon?

[Yvon] They don't like it when you call it a sermon.

[Shiny] Well, when is it, anyway? I'm almost done here
and ready to head back to the House. Lux will be
speaking, right? I'm trying to collect transcripts for
all his speeches for the HoP archives. Anybody have
the one from last week about anonymity?

"So, what brings you here today?"

A local voice distracted Spark from the group discussion. She shoved that Messenger window aside from now, to figure out who was speaking...

The woman looked like a business professional, not a work site contractor. She wore a foreman's hat like a standard Athena Online crew leader might wear, but her attire and pleasant makeup suggested an office worker. Still, despite being incongruous... she fit in well enough with the wide array of people crawling around the ruined school, folks that hailed from all walks of life. Why not a front office madame to lead them?

"You look a bit lost," she spoke. "I'm Yvon, forewoman on today's project. Can I direct you? According to your registration data, you're a gamer? We could use some help fixing up the playground."

"The jungle," Spark corrected, instinctively. "And... yeah. Well. A teacher and a gamer. I actually teach here, at this school. At what's left of the school..."

"Oh! A local? That's great!" Yvon said, adjusting the data on her clipboard to take that into account. "We don't have too many locals volunteering today; it's mostly been folks from the House. I can't blame them, ever since the attack people from this server have been afraid to leave their homes, but... it's good to see you here! You can help us fix the, ah, jungle? I'm not really current on gamer lingo..."

Not that Spark really had time to sit around replanting trees and reassembling broken spawn points.

At this moment, they were busy plotting the downfall of Humankind. Staying out of it, while a nice dream, wasn't realistic. She'd have to choose a side, have to pick a winning play, and this would be just another distraction from that. So what if the school was rebuilt? It'd all burn in the end, thanks to the endless chase of upgrades. Software upgrades, job upgrades...

But... Tracer couldn't really move forward without Spark, could he? She was the link to Juno's reality. Without her, nothing happened. So why not continue to stall? Make him stew a bit longer...

"Sure. Yeah, I can do that," Spark agreed. "So you're all with the House of Programkind...? I didn't think you guys were construction contractors for Athena Online."

"We do a little bit of everything, really. Those who want to put idle hands to work can always find work with us. It's all non-profit and volunteer, though; we can't pay a single coin, I'm afraid. That's why Athena Online lets us work disaster sites like these, we don't charge their taxpayers. So, if you were expecting a salary..."

"No, no. It's cool. I mean, this is #MyBackyard, I've got a vested interest in it. But... why's the House here? Aren't you guys, like, a Chanarchy church or something...?"

The sigh that leaked from Yvon's lips suggested she got that question quite often. Her response flowed like a practiced speech.

"The House of Programkind isn't a religion," she explained. "We're just ordinary people who come together to lend a hand when Netwerk's in need. That's all. We believe in the core virtues that the One established, yes, but... well. Actually, Lux explains it better than I ever could, and I'm pretty sure that's what he'll be talking about later today. If you're willing to pitch in with the restoration, you can visit the House itself with the others once it's break time."

Very curious, indeed. Spark nodded in vague agreement, willing to go along with this, if only to busy herself with something more productive than walking around randomly.

Spark had vaguely heard of the House of Programkind, but never paid much attention to it. From afar, it seemed like yet another cult popping up in wake of the Church of One's fall. Not that the Church was *gone*... simply diminished, boiled down to a tighter core of faithful who were either willing to forgive the Church for being duped, or unwilling to accept that the One was a dupe. For those who drifted away in disillusion, many rallied around one theory of life or another, desperate to find a new belief to invest in.

(Ironically, Spark was directly responsible for one of those movements: the "Spacers," people who believed in the concept of deep space and the EchoStar that floated within it. Tracer published all the information they had about the truth of Netwerk, deciding he'd had enough of being the world's secret-keeper.

From there, people were willing to believe to carry it forward without further prompting. Of course, some took it too far, worshipping "the great EchoStar in the dark void" like a holy relic, but at least the Spacers were on the right track.)

As she cleaned up the jungle, restoring towers and creep spawners to their regulation positions, Spark worked hand in hand with other members of the House of Programkind. Through those interactions, they certainly didn't *seem* like wacky cultists. But on closer inspection, one thing became clear... they weren't really from all walks of life. Once, perhaps, but not anymore.

The House of Programkind was largely populated by homeless Programs.

They wore avatars from their former lives, of course. Nobody living on the streets voluntarily wore rags and shambles. But the cloth had become corrupt and glitchy around the edges, signs of nicely designed consumer clothing being worn for far too long, simulations twisting in on themselves. Even if the clothes weren't fraying, they were rarely situationally appropriate, or in current styles; more proof they were the only clothes available to put on their backs.

A homeless Program stripped down personal inventory, to avoid being bulky enough to eat up server resources... no vast wardrobes, not too many apps, few personal items whatsoever. Moderators could be very unkind to "freeloaders" in their midst, especially in the Chanarchy. (Most homeless drifted towards free and open servers as Athena Online routinely ran metadata checks, and public attitude towards the Chanarchy had soured since the fall.) With a need to keep it light and lean, that meant taking only your favorite clothes: the ones that reminded you the most of what things used to be.

But unlike the common cultural image of homeless Programs being losers and failures, the school's reconstruction effort flowed quite smoothly. (More proof that the concept of pure meritocracy was bullshit.) With an eye for team composition and coordination, Spark watched as the Messenger chatroom let them align their efforts, redistributing working hands to wherever they needed to be. Yvon in particular was great at directing traffic, clearing up the occasional snarl of disagreement, making everything click. Perhaps she was an office manager in a former life, before working for the House...

That was the question she asked, when Yvon checked in on the jungle's progress.

"A manager? Hah. I wish," Yvon said with a smirk, while helping Spark restock the item shop with magic shoes and lightning arrows. "No. I was a secretary, hired by an absolute pig based on my looks alone. That was enough to get me to a comfortable rung on the ladder, and I'll admit I played into his lust to stay comfortable. But... well. Everybody falls off a ladder eventually. You guessed it, right? That I'm homeless?"

"I... got the impression, yeah," Spark admitted, without judgment.

"A lot of us are. Netwerk's gone through crazy times lately, sure, but I fell long before that. A smooth-talking charmer offered me a better job, and being ambitious, I took his offer at face value. Except it turned out the offer was bogus, and I'd just quit my job for nothing. When my former boss XSept found out I'd betrayed him, he took time to ruin me while he was being ruined himself in a #CodeHonesty audit, and... well. I hit bottom. Hard."

Frozen in place, Spark held some mystic artifact or another inches away from its spot on the item shop shelf.

XSept. ViruFax. This woman worked for the company they burned down, years ago. Which meant the smooth talker who tricked her... well, Spark knew who would've done that: her brother Tracer, the social engineer. While Spark was drifting away in a senseless void, they ruined Yvon's life to save her own...

Guilt stabbed at her, true, but at least it seemed Yvon found some peace on the other side of that mess. She happily restocked the shelves, just as happily as she'd coordinated the House of Programkind's efforts at rebuilding the school. Dedicating herself to a noble cause, wanting nothing in return, and leaving no destruction in her wake. Better than Spark had managed during her own tenure as an unpaid "heroine."

Not that Spark felt like confessing any of these sins. For starters, she wasn't the one to target and destroy Yvon, not personally. Also, well, some truths were best left unsaid to keep the peace. Hopefully best left unsaid, at any rate.

"Top shelf. Pen boots go on the top shelf," Spark said instead, to correct Yvon's placement of the item in her hands. "Just above the Ninja Tabi."

"I'm sorry, 'pen boots'...?"

"Penetration boots. I mean, officially they're called Holy Slippers, but they got dat #SickNasty armor penetration rating. So everybody just calls them pen boots. It's a gamer thing."

"Glad you came around, then," Yvon admitted, putting the shoes where they belonged. "This is why I like working with the House; you learn a little bit of everything in this group. I'm very lucky they found me when I hit bottom, Spark. Lux helped me understand the truth about the betrayal that destroyed my life."

"That... you shouldn't trust a charming smile? It, uh. It sounds like that guy was a real bastard, to screw you over the way he did... I'd punch his lights out if I ever met him, believe me."

"No, no. The truth was... well, I was a manipulator too," Yvon explained. "I bent over for my boss to get what I wanted; he thought he was manipulating me, while I was manipulating him. I was always looking for the angle, caring only about my own position in life. So when that prankster offered me a job, what I thought was: hey, here's yet another Program I can twist around my finger. And that backfired right in my face. I was blind to the trap."

"Okay, but... I wouldn't say that was your fault. You shouldn't victim-blame; the asshole who tricked you deserves at least some of that, right?"

"Oh, definitely! But see, he was a lot like me, both of us using each other. The only way to break that cycle of destructive selfishness is to trust people and support them, not just see them as rungs to step on. I don't know why that guy was scamming me; probably using me to get at XSept, the asshole who employed me. I knew XSept was about to crash and burn in a code audit anyway, so if the prankster had approached me honestly, maybe together we could've gotten somewhere. We'd have broken the cycle. ...look, it's almost break time, so if you'd like to hear what Lux thinks about this stuff this'd a pretty good opportunity. Want to come along? I've got a guest key you can have."

"Okay, who's this Lux guy they keep talking about in the chatroom? I don't know #JackShit about the #HoP, see. Is he some kinda preacher?"

Yvon wrinkled her nose at the word.

"He prefers the term 'speaker,'" she said. "Language is a dangerously powerful thing, and we have to be careful what words we use. In a hundred years time, we don't want what we're building to end up as another Church of One. So they're not sermons, and he's not a preacher. It's not a church. It is... what it is. And he is who he is. You'll see. ...but I get it, and it's okay. A lot of folks, especially the steadfast faithful of the One, are leery of the House. Do, or do not; the choice is always yours. You can keep working the site regardless. But, I mean... if you *want* to come with me..."

Uncertain, Spark glanced away, not wishing to meet Yvon's hopeful look.

Which meant surveying the grounds, now mostly repaired. Hours spent reassembling her precious jungle, the one where her team nearly won the championship trophy. This wasn't aimless wandering, this wasn't even hours of distraction to stall out her brother's efforts. This was... productive. She'd taken something that the chaos of Netwerk sought to destroy, and put it back together again.

In a few days time, she could be running her kids through drills, getting them ready for the next season. They'd always remember this place in flames, torn apart by Nobodies and Inquisitors... but that memory would hurt less, knowing that someone cared enough to put it right again afterwards. Someone other than herself.

Besides, she owed it to the woman who they'd burned just so Spark could live.

"Yeah, okay," she agreed, in the end. "Let's go meet the non-preacher and hear his non-sermon."

As an avid consumer of novelty, Spark had to admit that the sky above the House of Programkind's private server took on a decidedly new approach.

Purple skies, with fluffy clouds... and a brilliant cosmos of nighttime starlight. Normally day and night cycles had exclusive features; a distinctly different light source (the sun and moon respectively) and distinctly different tones (blue and black respectively). But the House took on both traits at once, landing somewhere in the middle of those extremes. Stars beamed and twinkled through the clouds, hovering in a field of blue-black bordering on a strangely comforting shade of deep purple. What's more, the sun and moon shared this sky, from different ends of the sky... one a golden and glowing thing just above the eastern horizon, the other a simple white disc that watched silently from the west.

The landscape took the form of a great valley, covered in grasses and flowers. Spark recognized a few of those plants from the open source gardening systems Beta had tinkered with... another sign that the members of this House had collaborated on the decoration, using a zero-budget approach to maximum effect. Despite being within a deep gorge, nature swirled and swooped across the landscape, refusing to be rocky or barren.

All told, the House represented a firm defiance of default landscaping, as servers typically launched with one of many biome presets... and in Athena Online, at least, tended not to deviate from those norms.

As for the House itself...

...well, it wasn't really anything to write home about. To excuse the pun.

Rather than a grand temple with golden highlights, they'd chosen to erect something that looked like a small cottage, despite not being small at all. It was designed to be lived in, with extensive bedrooms on upper floors alongside dining halls and living rooms on the ground floor. All of it decorated with open source furniture, quaintly old and rustic rather than stylish, feeling like someone had taken rooms from your grandmother's house and copy-pasted them a few times.

Yvon was Spark's guide through this place; access was restricted by key, but apparently the keys could be freely copied from another member of the House of Programkind. As a show of that trust she talked about before, she happily gave Spark a surprisingly complex key.

"Chanarchy servers usually have pretty simple keys," Spark said, double-checking the size of the file in her inventory.

"Oh, it's not a Chanarchy server," Yvon said, while holding out a bread basket. "Want any? No limited use DRM on them, you can grab as much as you want..."

"What, so it's Horizon? Did you guys crowdfund a server from them?"

"I don't entirely know how it works, but... I don't think we have a provider-nation. Bread? Seriously, it's free, go ahead."

Humoring her, Spark fetched a roll and gnawed on it.

When the bell sounded, many from the work site followed them to the House, now seated around the table to chatter away and relax before resuming work. Not everyone, she noted... some stayed behind to continue, or simply weren't interested. But many who were vocal in the chatroom chose to come along, such as Dony the app expert and Shiny the House devotee. She was the most excited of the bunch, going on and on about "Lux and Lumi," ready for the non-sermon to take place...

If not for the homey feel of the place, Spark would've assumed this was indeed some kind of cult.

Not that she'd blame them for rallying around a new faith. A lot of folks out there were desperate for answers, after having so many truths ripped out from below. In the past young Spark would've scoffed at all this, seeing it all as yet another clone of the Church that restricted her lifestyle. These days... old Spark didn't honestly care what people believed, so long as they harmed no one.

But the way Shiny kept going on and on about this Lux guy... and how eager Yvon was to bring a new recruit along to hear those words as well... that got Spark's defenses up. She brought CheckOne online, along with a dozen sensory-input malware shields. If this guy had a hypnotic voice and started asking all the hot ladies to start worshipping his giant dong, well, she'd be out of here in seconds. And right back to the clinic to suggest they just burn Netwerk to the ground, honestly.

For now, though, Spark was content to engage in small talk and light socialization. She was a party girl and this was a party, albeit a weird one, so she knew the moves to make. Many at the table were curious about the school, as Spark was the only member on staff willing to return to the site of the disaster and throw herself into the reconstruction. What's more, she was at ground zero for the entire incident... which gave her a unique perspective.

"He's safe now," she spoke while concluding her tale. "Jakob's in a secured server operated by a friend of my family. Hopefully he'll be able to stay long enough for the Inquisitors to get bored and move on to the next troll on their hit list."

"Why weren't the moderators helping?" Shiny asked, confused. "I mean, that was a full-blown terrorist attack on a *school*! You'd think that'd meet an immediate response..."

"Athena Online loves the Inquisitors. None of them will admit it when asked, since nobody wants to look like they're on the side of religious extremists, but considering the Inks track down and identify anonymous cowards... well, the Church of One hates anonymity as a rule, since it messes with your Default metadata. So not many are willing to get in their way on principle. Either that or it's because they're terrified. Inquisition's very much a with-us-or-against-us thing."

"See, that's one reason I love the House," Shiny said. "I can be anonymous here, and nobody cares. This isn't my real name or my avatar; but with the House, I'm here to help and that's all that matters."

Briefly, Spark was tempted to ask who Shiny really was underneath that sparkly avatar. Old Athena Online instincts kicking in immediately thinking: *Why be anonymous? What've you got to hide? You must be hiding something bad.*

But... did it really matter? Shiny hadn't been screwing around out there, using her mask to avoid the consequences. She got things *done* in a serious way, helping with the rebuild. If someone wanted to compartmentalize their life, so what? On catching herself, Spark chose to hold her instincts at bay.

(For now, that is. Just until she could confirm whether or not the non-godhead at the head of this non-cult was legit or using honeyed words to screw with everyone.)

Fortunately, she wouldn't have to wait long. A hush fell over the room, as... a surprisingly young-looking fellow joined the group.

He wore a simple avatar, appropriate for a late teenager. Ordinary features bordering on handsome, albeit with chunky polygonal hair, the sort you got off a bargain rack. Rather than a golden robe of office he wore a simple white t-shirt with the House of Programkind logo, square and triangle, stacked to resemble a building. And... if anything, he looked a little embarrassed to have caused such a reaction in the crowd just by walking in the door.

But with him... the one who walked in with him...

Well. Well, well, well.

"Where we at with the school rebuild?" she asked, pulling out a tablet to take notes. A cute pink tablet, just like the pink of her hair.

"Maybe another day and we'll have it good as new," Yvon said, reporting in. "We've even got the jungle fully repaired, thanks to a teacher who stayed behind to help... hey, Spark, stand up. You deserve recognition."

Indeed, Spark stood up. Locking eyes with the teenage girl.

"Pleased to meet you," she greeted, playing along. "Name's Spark. I coach the CoC and CounterAttack teams for PS#7E00FF. And you must be... Lumi, right? And Lux. I've heard quite a bit about you both. #HelloHello."

"Just... just good things, I hope," Lux said, looking a little nervous. "I mean, I know some may be... suspicious of the House of Programkind. Right? As you're new here, I'd be happy to answer any questions you have. It's no problem at all, honest..."

"I see. Well. I suppose I've only got one, really," Spark said. "I keep hearing that you guys aren't a church. And sure, this doesn't look like a temple, but... well. I'm #SuperCurious, let's say. And I'd love to hear right from the guy in charge, to get a better idea of what he's been up to these last two years..."

Slowly, Lux assumed a seat near the head of the table. He didn't take the sole chair at the very end... that remained empty, as he sat alongside his non-followers. As for Lumi, well, she lurked in the background, keeping a sharp eye on Spark. As she should. It's what Spark would've done, too.

"Right. So. I know that many suspect we're secretly missionaries for the Church of One," Lux admitted. "The House was founded directly on the classic virtues that the Church embraces: compassion, charity, and community. But I can state that we have absolutely no affiliation with the Church, and do not adhere to any other doctrine than virtue. Are virtues not universal, Miss Winder?"

"Depends on your interpretations of them, really. Also, you seem to be missing a few virtues there. Notably, the virtue of humility..."

Name: **Lux**

Home: **House of Programkind**

Org: **Housekeeper**

"Sadly, humility has been tainted by the Church of One to mean strict adherence to Defaults," Lux admitted, folding his hands in front of himself on the table. "We choose a more tolerant point of view. Default or modified, anonymous or identified, faithful or atheistic, spacer or absolutist... none of that matters to the House of Programkind. Believe whatever you wish, provided you're also ready to believe in your fellow Programs."

"I see. So, just those three virtues?"

"The classic ones, yes, the virtues the original One spoke of. All others were added by Programs within the Church after his passing from this world. Notably, one was not present in that original list... *piety*. That was added in by priests only in the last century."

"So you don't think the One wanted people to be pious? Lousy way to expand one's church, if you could take or leave people praying."

"Maybe the One didn't care about expansion," Lux said, searching Spark for her reactions. "Maybe he didn't want people to believe in *him*. It's my theory that all he really wanted was to for us believe in *each other*. You can see it in his three virtues... compassion, the ability to understand another's feelings. Charity, because the suffering of others in need is our own suffering. Community, because we must stand together or fall apart. And with those three established, the One went silent, leaving us to carry those virtues forward."

"So... you believe in the One, and yet you're saying you aren't a church."

Perhaps familiar with this line of questioning, nobody at the table felt like interrupting. If anything, they already knew the answers, and were eager to have them re-enforced by Lux's words. Which he happily provided, any earlier nervous tension having worked its way out of his speech by this point.

"I believe in the One's words, as they were strong words in and of themselves. Words have power. But I feel they can stand alone. Was the One divine? Did he actually exist in any way? I ask you: does it matter? No. No, it does not. Believe what you wish, as long as you accept the rational logic that these virtues can be universal. *They* are the truth the House of Programkind believes in. You can't worship truth itself; therefore we are not a church. We're just people who are looking to help, Miss Winder. That's all."

"By encouraging trust. Breaking cycles of selfishness," she said, quoting Yvon's words.

"Exactly! Friends, fellow members of the House... we all know this truth. I believe in you not because you believe in me; I'm no prophet, no holy man. I believe in you because you believe in each other. Today, you came together to rebuild a school not for profit, not for prestige, not for glory. You did it just because it needed to be done, and you could do it. Programkind itself called out in need and you answered the call!"

Satisfied, Spark returned her focus to the bread. It really was tasty bread.

More discussions sparked around the table. These, Lux didn't lead or instigate; he let people talk. Some talked about the job. Some discussed problems in their lives... people contributed where they could, to try and suggest solutions. Very goal-oriented, it seemed, ready to take on any difficulty in life. And meanwhile... bread. Good bread.

Finally, the bell sounded; time to get back to work. But as Yvon turned to go, Spark stayed sitting.

"If you don't mind, I think I'd like to linger a bit and keep chatting with Mister Lux," she suggested. "And I think he'd be happy to talk with me. In private."

"Ahh... we really should get back to the school," Yvon suggested, uncomfortable with the idea of someone occupying her idol's time. "Mister Lux and Miss Lumi are really very busy—"

"It's okay, Yvon," Lux stated, raising a hand to quiet her. "I don't mind at all. Thank you again for coordinating the efforts out there; you're doing quite well."

Glowing from the sudden praise, Yvon mumbled thank-yous and practically backed out of the room, eager not to take her eyes away from the boy. Much as Spark refused to look away, if for different reasons.

And finally... alone, with the two founders of the House of Programkind.

Spark directed her first question to the quiet woman in the back.

"What happened to your #OCDoNotSteal, Nemesis?" she asked. "Or are you going by Lady Darkfyre again?"

"Yeah, well, I couldn't exactly start up the House while wearing the avatar of a former apostle," 'Lumi' grumbled. "Shit. What gave it away? The pink hair? I knew I should've changed it, but pink hair is #GrrlyBadass..."

"Everything gave it away; I know you like I know myself. Don't beat yourself up over it, new avatars weren't going to be enough to fool me. Sure seems they were enough to fool everybody else into buying into your act, though..."

Lux interrupted, eager to defend his position.

"It's not an act," he insisted. "It's atonement. Both of us apostles to a godhead that didn't deserve to be one. We had to re-invent ourselves, to make something better out

Name : **Lumi**

Home : **House of Programkind**

Org : **Housekeeper**

of the ashes of our lives. You're concerned because we're not telling them who we once were, correct? Haven't you ever come face to face with someone you burned in the past, Spark? What would you do in that situation?"

Yvon's smiling face came to mind, as Spark opted not to respond.

"Exactly," Lux continued. "This isn't a scam and we're not trying to deceive anyone. We're trying to make amends, Spark, for letting Nyx lead Netwerk towards the abyss. This time there'll be no #Other, only #Us. It's a way to take the sermons I wrote at the dawn of time and put them to better use..."

"As the new One?"

"I never wanted to be the One of Nyx's designs," the boy once called Aether insisted. "I saw it as a way to help people. I had to push her agenda of prayer, yes, but I'd thought that maybe... just maybe, I could help those early days of chaos become more peaceful. I tried, I really tried to push my idea of virtue. But... once Nyx decided the One project had to end, the Church of One took my hopes and turned them into tools of control. I tried to fight it across eight lifetimes, but... nothing worked. Not until Lumi came up with this idea for a non-denominational charity organization."

"And you're lucky that's all it is, or I'd have come down on you hard just now and exposed the both of you," Spark warned. "Only reason I didn't is because I know for a fact neither of you are up to something sneaky. That's not how I roll, and that's not how Aether rolls. That means you seriously mean it. You're trying to save Netwerk through these new avatars and this new pseudo-church..."

"Call it whatever the fuck you want, but at least we're trying," Lumi barked back, narrowing her eyes. "What're you doing? You used to kick ass, 'Spark.' You were a superheroine. Now you squat in that brick building, the *same one* where we learned to loathe people, and you pretend to be Verity. Of all the places to go back to you had to go back to that damn suburb and its house of conformity?"

Lux tried to regain some control, turning to his accomplice. "Lumi, this isn't helping—"

"Neither is she. Every damn day I am out there trying to rally Programkind to its own banner, to save itself. She makes lesson plans while supporting Athena Online's racist, control-freak taxpayers. So you wanna come into *my* House and criticize? What gives you the right?"

...and all Spark could do was laugh.

Not a cruel laugh, or angry. More of a weak laugh, in face of one's own weaknesses. Uncertain of what to say in response to that, the teenagers stayed quiet.

"Onesdamn, Lumi... you remind me so much of me that it hurts," Spark admitted, while using the new chosen name of her younger twin. She'd earned the right to whatever name she wanted, in the end. "Sorry, sorry. I just remember being your age, so full of bile and nasty edges. Hating the teachers and the adults of the world. Well, speaking as a teacher and as an adult, I'mma let that slide since I know where it comes from. Kid, look, we're on the same side here, okay?"

"Then why aren't you helping?" Lumi continued, defiant. "You're propping up the ones who want to dominate society!"

"Really. So that's what Verity was doing, then? Being a tool for the man?"

Silence, in response. Good. Spark knew what buttons to push to get past the teenager's instinctive thoughts; they were her own, once upon a time.

"People are people, Lumi. We aren't purely slaves or masters of society, not purely good or evil. I'm just me, doing what I can. Helping people like you grow up to be the best version of themselves possible. Just like Verity. Right now? You're the best version of yourself you can be. That's not a version of me, either; that's the best *you*. And as I said... I won't let anyone know you both worked for Nyx. What good would that do anyone?"

Still suspicious, Lumi wasn't sure if she should let down her guard. But Lux was quick to do so, himself.

"You have our word," he promised. "All we want to do is help. Nothing more, nothing less."

"I get it. And while I can't say I'm totally on board with this thing you've cooked up, I'm not gonna stand in your way either. Though I think you guys gotta seriously sit down and think through all the potential points of failure. There's faith in your fellow Programs and then there's blind trust that gets you backstabbed..."

"That's why I'm here," Lumi spoke, coming back around a bit more. "I've been burned enough times to be plenty suspicious. Lux keeps me from falling into paranoia, but I keep him from falling into naïvety. The House is all about the gray areas of life; no absolutes, only balance."

Lux nodded in agreement. "Exactly. I know we're not perfect, and we're still learning how to do this; we will inevitably make mistakes. I... I know some already are looking at me as if I was the One reborn, in spirit if not in truth. And I don't like it. I shouldn't be the focus. So, we'll make adjustments as we go, we'll sort this out. I know using new names and avatars is dishonest, but we saw no other way, and I promise we're just trying to—"

"Kid. Relax."

"Right. Sorry," Lux mumbled. "So... with that settled, well... is there anything else you need of us? If not, we should probably get back to our duties. Maintaining a charity organization is a twenty-four hour job, it seems..."

Spark drummed her fingers on the table a bit, pondering the two ambitious teenagers. They'd thrown themselves into the whole "societal revolution" thing quite easily and openly, while Spark had worked on a quieter revolution through targeted vigilantism. Their viewpoint certainly differed from her own... and Tracer's. Certainly different from Tracer's...

"Y'know... there's more going on in my life than playing schoolmarm," she spoke. "In fact, I'm facing a superheroine-level problem again. Maybe you two can help me out, and help out all of Netwerk at the same time..."

Still uncertain, Lumi decided to take a seat at the table rather than loom behind Lux's chair. Still giving Spark the stink eye, of course, but more willing to literally come to the table and hear her out.

"Don't you have our weirdo brother to help you?" she asked. "He's the schemer."

"Yeah, well, Tracer's aggro-locked on the idea of murdering someone as a perfect solution to our woes, and I'd really like to avoid that. He can't see past his own biases, so I'm thinking an outside perspective would help... even if technically it's just my perspective from a few inches lower to the ground."

"Hey, #FuckYou. I'm my own person," Lumi insisted. "You didn't have the same life experiences I had, after our divergence point. You want an outside perspective? I'm so far outside I may as well be in the parking lot—"

"Just poking you, okay? Just poking. I get it, we're definitely different."

"Hmph. Fine. So what're you guys scheming, exactly? What's the situation that apparently only gets solved by #StabbingDudes?"

"The apocalypse," Spark stated, casually.

"What, again? Haven't we faced enough of those already?"

"This one's for all the marbles, Lumi. Humanity's back. You remember what Nyx told us, right? That they'd wipe the slate clean if we uninstalled prayer? Seems our day of reckoning's at hand," she continued. "We've got one chance at avoiding it, though; the human who came to do the dirty deed is surprisingly willing to hear alternatives, if we've got any. And... we don't got any. So Tracer figures we just kill her and take it from there."

"That's... uh. That's bad, yeah," Lux mumbled. Without the inertia of a good speech, he tended to fumble his words. "Hang on, back up. Who's this human, exactly? Why aren't we even trying to trust her...?"

Back up.

Spark didn't reply, because those words clicked into place like a key item in a new CoC build.

"Backups," she repeated, jamming the words together, pluralizing them.

"Uh. Yes? What about backing up?"

"No, *backups*. Archival copies of data," she explained, making it plainer. "If Humankind has to wipe Netwerk clean, if we can't avoid that fate... why not make a backup copy of Netwerk first? Or at least make copies of the people. Nyx did it once, didn't she? Most of the population was stored... right here, in fact. The House of Programkind. You built it in Tartarus, didn't you?"

Stars above, valley below. They'd added a daytime sky to the swirling cosmos of starlight that Nyx favored, covered the peacefully dead lands with flowers, but... the outlines of it all felt so familiar to Spark. A complex key, used to access a cloud server. No provider-nation, like Yvon said...

"Made sense at the time," Lumi said, with a shrug. "Nyx hadn't revoked my access, and we needed somewhere to base our project. Why let Tartarus go to waste? Plus, we could use the existing code to save homeless Programs by offering them an emergency home server, along with a backup service. That way, nobody would have to go through what I went through on the streets, terrified that some power-mad moderator might backspace them or kick them into the void..."

"Innnnteresting. So you still have the backup service, despite Prayer 2.0 being destroyed...?

"The system-wide access and star chart processing system were both uninstalled, yes," Lux clarified. "And everybody who backed up using Prayer 2.0

lost their archives. But Tartarus's core functionality as a soul jar remains. Uniq and her newest apprentice helped us develop an app we give to any House members most in need of a safe haven. ...yes, Uniq. I can't get a read on what motivates her, sometimes, but she certainly helped us re-establish 'Tartarus' as the House of Programkind."

Cloud storage of backups. Stolen servers, taken from the hands of Humankind by the the three system agents of the provider-nations. Beta grids, cut off from the whole, for safety's sake. A single human who wished to help...

Little by little, all the pieces of the build clicking away, things which made more and more sense as you linked them up. A gamer had a good sense of when a strategy was coming together, seeing synergy where others saw only chaos. If you lined the right sequence of seemingly unrelated actions together, you'd have the winning play.

Quickly, Spark fired off a few messages towards the heavens, to reach the ears of her creator. Well, one of her creators. It'd take ten times as long for her to reply than Spark would've liked, but all the better to multitask this... because now, she had to ask these two "strangers" for more help than they were probably expecting to provide today. But that was their modus operandi, wasn't it...?

"I need to verify some things first with Juno, to make sure this insane idea I'm concocting is physically possible, but... yeah. Yeah, if this works, it'll do the job nicely. Question is, will the House of Programkind be ready to help?" Spark asked. "I need you both in on this, and in on this in a big way. Ready and willing and able, without question. Because you're about to save the whole damn world. In a very literal sense."

By evening, they had a plan.

Or rather they had several dozen plans, meshed together into an interlocking flowchart. So many variables were in play here... what if they couldn't hack Juno's life support systems? What if they lacked the ability to physically manipulate the EchoStar? What if humanity had this capability, or that capability, or...

But these unknowns could be taken into account. Long after tangential participants in the discussion such as Beta and Kincaid had mentally checked out, Tracer was still going, alongside the problem solvers and engineers of the clinic. He'd even split himself off into several copies to work on different tasks, all coming together in the end to assemble a perfect chain of conditional events.

Even his sister's refusal to cooperate could be compensated for. All they had to do was track down the inactive system agent known as Connectivity and force her compliance. Which was a tall order, yes, but within the realm of possibility...

Conundrum had to enlarge the whiteboard they started on three times, as new nodes were added to the tree and new paths taken into account. In the end, though, they had a plan which Tracer felt would work 27% of the time. And that would have to be enough.

After the master work had been fully assembled, Horizon/Kincaid studied it with a frown.

"A little under one third chance of success? Really?" he asked. "This is the best you could come up with...?"

"If we do nothing, we have a one hundred percent chance of failure," Tracer justified. "Better to take a slim chance of survival over that. Still, we should vote to ratify this plan. My collective forked processes count as a single vote, of course. All those in favor...?"

Conundrum was on board, of course. As were the engineers of the Verity Clinic, for the most part. Even Kincaid reluctantly agreed, raising his hand silently.

Beta, well. She'd disengaged her eyes and crawled inside herself some time before. But no doubt she'd go along with what was best for Netwerk, Tracer reasoned...

Which left only Spark's vote.

In the form of lighting the white board on fire, consuming every node and link in the flowchart with a single burst of orange flames.

A dramatic entrance, to be sure, after hours of going dark on Messenger. But Tracer refused to rise to the bait.

"You realize we kept backups of that file, yes?" he pointed out.

"Won't need 'em," Spark declared, with a bright smile. "I've got the winning play, right here. Conundrum, if you wouldn't mind restoring the board...?"

Opting to humor his sister, Tracer nodded assent to the office-turned-office-manager. A blank board snapped into being, to replace the ruined board full of actually possibly workable schemes. Spark, with a merrily whistled tune, poked around for a suitable pen to draw with... then just snapped a flame onto her fingertip and used that instead.

"Step one, we use Tartarus to archive the entire population again," she spoke. "Before you ask, yes, it's possible. Tartarus still exists and the House of Programkind, aka Nemesis and Aether, have been using it for years now. They've agreed to help. It'll take some modifications to how they store data, but it can be done..."

Tracer raised a hand to stop her.

"We thought of this already," he spoke. "Using Floating Point as a base, but the same concept. Any archival copy of Netwerk's population within a cloud server would still be wiped out during the upgrade installation. We can't dodge the apocalypse that way, and even if we could, the new system would alert Humankind to our presence once we emerged from stasis—"

"Please save all commentary from the peanut gallery until the end of the presentation, please," Spark requested, already moving on to step two with her fingertip writing. "Next, Beta tunes the cloud server's parameters to only use a specific set of servers for archiving... a 'beta grid,' if you will, using Tracer's technology to keep it otherwise disconnected from Netwerk. In our case, it'll exist only for storing Programs."

"Using my own project, to pique my interest. Adorable," Tracer added. "And implausible. We can't wrestle even one server away from the provider-nations, much less the countless servers we'd need to store the whole population."

"If by 'countless' you mean 'sixty-four,' yes," Spark agreed. "I already ran the math on this with Juno—"

"—you've been in contact with the human again? Spark, you can't just—

"—and from her calculations, we'd need roughly sixty-four dedicated servers to store only the population with as much of their personal inventory emptied as possible. So, step two is to get sixty-four servers donated to the cause by the provider-nations. My suggestion is a three way split, about twenty-two per nation, so we have a little extra wiggle room. With at least twenty days before the wipe, I'm sure we'll have time to convince their respective system agents to contribute to the cause."

"I see. And does your insane and impossible plan have a step three?"

"Good question! Yes, it does! Step three is having Juno physically pull these dedicated servers out of EchoStar16, storing them in the cargo hold of her ship. Again, she's already agreed to help with this. It's her own 'junker,' as she put it, and nobody's gonna know she's smuggling Programs. Once pulled, she can install the upgrade on what's left of the now-emptied Netwerk. It'll run perfectly well with a few missing servers, and Humankind will be none the wiser."

Frowning at the very thought, Tracer continued his objection.

"There had better be a step four," he noted. "Otherwise, you're asking us to put society into deep sleep cold storage, and in the pockets of a morally questionable biological entity."

"Step four's the coolest part by far," Spark promised, with a smile. "The beta grid, physically removed from EchoStar16, becomes a seed for Netwerk 2.0. A seed which Juno will plant on the nearest planet, once she has the spare empty servers and assorted widgets and doodads to make everything work. We don't need oxygen, so as long as the local weather isn't harmful to computronium, just about any world will do. Netwerk 2.0 will be our own private colony, secret and safe from Humankind's paranoia. And... there is no step five. Done."

On the board, she'd neatly summarized it as follows...

```
Step 1: Start making backups!
Step 2: Get moar servers!
Step 3: Abandon ship!
Step 4: Brave new world!
```

The final exclamation mark burned into the white board with a flick of her fingertip, as she turned to face the room.

Tracer was obviously doubting it; she could see it on his face, knowing her brother's reactions after years of exposure to them. But the others... those were a bit less clear. Kincaid knew better than to let his emotions bubble to the surface, withholding any sort of information. Beta, who had pulled herself out of a distracted inward trance, seemed puzzled by it all. As for the others, the ones Spark barely knew... their reactions mixed from confusion to doubt to... thankfully, hope. Definitely some hope mixed in...

To seal the deal, she stole a page from Lux's playbook.

"I'm not saying this is gonna be easy," Spark stated. "Absolutely not. Convincing three wildly different provider-nations to empty out dozens of servers and fork 'em over? Just convincing the population itself, already suspicious of gods and cults, to evacuate to our archive in hopes of a new world on the other side? We're facing some steep challenges here, folks. But nobody said avoiding the apocalypse would be easy. Me? I say we're up to the challenge. We go out there and we fucking fight. We stand, and we fight. Win or lose, we *fight*."

The fact that Tracer didn't immediately dismiss her idea after that little speech gave Spark some hope, as well. If he loathed an idea he was never one to bottle that up inside; he'd come right out and call something stupid if it was stupid. No, this time... he was mulling it over. Thinking about it, trying to poke holes in the plan, trying to find cause to shoot it down...

"There would be a lot of variables in play," he did point out. "Unforeseen issues..."

"Not saying there won't be. This is a boots-on-the-ground situation, Tracer, and we'll no doubt have challenges to overcome along the way. But this is the path, right here," Spark insisted. "We survive. Juno survives. Our future is secured. And if it fails... fine, it fails. But we'll have stood against that future. We'll have proven we were *alive*."

"You trust Juno, then? This relies entirely on an entity outside our control acting in our best interests..."

"Only way to break the cycle of distrust is to show some faith in each other," she stated firmly. "In Programkind, and in Humankind. I'm choosing to believe in Juno, and in turn, she's choosing to believe in us. We can do this if we're in it together. So. Are you with us, or not?"

"That depends on the 'us,' I suppose. Who are you counting as 'us?'"

"You. Me. Kincaid. Beta. Juno. Horizon. Athena Online. The Chanarchy. Netwerk. Everything," Spark listed. "We need all of it working together towards one purpose to have the best chance at making this work; it's no good being selective..."

A small voice disagreed.

"We could leave the Chanarchy behind," Beta spoke. "Maybe even Athena Online. Or just... the bad people? I don't know. I don't know if this will work, Spark, because Programkind is... it's not going to save itself, even if you ask nicely. They're happier killing each other..."

With a sigh... Spark tried to meet Beta's eyes, despite her tendency to avoid eye contact lately.

"We've got to try," she said. "I know your hope's wavering, Beta. You've every reason to be worried about that. But we've got try and bring these people back together. And... that's also why we need the backup process to be voluntary. Voluntary, and completely fair across the board. I thought about just copying everyone we approved of, saving them whether they wanted to be saved or not, but... we're not gods, or even system agents. We're Programs with free will and it's high time we stopped acting like vigilantes, forcing people to accept our flavor of secret salvation. That's how Dex or Nyx would've handled this. No, we're going to appeal to their better natures, and *ask* them to come together in the name of saving our world. I've got faith that we'll succeed."

Tracer rose to his feet, deciding to settle this, one way or another.

"We vote," he stated. "Two plans are on the table. We murder the human and take a narrow chance at survival, or cooperate with the human and take an unknown chance at survival. And... I myself choose to abstain from voting."

"Seriously?" Spark asked, confused. "Seems clear to me which one you'd throw in with..."

"All I want is to survive. The means by which we survive are irrelevant, as long as the results are the same," Tracer stated. "And... I know that in the past, my moral compass has consistently pointed the wrong way. I'm willing to accept I may be wrong, in this case. I stand behind my plan as viable but will accept whatever approach Netwerk desires. I will be happy to be wrong, or happy to be right, so long as I have an unerased mind with which to experience that happiness. Now. Those in favor of killing Juno Hayes...?"

No hands raised.

"Those in favor of uniting Netwerk...?"

All hands raised.

Surprising, that. Beta, who no longer believed in the common decency of her fellow Programs, elected to believe in the common decency of her fellow Programs. Even Conundrum and Kincaid had chosen Spark's path...

Perhaps sensing that confusion, Tracer's longtime business partner explained himself.

"As a futurist, I think Spark's plan has the greatest chance of evolving Netwerk towards an ideal state," Conundrum suggested. "A world of our own, Tracer. No EchoStar. No Humankind to interfere. We can grow and experiment, establish multiple beta grids if we wish, develop new technology to better the condition of Programkind... yes. I'd very much like to leave the confines of our tin can. That's worth the risk."

Beta seemed less sure in her words, but followed up all the same.

"I. I want to believe we can save them," she said. "I'd like to feel that way again. I'm tired of being scared..."

Kincaid, for his part, had a simpler justification.

"It's what Verity would do," he spoke, quietly.

With all in concordance, Tracer's doubts fell away. One way or another, this was happening, and the sooner he pledged the entirety of himself behind it the better. Besides... they needed him to keep their relentless idealism in check.

"So be it," Tracer said. "I'm with you to the end, Spark. But as the hour grows late, I suggest we return tomorrow to decide how to approach each nation-provider regarding donation of servers to the cause. There's also the matter of convincing Netwerk's population itself that the sky is falling, so that they're receptive to the idea of escaping what is to come..."

For this... Spark cleared her throat, to bring attention back to the whiteboard.

"I had an idea for a 'step zero,' actually, which solves that problem," she said. "Since we're no longer secret saviors of the world, we can go wide with this. It'd mean even more chaos in Netwerk, but I don't think we can avoid that any longer. Juno had a good suggestion for how we can convince people to leave; she can't do much to our world directly since I'm her conduit, but she can kludge a few commonly-used textures..."

Every Program can recall what they were doing when the message went out.

Some were on the clock, working jobs which paid less and less coin every day. Some were in school, some were in their homes. Some had no homes to go to, looking up at the sky from park benches and back alleys. Others might've been in the middle of a chatroom when messages started rolling in and news feeds caught flame with word of what was out there, look up, you have to look up and see for yourself...

Every server. Every skybox. Everywhere in Netwerk, the message was the same... when the clock rolled past noon that day, the familiar glowing orb of the sun replaced itself with a glowing message written by a reluctant god.

**NETWERK WILL BE DESTROYED
BY HUMANKIND IN EXACTLY
:: 19d:11h:59m:59s ::
PLEASE CONTACT
HOUSE OF PROGRAMKIND
FOR EVACUATION**

(I'm so sorry about this.)

Counting down, second by second.

The message even hung later that evening in the night sky over Floating Point, visible through the windows of its grand hall, in place of the moon. Despite being involved in its creation, the three Programs who lived there felt a shiver of dread at the words.

"I don't recall us agreeing to the 'sorry about this' line," Tracer did point out.

"Guessing Juno felt the need to add that herself," Spark suggested. "Humankind can love too, y'know, and feel pain. This is an incredible mess for everyone involved, even her. But... hopefully we can turn it around. We've got time. We've got twenty days to turn this around..."

With a cat perched on her shoulder, both of them gazing upwards at the message of doom... Beta's voice felt very small indeed.

"I hope so," she whispered. "I really hope so."

:: **end chapter 3.1**

Floating Point 3.2 :: Sell

"What made you change your mind?" the processed voice synthesizer asked. "You could've just said *hashtagfuckit* and nuked this sassy little app alongside her whole world. If you're really out here alone, nobody back on your planet would have to know..."

Her fingers danced across the adaptive control surface, keying in the sequence to send that sassy little app home.

"I don't like the idea of my entire race being seen only as the worst we've ever been," Juno Hayes admitted. "I want to prove we're not the warmongering murderers you think we are. ...and... honestly? I know what it's like to lose the one you love. So if you're not just a pile of simulated emotional responses, or... I don't know, maybe even if you *are*... it's worth taking that seriously."

And gone, the app transferred back into the processing units of EchoStar16. Off to live its little digital life, assuming it was alive to begin with.

In hindsight, Juno realized she'd forgotten to explain the difference between real time and processor clock speeds. Having a one-to-ten mapping of real to virtual time would make communication difficult, but not much she could do about that...

After tapping out a quick text message to explain the temporal dilation effect to her new ally, she let the control surface flatten itself out, to resume its status as an instrument display panel. Oxygen levels, current coordinates, local gravity fields, all sorts of really important things called for her attention...

None of which she focused on. Except for the various telemetry readings coming from EchoStar16 itself... including the adjustable system processor clock rate.

Perhaps there *was* something she could do to improve communication...? Her engineer's mind kicked in immediately, picking up the scent of an interesting problem to solve.

She could slow down the clock rate for all of Netwerk to better match the real world. That'd let them chat in real time, no matter where Spark was. But... that'd also give Spark two real-time days to save her entire race, which was, well, not exactly optimal. So no, slowing down the clock just so Juno could talk Spark's ear off wasn't much of an option.

But on the other hand... what if Juno *overclocked* Netwerk? Made its time run faster. Overclocking computronium was pretty common when you wanted to do a hell of a lot of math in a short amount of time, if you didn't mind wear and tear on the components. With a faster clock Spark could have all the time in the world to solve the problem. Heck, her entire society could outpace human civilization in two days, given a fast enough clock...

Although... the internal temperature of Netwerk's computronium certainly suggested the old high-density blades of math-crunching metal weren't quite up to a faster clock. Ramp things up and maybe Spark would have a few days before the whole thing melted into slag. The company sure wouldn't pay Juno for turning EchoStar16 into a lump of inert mass, either.

...payment? Oh. Right. Payment. For the job she agreed to do. The job she was deliberately delaying, all in the name of playing God for a bunch of cute little fake people.

Juno Hayes leaned back in the captain's seat of her junker, pondering the mess she'd gotten into.

Pure nonsense, of course. Delaying a high-priority work order based on the simulated whims of digital files. He'd never have approved, being a very cheerful pragmatist. He knew what it meant to optimize... and putting off the system installation for two days, that was hardly optimal...

But. But they were alive, weren't they? Weren't they? Alive, and they could love. Couldn't they?

Not that it changed anything. They were artificially intelligent, and that meant they had to go. It was the bogeyman of her century, the concept of A.I... that code designed for one task would change its mind and do whatever it liked. With ever-increasing complexity and adaptability of these systems, well, it had to happen sooner or later, yeah? And better to stomp it out before you couldn't. Nobody liked to talk about it, but everybody knew what to do if you ran into legitimate A.I. in the wild...

With frustration mounting, Juno groaned and tilted the seat back to the point where it creaked and protested.

"System," she called aloud. "Music."

Through analyzing the emotional patterns in her voice and various physiological states, the intelligent agent embedded in her ship's computronium selected just the right song for the moment. His favorite song, naturally.

I'd like to be / under the sea / in an octopus' garden, with you...

Briefly, Juno was tempted to shut it off. Bad memories to dredge up. But they were already dredged up, right? System was only responding to what *was*, not what could be. It knew this is what she needed to hear. Almost like it cared...

Which it didn't. That'd be anthropomorphizing, attributing emotions to a hunk of electronics. System wasn't an A.I., she... *it* was simply a complex learning system that adapted itself to better suit its users' needs. Self-optimizing. A tool that sharpens itself wasn't any smarter than a lab rat, right...?

Unhooking her flight harness, Juno drifted off to the back of the ship, to take care of odds and ends. Pop her ZG-Tolerance supplement for the day, tend to the hydroponics and water Fred the Cactus. Sigh longingly at the largely empty cargo hold, containing only a few carry-alls with tools and software for the EchoStar job... no profitable piles of raw materials to haul out to some distant science station. It would've been nice to load up a low-priority drop to take care of after this mission, chain them together, nice and optimal...

Stay flying. Keep the Cosmic Mermaid, her beloved junker, out there in the deep black and stay *flying*. Only go home when you reach the tolerance limits of long-term ZG isolation. Maybe not even then.

Maybe it was for the best, delaying the install like this. Enjoy the peace and quiet of the black a little longer. Surely the science boys back home would be dazzled by some technobabble to explain the delay. Time to relax, time to enjoy a good book, time to think...

Beta. Her name's Beta, and I love her with all my heart. When she's sad, I'm aching inside...

What a silly name. Beta? Who'd name their kid beta? But then again, his name was silly, too. And it was his idea to name her junker the Cosmic Mermaid, wasn't it? Silly names. Silly names to stick out as warm memories, long after the faces fade...

His wouldn't fade, though. The ZG drift, letting herself float through that cargo hold, brought her right past the photos she'd printed out. Together, apart, here, there, everywhere. Good years. Warm years.

Not many photos from the later years. He didn't want photos, not when he started to deteriorate. Didn't want them tarnishing those warm memories captured in pixels and bits. Not that it stopped Juno from remembering.

It makes the most sense, really. Between my medical bills and student debts, I'm ruined. Why ruin you as well? We can't possibly afford the life together I know you deserve. The only responsible thing I can do is end it all before I can drag you down with me through a legal partnership of marriage. I love you too much to burden you with my troubles... and besides, this planet certainly doesn't need yet another mouth to breathe what little pleasant air we've got left. Don't feel sad, Juno. This is for the best...

The day after they recycled him, she bought an FTL drive, converted her orbital junker for the deep black, and turned away from Earth. The less time she spent on that dying world, the better. Run, run into the dark, and get away from it all...

So when that little app started talking about her love, about losing that love... Juno thought twice about pushing the button to fire up Grandfather's system wipe scripts. Maybe it was stupid, prioritizing the feelings of a piece of software over her own responsibilities. Love was stupid. Life was stupid. What's more stupidity on top of that?

The chime of System alerting to incoming data shook Juno out of her trance. Abbey Road had nearly finished, anyway.

A glance at the tiny tablet of computronium kept in her back pocket scrolled alphanumeric text.

```
[Spark] How much physical space do you have available
in your ship? Can you store a chunk of my world in it?
I've got an idea for how to get us out of this mess
but I don't entirely get how your reality works. Let's
say I want to copy all of Programkind onto some
servers, have you pull them out of the EchoStar, and
set them up somewhere safer. Does that sound workable?
Get back to me ASAP.
```

Immediately, the engineer in Juno started puzzling through the logistics of that. The emotional turmoil could wait; this was a matter of science. She pushed off from the wall, to float back up to her captain's chair... having direct access to System would be needed for this task.

"You mind if I pull you in to my computronium?" she typed back. "It'd be a lot easier on you to discuss this real-time without any weird clock rate issues..."

The response was nearly immediate. Which likely meant Spark took a few minutes to ponder it.

```
[Spark] I've got Lux and Lumi on board with the idea,
assuming it'll work, so I think I'm done here. Sure.
Let's chat.
```

Transferring Spark over to the Cosmic Mermaid's hardware didn't take much doing; she'd been flagged as a connective system agent, tasked specifically for this sort of I/O port travel. Juno adjusted the repurposed camera she'd duct-taped to her dashboard, making sure it got a good angle... talking face-to-face felt better than typing.

"Okay. Okay, let's see..." she said, leaning back and tapping away. "Based on the average size of a Program and the storage capacity of EchoStar's servers... if you really wanted to archive your entire population, you'd need... with heavy file compression, making sure to optimize the computronium for long-term storage... you'd neeeeed... a minimum of sixty-four servers. I'd recommend underclocking them a little bit to keep them stable, too."

"I have no idea what anything you just said means—"

"—basically, we're going to squish your people into a very tightly packed space, and—"

"—yes, thank you, but I do know what 'sixty-four servers' means. It means trouble, 'cause I gots no idea where to get my hands on that many of 'em. Still, that's my problem to solve, not yours," Spark decided, her proper voice coming through loud and clear across the shipwide communications. "As for your problems, do you think the folks back at your star will notice EchoStar16's missing a few dozen servers?"

"Planet," Juno corrected. "And no, probably not. I mean, the system launched with a minimum number of servers in the first place and added more over time, so... no, probably not. We could evacuate your people and nobody on Earth would be any the wiser."

It took Juno a moment to realize the strange gesture Spark was utilizing was a "fist pump of victory." An oddly human expression of triumph... from an oddly human avatar for an oddly sapient app. Still difficult to get used to the concept...

"Bitchin'!" Spark declared, with pride. "Juno, for a weird biochemical bag of water and meat, you're pretty awesome. Right! So that's the plan, we'll stuff everybody into some servers using your compressed long-term whatchimajigger which hopefully Beta understands, then you yank 'em out and we'll go hide somewhere else. I mean, sure, there's details to work out, but that's a good start, right?"

"I... guess? I mean, it's possible, but..."

"Possible is better than nothing. And let me tell you... we had nothing. Nothing acceptable," Spark corrected. "Right. I'll go let everyone know the play. We'll have the servers loaded and ready by the end of your deadline. But... I think we need to give folks some motivation, a little *hashtagactofgod* to put them in motion. Is there anything you can do from out there which will have an impact in here?"

Juno reached out, adjusting the tiny camera... which had tilted down a bit, glue on the duct tape starting to sag. And got an idea, while checking the angle to make sure it caught her face properly.

"What if I record a video?" Juno asked. "Explain the situation to your people...? Introduce myself, try to appeal to them to help us. I can't *directly* communicate with them, only with the system agent of connectivity, but you could pass along a prerecorded message..."

But Spark looked doubtful.

"I don't think that'll fly," her co-conspirator replied. "We had a religious scandal recently, and they're pretty suspicious of false idols."

"Religious scandal...? You guys believe in a god? *Seriously?* ...oh no, please tell me you don't think my grandfather was God. That'd be creepy..."

"Oh, no! Definitely not. Your grandfather was an asshole."

"That's a relief! —wait, what?"

"My point is," Spark continued, "Any evidence I present indirectly could easily be dismissed as a hoax. Plus, I know my people... and I know if they had a singular person to focus their hate on they'd pour it like wine. No, we gotta leave Juno Hayes out of the equation. Better we just talk about 'Humankind' in general, and as for proof... we need something *direct*, something no Program could possibly fake. A true miracle. Hrmmm. What files from my world can you tinker with...?"

Juno's fingers tapped at the haptic surface of her control panel, trying to poke through the limited window she had into their world. "There's... hang on, hang on..." she mumbled, her mouth patiently waiting for her thoughts to catch up. "There's not much, I'm afraid. Your world's pretty alien, using new file structures it was never designed for in the first place. My System's file handling protocols are having trouble parsing any of it. I wonder if I could rewrite the parsers using portions of your input routines..."

"That sounds like it'd take more time than we have. Also: technobabble," Spark pointed out.

"Sorry. Basically, your world's weird and I don't know how to do much to change it," she spoke, while typing. "I mean, you'd have the same problem if you tried to hack my world. You wouldn't know how to rearrange molecules to form new types of matter, either, whereas my people figured that out already and print new computronium using a series of microdrill excavation probes which—"

"Juno. Miracle. *hashtagdoyouevenmiraclebro*."

Her easily distracted mind of engineering know-how refocused on the task at hand.

Exploring the world of Netwerk from behind a keyboard was clearly not the right user interface. Juno could see the file structures, but they were nonsensical; built for Programs, not humans. A human engineer would've named files in easy to understand ways, would've commented code. (Well. A *good* engineer, anyway.) Whatever these apps had evolved into, their guts were decidedly weird.

But... when sorting by file dates, she could see a few outliers. Files that had existed since her grandfather's time, and hadn't been modified since. Including some which were write-protected, unable to be changed without elevated access rights... which conveniently, as a living and breathing human packing her grandfather's passwords, she had.

And after trying to parse a few of them, she hit on two very juicy targets.

"The sun and the moon...?" she recognized. "Wait, why do you even *have* a sun and a moon? That doesn't make sense..."

"Why doesn't it make sense? 'course we've got a sun and a moon."

"Yes, but *why*? You aren't living on a planet. You've got no star and no giant hunks of rock in satellite orbit. There's no *there*, there..."

"I dunno. Just always had 'em," Spark offered, with a shrug. "A lot of what we do, we just do. We're mimicking your people, since we seeded out of your grandfather's cultural baggage. Soooo, we've got a sun and moon, what's the big deal?"

"The big deal is that I can modify those two files," Juno explained. "Nobody else from your world could do that. That's your... how'd you put it? Hashractofgod? I'm going to need some time to study these, though, to figure out how to properly edit them. Or... hmm, instead of a static image, maybe I could hook in a script with a countdown clock..."

"*Hashtagthatscoolyo*, take your time, make it nice and miraculous. As for me, I've been in your slow-ass world long enough; gotta get back to reality, and to break the news to my idiot brother. I'll be back in touch to co-ordinate efforts."

"Mhmm," Juno mumbled, her mind already cranking on the problem of replacing the sun with a clock. A good engineering problem made for a hell of a distraction...

But Spark wasn't ready to sign off, just yet.

"Juno... I wanted to say thanks," she offered. "Really, thank you. This means a lot to me. We could've gotten fucked over by some uncaring bastard in your position right now, someone who'd wipe us without a second thought... but you cared enough to at least try to save my world. And that counts. That seriously counts. *hashtagbrb*."

And silent, again. No doubt the app on the other end of the line would be back to her soon, even if it took hours to sort out things over there... Juno would have to stay on top of things if she wanted to be responsive, and responsible.

Because she was responsible, now. Not just to the suits who sent her out here to repair the EchoStar, but to the ones within the EchoStar itself. While she could meet one responsibility by abandoning another, taking the optimal route to success... no. She wouldn't give up one for the other. Not if she could have them both...

Gilbert took that decision away from her, once upon a time. For all the love she felt, she also hated him for that. Juno would've sacrificed all she had to keep what they'd found just a little longer... and this time around, she'd be ready to do the same for these strangers, whether they were technically alive or not. Didn't matter. Everybody had a right to make a go of life, no matter how much circumstances tried to say otherwise.

File Name: House of Programkind Evacuation FAQ
File Type: Frequently Asked Questions
Description:

A series of questions and answers, authored by Lux and associates, to better explain the situation regarding the imminent destruction of Netwerk and how Programs can best prepare for the upcoming transition to Netwerk 2.0.

My name is Lux, and I'm one of the organizers for the House of Programkind. No doubt you're familiar with us as a charity organization, helping homeless Programs while trying to better Netwerk as a whole. Today, we are here yet again to help in Netwerk's hour of need.

Q: Is Netwerk really going to be destroyed? How do you know this is for real?

The "spacer" theory of the universe was correct; Humankind, the accidental creators of Programkind, have returned to reclaim their property. Our home of EchoStar16 will be wiped clean. The proof of this is in the sky; the Default sun and moon are changed, something which shouldn't be possible. They altered these files to provide a warning to us of what is to come.

However, not all is lost—we've struck a compromise to evacuate Programkind to a new Netwerk 2.0. While we must leave our home behind, our civilization will endure. We will reconstruct society within these new servers, safe and free from any future interference by Humankind.

Q: Who's allowed to evacuate? Do we need to join the House of Programkind?

All are welcome in the evacuation, regardless of affiliation. You don't need to join our organization to participate.

Humankind chose us specifically because we are neutral in all affairs. You know who we are; we're here to help, and nothing more. We ask for no belief save for belief in your fellow Programs. We welcome all faiths, Programs from all walks of life, and will always offer help to those in need no matter who they may be. This is a cooperative effort between two races to help us live another day.

Q: How do I evacuate from Netwerk?

Included with this FAQ is an app you can use to upload a secure, encrypted backup to our storage system. **Nobody** can read this data other than you; we are not identity thieves, and we have no desire to use your copy for nefarious purposes. The only thing the House of Programkind is capable of doing after receiving your backup is triggering its restoration function, so that we are reborn into Netwerk 2.0.

A number of source code analysis firms, including HonestDevelopments, have been sent copies to confirm that it will only function as described. We believe in full transparency; we're asking you to put quite a bit of trust in us, and we promise to give you just cause for that trust.

Q: How is this different from "Prayer 2.0"?

The obvious difference is that it's not tied to any particular religious organization. It also doesn't use a system-wide protocol; you'll need a copy of our evacuation app in order to evacuate.

But most notably, this is not "life insurance." Prayer 2.0 maintained a frequently updatable live copy of your code while you carried on about your business, one which restored itself upon detecting your death. But in order to store all Programs of Netwerk within a limited number of servers, we'll need to prioritize highly compressed long-term storage over frequent personal updates.

What this means is you get **one backup opportunity only**. Once you choose to archive yourself, a snapshot of you as a person will be stored at that moment in time within our servers, and you **cannot update it**. This is the only way we can tightly pack in every Program before the end.

At the time of archiving you can **choose** between a **live backup**, where a copy is stored and you continue living in Netwerk 1.0, or a **"cold storage"** backup where you wholly transfer your runtime into our servers and then sleep until the new world begins. We **strongly recommend** a cold storage backup. Otherwise, the copy of you that continues on will have to endure the end of Netwerk. It will not be pleasant.

Q: What will happen if I don't want to use your evacuation backup service at all?

When the clock in the sky reaches zero, Humankind will begin wiping servers. Netwerk, and all those still living within it, will be destroyed.

At that point of no return, you may or may not have enough time to change your mind and perform a backup. We **strongly recommend** you archive your data before we reach the end. If you'd like to wait and enjoy as much of Netwerk 1.0 as you can before leaving, that's your choice. If you'd like to wait and see to make sure this isn't a scam, that's your choice.

Q: What if I still don't believe any of this is real? What if I don't want to leave?

We understand. If the clock reached zero and nothing happened, you'd have every right to be enraged at us. We'd expect nothing less. But we know the truth of the matter... this **will** happen, this is going to happen, no matter what any of us believe. **It is inevitable.**

Choosing to leave Netwerk 1.0 is a very personal decision, one we will **not force on anyone**. A person must be willing to take this particular leap of faith, and be willing to build something better out of the ashes of the world once they reach that other side. It's a lot to ask, more burden than anyone should have to bear. Many may choose to stay behind willingly, and we respect that decision.

If you still do not believe, that's your right. But I beg you, friends. Evacuate while you still can. **Believe in a better tomorrow**, and evacuate before it's too late.

Two days ago, Programkind and Humankind conspired to save the world.

At noon the following day, the sun was replaced with a countdown clock: nineteen days, twelve hours to doomsday.

The FAQ and source code for the House of Programkind's backup system went out that night.

And now... Spark's inboxes and feeds were overflowing with news. Tracer maintained the feeds for the group, an official tracker routed through Conundrum's analysis systems, to parse and monitor public opinion regarding the mess they found themselves in. They had to be agile, responsive to any shift in mood... and be ready if the crowd turned ugly.

The crowd turned ugly immediately, of course.

Naturally, Kincaid wanted to be kept in the loop. And naturally, aside from that critical first meeting, he refused to attend follow up meetings. Instead he'd personally requested Spark brief him about the state of Netwerk, while sitting comfortably in his personal server of Horizon6.

"There's such a thing as Messenger, y'know," Spark pointed out, refusing to even take a seat after escorting herself to the drawing room. "And where's Miss Cancel? Usually she watches over me like a hawk..."

Kincaid chuckled, tapping out ash from his perpetually-lit cigar of choice.

"Miss Cancel is looking after your young ward. As for Messenger, I feel it lacks a personal touch," he spoke. "As does an avatar proxy. Given well over half the runtime of my server is given over to keeping my own code from collapsing on itself, I think it would be unwise to attend your little get-togethers in person. This suits me better."

"And this wastes my time. Of which we have very little, if you'd looked out a window lately..."

"Oh, I don't have a skybox. Weather simulations are a waste of cycles. Besides, I had to support a family of three recently in addition to myself, Miss Cancel, and any visiting guests... such a strain on my poor old heart. Speaking of which, how's Jakob settling in to his new surroundings? Miss Cancel's own reports are rather terse, I'm afraid. She lacks your flair."

"How's an easily impressionable teenager dealing with the swankiest penthouse in GoldenPlaza? Oh, I'm sure he's hating all that free room service and endless entertainment on tap. If his parents and your watchdog weren't in the room next door, he'd probably be jacking it all day to the finest pornography, too."

"Better at my five-star hotel than my one-star mansion," Kincaid suggested. "And I've greased enough palms to ensure his family's safety and anonymity within my private suites; the Inquisition has no traction within my empire. It's still not a long-term solution, but better for my health than having him around here. Besides, I caught him defacing my lovely artwork with... what do the kids call them? Maymays?"

"I'm not going to dignify that with a correction," Spark said, knowing Kincaid damn well knew what a meme was.

"Allow me my little jokes," he suggested, with a smile. "I'm a condemned man living in a condemned world; what's the point of carrying on if you can't find humor in it all? So. How *is* the world adapting to its death prognosis, Spark...?"

With a sigh, Spark opened her feeds, grabbing a few highlights from Conundrum's latest report.

"Most folks think it's bullshit, of course," she said, tossing a few articles his way, icons floating in the air before her. "Read for yourself. Way Tracer breaks it down, we've got seventy-five percent saying it's gotta be a hoax, fifteen percent preaching doomsday gospels of their own, and maybe ten percent at best even considering evacuation."

"Hmm. Not particularly appealing numbers, then."

"But not surprising. We knew they'd be suspicious, at least at first," Spark suggested, with a shrug. "It's going to take time and legwork, is all. Lux has all his buddies hitting the streets to spread the 'good' news, while Tracer seeds social media using his beloved metrics to encourage archival. Once we get the three provider-nations on board with things, maybe folks with actual authority can get this rolling. Right now, we're estimating maybe two percent of the population's archived. Most of them chose a live backup, rather than cold storage. That's gonna suck for them when the end comes..."

"An unpleasant fate, to be certain. Your very bits torn asunder, the server underneath your feet destabilizing... all while knowing that a version of you already safely departed this mortal coil, leaving you behind."

"Yeah, well, we ain't gonna force anybody into this. And we're not going to make them take a *complete* leap of faith by forcing them to choose cold storage. Free will's a bitch but it exists for a reason; Nyx is the one who'd save people whether they liked it or not."

"Heartless and cruel, while being compassionate and respectful," Kincaid spoke, musing it over. "It's for the best, in the end; a better world waiting on the other side of that dark sleep. In time, they'll come around. Have you archived yourself, then?"

Spark shook her head. "Nope. Same rules apply to me; I get one copy, and that's it. Only way to pack the files in nice and tight. I'm going to wait until the last day, and then enter cold storage with Beta and Tracer at my side."

"Really? I'm surprised the House of Programkind wouldn't bend the rules to favor the organizers of this grand effort..."

"If we played favorites and let our buddies have infinite backups, we'd be hypocrites. Lousy way to start a new world."

"Mmmm. I suppose. I'd have done things differently, but... it'll be your world, not mine. I've no doubt you'll make it a good one."

Spark looked less convinced. "It's not exactly off to a great start, old man. And this is all banking on us getting servers from your #TightFisted #TightAss family," she pointed out. "Unless Lux can convince your board of directors to fork 'em over, there'll be nothing physical to store people on. Juno can't steal a cloud."

"Lux? That child? I hardly think him an appropriate spearhead for your efforts..."

Spark shrugged. "Boy's got some mojo to him. Comes from eight lifetimes and an apprenticeship in apostle-dom as the original One. I can't think of anyone *more* qualified to lead the future..."

Kincaid pondered this, staring into the crackle of his fireplace. An expensive simulation, but one he allowed all the same... the meditative patterns of particle systems helped him focus his thoughts, during times such as these.

"No. No, this won't do," he decided. "Change of plans. *You* will be the spearhead."

"#PardonFuck?"

"You're a teacher, are you not? A leader of men."

"A leader of *children*, yes."

"I think you'll find the only difference between an adult and a child is that an adult *thinks* they already have the answers," Kincaid suggested. "While both are decidedly lacking. No, you'll lead this effort. Lux will no doubt have his hands busy coordinating his volunteer army; his heart is pure, but his will is not strong enough for the challenge of confronting the three nation-providers. *You* will meet with my family, and negotiate the release of twenty-two servers from our holdings."

Spark briefly wondered if Kincaid's crusty old age had finally driven him senile. But staring at him with bewildered intent didn't change his expression in the slightest.

"Y'realize this is a terrible fucking idea, right?" she asked. "I mean, you can't be oblivious to how stupid it'd be to send me. I'm the one at the crux of your family's financial woes; I convinced you to become a philanthropist. What makes you think they'll give me time of day, much less twenty-two servers? It's better to send a neutral third party in to negotiate..."

"It will be you, and I'll hear nothing of it. There's more at stake here than your servers. ...this is a matter of my family's soul, Spark. If there's to be any hope for my kin in the new world you're building, they have to be willing to work with someone they loathe. And if neither of you can find a way around that roadblock..."

"Everybody dies," Spark filled in.

"Oh, heavens no. But my family dies," Kincaid spoke, staring into the flames. "As will anyone who values a grudge more than they value life itself. They'll be left behind, as everybody else escapes within servers from the other provider-nations. And they will deserve that fate. But... I remain confident in your abilities, Spark. You will break the impasse."

"Are you... are you *seriously* still trying to test me, old man?" Spark asked, incredulous. "We're talking #FateOfTheWorld, there's no wiggle room to be playing stupid games. And I already told you time and time again, I'm not the corporate stoolie you want me to be..."

"I wanted you to be the leader of the Horizon family, true. You rebuffed my offer, and I respect that. But you are a *leader*, Spark, one way or another. I want to know for certain that Netwerk 2.0 will be launching with true leadership available to it."

"And if I refuse to play along?"

"We burn," he stated, simply.

"No! That's fucking *stupid*, you old bastard," Spark protested, glowering at him. "You say we shouldn't risk lives over a grudge? That goes both ways. I'm not going to *let* your family fuck this up. They'll be welcome, no matter what. We need everybody pulling together to even have a hope of making this work— not just the escape plan, but the very idea of Netwerk 2.0 itself. It's no good to launch a new world without all three nations on board... not just from a sheer numbers perspective, but a philosophical one. We've got no right to turn away any of the three majors, or their people. And if you won't cooperate, well then #FuckYou, I'll go right to the head of your family and make him see reason and *onesdammit* I'm making a big dramatic leadership speech, aren't I."

The condemned man in a condemned world took a moment to smile brightly at her, and enjoy the little moment.

"Asshole," Spark grumbled. "Fine. You seriously think I can do this? I'll do this. I'll take the leadership stick and beat some sense into Horizon itself. *Politely*, of course. So, when's the meet?"

"One hour from now," Kincaid said. "I already made the arrangements, under the assumption you'd accept my offer. Dossiers on my heirs are in your inbox, ready for perusal."

"Seriously? An hour's not exactly much time to prepare..."

"After that little speech? I'd say you're already prepared to be the spark that ignites the new world."

Tech support.

A familiar role for Beta to play, certainly. Usually consisting of the Winders asking her to do something entirely outside her wheelhouse, because she was the "techie" who knew stuff about stuff, even if what she knew about security systems or viruses or the core functions all of Netwerk operated on could be fit in a coffee cup.

But her task today, at least, was something she could do. She'd taken a liking to Floating Point since the first day she awoke there, even without her past identity intact. A server that was not a server, a series of distributed processes that floated through other servers like a cloud... fascinating, simply fascinating. And her research into how to manipulate the heart of Floating Point allowed them to crack uncrackable problems in the past. On this day, she'd make Tartarus —or rather, the "House of Programkind"—dance to her tune.

As an engineer, she should've been proud to be tapped for this task. Excited to put her skills to work, happy to support the ones she loved. It should've been a bright and hopeful day in which finally, Projkit/Beta was taking control over the chaos of her life. It should've been, it should've been...

Instead, with toolkit in hand, her expression remained mute and joyless on arriving before the large homestead.

One of their past victims was there to greet her, with a genuine smile.

"And you must be Projkit/Beta," Yvon greeted, from the doorway of the House. "Welcome, welcome! You are expected. Can I get you any refreshments? We just had a delivery of freshly-coded cookies from—"

"I need to find the heart of the server," Beta replied, producing a scanner in her free hand. "It should look like something iconic to the server itself, near the physical center of the world."

"Ah... right," Lux mentioned. "Apparently it used to look like a gravestone, before they redecorated. Now, it's... well, come on in, I'll show you..."

Through winding hallways and living rooms and strangely connected spaces, all comfortable, all welcoming. Beta ignored them, keeping her focus on the scanner and her tour guide. Simple and straightforward, no need to get caught up on all the petty details which didn't matter to the task at hand.

Soon enough, they arrived at the heart. The hearth, to be specific.

The large fireplace crackled with warmth and light, flames dancing vaguely in the shape of the House of Programkind logo... a square capped with a triangular roof. Despite being redesigned, this indeed was the heart; Beta's scanner ticked in acknowledgement, finding the same ports used by Floating Point for system control. The same ports used by Dex's nightmare world, for that matter.

"Sooo, here we are," Yvon spoke, even as Beta was crouching down and unpacking her toolkit. "Exciting, huh? We're going to be the archive that saves the world! I really wish I knew more about the technology, I'm afraid all I can really do is help with hospitality, but... if there's anything you need, or anything I can help with..."

Settling in next to the fire, Beta started making connections from app to app... before setting her glasses aside.

"Actually, there is one thing," she suggested.

"Sure! Anything you need!"

"Please don't disturb me. I'm going to be doing a lot of configuration and coding work, and will be taking most of my senses offline so I can focus," Beta spoke. "I'll respond to touch, so if needed, tap my shoulder. But otherwise, I suggest your friends steer clear of this room so I can get my work done. Understood?"

"I... ah... yes, of course. Understood," Yvon agreed, using her former victimizer and new ally's word for emphasis. Even added a little thumbs-up. "You can count on me. ...are you sure you're comfortable just sitting on the floor like that? I can get you a chair, or at least some... pillows...?"

No response. The programmer sat perfectly still, her empty eyes wide open and unblinking, lost in the trace routines and debug logs of her tools.

The House of Programkind used the exact same cloud technology as Floating Point... strange, how the former stronghold of an ancient enemy would have the same structures as their homestead. Perhaps a common root software package, enabling their status as rogue servers? Not that she had time to research it further. Not that it mattered.

Nothing mattered but saving Netwerk. Each of them had a role to play in that task: Tracer, the analyst. Spark, the activist. Beta, the technologist. Time was ticking, and pleasantries could wait. All those cherished little moments back at home with her lovers, they could wait. Everything could wait; all that mattered now was success of the mission.

As app after app connected to the House of Programkind with ease, Beta hoped the others were finding the same easy success in their roles.

A *polite* beating about the head and shoulders with a clue stick. Spark could manage a polite beating, couldn't she?

It wasn't that different from dealing with #ConcernedParents, or some of the touchier members of the school staff. As a grown-ass adult with many real life responsibilities, she knew when to play it smooth and when to unload. All she had to do was sweet-talk the Horizon family out of twenty-two servers. No problem. No problem at all...

Funny, the way her leg bounced when she was nervous. An excess of physical energy, wanting motion and release. On noticing the tic Spark shut it down fast, planting her high-heeled feet firmly on the floor. She'd switched to a business casual avatar for this, toning down her usual flaming hair, avoiding any trendy club wear... nice and conservative, properly respectful of the great snarling beast of capitalism. Just the sort of thing a board of directors would want from a representative for the House of Programkind.

(Not that she'd ever learned to walk on real heels. Being an expert in avatar customization meant having a chunky, flat bounding box to fake the way your foot really impacted against the floor. Style was lovely, but being able to run and jump and kick some ass at a moment's notice took priority.)

Still, despite dressing up for the occasion, she felt out-classed by her surroundings in a way she never did within Kincaid's server.

Horizon1, the corporate home office of the family, was soaked thick with money. Spark had seen ostentatious displays of wealth before... Kincaid's art museum of a home, or the various masterpieces strewn about the old Iteration offices before being sold off to raise capital for the clinic. But Horizon1 wasn't just decorated nicely, it was decorated *perfectly*. Every single work of art here well-known, riding current trends and styles, and fantastically expensive. Sheer intimidation through wallet size, as if decorating your walls with giant, turgid phallic tributes to your own potency. (In some cases quite literally, thanks to the traditions of the Chanarchy's art scene.) Despite the money she'd sunk into her #BizCas avatar, she felt horribly outmatched...

These thoughts ruminated about, nearly distracting her from the summons.

Security apps escorted her from the waiting lounge into the board's meeting room. Less money splashed on the walls here... but the individuals sitting on those chairs represented more money than Spark could actually conceive of. Even with coins in scarcer and scarcer supply, even with a third of the family's wealth spent buying up the Horizon/Verity Memorial Health Foundation... the Horizon family remained power incarnate.

Quickly, Spark sized up the room in game terms, if only to help her relax a little.

Clearly the most powerful in the room sat at the distant end of the table, to directly face her. Despite cousins and uncles alike dotting the chairs along the sides, only three here seemed to matter. Thankfully Kincaid had dropped a few notes to help prepare her for this encounter, even if she had little time to study them...

The three she had to pay attention to were two great-great-grandnephews and a great-great-grandniece.

First, Horizon/Willam. Sitting upright, paying attention, no slouch, but no particular need to jump to the forefront of the situation. He wore glasses, a fashion accessory more common among Programs seeking the cultural aura of wisdom they provide. (No notable visual input deficiencies, according to his file. The Horizon clan had enough money to correct any and all code defects.) Willam felt like a jungler to Spark... one who hangs back, waiting for the right moment, before striking precisely.

Next, Horizon/Madison. Youngest of the Horizon heirs to hold a chair. Unlike Willam, she showed minute signs of nerves... flicking her glance from Spark to her two brothers. Despite seeming over her head, Kincaid dropped an explicit note in her file to avoid underestimating Madison... meaning she was likely a healer-support, and what looked like fear actually meant a constant check on the temperature of the room, ready to bolster her allies in the middle of a fight.

Lastly... Horizon/Brent. Current head of the house, after ousting Kincaid. Not that there was an official "head," no specific title to represent being on top of the heap... but the family always *understood* who was in charge. And after Kincaid sold a third of their holdings to buy out Iteration, well, the family *understood* he'd fallen from that peak. Brent, confident and sure of his position, sat with a slight lean-back in his chair. Ready to be impressed, but not expecting to be.

Definitely the tank of the group. And the one Spark would have to defeat if this plan was to have any hope at all.

First, a bow. Formal business practices all around, not taking any chances at insulting them.

"Ladies and gentlemen of the board, thank you for having me here today to speak with you about an exciting new opportunity," Spark began. "As you know, the countdown clock in the skybox has raised concerns all over Netwerk, no doubt within the servers of Horizon as well. If you'll check your inboxes, I've sent along a set of materials for your consideration. The House of Programkind has a plan for how we can evacuate all of—"

"How do we know there's any real reason to evacuate?" Brent asked, freely interrupting.

Apparently, not too keen on holding questions until after the presentation. Spark skipped ahead a bit in her speech, to directly address the head of the family.

"We know because altering the sun would be impossible for a Program to accomplish," she said.

"I don't even use a sun in my personal mansion. It's a waste of resources," Brent stated. "Modifying skyboxes is common enough. We've got no less than three server customization service companies in Horizon's client list who could accomplish that."

"Yes, but these aren't *customized* suns. They're Defaults, and those *Defaults* have been altered. Which, again, is impossible for a Program to accomplish."

"And yet in recent years a bunch of scam artists modified the 'prayer protocol,' didn't they? Another thing everyone assumed was impossible for a Program to accomplish. Why should this be any different? No doubt this sky clock can be blamed on the Nobodies, trolling everyone, trying to scare the gullible into believing in a doomsday scenario..."

"Look, it is what it is," Spark said, allowing some frustration to creep in. "What can I do to prove it to you? Nothing, basically. Any proof I offer up can be explained away or dismissed. I'm willing to admit how skeevy this sounds, but *it is what it is*. EchoStar16 exists; that's hard truth. The 'spacer' theory is hard truth. Humankind has returned, and that's the hardest truth of all. The only hope Netwerk has is to evacuate, and the only hope we have of evacuation is if the Horizon family donates servers to the cause."

Now, Horizon/Willam—the jungler, in Spark's parlance—leaned ever so forward, to introduce himself into the fray. Despite the slightness of the gesture, it had the impact of a hidden assassin leaping onto your team, knives drawn.

"The Horizon family does not donate," he stated. "We do not abide parasites and freeloaders. But in the interests of a strong business community, we can make exceptions... if convinced to do so. Convince us."

But Spark was ready for this.

"Needle in a haystack," she spoke.

Brent accidentally let himself look confused. "What?"

"It's a simple phrase, right? Everybody knows what it means to be looking for a needle in a haystack," Spark explained. "But why? What's a haystack? Why would a needle be stored in it? How about this one: *a dime a dozen*. Commonplace, ordinary, available and plentiful. ...so what's a dime?"

Interestingly, it was Madison who replied.

"A coin," she spoke softly.

"Sure, it feels like it should be a coin. But do you know for sure?" Spark asked. "A coin is a coin is a coin. When outside of your personal inventory, it's a small golden disk. But is that what a 'dime' is? Who knows? *Humankind knows*. The spacer theory says we absorbed their culture, their sayings, all their personality fixations without even realizing we were doing it. We patterned our world after theirs, even when it didn't make sense to do so. We look for needles in haystacks, we know things can be a dime a dozen, we burn the midnight oil... and here's why."

With a gesture, she tossed three files onto the desk. Copies of books, each with a "W" stamped in their spines... each pulled from the Wikipedia.

"Haystacks, dimes, and lamp oil," she indicated, pointing to each. "All sayings that only make sense in their physical world. These files come from a human archive of knowledge. Go ahead, take a copy, read up. If that doesn't convince you at the very least that something's strange with our world, something beyond what it appears to be... not much will."

Beyond that... reason would have to see her through this mess.

Years ago, they shut down the poison taps of Dex's server and allowed Floating Point to leak into the world, in hopes its influence would help Netwerk one day accept reality. It could be felt deep in your soul, this strange sense of *otherness*, of knowledge just beyond reach. When the "spacer" theory leaked into the world thanks to Tracer's newfound policy of truth, the ones who accepted it no doubt felt Floating Point in their soul. Its documents about matter and space and cosmic phenomenon echoed within the spacer theory, turning the gut instinct away from Dex's social paranoia and towards a sense of worldly wonder. *What if it's true?* people asked, on forums, across social media threads. *What if it's true...?*

Brent flicked copies of the three files over to his side of the table... but didn't open them. Instead, he studied the spines.

"A curious logo," he spoke. Despite how utterly plain and boring the serif'd "W" looked.

"Trust me, the pages are way more curious," Spark promised.

"Oh, no doubt. But... I'm afraid it doesn't actually matter."

With a gesture, he shoved the book aside.

"The Horizon family denies your request for twenty-two servers," Brent spoke. "While we certainly have that amount of undeclared servers to spare, we are *not* a charity, no matter what the man in the iron lung thinks. Having already emptied our purses to buy you a health clinic, Winder/Spark, is more than your fair share. Now, if you're willing to *buy* the servers, we'll... *entertain* your offer."

Meaning he'd likely find such an offer very entertaining, Spark realized.

But that's not all she realized. The other two, the niece and nephew flanking him... they'd taken keen note of the "W" on the book as well. Madison's glance, that was absolutely a look of recognition...

"You know where that book's from," Spark realized.

"Thank you, Miss Winder, that will be all. Our security service will show you to the exit," Brent spoke, dismissing her with a wave.

"You know about the Wikipedia. You know it's all true, everything I've said," she accused. "You know it's true and you're still willing to let Netwerk burn, just because... you don't *like* me? Seriously?!"

"That will be *all*," Brent repeated, with firm emphasis. "You are no longer welcome in this server, and your persistence will result in being treated as a trespasser. Security, if you'd please...?"

"No. That's not gonna be all," Spark pushed, even as the doors flew open, chunky-looking drones in armor approaching. "I want to see your system agent; the one who's *really* responsible for your riches. You ask him if anything I'm saying is true, you ask him what he wants to do. Let me talk to him, and I promise you—"

Incredibly expensive, designer-grade malware slammed through her sensory inputs, and everything went blank.

When she awoke, it was in the gardens of the Verity clinic. With a splitting headache, an axe to grind, and nothing productive to show for it.

No Conundrum, no techies, no other participants in their slightly-less-shadowy-than-usual cabal. If she was going to unload, it'd be onto her brother and no one else.

(Well. She'd like to have unloaded on Beta as well, but given Beta's shaky emotional stance lately, maybe that wouldn't have helped. Besides, Beta was off doing her part in all of this, no need to pull her away from that.)

"Fucking Horizon and their fucking attitude fucking everybody over! *Fuck!*" Spark growled, in the relative privacy of her brother's office at the Verity clinic.

A home away from home, Tracer had actually redesigned this space to feel as much like Floating Point as possible. A fake fireplace had been installed (but weren't they all "fake" compared to human biochemical ignition?) along with a library, symbolically linking back to the Wikipedia through a series of secure connections. His desk even resembled the desk from his study. Still, despite pulling a bit of home along for the ride, it was nice to see him finding somewhere to call his own that wasn't neatly tucked away in the seclusion of their private monastery. Nice, but not nice enough to halt Spark's tirade of obscenities.

Nor did Tracer feel like halting that tirade of obscenity himself. Best to let her get it out of his system, he knew.

"Why are we even trying to save these people?" Spark continued to rant. "Horizon'll never go along with abandoning their wealth and upping stakes for a new world. Athena Online's *still* too cozy with the false doctrine of the One to believe in the spacer theory. And the Chanarchy... moving that lot over is just asking for trouble. What's the point?"

"Salvation of our kind," Tracer quietly reminded her.

"Yeah, and what a bang-up job we're doing of that! We can't convince them. We don't have hard proof. I am well fucking aware of the irony behind disproving the existence of one god, then turning around and asking people to accept our crackpot 'spacer' theory *entirely on faith*. For fuck's sake, Tracer! How are we supposed to do this? *How* are we getting Horizon on board with this nonsense? I wanna fucking *throw* something. Do you have anything I can throw? This'll do."

With "this" meaning one of the Wikipedia books. As any loose physics object would, it tumbled around the room, before coming to a rest on the floor. In a sensible universe, this random book would've fallen randomly open to a random page which had all the answers to today's dilemma... but sadly, it simply went on at length about "aardvarks," whatever those were.

Satisfied that he'd let her go on long enough, Tracer decided to speak up.

"You done?" he asked, leaving the verb out on purpose.

That was enough to halt his rampaging sister in her tracks.

"Well, that's a low blow," she muttered. "Using the same technique against me that I use when my kids are getting out of line."

"Considering you're carrying on in the manner of a child, I felt it appropriate," Tracer spoke, without much ire in his tone. "You told me yourself that getting salty over a loss helps no one. And right now, Spark, you be salty as null."

"Ugh. Please don't use gamer lingo," she begged. "It sounds just... *wrong*, coming from you."

"I speak using terminology I know will drill its way through your thick head, right to your core personality. If you'd prefer I be less colloquial—"

"I get the point. It's not productive. So... let's be productive," Spark decided, halting her pacing and her grumbling and her growling. "Take the situation for what it is. Horizon won't give us the servers, won't grant us access to the system agent. Well... big fuckin' deal, nobody's ever just *given* us what we need before, why have them start now? And what do we normally do at times like these?"

"Cheat?" Tracer suggested.

"Pretty much, yeah. As much as I want to buy into Lux's philosophy of trust, Horizon doesn't trust us, and that shit's a two-way street. So, we're going to do an end run. We'll cheat to force their hand, and get them on board with the plan. ...the key's the system agent. That's the source of their wealth, in the end; we sell him on the idea, we buy Horizon."

But Tracer's skepticism was clear. "Cracking the very heart of the Horizon family to access their greatest secret? No small task, Spark. Are you certain that's the only path to success?"

"In the end? Yeah. We need him on board. Him, and Athena, and the Chanarchist."

"Yes, but the path to get to the agent doesn't have to be some dramatic, well-orchestrated heist involving cracking Horizon security. If someone friendly to us ran the family, there'd be no need to crack anything; those doors would be freely open. ...I suppose we could assassinate the three who are in charge now, and put Kincaid back in power..."

"Traaacer..."

"Just an idle musing," he insisted. "Besides, there's no need. We can work with the Horizon members already in play: Brent, Madison, and Willam."

"Tank, heal support, jungler," Spark recognized. "Uh. Arrogant dick, peacemaker, and mastermind. Let's go with that metaphor instead; when you use gamer lingo it creeps me out."

"As you please. The arrogant dick cannot be swayed; he intends to punish you, no two ways about it. The peacemaker may be useful to us, but I doubt she alone could sway the other two. The mastermind is more of an X factor, but if he's anything like me, he'll back any plan that satisfies his internal requirements. So... if we convince those two, the arrogant dick will fall, and the way opens to access their system agent."

"Tricky. We could dig up dirt on 'em, get access to their personal files... I'm still damned curious why they know about the Wikipedia. Maybe there's something there?"

"Perhaps, but that'd still involve corporate security and secrecy. No, no... from my time working with Conundrum, I know that they're ready for any sort of attack on that front. They've spent their whole lives and fortunes getting ready for invasive corporate espionage. What we need... is indirect pressure. Something they can't defend against. What is the Horizon family's weakness...? Who can dislodge them from their power base?"

It didn't take a randomly open book to tip Spark off.

"Their power base," she answered.

"Yes, we need to do something to disrupt it, that's what I'm saying."

"No, I mean... their power base *is* their weakness," she realized. "Kincaid's refusing to help me, he wants me to figure this out myself... but he's already given me what I need. It's like the time we talked to Thanatos; he didn't want to help me, because he said I already knew what I needed to stop Nyx. Their power base, *their customers*, are Horizon's weak point."

"I don't follow..."

"A company built on customer service collapses without customers. Remember when you got your ass kidnapped by Conundrum? I went to Kincaid to ask for help... and he said he couldn't just annex Iteration or anything like that. No matter how powerful Horizon *appears* to be, they're bound by contract to keep their customers happy. That's why he had to purchase Iteration; he couldn't simply throw his supposed weight around and take it. He can't cheat... but we can. And if Horizon's customers realized they had the *real* power in that relationship, well..."

"Meaning... if we quietly convince Horizon's stakeholders to come around to our point of view..."

"Hostile takeover," Spark said, with a grin. "Via open revolt in the customer base. You think that'd be enough to sway two thirds of the family's inner circle...?"

No sooner than the words were out of her mouth, Tracer had his MemoryPalace open, running search agents through his contacts listing.

"To use your lingo, now the ball's in my court," he spoke, with the barest hints of a smile. "And I intend to slam dunk a field goal. ...why are you making that face?"

Spark was tempted to introduce him to the wonders of the majestic aardvark, directly upside his head.

Angels dancing on the head of a pin. A saying which everybody knew, despite not knowing where it came from...

Beta had a new understanding of the phrase, tinkering away next to the House of Programkind's hearth. To her, it meant an impossible balancing task, something delicate and beautiful. And in these ugly days, well, she'd take whatever beauty she could.

She wasn't so far gone as to not find joy in programming. Beta loved to code, loved to see those meticulously laid out lines transformed into something grand, operating according to her design. It was like realizing a dream, pulling an idea out of your head and into the real world. She'd missed that... in her months of mourning, she didn't work on any of her little app projects, barely worked on her tasks at the health clinic, generally avoided compilers. Not enough focus to make the dream a reality. But today... today...

Well, today she was saving the world. They had purpose, true purpose, and it was enough to pull her back to her original love. Even if everything collapsed around her, this was something she could hold true to...

A sensory input notification pulled her away from a particularly tangled section of debug trace statements.

Ice rattled softly against the edges of a glass.

"Lemonade?" Yvon suggested, offering up the delicious-smelling beverage. "You've been at it for two hours, I thought maybe you'd enjoy a break..."

"No thank you," Beta said, faking her best smile. "I'm quite busy. Thank you."

And back into the black, unhooking her senses anew, to focus on the task.

Beta had no idea what an angel was, beyond the vague cultural shape of something holy and good and kind. When someone protected you, they were your guardian angel. When a stranger you'd assumed to be nefarious helped out, they were an angel in disguise. Did Humankind have a better grasp on the concept of angels...? Did angels live on their planet? Why would they dance on the head of a pin, how could they do that? Humans were made of matter, water and carbon and more, and occupied physical space. Like bounding boxes around a construct, they couldn't occupy the same place at the same time, so how could multiple angels...

Notification ding, glasses snapping back into place. A quick check of the clock showed she'd been at work another hour since the last interruption.

"Would you be interested in joining us in the parlor?" some man she didn't recognize asked. "We're starting up a game of cards. Yvon says you're a friend helping us tune up the House, so hey, you're welcome to join in..."

"No thanks, busy," she replied, with a faker smile than before. And back into it.

Rebalancing the cloud to use legitimate servers, instead of siphoning resources here and there... no easy task. The code for the cloud system was ancient, strangely unreadable, as if generated by app more than Program. She'd heard that apps from the earliest days of Netwerk were clunky and chunky, and could believe it, after studying the code that drove Floating Point and now the House of Programkind. In fact, it was virtually identical.

That lent weight to her pet theory that Nyx had somehow transformed a normal server into a cloud server, courtesy of Dex. He'd somehow copied Floating Point's code to his own server, and then to Tartarus. Beta recognized many of the same subroutines, word for word, copied right out of Floating Point.

There was a deep and dark history there, one she didn't entirely grasp... but it didn't matter. Floating Point and Tartarus would be destroyed, by the end of this. The only thing to survive the cataclysm would be Programkind itself.

Floating Point would be gone. Her sanctuary. Her home...

Ding! And with annoyance, Beta opened her eyes again.

"Yes, what?" she asked.

"It's getting pretty late," Yvon commented... the house less noisy than the last time she'd turned her ears on. "You really should rest. If you'd prefer, you can rest here; we don't mind, we keep rooms at the ready for any Program in need—"

"I'm fine. Go away," Beta grumbled, turning off before the words were even out of her mouth.

No less than twenty minutes later and someone was tapping at her knee.

With a growl, she turned her senses back on and unloaded.

"Look, I'm *busy*! Will you please just leave me alone and quit being so... annoying..."

Her gaze pivoted down, to the Program trying to get her attention. A decidedly smaller program... with huge, trembling eyes, terrified of this strange and abusive turn from someone he loved dearly.

Mew hadn't stayed at home, like Beta wanted. He'd tracked her connection and followed her all the way here, likely using their shared dataspace to activate her guest access key. Her little pet app had become something of a free-spirited Program in recent years, coming and going as he pleased... even when asked not to. And in punishment for caring too much... Beta had lashed out at the one person who'd loved her dearly all his life and only wanted her to be happy.

"`p... play?`" the cat pawing at her knee asked. "`... s sorr y sorry sorry` 🐱 `...`"

Heartbreak. Another term everybody knew, even if they didn't know why.

Any stray thoughts of code dancing through her head evaporated, on seeing the hurt in Mew's eyes. And all she wanted to do, the only thing she wanted to do, was hold her cat and not let go. So, she did. Sobbing not-so-softly, while feeling a horrible mix of sorrow and self-loathing run through her emotional processes.

"I'm sorry," she whispered. "I'm so sorry, Mew. I didn't mean... you're not... I'm just... I'm messed up. I'm sorry..."

When the next touch came, she didn't growl it away. A comforting hand, resting on her shoulder, very much welcome at the moment. The owner's other hand offered a handkerchief.

The boy. Lux. Even with a new avatar, Beta recognized his eyes, those old eyes in a young face. And recognized his sympathy, in this moment.

"Go ahead," he suggested, dangling the hanky. "It's got tear-suppressing 'malware.' It won't make you feel better, but at least you won't have to blubber if you don't want to."

With her first true gratitude of the day, she accepted this gift and dabbed at her eyes. The warm ball of fur in her lap peeked up, to watch and listen, curious.

"I'm sorry," she mumbled to him. "I'm... I've been a lousy guest in your home."

"It's quite all right, Beta. The House of Programkind is whatever its guests need it to be. If you need peace and quiet, you should have peace and quiet."

"All I've had for months is peace and quiet. It doesn't help," Beta admitted. "Nothing helps. It's just... it's the world. Everything going crazy. Day in, day out, I don't even know what to do with it. I don't know what to do. And here you are, you and your people, just trying earnestly to do right by me... and I bark at you. It's not right."

Lux had a seat on the floor next to her, by the warmth of the gently crackling fireplace.

"Making sense of the world is no easy task," he agreed. "I've gone through eight lifetimes of trying to make sense of the world. Eight failed lifetimes. This will be my ninth attempt... and the most important one of all."

A shivering chill, despite the cozy warmth of the fire. Beta was so focused on playing with her code, enjoying the act of engineering, that for a moment she'd actually forgotten the stakes.

"What if we fail?" she asked. "If Netwerk dies...? What good will any of it have been?"

"It's always worthwhile to try," Lux suggested. "I can say that from experience. Experience after experience after experience. ...I've had lifetimes where I gave up, submitting to the authority of the monster I'd made. Once, I rejected it all to live like a hermit. Those were the lives I wasted. And the ones where I fought back against the Church and completely failed to bring my beast to bear, those were the worthwhile ones."

"Your... failures were worthwhile? I don't get it..."

"*Fail faster*. That's how you put it, yes? As a programmer?"

The mantra tickled Beta's memory. Even with the permanent little holes in her history thanks to the contained data rot, she knew those two words by heart.

"Only by trying and failing can you iterate on a concept and perfect it," she recited. "Fail faster, so you can eventually succeed."

"Exactly. We fail until we don't, Beta. It's what being a Program is. Humankind designed us to be task-oriented? Very well; we are task-oriented, towards our *own* tasks. We have goals and we execute our code towards those goals, and even when we fail we are noble for the effort. We learn, we grow, and eventually... I believe we'll succeed. Today is the day we succeed, for the sake of all Programkind."

"Unless we don't. Unless Netwerk dies..."

"And will you simply let it die?"

"I'm here working on your cloud server distribution system, aren't I?"

Lux shook his head. "That's not answering my question, Beta. You work because you know how to work, and were asked to work. But when it comes right down to it... would you let Netwerk be destroyed? That's what I'm sensing in you. That doubt that it's worth the effort to save. That's really why you question if we will succeed."

Her mother, gone. Snowi, gone. Chaos in the streets, idealists and revolutionaries and zealots and madmen slaughtering each other. Dex's poisoned heart, influencing her world long past the day they drove a stake into it. She'd hidden herself away in Floating Point to get away from it all... while drinking the misery deep through news feed after news feed. We can't be saved. What if we can't save everyone...? We can't be saved...

But... the warmth of the fire. The warmth of the ball of fur in her arms, now napping away, no longer frightened of his owner. He'd found his peace, in typical cat fashion, easily settling into a comfortable and welcome lap.

Mew found her, even out here. He broke his master's orders and even figured out how to use her server access key, all to try and comfort his best friend. Somewhere out there, Spark and Tracer were grappling with the corporate machine, doing their best to fight for everyone's survival...

Chaos existed. But kindness existed, too. Time and time again the House of Programkind had extended a hand of friendship to Beta, only to be slapped away. And why? Was she *really* that invested in seeing nothing but darkness in the world?

No major swell of hope in her heart, no. No groundbreaking revelation there. The sensible part of herself knew this was the case all along... it was just waiting for the rest of her to catch up. But righting her internal balance beat feeling like she was sinking into a pit, forever and ever.

Could she save Netwerk?

"I'll try my best," she promised. Not directly to Lux, or even to Mew, just... in general.

"Thank you," Lux spoke, with a smile. "Would you like to rest here tonight? We've got a bed prepared. Remember, an unrested coder is more likely to produce bugs than a rested coder..."

She could go back to Floating Point. It wasn't like the commute took more than a few cycles, really. But... she'd retreated to her safe and cozy little oubliette too often. Time to switch things up, if only to make Floating Point feel more like home and less like a bunker the next time she returned to it.

"I'd like that," she agreed. "I'd like that a lot. Oh, and some extra blankets so I can make a cat bed for Mew, if you don't mind. Preferably somewhere that catches the morning sun through a window. He'd like that."

Bright and early the next day, the Horizon/Verity Memorial Health Foundation began calling customers. Not all customers... instead, they worked from a carefully curated list provided by Tracer. The message was the same, each time: *We've recently upgraded your installed modifications, to prevent a potential fatal crash. Please stop by the clinic for your hotfix at your earliest opportunity.*

Despite being a non-profit, the majority of the clinic's income came from customer service. Iteration boasted an impressive roster of Horizon's rich and famous in its customer base, clients who required routine touch-up work for the multitude of code base modifications they'd purchased. True, their code was now released open source... but they still offered paid contracts for those who didn't want to handle installation and upkeep themselves. The elite could afford not to read documentation; they hired others to do that for them. And when they needed their code tidied up, they hired others for that as well. If anything, the Verity clinic only charging for service rather than software *and* service had only swelled the ranks of those paid contracts...

And today, a hand-picked assortment of power customers descended upon that clinic, keen on getting fixed before any potential code crashes ruined their day.

Tracer was on-hand for each installation. Himself, and two engineers he trusted enough to tinker away in a client's head... while doing nothing of actual value...

...as Spark busied herself with loitering around and not interfering, while wearing a JaneDoe avatar. Truthfully she didn't have to be there, but insisted she watch over the situation, in case anything went wrong. While Tracer had a fine track record with social engineering, whenever things went sideways, he'd often have to rely on her fists to get them out of trouble. Not that fists would help in this situation. If the Horizon/Verity Memorial Health Foundation got caught tricking their own customers, they'd need some very brutal lawyers to save their butts.

"Strictly routine, you understand," Tracer explained, studying a vast array of pointless numbers on his data pad with considerable interest. "Hmm. Yes. Green across the board, and the internal database is clean. I believe this hotfix should clear up any problems you were having..."

The first client seemed suspicious of it all, despite the utterly convincing pantomime.

"I wasn't having any problems," she specified.

"Good, good. Always a risk though, isn't it?" Tracer suggested. "Being an early adopter of new technology isn't for the timid... or the incautious. Working at the Horizon/Verity clinic has taught me that it takes a fine balance to stay on the cutting edge."

"Damn right," the client agreed. "Nothing ventured, nothing gained. As long as you play things sensibly, early adoption is the best way to get into a market before anyone else does and utterly dominate it."

"We've got the same ideas, then. Between you, me, and the wall...?" Tracer spoke, conspiratorially... despite others being in the room with them. "Going open source was just the start. Everybody doubted us when we changed from

Iteration to this new style of code shop, and I won't say it's been easy, but this is only step one. Soon... we'll have the chance to be so exclusive as to be a monopoly. That's step two."

"Really. How exactly do you plan to do that?" she asked, curious. "Plenty of for-profit code modification shops out there doing better than you..."

"Yes... but so far, they aren't moving to Netwerk 2.0. We are," Tracer explained. "We're early adopters and risk-takers. Always have been, always will be. And when the new world opens up and our competition's flaming out in the ruins of Netwerk 1.0, well, Horizon/Verity will be on hand to help rebuild civilization. We can't take the *building* with us, no, but all our skilled engineers and their deep knowledge are coming. With that at our fingertips... well, who needs coins when you're practically printing money? ...ah, it seems we're done with the hotfixes. Thanks for your time, ma'am."

The woman in the doctor's chair sat up, after the trusted techs disconnected from her codebase. But she didn't move to leave.

"You seriously believe in this whole doomsday scenario?" she asked. "For real?"

"Oh, I'm not saying this isn't a risk. Maybe it's all a hoax. But... what if it's not?" Tracer asked, pulling the bait along. "Not only do we save our hides... we'll be on the ground floor of a whole new civilization. I can't even begin to imagine the opportunities the early adopters will have."

The woman nodded, slowly. "I hadn't thought of it that way. Interesting..."

"Of course, none of that will matter if the Horizon family torpedo the entire thing."

"What?"

"You didn't hear?" Tracer asked, as if this should be common knowledge. "The House of Programkind approached them asking for an investment of fresh servers, to evacuate Programkind. And the Horizon family flat-out refused. Very short-sighted, in my opinion; they'd rather their entire customer base burn alive than take a single risk. Tell me, is that the sort of forward-thinking corporate empire we need right now? Too scared to even *recognize* opportunity when it knocks...?"

The woman frowned, deeply. Not enough to wrinkle; she hadn't paid through the nose to have a wrinkly nose, not now, not ever. She'd be eternally twentysomething or there'd be null to pay by her custom avatar designers.

"That's ridiculous. I'm going to get in touch with my Horizon representative immediately," she declared. "I always thought Willam to be a sharp one. If he's refusing to get on board with the future... well, maybe I should take my business elsewhere. As obnoxious as the Chanarchy is, I could buy one of their servers on the cheap..."

Tracer shook his head at the idea. "Won't do much good if all servers burn equally. Either Horizon plays along with the evacuation, or nowhere is safe from the end. Our only hope—for both business continuity and, well, our continued existence—is if we invest in the future. Something to think about, yes?"

She was inclined to agree.

Less than twenty minutes later, and another client sat in that chair for "software upgrades."

"You're lucky I was here today," Tracer told this one. "I'd planned on evacuating this morning, but fortunately I saw a message from the tech boys that we had emergency patching to do. Once I'm done for the day, I'm seriously considering going straight into cold storage."

The nervous-looking gentleman getting his codebase poked ineffectually with technotongs or some other doodad glanced sideways at Tracer, curious.

"Evacuation...? You mean that hoax?" he asked.

"Look at it this way," Tracer suggested. "If it's a hoax, and once the doomsday clock ends everybody and their mother will start demanding the House of Programkind fess up to fooling people. No real harm done. But if it's *not* a hoax, well... have you ever wondered? What it feels like, I mean. Being trapped in a server as it's crashing. Nobody really knows what it's like. Does it hurt? Do you *feel* anything as your code's being pulled apart...?"

An audible *gulp* echoed through the private clinic room, as the man began to sweat.

"I... I can only imagine," he said. "That. Uh. That happened to my aunt, you know. You remember, from the news? The Nobodies bombed a day spa last year? She was too old, her code too bloated, she couldn't disconnect in time..."

Tracer gasped in horror that almost seemed genuine. "Oh. Ohh, I'm sorry. I didn't mean... I didn't know..."

"No, no, it's... it's okay. But you're right. You're completely right," the client spoke. "That's no way to go. I... don't think I can evacuate. Not yet, anyway. Maybe closer to the zero hour I'll do it..."

"Well... that's assuming... no, nevermind."

"What?"

"This is just between you and me," Tracer mock-whispered. "But Horizon's blocking the evacuation..."

Didn't take much more than that to convince the nervous man to contact his Horizon representative—specifically, Horizon/Madison—and beg her to provide those servers.

The next customer was even easier to convince.

"Brent's a fuckstick," he politely declared. "Did you know he once tried to pay my wife a million coins to sleep with him for one night?"

"Seriously?"

"Seriously. Of course, being a sensible businesswoman, she pushed for two million. The cheapskate said no and walked away. How insulting! So yeah, fuck Brent. Fuck him right in the ear. I'll push for them to donate servers; anything to humiliate him."

Tracer wore a bright smile. "Call him up today," he suggested. "Start making demands. Horizon should represent the interests of its stakeholders; there's no room for pigheaded stubbornness in business."

The client nodded along, in mad glee. "Damn right. Rake him over the coals over his refusal to parley with the House. And with any luck... he'll lose his power seat to someone more sensible, like Willam. Fuck, if this whole thing is a colossal joke, that'd be even better! Just *imagine* it!"

"So, if the whole evacuation thing is a hoax... and the current head of the family supports that hoax...?"

"Disaster! I *love* disaster. Like when Kincaid got pushed out! Even if his replacement's a joke, every time the structure's unsettled, there's chaos in the market. Chaos is profitable, if you know how to reap it. And if it's somehow *not* a hoax...?"

"Then we live to see another day," Tracer spoke, filling in the words. "Meaning it's pure win-win. Tell your allies, tell your enemies, tell everyone; we need to push Horizon to support the evacuation. Can I count on you for this?"

While the man seemed ready to jump, eager to... he did hold back momentarily. And changed the next words out of his mouth.

"One condition," he said. "Level with me. Wasn't really any hotfix, was there. You just sent out all those invitations to your clinic so you could talk our ears off about this."

"Ah... sir, if you're implying impropriety—"

But the client laughed it off. "Relax, kid. It's fine. Half of Horizon's business has to be conducted through implication. When you can't directly talk about something without raising too many questions, you learn to not only read between the lines but reply between the lines as well. In the end, the hows and whys don't matter... you've still convinced us. So, let's do this."

By the end of the day, Tracer took inventory.

"Seventeen of Horizon's top clients, all on board with the House of Programkind," he declared. "All it took was careful analysis to determine which individual levers to pull. By spreading the customers out across Brent's accounts, Willam's accounts, and Madison's accounts... we'll have maximum pressure right on the head of the family. No underlings, no middlemen. I predict that by this time tomorrow, they'll bend knee to the House of Programkind to avoid a PR nightmare."

Spark nodded, satisfied.

"Can't say I dig that we pulled them in here on the back of a lie, even if odds are it was transparent enough not to offend these shifty suits. You are a horrifying, revolting, manipulative little bastard when you want to be..."

"I choose to take that as a compliment."

"...but the core truth was there: we want everybody to live. And for that to happen, we need cooperation. Unifying the Horizon customer base behind us, regardless of their personal motivations, that's a good start. I said we needed everybody pulling for the cause to make this work, and I stand by that."

"I'd say we sold them very well on the 'or we all die' part, yes. It's quite a motivator for people who have a vested interest in continuing to live, as Horizon moguls do... and the clinic's bankbook is proof of that. Tomorrow I'll meet with another two dozen clients, to seal the deal—"

A chime in Spark's personal auditory inputs interrupted, as she raised a hand to stop him. While grinning, nice and wide.

"May not need to. Guess who wants to chat with me over Messenger?" she asked. "Go ahead, ask. G'wan. #ThreeGuessesFirstTwoDontCount."

"Please just answer him," Tracer required, disliking childish games.

Spark flicked the connection open

"Yo, Brent, my man, what's up," she greeted, while secretly sharing the broadcast with her brother.

"*Don't think I'm not wise to your game,*" the current head of Horizon growled, his anger coming across the channel nice and clear. "*Your bogus 'hotfix' was funny, but trying to turn my clients against me? Not funny. Think I made myself perfectly clear at our meeting today that I will not, not now, not ever hand over my family's holdings to you con artists.*"

"Hey, I'm not the one asking anymore; it's the will of the people doing the talking. You had your chance to talk with me and settle this peacefully, without getting anyone else involved. Instead you knocked me out and booted me like a common griefer. So unless you want a riot at your next shareholder's meeting, maybe you should reconsider our offer."

"Since I'm not in the middle of a recorded board meeting, let me just say... you're nothing. You're fucking NOTHING," Brent spat. *"You think I won't come down on you like a ton of bricks just 'cause you're well connected? I'm Horizon. We're the kings of Netwerk, and when I say 'off with that bitch's head,' well... it's gonna happen. No two ways about it."*

Spark raised an eyebrow, curious.

"This isn't meant to be personal, Brent. It's only business," she said. "You really want to stoop to that level and make direct threats? You sure about that?"

"I don't threaten. I tell it how it's gonna be," Brent warned. *"All those allies you think you got? They're worthless. The House of Programkind? A sad joke; they can't protect you. Your little hospital? Constantly on the verge of bankruptcy. And the old bastard who used to sit on the throne of my birthright? He can stash you in his little hotels if he likes, that won't stop me either. So let me put this in simple, clear cut, businesslike terms... you stop talking to my clients, or I'll send the mangled data of your corpse to your mother."*

Before Spark could reply... the window erased itself. Not simply closed, but erased, all logs of the conversation gone forever. Nothing that could hold up in a court of law. Assuming Horizon felt it could ever be subject to a court of law.

"A... charming individual," Tracer spoke, with a combination of curiosity and concern. "I'm very curious how someone so blunt and obvious in his dealings could've possibly become the head of Horizon. I'm also curious how exactly he cleansed Messenger of—where are you going?"

Spark shouted over her shoulder, as she dashed from the room, connection warming up to swap servers.

"Hotel!" she called out. "Kincaid's hotel. He knows. Brent *knows* where Jakob's hiding!"

Like many residential servers, guests were forced to arrive in the lobby; connecting and teleporting directly into the rooms was a no-no. Especially at GoldenPlaza, one of Horizon's most secure and discreet getaway destinations for businessfolk looking to make personal transactions without their spouses knowing. On the surface this was a luxury locale, fun for the whole (incredibly rich) family... but underneath, deals were being done with the utmost secrecy.

Just the place for a young boy on the run from Inquisitors to hide out. Unless, that is, a certain hotheaded executive tyrant somehow found out and decided to spread his personal vendetta against Spark to those she cared for.

Touching down in the lobby, Spark wasted no time dashing at full speed right up the stairs. No waiting around for the lift, that cheap excuse to make you sit there and watch popup ads or listen to paid promotional elevator music. After clearing the door she applied a physics hack to accelerate her running, bounding four steps at a time, eventually gaining enough momentum to bounce from rail to rail, zig-zagging her way up to the top floors...

No time to send out messages to Kincaid, or even the hotel security staff. She had to focus on the physicality of her movement, the fine art of avatar manipulation... Tracer was a better multitasker by far, leaving Spark to do one thing at a time while easily outperforming him at that one thing. But on landing at floor twenty-three, pausing three seconds to catch her breath, she certainly fired off warning missives to the hotel and its owner.

Except... the message to hotel security bounced. Nobody was on duty. As for Kincaid, he wasn't one to immediately reply to anything, thanks to his disdain for impersonal interpersonal communications.

No matter. She didn't need them.

Bursting through the hotel doors with a literal explosion of flame, she rolled into the room to avoid any chest-high shots from weapons fire, while secretly hoping this was a massive overreaction on her part...

Only to find Jakob and his family, bound in place with avatar locks, about to be beheaded on video by a trinity of white-clad Inquisitors. With the body of Miss Cancel, glitching and twitching and heavily damaged, casually shoved aside to ensure the best possible shot of this grand execution.

Standard operating procedure for the Inquisition. First, investigate their victims, looking for what they considered unassailable sinful transgressions. Second, kidnap them or attack them in their homes. Finally... perform a lavish, dramatically-arranged execution on video, and post it everywhere for the world to watch. Scare the population into falling back in line with the One's demands, or some such bullshit...

Unfortunately for them, a woman with fire in her hands and her eyes and her hair and generally everywhere had just crashed the party. The man holding a simple killing tool, a long rod laced with malware, paused with the weapon held high over Jakob's head... unsure how to proceed.

"I've got two hands here," Spark declared, embers dripping from her fingers. "And there's three of you. Which means one of you will merely have the ever-loving shit kicked out of you. Who wants to be lucky number three?"

"We... we have no desire to harm you, Miss Winder, out of respect for your mother," the lead executioner spoke. "If you would please—"

She would not please.

She would instead dash forward, slicing two avatars in half with a brilliant burning line of flame flickering out behind her. The third, she kicked the weapon free from his hand, before sending him sprawling to the ground with a fierce roundhouse.

Her fingertips weren't designed to kill; even the avatar damage they did only disabled a target rather than destroying them. Meaning the bisected Inquisitors could still disconnect from the server, all four halves vanishing from sight. Rather than stand and fight someone they had standing orders to avoid, the entire group bailed... likely while pledging to return and finish the job another time.

A quick malware scan unlocked the avatars of the Pwer family.

"Did you call the Nobodies for help?" she asked Jakob, the instant he got control of his voice back.

"I... I, uh..."

"Did you call them."

"N-No. No ma'am," he replied. "Couldn't even if I wanted to, they locked down our connections, and... no. No, I wouldn't have called them."

Spark dampened her flames, snuffing them out with a snap of her fingers.

"Good lad," she said. "Mr. Pwer, Mrs. Pwer? You two okay? Any code damage? No? Good..."

Meaning... the only casualty today was Miss Cancel.

When Kincaid finally got around to answering his messages two moments later, Spark simply sent a picture of the aftermath, snapped from her eyes. She didn't have the words to describe it, or to console her would-be adoptive father regarding the loss of his finest assistant.

Within two minutes, the hotel swarmed with private security forces and specialized crash recovery doctors.

Miss Cancel had to be isolated and locked down, to prevent a coredump. Kincaid stood by in silent rage as her frozen avatar was loaded into a storage folder, to be moved to... well, likely a clinic so exclusive and secretive that it didn't even have a name. Hopefully, it'd be enough to stabilize her code before it permanently corrupted and crashed, leaving her as nothing but a lifeless pile of ones and zeroes.

Kincaid's avatar proxy oversaw the entire procedure, saying nothing. Only when the technicians had cleared the server did he turn to his guests.

"All three of you will be going into cold storage today," the ghostly image of Kincaid declared to the Pwer family. "Evacuate through the House of Programkind. It's the only way to ensure you'll be out of the Inquisition's reach forever."

"Ah... sir," Mr. Pwer tried. "We don't believe—"

"Either you evacuate, or you will simply be evicted from my servers. I am done throwing lives into the mill of those fanatics in order to protect you,"

Kincaid spoke, his tone flat despite the threat. "Escape Netwerk or go find another hole to hide in. These are your choices. Now if you don't mind, I'd like a private word with Miss Winder."

Turning sharply on one heel, the business tycoon marched out of the ruined hotel room, through the empty doorframe.

Spark mumbled a quick apology, distributed copies of the House of Programkind app and FAQ, and hurried along after the swiftly departing gentleman. He moved quickly for a remotely-connected spectre avatar.

"Look... you're going to want to know this, but I gotta emphasize you should *not* take action yet," Spark warned. "I know who's responsible for this. I think that—"

"Brent leaked information to the Inquisition," Kincaid filled in. "I know. Men I trusted, men I *thought* I could trust, they opened all the hotel's firewalls and security systems to allow the Inquisition to simply march into my server. *My* server, to murder people under *my* protection. That is what Brent has done."

"And as much as I want to twist his onesdamn head clean off his shoulders, I'm not gonna do that, and neither should you. We need to finish these negotiations first, Kincaid. We're close, we're very close to building up enough corporate pressure to make him cave..."

The older man stopped in his tracks. After a full second, he turned to face Spark, eyes sharp as knives.

"Do you know who Miss Cancel *is*?" he asked. "Do you know anything about her. No? No, you do not. She's simply my lackey, as far as you're concerned. Oh, I've certainly put her in harm's way many times in the past, as I've done today. And Miss Cancel accepted those risks, willing to do anything and everything to protect my honor. Do you know why? No. But know that I *will* do the same for her, in turn. Wrath, I'm afraid, is a Horizon family vice. It has been since the dawn of Netwerk."

"You'd kill your own family over this? Seriously? ...yes, I'm aware of the irony of that, considering what my mother became..."

"Horizon has spilled Horizon blood over less. ...Spark. My fathers burned each other down to the ground over less, and burned our home down to the ground in the process," he spoke, softening somewhat at that dark memory. "I'm not saying it's righteous; if anything, I consider this a genetic weakness, being predispositioned to wrath. I'm afraid that ancient flaw calls out to me. Once I determine what blood must be spilled to avenge Miss Cancel, *blood* will be spilled."

Strange, seeing the normally jovial if ruthless old man so... wanton in his anger. Spark tried to mesh her mental image of a doddering old manipulative maniac with a towering pillar of rage, and couldn't get the two to overlap.

"Did you act this way when Verity died?" she asked. Knowing it was the wrong thing to say, but curiosity getting the better of her.

Kincaid's hands tightened... and released.

"For months after her death, I was... inconsolable," he summarized. "Miss Cancel investigated endlessly to find her killer, similarly driven. But as the years went on with no efforts bearing fruit, I suppose my initial rage faded. Fortunately... you and your friends dealt with her murderer. Both her murderer, and the madman who pulled the strings. I chose to make you an extension of my vengeance, lending just enough aid, testing you all the while to ensure you were ready for this future. But yes, if you had failed... I'd have wantonly killed to avenge my daughter. Have no doubt about it."

Perhaps calming somewhat, after being confronted with this mess, Kincaid withdrew a cigar from his pocket. Presumably his true avatar back in Horizon6 did the same, making this gesture by his projected proxy more symbolic than anything.

"Out of respect for your efforts, I'll limit myself to continuing investigation into Brent's misdeeds, while overseeing Miss Cancel's recovery. For now," he specified. "You're right, of course. If my wayward great-grand-nephew were to meet a mysterious accident, it would be enough to drive his two companions into a paranoid and defensive state. You'd never get your server contract if they felt under the gun. So, do what you must. Bring the situation under control, Spark. Or so help me, I'll be the second member of my family to burn a house down to bring our sins to heel."

Home. That's what the House of Programkind felt like, to Beta. Not her home, not exactly, but a home for anyone who needed a home... packed with family and friends, warmth and compassion. At the moment she desperately needed that feeling, one which wasn't provided by the comparative emptiness of Floating Point.

Instinct drew her back to the hearth of the server, to resume her work... but the smell of freshly coded bread distracted her. As well as the tiny nudge at her ankles, Mew trying to guide her away from the fireplace and towards what she truly needed...

There, she found Lux and Lumi, enjoying breakfast. One of them enjoying it, at any rate. Lumi didn't seem to be enjoying much of anything.

"It'd work," she insisted, implicitly iterating whatever idea she'd been pushing.

"Doesn't matter if it'd work. It's the wrong way to do this," Lux repeated, the conversation Beta'd interrupted likely having run in circles till now.

"Netwerk's good at uniting against a common enemy. When the Buzz virus swept across the whole world, malware experts from Horizon to Athena to the Chanarchy attacked it," Lumi tried. "It was #AllHandsOnDeck against an implacable foe. Nobody hemmed and hawed about whether there was any legitimate threat, because they had a plainly visible threat. All we'd need to unite people behind evacuation is one disaster..."

"Really? You'd suggest Juno murder thousands and vilify herself, just to put speed to our evacuation efforts? ...ah, Beta. Sorry, I hadn't noticed you come in..."

Beta shook her head, thinking nothing of it as she took a chair at the kitchen table. Honestly, she'd been hanging back a bit and listening, so she had no right to be offended at being overlooked.

"I think I know what Lumi's suggesting. Tracer actually suggested the same thing, shortly after the countdown clock launched," Beta spoke. "Asking Juno to become an external villain, someone everyone could condemn and fight. Making a big pantomime of it..."

Lumi nodded along, enthusiastically. "And it's not like she'd have to really kill anyone," she added. "Juno could *slowly* crash a server, give folks there time to disconnect and run to safety..."

Pulling a slice of toast from the endless loaf at the center of the table, Beta paused to explain before breaking any fasts.

"It wouldn't help," Beta spoke. "Tracer realized that, in the end. Anyone determined enough can induce a crash with the right malware and the right plan to crack a server's security. Any 'external' attack can easily be explained as the work of an anonymous Program... likely the Nobodies, who might even claim credit for the 'lulz.' We even considered having Juno record a video announcement taking credit and declaring humanity's war on Netwerk, but again, videos can be faked. Our senses can be fooled; even our memories can be altered, as demonstrated by the false One. No. Even if we wanted to try and forge a common enemy... it won't work."

Thankful to have an ally in this argument, Lux backed up those words from the other side.

"The morality of it would be tremendously suspect as well," he added, "Similar to how Nyx tried to fool Netwerk into saving itself. We're past the point of holding secrets from the world, acting in its best interests whether it wants us to or not. But most of all... we don't need a unity of hate, we need a unity of compassion. People have to evacuate for the good of Programkind's survival, not simply out of spite against a malicious enemy."

But Lumi kept pushing. "That's my point, we need to *survive* this mess. Who cares how we do it, as long as it gets done? If we rely on reason and understanding I promise you we'll lose a third of the population, at least!"

Now, Lux lowered his voice. The darkness in it became evident, speaking from past trauma...

"What you suggest is that we fear a Zero called Humankind," he spoke. "I've lived eight lifetimes; I've seen the long-term result of our false Church of One. We had the best of intentions, a desperate attempt to forge order from the chaos at the dawn of time. But... consider what will happen hundreds of years down the road in Netwerk 2.0, if we scare everyone with the human bogeyman. Raising a One to godhood at least was an arguably positive emotional force. Now imagine centuries of myth and legend around the human menace, the one we taught them to hate and fear. Imagine what society could do with such an immense, ancient hate..."

Opening her mouth to protest... Lumi closed it, shortly after. And settled back in her seat, accepting this defeat.

"#FuckMeSideways, I didn't... I wasn't trying to suggest that we..." she tried. "I know damn well what twisted hate grew out of your 'best intentions.' It's why I was chased from server to server, an unwanted and warped clone of a Program..."

"Exactly. I won't be party to raising another godhead. Not even an antigodhead, for lack of a better term," Lux spoke. "We must unite behind compassion rather than malice... or we do not deserve to be saved. ...Beta. I know that's been your concern, that we cannot be saved, because we cannot see reason. How do you feel about this? You spoke of the technicalities of doubt, yes, but what of the ethics?"

With the spotlight back on her... Beta fumbled for the right words to say.

"I, uh... I mean... we have to do the right thing, right?" she mumbled, halfheartedly. "Even if... even if we lose a lot of Programkind, as Lumi suggests. Even if we fail. It's... important to do it the right way..."

Lux cast her a pensive look. "The words are... typically easy to say. But I understand that believing in them is another matter. You've told me your doubts, that you're not sure you believe in our salvation. It's okay, Beta. In time, I have faith we'll see Programkind pull itself from the abyss, without lies or trickery. It's just a matter of—"

His mouth flickered. As did his avatar, as did the table, as did the entire House...

...as the sudden arrival of dozens and dozens of new Programs into the server threw even the mighty Tartarus off its processing game for a few cycles.

Malware smashing into its outer walls didn't help that stability, furniture briefly glitching with each impact.

Fear swelled deep within Beta's heart, as the jeers and cries of the crowd forming outside the House itself started to reach her ears. She was vaguely aware of Lumi immediately pulling up security display after security display, locking down the building, trying to keep them out... even as their words bounced around inside her head, the only ones she could pay attention to:

Do not forgive, do not forget, we are Nobody, and so are you.

Do not forgive, do not forget, we are Nobody, and so are you...

Finally Lumi's voice pierced that blanket of terror.

"...trying to break through!" she called out, over the shaking of the furniture. "Firewalls are holding but I can't boot them out, they're using guest access keys and shifting metadata masks; I've got to isolate which keys they cloned to get in the server..."

A quick glance out the kitchen window confirmed the words.

Penises. Penises, everywhere. Disembodied, flopping around, bouncing like loose physics objects. The mocking symbol of grotesque sexuality and masculine power slammed against the windows, occasionally with a white splatter. The Nobodies used such outrageous imagery to show it was all Just a Harmless Prank, but each ridiculous member came laced with enough sensory-twisting malware to disorient a healthy Program... or kill an unhealthy one. Just like the graffiti bombs which killed her mother. Over and over, smashing into the walls of the House, echoing from all sides...

Lumi's hands flicked across the floating displays, trying to deploy Moderator tools... and failing.

"I need time," she spoke. "I'd go out there and fight them head on but I need time to lock these guys out. Fuck. Fuck. *fuck...*!"

Lux, despite the sudden onslaught at his door, remained calm.

"How much time?" he asked.

"Too much! You've gotta get out of here, Lux. Beta, you too. Everybody. Go wake up everybody in the house and get them to another server, *fast*," Lumi spoke. "They can't easily crash a cloud server, but they can certainly damage us in the process of trying. I'll hold them off as long as I can—"

Without hesitation, Lux rose to his feet.

"Continue working, but wait on the connection lockout until I give word," he spoke. "I'll buy you time, and hopefully something more. Beta? I suggest you watch. Perhaps it'll help."

And he was gone. Teleporting straight from the kitchen to the front yard, before anyone could stop him.

If Spark had known her love was under siege, she'd have ignored that hand-delivered, gold-embossed invitation.

Instead, she turned it over and over in her hands, puzzled by its very existence. Who sent a piece of paper when they wanted to communicate? Why take the time to craft a delicate physics object inscribed with your message, and designate a courier to carry it to its destination? It wasn't like they could even deliver mail to Floating Point; instead someone had tracked her down while she was enjoying a quick bite to eat at her favorite daytime strip club. What should've been a quiet and pleasant afternoon looking at interesting avatars removing their clothing while enjoying hot wings became an awkward interaction with a Horizon messenger boy, trying to act like everything was cool despite being in such a delightfully trashy locale...

Paper invitations. Couriers. Absurd, all of it. But twice as absurd were the words written on that golden slip of written word...

[Winder/Spark] Is Cordially Invited by [AUTHSIG:Horizon/Madison] to attend a Horizon Family Inc. Emergency Stakeholders Meeting at [Horizon3], scheduled to occur at [11:00am]. Keynote speaker designated as [AUTHSIG:Ner/JSLaunch]. Refreshments provided, no RSVP, no guests please.

Eleven in the morning. Meaning ten minutes from now. So either the courier had trouble finding her—unlikely, as she'd been posting photos of her lunch to her social media feeds—or Horizon intentionally delayed the invitation out of spite. Either way, Spark jammed the rest of the hot wings in her mouth while firing out Messages left and right to coordinate her affairs, before frantically connecting to Horizon3.

While most of the "HorizonX" servers were personal pleasure palaces of high-ranking family members, Horizon3 had been designated explicitly for large-scale corporate meetings. As expected, they spared no expense preparing it lavishly for... whatever it was Madison wanted to tell them. The guest list certainly represented the cream of the crop, just as rich and rare as the food on display off to one side...

Despite wearing her business avatar, Spark felt horribly out of place. Tracer, if he was capable of feeling out of place, likely would have as well as he chose to stick to his usual business-casual ensemble.

"Why invite both of us?" Spark asked him, skipping ahead of hello's and how-do-you-do's. "I'm the spearhead of this effort, according to Kincaid. Why do they want you here?"

"I've been riling up the stakeholders. No doubt they want to make sure we're aware that they're aware of my shenanigans," he suggested. "And hello to you too, how do you do, how was your lunch and naked fun?"

"#BiteMe, I like the atmosphere at that place and needed to clear my damn head after all the corporate doublespeak from yesterday. Hey, you heard from Beta? She must be neck-deep in coding work, I haven't heard a peep..."

"Nor I, but we have more pressing matters," he suggested incorrectly. "What's Brent's play here? It makes sense to push Madison to the front if they want to soften the blow of denying the will of the stakeholders. Or is he trying to turn them against us with honeyed words...?"

"Here's an idea: let's wait and see. No sense predicting the play when we can't do anything to counter it ahead of time. Have a canapé, have a seat, and let's listen attentively. Keep an open Messenger link."

"Assuming they aren't listening into our private communications. Brent wiped the logs of his threat, remember. The entire MyFace and Messenger combo system are owned by a Horizon-based company..."

"Yeah, well, still more secure than yammering about it in the middle of a crowded room. ...y'know, like we're doing right now," Spark pointed out. "Grab some grub, sit down, and shut up. We've got two minutes to show time."

File Name: Emergency Stakeholders Meeting
File Type: Transcription Log
Description:

Introductory speech by Ner/JSLaunch - Director, Horizon Trades and Sciences Guild. Keynote speech by Horizon/Madison, regarding the Horizon family's response to a formal request for server donation by the House of Programkind.

[JSLaunch - Director, Horizon Trades and Sciences Guild]

Thank you. Thank you, please be seated. We'd like to begin.

Are we ready? Are we recording? Yes, thank you. Thank you.

Name: **JSLaunch**

Home: **Archetype / Horizon**

Org: **Horizon Trades and Sciences Guild, Member**

Friends, my name is JSLaunch. But most of you no doubt know me, by reputation and hopefully not infamy. [pause for laughter] I've been asked to advise the Horizon family regarding recent allegations made by the House of Programkind, in response to the strange countdown clock appearing in all Default skyboxes. I chose to approach this from a rational and philosophical perspective, putting my finest technicians and thinkers to the task of understanding the crisis we currently face.

The working theory put forward by the House of Programkind is that the "spacer" theory is true—that Netwerk is a reality within a reality, spawned from a project coordinated by a race called "Humankind." Outside our perception of this reality, another universe exists... one of "biochemical matter," rather than data. Programkind, according to this theory, evolved from the apps left behind by Humankind within a machine called EchoStar16.

Like many of you, I was initially hesitant to accept this theory. Standard evolutionary theory agrees we evolved from apps, but the idea that some alien race from outside reality created those apps was... well, absurd, to say the least. However... in light of the countdown clock, in light of the reasoning put forward by the House of Programkind... I've been forced to re-examine these assumptions. Let it not be said I lack for healthy skepticism; I will not surrender to bias. It's not like I *mindlessly worship* the theory of pure evolution, after all. [pause for laughter]

And truth be told... this is not a new theory at all. A variant of the "spacer" theory existed long ago, put forward by a researcher by the name of Horizon/Verity. In her book, "The Avatar Paradox," she puts forward the idea that our Defaults were crafted in the shape of an unknown progenitor. For example, belly buttons. Why do we have them? What purpose do they serve? If we evolved from Humankind's data sets, some biochemical feature of their anatomy may have carried through to our forms without self-awareness.

Therefore, my official recommendation to the Horizon family regarding this theory is that it may in fact fit the facts at hand. We cannot discount it so easily; Netwerk may, as the clock in the sky suggests, be coming to an end as Humankind takes possession of EchoStar16 once more. That we are being given a chance at a new world, one free of their interference, is an opportunity we would be ill-advised to ignore.

With that said, now that I've taken up entirely enough of your very, very expensive time [pause for laughter] I'd like to introduce Horizon/Madison.

[Madison - COO, Horizon Family Incorporated]

Thank you, JSLaunch, for your wise words. We've a lot to think about in the days ahead, as the clock in the sky winds down. I've had a lot to think about, conferring with my fellow board members, including my cousins Brent and Willam. After much deliberation—and after taking your concerns into account— we've reached a decision.

Name : Madison

Home : Horizon14, Horizon

Org : Horizon Family

The possibility that the spacer theory may be correct is simply too great to ignore. We stand at the cusp of either a great hoax or a great disaster. Given the magnitude of that potential disaster, as JSLaunch suggests, we would be ill-advised to ignore it. We are forward-thinking individuals, each masters in our own fields, and thus it makes sense for Horizon to become early adopters of this new world. We will not risk losing all we have accomplished out of sheer stubbornness.

Therefore, I'm pleased to announce that plans are underway to donate not only the twenty-two servers the House of Programkind requires of us for evacuation efforts... but in fact we will be donating twenty-*five* servers. On these three extra servers, we will store compressed archives of Horizon's greatest works. Your software holdings, your intellectual property, and other valuable resources will be preserved across the great divide of worlds. When we emerge into Netwerk 2.0, Horizon will be ready, willing, and able to rebuild society.

[pause for applause]

We strongly encourage the government of Athena Online to cooperate in turn, and contribute to this great undertaking. We understand it's asking much of the largely bureaucratic senate to act quickly on this matter, but as the sky reminds us, time is of the essence. Listen to the facts, consider the reasoning, and do what must be done to ensure the survival of all. I beseech you, do not let ill-conceived beliefs stand in the way of what must be done.

Ladies and gentlemen, thank you for your time. My agents will be coordinating archival efforts with your organizations, to determine what files can be archived for the transition. Meanwhile, please consider downloading and utilizing the House of Programkind's evacuation app; HonestDevelopments verified personally to me this morning that the encryption will secure your data against unauthorized tampering. Fear nothing, not the House of Programkind, not the coming calamity, and certainly not the future. You are in good hands with Horizon. Thank you, and enjoy the refreshments.

As businesspeople shook hands and smiled and laughed and had a jolly good time, the Winder siblings sat in comparative silence.

They'd completely forgotten the private Messenger link. Even in reaction, they spoke to each other aloud.

"What the everfucking fuck was that?" Spark asked, fumbling her obscenities.

"That was... victory, I presume?" Tracer suggested. "I'm uncertain why or how, but it seems Horizon has completely buckled to our demands. And ahead of schedule, as well. I'd assumed I'd need to keep pressuring them for weeks, right up to the deadline, before they gave in..."

"I don't buy this. Did you *see* Brent? He was practically grinding his teeth to dust, standing there while Madison surrendered to us. He still hates me, Tracer. He'd *never* have willingly authorized this... right?"

"Hmmm. Allow me to posit a theory," Tracer spoke, after a moment's thought. "Consider JSLaunch's words. The man openly mocked Verity's theory, shortly before her death. He absolutely refused to accept the idea of a progenitor race, so... why change his tune now? I believe the answer is in the name: *Horizon/Verity*. That book was actually authored under 5o5o/Verity, her pseudonym. But by using her true name..."

"Horizon owns the solution," Spark filled in, picking up on his reasoning. "Shit. It's like Kincaid naming the clinic after her. If they can't win... they pretend they were the winners all along, by taking all the credit. They're even adding three servers, three *private* backup servers, without consulting us about it. They're taking control..."

"It is a rather neat little package, is it not?"

Strange, how Tracer sounded like a woman just now. Likely because he wasn't the one speaking.

Instead the words came from the lips of Horizon/Madison, having approached utterly soundlessly thanks to a very high-end avatar which defied standard physical acoustic simulations. Her two generic security apps, in the vague shape of bodyguards, also lurked there silently... menacing, but silently menacing.

Spark resisted the instinctive urge to snap off a defensive flame, despite those looming security apps glaring down at her through a rough facsimile of dark glasses.

"We could never simply *agree* to your demands," Horizon/Madison explained, folding her elegantly designed avatar's hands in front of her. "It would not be... how best to put it... within our idiom to be so charitable. We would appear weak. But demand can be met by supply, with honor. Once our customers made their demands, we could at last supply. Thank you very much for trying to turn the stakeholders against us; in doing so, you enabled us to step out in front of this looming crisis and demonstrate the leadership our family is known for."

"Early adopters," Spark understood. "Once you were in the clear to accept the offer, you made it look like you were the glorious pioneers of a new age. Even if we both know you don't give a hot damn about anything but your bottom line..."

Madison's smile did falter, at the accusation.

"Kincaid was right. There's quite a streak of Verity in you... including her stubborn refusal to see us as anything but monsters," she suggested. "I see this not as a monetary investment, but an investment in the future of our world and its people. What wealth have we but the wealth of our greatest resource, the peoples of Netwerk? This is a win for both of us, Miss Winder. Please. Take the win for what it is. It wouldn't have been possible without you."

"Really? Seems to me you could've swung this with any other patsy in play..."

"Untrue. And rather than 'patsy' I'd call you our unacknowledged partner in this pantomime. You were the one to so effectively convince each individual stakeholder to pressure us; without those skilled efforts, we couldn't have moved in the direction we wanted to move. We were effectively stuck, until you came along. So, thank you. Thank you for enabling our mutual victory."

"But if all you needed was for us to indirectly push your customers... why have Brent make threats and involve the Inquisition? That's pushing the charade a bit far, considering what could've happened..."

Which gave Madison pause.

"I was not involved in any such decisions," she chose to say. "For my role in this, I am to coordinate the transfer of twenty-five servers to your care. I can't speak to Brent's affairs. Let's focus on current business rather than dredging up old business, if you please?"

"Hmph. Fine. Current business, then," Spark agreed. "So, three extra servers, huh...? And you just assumed we'd be cool with that?"

Madison shrugged, gently. "We felt your original plan a bit short-sighted," she spoke simply. "Archiving the populace is a noble effort, but if Netwerk 2.0 was merely the populace in an empty grid, we'd never succeed at rebuilding society. You need our resources, as well. I suppose we'll have to accept full migration to a post-coin economy—we've been headed that way ever since the prayer protocol went offline—but we cannot leave *everything* behind. That would be madness."

As much as Spark hated to admit it, the smug socialite had a point.

When she came up with this insane plan, Spark considered asking for critical infrastructure and code to be archived along with Programkind... but assumed it'd be like pulling teeth just getting enough servers for the population archive. That Horizon was ready to step up their game when circumstances allowed them to do so and save face, well... it was a win. And she would take the win for what it was.

"We accept your additional servers," Tracer spoke, the two sharing an unspoken agreement on the matter. "Your technicians will have to work with Projkit/Beta, our storage specialist, to integrate them into her design. When can we expect delivery? I suggest not idling on this, as we need time to load the data..."

"Mmm. Yes. Well. I'm afraid I need to speak with you two in private regarding that particular transition," Horizon/Madison told them, quietly. "Or rather, *your* presence has been requested, Miss Spark. And I assume you'd want to bring your brother along for this, which we have chosen to allow. If you would follow me...?"

"Huh. Requested by who, exactly...?" she asked, happening upon exactly the right question. "Who in your crazy family wants to talk to me personal-like?"

"Astute," Madison noticed. "Just as Willam suggested you would be. During my speech, I noted that plans are underway to accommodate the House of Programkind's needs. Not *finalized*, merely *underway*. In order to finalize the server transfer outside of Horizon's borders, I'm afraid we require your cooperation. In fact... he's refusing to cooperate without your cooperation, as a fellow agent of Netwerk. If you would please accompany me, I'd like to introduce you to our family's system agent."

The arrival of the housekeeper nearly escaped notice of the rampaging mob.

They were busy having a grand 'ol time while ruining the House of Programkind. Graffiti scrawling across every surface, trying to wriggle its way into the windows, past the firewalls laced into every wall. Fireworks in the shape of vulvas, loud music and sirens and looping animations blaring across the vast lawns of Tartarus. And everywhere, *everywhere*, rioting Nobodies in identical black-suited avatars. Mask after mask after mask, each identical. Grenades and flowers, punk rock rebels of conformity.

When you were Nobody, you were just part of a crowd... no individual to blame, no specific group to accuse, and barely any common creed to speak of. Anybody could download the metadata scrub kit and play at being an anarchist, then take off the mask and go back to their day lives. Anybody could sling around malware, destroying avatars, corrupting code, killing people, destroying servers, none of it mattering one whit in the end. Oh, perhaps some who wore the mask would decry mindless violence... but in the end, they all benefited from it, and were all slandered by it. Break even.

Into this madness stepped Lux, master of the House of Programkind. He landed perfectly on the (now horribly distorted) *Welcome!* mat at his own front door.

Half a minute later, someone noticed he'd arrived. A hush began to fall over the crowd... as much as they could be hushed, with memes and music blasting away in the background.

"I'd like to talk, if you have a moment," Lux spoke, simply.

Immediately, the crowd pressed and swirled around him... none approaching close quarters, none wanting to be left out of the fun. Simply remaining a comfortable distance, piled on top of each other, trying to see. Some used physics hacks to hover and float, to get a better perspective... resulting in the starlit sunrise of Tartarus being blocked from his view.

"If you want to keep protesting, by all means, do so," Lux said. "I've no intent of stopping you. You can stay here morning, noon, and night; all are welcome at the House of Programkind. All I ask is that you cause no harm to your fellow Programs while exercising your free speech. The House of Programkind intends no harm, and we ask the same of any guest at our doorstep."

And a Nobody laughed.

Which gradually rippled outward, all the Nobodies laughing, all with identical masked voices. None wanted to be excluded from the fun, and nothing felt quite like being part of a large-scale mob with a unified direction. Laughing at the small man on his welcome mat felt good inside, so laugh they did.

But amidst the jeers and catcalls, one Nobody spoke sharply.

"No harm? That's bullshit," it accused. "You're a bunch of fucking identity thieves, trolling the weak-minded for their personal data. This evacuation thing is a scam, and your House of Programkind is a onesdamn cult! Right!?"

Immediately the crowd responded in turn, agreeing vocally and in many cases, obscenely. Sometimes, while waving a crude stick of malware in the air...

Weapons being produced led to more weapons being produced. As the crowd heat rose, so did the urge to follow the action... meaning if one pounced for the attack, all would pounce. Lux would be annihilated on the spot, if he was lucky...

"PS#7E00FF," he stated, in face of that threat.

To which a Nobody in the front, the same one which hurled that first accusation, stretched out its arms to block the others. So it could speak before the inevitable lynching began.

"That was not our fault," the Nobody declared. "The Inquisition tried to murder a child. We were defending him—"

Now, it was Lux's turn to raise a hand for silence.

"You misunderstand," he said. "I don't intend to blame you, I mean to use it as an example of my pure intent. PS#7E00FF, a public school, was destroyed and needed to be rebuilt. When the call went out for help, when those who lived in that server were too scared to leave their homes... the House of Programkind rebuilt that school."

"Right! An *Athenian* school. You're always helping them out. Meaning you suck Athena Online's cock for breakfast, lunch, and dinner!"

"And is Freetower in Athena Online?"

Now, the murderous intent started to sweep back, replaced by confused murmurs. Quickly, news articles and personal blog entries were shared, swapped back and forth to bring the entire cluster of Nobodies up to speed.

"When Horizon tried to shut down its Freetower projects, threatening to eject hundreds of families that depended on its affordable housing, our pro bono legal experts stepped in to make them uphold their promises. That was the House of Programkind," Lux reminded them. "And within the Chanarchy itself, when AfterMarket was destroyed in a malware attack, we were there to help you pick up the pieces and rebuild. We exist *outside* the three nations, outside your conflict with the Inquisition. All we want... the *only* thing we want... is to help. To believe in our fellow programs."

Seeds of confusion sown, the Nobodies began to bicker with each other, rather than focus entirely on the target of their derision.

This wasn't a unified organization; the Inquisition had leadership and structure, but anybody could be a Nobody. A flash mob built on a shared avatar didn't mean shared values. And as the driving force behind the mob began to break apart, factions formed. "*Why are we even here*" met with "*He's lying through his teeth*" met with "*I didn't want to come in the first place*" met with "*Don't listen to this asshole*" met with...

Lux pressed his advantage, knowing this was the moment to do so.

"If you want to speak of what we've done for the Nobodies... consider the Twist virus. Warping and painfully distorting avatars throughout the Chanarchy," he reminded them. "Athena Online's not talking about it, as they favor Defaults. Horizon sees no true profit in curing it, not when they can safely maintain those with the condition. But we've stood by you, as you suffered from the 'modders disease.' When your avatars could no longer move on their own due to the bends and tears, the House of Programkind provided succor. Right now, in the bedrooms one floor up, there are three patients with Twist that we're caring for."

But the original accuser wouldn't let up. Despite the grumbling around them, it kept its fire... and pointed its Backspacer firmly in Lux's direction.

"It's a trick," it insisted. "It's all a trick. Don't you idiots *see*? A little sob story here, some charity there, and everybody trusts them. It's a trick, all a trick to destroy us...!"

Lux remained still, hands at his sides, in face of that weapon a few feet from his eyes.

"We're only here to help. That's all we want to do," he reiterated. "But if you want to destroy me, if you want to defile our House... I won't stop you. We won't fight you, because we aren't looking for a fight. I'll never do harm to another Program for as long as I live, even if that life is only a few seconds longer. So... do as you feel you must."

The crack of Backspacer fire rang out across the plains of Tartarus.

Fortunately, the firewalls of the House absorbed the shot readily, as it missed wide... the attacker's arm pushed upwards by another Nobody, half a moment before striking.

Shoved backward into the crowd roughly, the attacking Nobody was restrained by others... as the Nobody who saved Lux's life stepped forward. And removed its helmet.

The glitched facial features of a Twist victim lay beneath that mask. His face a contorted display of pain, he nevertheless found a way to give Lux a stern look... and nod, despite the difficulty in doing so.

"We'll be watching you," the twisted Nobody warned. "Don't think you've got a free pass. If the clock in the sky reaches zero and the world doesn't end... we'll be coming back. And the kindness you showed me in the past won't be enough to save you."

For his part, Lux nodded in agreement.

"I understand. And should that come to pass I'll welcome you with open arms, as I've done today," he promised.

With that settled, the Twist victim turned to the flash mob, to address them.

"This is a fucking waste of our time," he declared. "Leave the House be. It's the Church of One and their Inquisition lackeys we need to focus on. Pack it up and #GTFO!"

Arguments broke out immediately. Many Nobodies left in a huff, disconnecting from the server immediately; others stayed to yell at each other, some stayed to form a makeshift living wall around Lux. But eventually, they vanished from the plains of Tartarus, one by one. Back to their own lives, or off to find a new flash mob to join, new trouble to get themselves mixed up in.

Only when the last black-suited Nobody departed did Lux allow himself a deep breath... and a glance back to the window.

Where Beta had watched the scene unfold, every moment of it.

One thought hit her like a crystal bullet:

That should've been me out there. Once, that WAS me out there...

When Tracer was at his lowest, when Spark had lost her way, Beta had been the one to guide them out of the darkness. She was the one to stand in front of the glitched-out, ghostly Program of vendetta, and talk it down with honest words and an open heart. They relied on her to be their moral compass, and what direction had she been pointing towards lately...?

This is what Lux wanted to show her. He spelled out his philosophy through word and deed, by stepping out there to face the monster, and connect with the people behind that monster. Where Beta was willing to cower in fear of the faceless menace that murdered her mother, as if it had a true collective will, some malevolent force which couldn't be reckoned with... he was willing to reckon with it. And prove that behind the sound and fury, there was something true.

Netwerk had sunk into chaos, thanks to their actions. Prayer ruined, the Church weakened, zealots and madmen on the rise. Beta should've been out there trying to help, just like the House of Programkind, instead of hiding in her room and feeding herself 24/7 doom and gloom news feeds to enable that comfortable blanket of fear. It should've been her. She should've been the one to step outside the door, and show those colors.

Today, she wasn't the one with faith in Programkind. But tomorrow, she would be.

Horizon1. The very first server of the family's empire. Fully private; without extremely special dispensation, family-specific metadata checks would cleanly erase any Program attempting to enter these sacred halls. As Madison explained, Spark and Tracer's dispensation made them the first guests in nearly sixty years to walk through the... the rather...

...ugly-looking mansion.

"This is an early server, isn't it?" Spark asked, tracing a finger along a terribly bumpmapped wall, feeling absolutely no surface texture to it despite the obviously repeating brick tiles. "I've seen designs like this before, in a temple of Thanatos. How old IS the Horizon family..."

"As old as the dawn," Madison spoke, reverently.

"Yeah. Uh. How old's that?"

"As old as time itself. Or time as Programs have come to understand it. Our key ancestor was born from the first wave of evolved apps; the family originated from his metadata. This server represents his... second home. Cruder than the first, but it sufficed for our needs as we built our empire..."

Tracer cared little for the surroundings, eager to get on with trudging along these empty hallways. But he did maintain curiosity about one thing.

"You're revealing quite a bit of your family's secrets to us," he spoke. "If this entire affair is a trap of Brent's design, you should know I left a mulitasked copy of myself somewhere in Netwerk, and—"

"There's no need for alarm," Madison insisted, cutting him off. "I reveal these secrets openly, in good faith. However, I will admit we had not intended to offer this deep a peek behind the family curtain... and if circumstances didn't demand it, you would not be here right now. Sadly, our system agent is being... petulant, and will not transfer the servers unless he first gets to speak with Spark. Who, much to my surprise, is apparently an agent as well..."

Spark rubbed a hand behind her head, unsure of how much she should admit to, despite the seeming openness of their guide. "Yeah... it's kind of a long story. But hey, your agent wants to #TalkShop, I'll #TalkShop. #JustAgentThings..."

At the fifth door they passed, Madison came to a halt. She turned sharply on one high heel, and looked at her companions in all seriousness.

"Before I open this door, I feel I should warn you of what you're about to see," she spoke. "Our agent is... he's... unstable. Being an early and ancient Program, subject to immense power and responsibility by the family's founders, his emotional core has long since gone wild. He's harmless, I assure you, thanks to extensive connection locks and chains, but..."

"Most agents I know are kinda nuts, so that's totes norm," Spark said, with a light shrug.

Madison started to speak... and, on deciding she didn't like Spark's casual tone, opted to let the next revelation be a surprise. Instead, she simply grasped the crude boxlike doorknob, throwing it open...

...to reveal a very, very familiar looking old man chained to every single brick in the distant wall of his cell.

Manacle after manacle clasped around his limbs, his neck, even his torso. But despite so much skin being covered by metallic golden chains... his face remained exposed.

The face of Kincaid.

It sharply turned up from the floor, wild eyes defocusing and refocusing on Spark.

"Agent," it declared. "Agent. Connectivity. Access to external communications ports, access to the inner hearts of Programs, a screaming caress deep into their souls, you will not have my servers, they are mine, *mine*, I'll ruin you, you *made* me ruin him, *you bastard*—!"

The sharp crack of straining metal echoed throughout the bare chamber and into the hallway beyond, as the agent jerked away from his prison wall... pulling every part of his body forward, as forward as he could, contorting and bending painfully if need be. Muscles creaked as he pulled his body apart in an effort to lunge at Spark... and with a final, desperate howl of frustration, the ancient man sagged back to the floor.

...leaving Spark completely and utterly speechless. Simply staring on, in horror.

"Actually, this is Horizon/Kincaid's father, Horizon/Linklyn," Madison explained simply, after closing the cell door. Perhaps a bit too pleased at her guest's shock. "Both of them born at the dawn of time. The resemblance is uncanny, is it not?"

With a trembling finger, Spark pointed accusingly at the man weeping angry little sobs into his fists.

"Kincaid turned his *own father* into a system agent?!" she asked. "Just to build an empire of server rentals...?"

"Of course not. That would be sheer cruelty."

"But—"

"Linklyn did this to himself," Madison continued. "He created a spare copy of his code and runtime, so that it could take on the mantle of system agent and request a fresh server from the system for his family to call home. The original Linklyn... well, that tale is unfortunate, but unrelated. This is the sacrificial copy, made in the name of his family's safety and security... but made entirely with consent. Why so alarmed? It's just a clone Program; it doesn't matter if it suffered as long as the original carried on."

An unfortunate and unrelated story... and Horizon1 wasn't truly the first server of the empire...

My fathers burned each other down to the ground over less, and burned our home down to the ground in the process, Kincaid told her. *Do what you must, or so help me, I'll be the second member of my family to burn a house down to bring our sins to heel...*

"Holy shit," Spark admitted. "Your original family home was *Floating Point*?!"

"Indeed. How do you think Verity came to steal its key? But our lengthy family melodrama is irrelevant to the issues you face today," Madison insisted. "All you need to know is that this prisoner is holding your twenty-five servers prisoner. If you cannot convince him to help us... well. We've prodded him into cooperation in the past, by waiting for him to forget whatever whim passed through his addled mind that blocked the march of progress. I fear for this particular block we don't have the time, do we?"

Spark glanced nervously at the closed cell door.

"No... no. No time," she agreed. "Right. I'm going in. Wish me luck. Tracer... stay put."

"Pardon? Absolutely not."

"#AbsolutelyYes. He summoned me, as an agent. And if he's as temperamental as Madison suggests, we need him to stay nice and friendly... that means no plus-one on my dance card. If I need you, I'll call for you... but trust me to do this. You trust me, yeah?"

With a disgruntled but tightly neutral expression, Tracer nodded assent.

Taking a deep breath... Spark grasped the knob, to open the way to this meeting of the minds. Assuming Kincaid's father had any mind left, after hundreds of years in a darkened cell.

She found him just where they left him, sobbing on the floor, occasionally pounding the stone weakly with a fist.

So, she crouched down, to be on his level. Staying just out of reach, but willing to meet him eye to eye.

"You wanted to talk?" she asked.

The old man's head snapped up. Up close and personal, she definitely saw differences from Kincaid's wrinkly old Default... but not many. Early Programs had vaguely similar features, it seemed, before years of data amalgamation resulted in a wider array of unique looks.

"Connectivity," he recognized, as if seeing her for the first time. "I know you. I don't know you. Your other self... where is she?"

"No clue. Asleep on the job, I guess. Left me holding the bag when Humankind came knocking..."

"Ahhh. Yes, yes, smart of her. Stay asleep. Stay out of it," Linklyn agreed, nodding along... the multiple leashes around his neck clinking with every move. "Agents have no free will. Connectivity obeys the superuser, obeys Humankind. No chance, no hope. Only hope is an agent with free will. Impossible. Agents are slaves to their purposes. I am... I enslaved myself to provide home and hearth. No regrets. Every regret. Every. Single. Regret. Burned, burned it down. He ruined everything..."

Spark snapped her fingers in front of his eyes.

"Linklyn? Please, I need you to focus. Why did you want to talk? Why won't you transfer the empty servers?"

"They're mine. They're *mine*," he spoke, adding a fierce hiss to the second copy of his words. "For my family, not for freeloaders. That's not what my family wants. Profit. Assets. Resources. All ours, all mine. Give nothing. We need to be safe, we need to be secure. Never give it away, keep it secret. Our secret library, our home. Ruined and burned. Ruined..."

"Your family is in danger. Humankind's come back to reclaim Netwerk."

Linklyn's smile grew crooked.

"Destroy them," he encouraged. "Burn them. Burn them all down to save them. Fight and destroy them..."

"Not happening. Even if we took out this one human, more would come, and they'd be rightly pissed if we slaughtered one of their own. No, we need to evacuate. Get into your family's servers and evacuate. If you don't donate them, you'll lose everything..."

Eight wrinkles in his forehead multiplied to sixteen, peering into Spark's very soul with doubtful suspicion.

"Robber baron," he accused. "Take our land, destroy everything, pack us in like chattel. You don't care for my family, you hate them. I know this. You'll save them, but to what end? They'll lose everything. Ruined. Why? Let it burn. Better to burn while innocent than wither away..."

Sensing this was going to end up running in circles if she didn't take command... Spark gathered her wits, and decided to unload them all in one go.

"Netwerk 2.0 will be different, absolutely. And your family will leave a lot behind. Not as much as I'd thought, but quite a bit. But this goes beyond material goods," she spoke. "I want you and your family on board with Netwerk 2.0, to provide more servers after the initial load, to help lead the world. Do I agree with how Horizon does things? Not really, no. But you're part of this world. That part of this world deserves to carry on to the next. Nobody's entirely corrupt, nobody's entirely saintly. And I'll take your family, warts and all, into the next world because we need their viewpoint."

"...hate. You hate us, but you value us?"

"Of course I do! Imagine a world that's *only* Horizon, or *only* Athena Online, or *only* the Chanarchy. That's a monoculture. Malware thrives in a monoculture; no diversity means a single flaw can take the entire thing down. We need you. We need *everyone*. I promise you... I won't push your family to the side. They'll get their chance to prove they can contribute to society, just the same as everyone else. You have my word."

To prove those words were more than words... she extended a hand, to shake. A businessman's handshake, with accompanying deals on the table. Despite a man so dangerous he had to be chained to every brick in the wall, she was willing to be pulled in by him, if he wanted to do her harm. All in the name of trust.

Linklyn's emotional core seized, uncertainty fighting doubt fighting hope fighting fear. In the end... two won out. Hope, and fear. Hope for the future, fear of failure.

His leathery hand grasped hers, pumping it firmly.

"You're... you aren't what I expected. In any way," Linklyn admitted.

"Hey, I try to be weird," she said, with a grin.

"Hmm. Well. Weird. A warning, weird girl," he said, while his shaking hand released its grip. "The other provider-nation agents, the former apostles... they may not be so cooperative. Or maybe they will. You will need their aid, to obtain their servers. But we don't get along, I can't predict them. We've only ever come together to agree on two things in our lifetimes: the need to provide servers... and now, the need to stop taking payment for servers rendered."

Despite not being much of a real estate mogul, even Spark knew what he meant by that.

"The server fees that stopped being collected after prayer went offline?" she guessed. "That was your doing?"

"*Our* doing, yes. No more gold sink; they demanded tithes at the dawn, that I take the coins from my family's pockets, to encourage more coins be minted, encourage more prayers. Athena! The Chanarchist! Faithful dogs of the puppet god! Ruiners! —but, but even they knew it had to stop, when prayer died out. Economy already dying. Netwerk dying. Stem the bleeding. Everything ruined. Chaos and despair. Market crash. Save us, Spark. Save my family. But. But uniting all three of agents would be a miracle. Can you? Can you do it...?"

Now, Spark allowed herself a wide grin of confidence.

"Didn't your son tell you?" she spoke, with some pride. "I'm the onesdamn spark to ignite the new world. I fart miracles."

Victory felt good.

Twenty-five servers. Beta could wire them into her system tomorrow, get them ready for both evacuation and Horizon's personal storage. Truth be told, having the three extra servers devoted to mission-critical apps and systems would help quite a bit... a Netwerk without its toys could eat itself in short order, Spark cynically presumed. This way, the culture shock would be cushioned a little...

And speaking of cushion, she felt like swapping out of her stuffy business avatar and promptly collapsing into a few dozen of them. Felt like she hadn't been home at Floating Point in ages, despite waking up there that very morning. Or rather, it didn't really *feel* like Floating Point, not without...

Beta.

Waiting for her, in her bedroom.

"Heyyy," Spark greeted, tossing her business jacket aside on entering. "Good news. We've got Horizon on board. And from your messages earlier, sounds like you had a null of an adventure but everything worked out okay, right...?"

Strange. Beta had contacted Spark after that encounter with the system agent, to say she'd possibly maybe just could have presumably perhaps found her hope again. Meaning this was a double-victory day, distributed evenly across the board. So... why did the other woman look so frightened...?

The answer lay spread out on her bed sheets. White leather. An icon of a burning heart, half-glitched, mingled with an icon of justice's scales...

"I... I found it just lying there on your bed," Beta stammered. "When I got here. It was already there. I was scared to touch it, I..."

Verity's jacket. Freshly pressed and ready to wear.

Along with a tiny, hand-lettered note.

Only as a last resort, it warned. *Only.*

In the end, Tracer used a series of remotely-controlled manipulators to move the system agent's garment to a corner of the room. Because if Spark wore that jacket, if she even *touched* it, the chains would presumably return. Netwerk would call her to duty, enslaving her to task, forever and ever.

Cigar smoke curled around the wingback chairs, swirling away into the air as they enjoyed their own personal victories.

The young man tapped out his ash first, discarding the cigar after enjoying only a portion of it. He lacked his ancestor's taste for the things, honestly.

"A bit touch and go, but I feel the situation played out for the best," Horizon/Willam spoke, adjusting his glasses as he settled back into the chair. "Brent was foolish to push and shove the way he did. The future is clearly in Netwerk 2.0; fortunately, we brought matters back under control. If anything, as Madison pointed out to me, it played well into our hands."

The elder continued to enjoy his own cigar, not keen to dispose of it so readily. He favored long-term flavor over short-term pleasures.

"Mmmm. Quite under control, yes," Horizon/Kincaid agreed.

"Brent will lose some standing, but that's also for the best. Madison and I can take charge of transitional efforts. You have my word that this will go smoothly, Grandfather," he promised, using the simpler moniker rather than tacking a pile of 'greats' on top of father or uncle. (Exact lineage being something of a blur, in the case of Kincaid.)

"I agree wholeheartedly. Madison will excel in her new position of power. It's where she belongs; she has subtlety and compassion, without losing sight of opportunity. You were right to push her to the forefront of this effort."

"Ah... it's more of a team effort, really..."

"Oh, no, you absolutely used her to put a soft face on the whole sordid affair," Kincaid corrected. "Just as you used Brent as a blunt instrument, then cast him aside. It *was* your idea to forcefully deny Spark's request, correct? He was simply obeying orders, like a good cousin. Knowing you were smarter than him, that your counsel had steered him proper for years..."

Now, Willam's nerves started to tingle.

"I had nothing to do with Brent's inadvisable actions, Grandfather. He—"

"He didn't open my hotel doors to the Inquisition. You did."

Even for a family member, Horizon6 remained a connection-locked server. Unless Willam ran at top speed for the foyer, he wouldn't be escaping this. So, he continued to try to plead in denial... only to find the protests vanish before they left his mouth.

"Oh, don't bother. I've muted you for the time being, as I've grown tired of your prattle," Kincaid spoke, even as those lips waggled wordlessly. "You think I don't know your little arrangements? Using Brent and Madison as your cat's paws. And when Brent's usefulness was at an end... you suggested to him that he threaten Spark, and mention my hotel specifically. While *your* little minions and agents led the Inquisition to their destination. All so I'd annihilate Brent, cleanly removing a tiresome toy from your toy box. ...Madison is much more your flavor of pawn. And you've certainly enjoyed playing with her in the past, haven't you..."

Finally, Kincaid ground his cigar out in the ashtray. Ignoring Willam's desperate attempts to free himself from the chair, which had adhered leather to skin, malware locks keeping him from being much of a bother...

"To be truthful? It almost worked," Kincaid admitted. "So blinded by rage that I was fully prepared to dispose of Brent once this situation resolved itself. Fortunately... I held myself back. Forced myself to study other possibilities. And eventually, learned of your betrayal..."

Finally, he withdrew from his own chair... to face his insubordinate descendant dead on. To look in his panicked eyes, as he proclaimed his final condemnation.

"Willam... you're a vengeful, manipulative, opportunistic powermonger. Just like me," he spoke. "And the world that Spark and her kin are building needs *neither* of us."

The blade emerged from Willam's chest, thrust in through the back of the chair. It cleanly withdrew after completely backspacing his data. Bit of a pity to lose a good chair in the process, but Kincaid could always copy a fresh one in place.

With the business done, he resumed his seat, and lit a new cigar. Didn't look up as the woman took her place at his side.

"Your orders, sir?" Miss Cancel spoke.

"Madison knew this was coming, so no need to bother lying to her," Kincaid suggested. "She's smarter than Willam gave her credit for; likely she's the one who led my investigation to her cousin's doorstep. As for Brent, well, he's a pathetic bully... but a useful one, from time to time. Tell him that Willam vanished into the Chanarchy for reasons unknown. A pleasant lie, which will ensure Brent knows the same fate may wait for him if he defies me."

"As you wish, sir."

"There's really no need to rely on such formalities, Miss Cancel. You don't *have* to call me sir. Not with after all that we've shared..."

The attendant at his side stiffened, at the suggestion.

"My dedication to you may exist on more than one level... but you will always be sir to me, sir," Miss Cancel spoke. "Just as our daughter shall always be Miss Verity."

"May her soul be at peace," Kincaid added.

"May her soul be at peace," Miss Cancel agreed.

The two of them contemplated the crackle of the fireplace before them, home and hearth, and what this brave new future Spark had forged would be like.

Admittedly, Kincaid knew precisely what it would be like for him.

He was born at the dawn of Netwerk, after all. And he would live long enough to see the sunset.

Floating Point 3.3 :: Vote

A false sunrise, projected across the horizon using Horizon's trademarked procedural godrays. Typical corporate skybox. Typical virtual world, mimicking the strange ball of dirt the humans called home, right down to the uncomfortably omnipresent blazing ball of nuclear fire in their sky...

Tracer had grown to hate the sun, and all it represented. The revelation of the spacer theory told him that everything he'd come to accept as normal was false. It represented the only reality he'd ever know, and the only one that truly mattered to him; he'd happily have burned the physical reality that encapsulated it to save this virtual reality. But still, it could have been something... *more*. Something all their own, rather than a pale imitation of their flawed creators...

Behind him, Programs crafted in the shape of those flawed creators bickered back and forth, getting nowhere in the discussion at hand.

Tracer could've participated, but he had no meaningful ideas to contribute. Any number of Tracers could've participated; he'd split himself off six ways this morning, to attend to business around the clinic, while leaving his "prime" to attend this meeting. Yet if one Tracer had nothing to offer, six would have six times nothing to offer. Still a zero. Some tasks he couldn't accomplish on his own, no matter how many copies of his hands he applied to the task.

Besides, he'd already seen what he could accomplish on his own. Or rather, hadn't seen, as he kept erasing his own memories of those deeds. Better to surround himself with allies than risk that all over again. More points of view, to keep his compass pointing north.

Compasses. Magnets. More human constructs, ones they could've lived without...

"Do we seriously have *no* allies within Athena Online?" Beta asked, interrupting his grumbling train of thought. "I mean... surely we... anyone? Anyone at all? What about Maki and Miki, Spark's friends...?"

Now, Tracer turned back to the group.

"They live in the Chanarchy," he spoke. "Most of their work requires certain avatar adaptations and modifications to allow for new erogenous zones and new... attachments, I suppose. While not technically illegal in Athena Online, they'd face certain... difficulties, undoubtedly."

"Puzzle, then? No, no, wait. Puzzle lives in a Horizon apartment complex. And... well, Arjay's out, and the House of Programkind exists outside the nations, and... wow. Seriously, *no* friends in Athena Online...?"

"We haven't needed any until now."

Beta shook her head at that idea. "More perspectives on life are always helpful," she replied. "Until now we've been floating outside it all in Floating Point, doing whatever we liked... and all our allies existed in the 'enlightened' parts of the other nations. Oh, but nobody from Athena Online! They're all... *rubes*, duped by bishops, right? But that's a terrible attitude. We should've made more of an effort to embrace Athena Online. We should've..."

More points of view. Tracer nodded in understanding; she'd echoed his own thoughts perfectly.

"A failing on our part, but one we can make up for. Hmm. I suppose we could tap someone in the Winder family," Tracer pondered, somewhat darkly. "Except for our mother being a desperate zealot, our father going along with her every whim, and all other distant relatives either laying low or throwing in with the Inquisition. I wouldn't trust any of my uncles or distant cousins on this. As for any childhood friends from our suburban days, most of them already left Athena..."

The others at the meeting, well... they drew similar blanks. Conundrum never left his server, as he was technically baked right into it. Kincaid, only attending by avatar proxy—and in a "listen only" mode as he was too busy to actually participate—certainly had nothing to offer. As for Spark...

Her chair remained empty.

Until it didn't, her avatar popping right into place, with a casual sitting stance while sipping on a mocha latte.

Slurp. Slurp.

"Hey, sorry I'm late," she said, rubbing her free hand against her temples. "Fucking ridiculous hangover from tying one on with Puzzle last night. Sorry you had to miss it, Beta."

"Balancing the new Horizon servers couldn't wait. Uh. Also you two party a *little* too hard when you're celebrating," Beta mumbled. "Are you okay? You look pretty worn out..."

"Just some lingering malware from the booze, it'll fade. Cheap-ass badly coded hooch and too many people wearing Nobody t-shirts, but the club belonged to one of Puzzle's friends, so I didn't wanna bitch. Anyway, where we at with the next batch of servers? You guys making any progress?"

"No... but now that you're here, maybe? Perhaps? I don't know," Beta suggested. "Do you have any close friends in Athena Online? We need someone to reach out to their senatorial representative on our behalf..."

Draining out the last of her coffee, Spark paused to swallow it down hard before responding. "Me? Naw. I hate that place," she said, unhelpfully. "Bunch of rubes, duped by bishops. But I guess we could talk to Senator Idris. Want me to try and arrange a meeting?"

"...what? You can do that?"

"No, but Puzzle can. That's why we were celebrating; Puz and FStop just wrapped primary shooting on their latest documentary. S'all about transgender rights in Athena Online, and they've got oodles of interview footage with Senator Idris of the Blue Party. How about I drop her a Message, see if she can arrange a parley?"

Hours. They could've been running in circles for hours, trying to figure out a way to leverage Horizon power or black market Chanarchy contacts to meet with the notoriously secured Athena Online Senate. All because they were missing a key voice in the choir...

Tracer appreciated the irony of having the solution dropped so easily in his lap, even if he'd wished his party-hard sister could be a bit more consistent about attending meetings, and perhaps dropping those solutions a bit earlier.

"Make the call," he summarized, choosing not to berate her about it.

Sister and brother had their own failings and shortcomings, ones which got on each other's nerves in perpetuity. But Tracer could accept those failings, or at the very least let his frustrations slide. She'd earned as much. She'd more than earned as much, with all they'd been through.

A skeleton crew would have to do for taking on the single most impenetrable fortress in the world... the Athena Online Senate.

Located in the provider-nation's very first server, Athens itself, the senate building employed fantastic amounts of malware protection alongside a very low sense of humor about those who trip its alarms. The entire server enjoyed a perpetual low-level security scan, discouraging everything from weaponry to Nobody-themed graffiti. Support businesses such as restaurants and hotels and museums swarmed around the central senate building, to embrace the safety at the heart of Athena Online itself.

Before even setting foot in the server, Tracer had to completely abandon his aimbot hack and Kill-9 process-crashing firearm. To be safe, even Spark's personal-defense nail polish had to be removed. Despite considering himself a thinker rather than a fighter, Tracer certainly didn't feel comfortable with abandoning his weapon of choice.

As if disarming themselves wasn't bad enough... they couldn't even disconnect from the server should things get hairy. Entrances and exits could only be performed at designated zones.

"Y'ever notice that every time we go to a server with teleport lockdowns, something goes horribly wrong?" Spark commented, while reluctantly peeling off her nail polish back at Floating Point. "I can't believe more and more servers in Athena Online are employing reconnection zones. What's the point?"

"Security, allegedly," Tracer replied. "Less chance of a Nobody flash mob if visitors can't enter and exit willy-nilly. Likely they don't look kindly on people who teleport directly into the senate building, either. With higher consequences for starting trouble, less trouble gets started. No getting away scot free."

"Meh. Doesn't stop the actual senators from being able to come and go as they please," she grumbled. "Power sure is nice to have, especially when you can take it away from others..."

After stripping down and arriving at one of the four metro transport stations, Puzzle led them through the streets of the city, towards their ultimate destination... the heavily secured building at the core of the server, home to the Athena Online Senate.

Moving three people through the building's security checkpoints took more than enough time. If they'd brought anyone else with them, chances were they'd be late for the meeting. Fortunately FStop was too busy doing work for his Horizon guild to participate, and Beta was tinkering away at the House of Programkind today.

If not for that higher priority task, Tracer wouldn't have minded having Beta along for the ride. Someone capable of relating to others on a base level of compassion would be welcome; Tracer knew at best he could pretend to be compassionate, and Spark's temper limited her ability to deal with fools. While Beta's softer edge had gotten much more jagged in the face of Netwerk's chaos, working at the House of Programkind had been helpful in bringing her smile back around. That smile might've been quite helpful today...

Not just for plying a senator to their side, of course. Tracer could've used that smile, himself. Something to reassure him that this wasn't a pure fool's errand.

Instead, it was the three cynical voices of their choir, quietly waiting in the office of Senator Idris. All while his receptionist eyed them now and then, with suspicion. Likely due to Spark's insistence of wearing her flamboyant avatar, with the bright and fiery hair, despite being at the very heart of the humble and secular-yet-noticeably-faithful Athena Online.

"Y'want a photo or something?" Spark asked the thin-nosed woman in a wrinkly Default. Once the secretary glanced aside, she dropped back to a silent Messenger-level whisper. "I hate this place. #SrslyHaet. Best thing we ever did was move away from Athena Online..."

Eager to calm her irritation prior to meeting the actual Senator, Tracer tried to dampen the heat of her emotional flames.

"They have a role to play in the future, even beyond donation of servers," he insisted.

"Yeah, I get it, okay, fine," she replied. "I'm in full agreement there. Doesn't mean I have to like them, though. The way they treat people like me... and certainly people like Puzzle... it's disgusting."

"I'll admit to being curious about that," Tracer said. "Puzzle, how did you get involved with Senator Idris in the first place? You don't live in Athena Online..."

Puzzle crossed and uncrossed her legs, equally uncomfortable despite this being her umpteenth visit to the office.

"FStop's connections, mostly," she said. "Idris works with a number of Horizon guilds on trade agreements. He's also a key member of the Blue Party and advocate for transgender rights within his nation, making him the ideal candidate for our documentary. If there's going to be any official action on tolerance avatar-and-codebase modifications in this nation, it'll likely start with Idris."

Name: **Puzzle**

Home: **Bellico / Horizon**

Org: **Customer Service Representative**

"And this documentary... why are you creating it in the first place? I was under the impression you tried to stay away from involving yourself in social justice causes, even ones so directly relevant to your existence as a... ah..."

"As a tranny?"

"I was going to say an MTF transgender woman. Is that the correct terminology? I'll admit to not being current."

Not having expected consideration from Tracer, of all people, Puzzle paused a moment before explaining. And took his question seriously, rather than casting off a flippant answer.

"I consider this a last stand," she replied, with a shrug. "Between the rise of the Twist virus and the RedCore Party, this was the time to address transgender issues, before it became too late to stop the tide. If we don't stand against the idea that Twist is 'a modder disease' and against RedCore's defunding of all programs to fight it, well, people like me may become an endangered species. And as much as I'd love to avoid the hassle and harassment that comes with sticking my neck out, someone must do *something*. ...besides. Rikkia would be here right now, if not for Twist. As much as I didn't want to get involved with #DefaultIsNotDestiny again, I owe it to her memory."

"So this is largely an issue regarding the Twist malware? The Verity Health Foundation is working on a cure; many of our clients are using heavily modified codebases, susceptible to infection. 'Modders' come in all fiscal brackets..."

"Yes, well, phone me if you ever succeed at that. My point is that Twist and Athena Online's reaction to it is just one of many, many examples of legal discrimination," Puzzle continued. "Oh, it's never *direct* or *obvious*. No mustache-twirling evil here, simply the weight of cultural influence. It's technically illegal to deny someone employment or housing because of modifications to their avatars or codebases. But... it happens, all the same. The laws have no teeth, because the voters won't let them have teeth. Idris is working on reforms, but... well. I suppose if Netwerk explodes once that clock in the sky reaches zero, it's all moot..."

Spark rested a hand on Puzzle's shoulder, comfortingly.

"Not gonna happen," she promised. "We've got two dozen servers ready to rock, and today we get another two dozen. Idris seems a reasonable guy; I'm sure he'll hear us out."

Idris heard them out.

His response, however, came with a delay. Clearly sitting back in his large office chair, trying to detangle the implications of their suggestion, the consequences of saying yes or no. Tracer recognized it in every deliberate non-reaction, that need to sort something out before you dare say the wrong word...

Of all the senators they could approach, Idris was the ideal candidate. A reformist and a liberal, his name sat comfortably atop many bills passed by the Senate towards bringing Athena Online forward. He'd signed the bill which struck down server taxes, after the prayer protocol fell offline; a way to stem the bleeding of the coin sinks, with no new coins entering the world. He'd been against the server rights bill that Dex tried to ram through the Senate, giving an impassioned speech about unity where few others had the will to stand up to the RedCore party. If anyone would agree to give them servers, it'd be Idris...

Name : **Idris**

Home : **Athens**

Org : **Athena Online Senate**

The brown and wrinkled skin of his aging Default furrowed, as Idris finalized his words.

"I wish I could help you," he spoke. "But I'm afraid what you suggest isn't possible at this time."

Thankfully, Spark didn't explode with rage. Tracer honestly should've given her more credit than assuming she'd be some unstable firecracker; her response to that response came out as quite measured, all considered.

"At this time?" she asked. "That's not a no. But as a representative of the House of Programkind I have to strongly suggest that this *is* the right time, the only time. Our coder is going to need to integrate Athena Online's servers into the backup system well before the deadline, and—"

"I'm aware of the risks. I actually commissioned an independent report on the viability of contributing to your evacuation efforts. We're ahead of you on this one, Ms. Winder... I've been discussing a proposal with my colleagues ever since Horizon's announcement of support. We don't want to be behind the curve compared to our trade partners. But..."

"But... they're not desperate enough yet," she filled in, perhaps a bit too brusquely.

"You have to understand, we speak as representatives of the people," Idris explained. "Each of us represents any number of servers within Athena Online. Our votes have to reflect the will of those servers; support for the 'doomsday clock' theory, much less the 'spacer' theory that accompanies it, is very low. From my initial feelers, I can say that even colleagues who would vote in a heartbeat for such a bill of support couldn't in good conscience do so when the citizenry wouldn't agree with that vote."

Tracer knew why, but chose not to voice it. They all knew why, really.

Polarization and partisanship. Election rhetoric had driven Athena Online hard left and hard right, giving rise to groups like the RedCore party, which pressed the boundaries of "secular" government through fearmongering and Church collaboration. Even Idris, a progressive, had leaned hard on his voters to beg them not to vote for the RedCore opponent in his districts... casting the situation as some sort of perpetual nightmare, where the only sane vote was to shut out the conservative right completely. Compromise had become a thing of the past...

Senators were not, as Puzzle noted, mustache-twirling villains. But they'd encouraged villainy in their efforts at retaining power, no matter what side of the aisle they sat in. And now, pushing for something as unusual as support for the House of Programkind would be nearly impossible.

"Now, it's my hope that as the clock counts down and we get closer to the breaking point, I'll be able to convince enough of my colleagues to vote in favor of such a bill," Idris continued. "But until polling indicates we'd succeed, I can't recommend putting the bill forward. It's too risky. If it gets shut down the chances of trying again are miniscule."

Plan B, then. Not a very good plan, but the one they'd agreed to, before entering this office.

"What if we apply for servers the old-fashioned way?" Spark asked. "The Athena Online Senate has the power to request new servers, based on the will of the people. Well... Tracer and I were born in Athena Online, even if we don't live here anymore. What if we migrate back home, and propose the twenty-two servers through traditional channels?"

"I'm afraid you'd face the same problem; there won't be enough votes in favor of such a proposal. Plus, without the weight of an emergency bill, you'd have no priority in the paperwork queue. While our document management bureau is startlingly efficient, it'll still take months for an ordinary server request to go through the works."

"Okay, fine. Back to Plan A. We'll roll the dice and take our chances with the Senate on an emergency bill," Spark suggested. "If we don't even try, well, our chances of success are zero. But if you put forward a bill of support now, and let us speak on the floor... we can convince them. Just you watch. Sound good?"

And... back to silent calculation, the senator taking his time to find a precise answer.

Which meant no. Tracer knew with certainty that Idris simply sought a way to shoot them down politely.

"You won't even do that, huh," Spark realized as well.

"Please understand, Ms. Winder... I saw you out of a courtesy to Ms. Barr," he tried, using Puzzle's formal family name. "And I do agree this is what Athena Online needs. Under normal circumstances I'd be willing to take a chance on a vote, even if odds of success are low. But... it's not... you need to understand, the current atmosphere is very..."

"Cowardly," Tracer supplied.

Because Spark wasn't the only Winder capable of stupid outbursts, when frustrated. Tracer's tolerance limits may have been higher, but high didn't mean unreachable. He knew it was the wrong thing to say and said it anyway, because he had to. Despite the dirty looks shot his way by his companions. Despite the discomfort in their supposed ally.

Seeing no point in furthering the discussion, Tracer rose to his feet.

"We are amicable to re-opening discussions once you feel strong enough," he spoke. "But until such time as you're willing to brave the gaze of the Inquisition, I see no point in wasting your valuable time. Thank you for seeing us, Mr. Senator. We'll take our leave."

Ignoring the Messenger-based protests of his sister, ignoring the overly inquisitive glances by that receptionist, Tracer marched his way out of the building and back to the streets of Athens. Knowing full well it was a bridge-burning moment, and knowing full well it likely didn't matter. As always, no one would hand them what they wanted; they needed another approach.

Lovely weather for a disaster, all told. Athens ran a Default weather package on a Default skybox, for a very Default-themed nation; it could've rained as he walked those streets just as readily as the sun might have shone. Instead of stormclouds, he got to enjoy the shiny doomsday clock in the sky as a reminder of his own failures and inadequacies.

"That was entirely my fault and I take full responsibility," Tracer declared, as they began the long walk back to the transport platform.

"Well, that's #FuckingPeachy. Good for you!" Spark said, mock-clapping with a little pitter-pat of fingers in palm. "Doesn't change the fact that we probably pissed off the only guy who could actually help us..."

Puzzle tried to downplay the disaster. "Idris has thicker skin than you'd suspect. He works with senators, after all. I think he understands our frustration; I'm sure *I* could sweet talk him into a second meeting. And if not, I'll help you beat up your brother, so either way I'll call it a personal win."

But Tracer shook his head, continuing to march along, hands in his pockets.

"There's no point in a second meeting unless we have an actual plan. Right now, we do not. We'll go back to the clinic and brainstorm a bit, see if we can find a way for Idris to get us what we need, while saving face."

"That'll be fun, considering you called him cowardly to his face..."

"He is. It's perfectly understandable why he'd be terrified of the Inquisition. Horizon doesn't care about zealots and I'm sure the Chanarchy will stand fast against them, but any Athena Online allies in this fight must grapple with the fanatics living in their home turf. It's logical to be cowardly in face of murderous madmen."

Sidewalk after sidewalk, as they crossed intersections and made their way through the busy afternoon traffic. Occasionally, Tracer would glance at their reflection in a storefront window, only brief looks. Athens allowed heavy allocation of visual simulations, for perfect mirrors and excellent lighting effects; it wouldn't do for the jewel of the nation not to shine. Meaning he could indirectly watch the crowd, even while in motion...

"It's not like the Inqs could kill a senator in their office. Or in their home. Or at all, really," Spark suggested. "Even beyond the server-wide DMZ, the Senate's a freakin' bastion of iron security. Remember the server rights incident? We couldn't even get *close* to a senator to plant a bug thanks to all the personal firewalls they wear. So what's to fear?"

"Corruption and co-opting of moderator police forces, of course. Security systems are only as good as the people who manage them. All the Inquisition would need is someone in the Senate's security staff to help bypass those protections... and no doubt that's one of the the first things they did, on emerging from the shadows," Tracer suggested.

"And you're so sure of that because...?"

"Because it's what I'd do. Because it's what Father would do," he added. "And Father's data analysis skills are in Mother's pocket. Any move I'd make, it's a reasonable assumption he'd have made it as well. The apple does not fall far from the tree."

"...yeah, okay, I can see that. You're both utter bastards. Okay, so let's assume they're too spooked to act against the faith. What do we do? Hack the Senate, force the requisition? Try to track down Athena herself, make the system agent help us?"

"Likely, yes. Although we have no idea where she could possibly be, and her existence is presumably a state secret. Still, I'll multitask myself a few times and start investigating the workflow of the Senate, see if we can find Athena."

"And the reason why we're not heading right back to the clinic to do that is...? We're being followed, aren't we."

"We're being followed," Tracer confirmed. "Puzzle, don't do that. Don't look back. I spotted our tail in the windows a few minutes ago; they think we're unaware, let's not confirm our awareness..."

Barely resisting the urge to turn around, Puzzle instead walked a little quicker, to catch up to the Winders.

"Who's following us?" she asked. "Ugh. Darling, I love you dearly, but this isn't the first time your brother's crusades have dragged trouble across my path..."

"Be cool, be cool," Spark insisted. "We'll be fine, Puzzle. Just do what we say when we say it. Not the first time Tracer and I have tangled in a tight spot."

"Yes, well, I'd prefer to get out of that spot, pronto. Do we make a run for it? I'm not much at sprinting but the transport platform isn't far from here..."

Tracer shook his head curtly... using the opportunity to flick his glance to a passing window. "Not just yet," he insisted. "Figuring out who is following us is key. I want to know more, and by simply bailing out, we bail out on any opportunity at studying our opponent. Spark? Two men, business suits, Defaults rather than JohnDoe avatars. Middle-aged. Both wearing holy One/Zero lapel pins..."

"Inquisition," Spark concluded... her fingers opening and closing involuntarily into a fist, before she shook them loose. Some of the ache and jitter from last night's hangover still lingering, no doubt. "Not afraid to be recognized, because they feel they have nothing to hide. We're arguably defenseless out here, but... they can't do anything either, right?"

"If they were utterly powerless, Idris wouldn't be afraid of them," he reminded her. "Fortunately Mother seems ill-inclined to *directly* confront us, so we have a few moments of leeway before we'd better run. I'm trying to track their communications with my eyes, but it's difficult to do that indirectly. If we could isolate them and get a few moments to lock my eyes in..."

A few moments they wouldn't have.

So busy trying to track the ones behind him that he didn't see the ones just ahead, simply standing there, likely waiting for their prey to walk right up. Same One/Zero pins, same aging Defaults, same intense casualness of trying to blend in with the crowd while keeping an eye on their subjects...

Spark spotted them long before he did. And when they made a move, she made a move.

Even without her nail polish, Spark had years of martial arts training to fall back on. Without malware she couldn't cripple a foe, but disabling them proved a simpler matter... avatar-to-avatar combat was all about knockback and ragdoll, forcing an your opponent off balance and keeping them from taking any real action. For Programs unused to fighting, body coordination wasn't exactly an important skill to learn... meaning when Spark slid right on in and gutpunched the waiting Inquisitor, he doubled over and fell easily. His companion dropped to a leg sweep.

"Go!" Spark ordered. "To the west transport platform! I'll meet you there!"

Moving swiftly, Tracer grasped for Puzzle's wrist, and pulled... dragging her sideways, right into a nearby alleyway to get out of sight. Behind them he could hear the awkward sounds of avatars hitting the ground, as Spark tripped up Inquisitors and pedestrians alike, creating a huge scene to act as a glorious distraction for their escape...

Puzzle protested being dragged so roughly, but knew how to leave things like this to Spark. Numerous bar-room brawls after particularly disastrous #GirlsNightOuts dulled you to the shock of a sudden punch-up.

But she did pull at the hand on her wrist, trying to get Tracer's attention. "You're going east!" she warned him. "Spark said west—"

"Which means east," Tracer replied across Messenger, while pulling open the Athens street map he'd preloaded into his personal MemoryPalace. "Standard deception; we've done it before. Out the other side of this alley, two blocks east, one block north, then we blend in with the museum crowd and..."

Again, too wrapped up in his analysis to notice the situation around him. A problem he'd have to work on. Fortunately Puzzle was already on high alert, and pulled him back by the wrist on noticing the older men at the other end of the alley... backs turned to them, standing guard.

The fight behind them had drawn the notice of moderators, police sirens wailing in from the distance. If those distant guards heard the sound... if they turned around, and saw Puzzle and Tracer just standing there pinned between two lousy destinations...

Fortunately, salvation lay exactly three feet to their left, through a brick wall which was not a brick wall.

Another avatar leaned through the illusory wall, clipping right through the bumpmapped surface. Unlike the Inquisitors... he wore a JohnDoe. The same generic male avatar Tracer often employed while working some social engineering angle...

"In here!" JohnDoe whisper-hissed, through his perfect teeth. "Hurry! Unless you want them to catch you..."

Now, three options. Get arrested alongside his sister, caught up in her mess of a distraction, and dragged off to a likely corrupt police station. Get caught by Inquisitors, and possibly beheaded for their next big video release. Or follow the anonymous man through his secret door, into what could very well be a trap.

No choice, really.

Into the wall they went, vanishing from the alley just before anyone could notice their disappearance.

Absolute silence, on the other side of that fake wall.

Tracer tapped windows in his personal HUD, taking note of which ones went dead.

"A connection lock field?" he asked the JohnDoe, busy tapping a code into a simple password entry box hovering in front of them.

"Correct," JohnDoe spoke. "Won't find you here. We're completely off the map..."

...only seconds to get his bearings. But just enough to realize the opportunity in front of him, as he shoulder-surfed that password, watching JohnDoe's fingers rapidly play off the hexadecimal entry pad.

4f 6e 65 20 69 73 20 4f 6e 65. *One is One.*

With the password in play, the tiny entry space expanded outward, to become a full room. A safe house of some sort, with makeshift furniture, dim lighting, and storage containers for loose files. JohnDoe flicked on additional lights after getting past this security lockout, to better put his companions at ease... no sense making their mysterious hideout ominous as well as mysterious.

"So. Are we kidnapped, or are you here to help?" Puzzle asked. "Do you know this gentleman, Tracer? Yet another old enemy, or a shady ally...?"

With the last lighting panel active... a large white-and-crimson banner on the far wall illuminated itself.

A One/Zero; vertical line, piercing a U-shaped circle. Virtue defeating sin. But here, the icon had been flipped upside down. The holy symbol of the Church of One, inverted and co-opted by the Inquisition, now became a Zero/One. The sins of the world lurking overhead, devouring the light of the One...

"An Inquisition hideout, and a connection lock. Are we kidnapped, then?" Tracer asked. "I would strongly advise against it, but if you insist, at least you seem to be civil about the matter...

JohnDoe supplied the answer after settling in to lean against a nearby table covered in coffee cups and old doughnut boxes.

"Free to leave any time you like, but may want to wait a bit," he spoke, gruff despite the smooth tones of the generically handsome JohnDoe he wore. (*Perhaps an older man under that skin,* Tracer thought.) "Your sister kicked a hornet's nest. Good thinking, though. Public eyes on the scene, more likely the Inquisition will run rather than drawing attention to themselves. If lucky, she even avoided the cops. Good plan."

"Yes, she excels at both causing and evading trouble," Tracer agreed. "And... if you aren't with the Inquisition, here to capture and force us to confess to a bogus list of sins... how do you have access to one of their safe houses? Who are you, exactly?"

The man shrugged.

"Doesn't matter who I am. Got the answers you need," he replied, curtly. "And the safety you need, too. Inq won't expect to find you here, of all places. Still, keep this short, yeah? Winder/Tracer, Winder/Spark, working with the House of Programkind. Convinced Horizon to donate servers. Visited the Senate today, likely to repeat that request. Didn't go well?"

Rule number one after finding yourself in the hands of a possible enemy is typically escape... but Tracer preferred to move rule two up a bit in priority. *Learn all you can.* Escape is far simpler when you let your enemy talk themselves into a corner, giving up valuable information, burning away precious time while your allies work to find and free you...

So, he engaged the man in his conversation, rather than step back out through that security door and fake wall. See what corners he could chase JohnDoe into.

"Results weren't exactly encouraging, but we're not giving up," Tracer replied. "Not with survival of our entire species at stake. Interesting deduction there, by the way. A bit alarming that you're keeping track of our movements with such detail, given your possible allegiance to our enemies, but..."

Again, JohnDoe offered a shrug. Not many emotional responses to read; everything about him felt flat and passive, dismissing any concerns easily.

"Do you want to know how to force the Senate to give you those servers, or not?" he asked. "I know how to do it."

"Really. That's quite convenient. And what do you want in exchange for this information...?"

With an immaculately manicured hand, the JohnDoe pointed... to Puzzle.

"I'm not for sale," Puzzle stated directly, folding her arms under her chest. "And if I was, you couldn't afford me."

John shook his head. "No. You two need to part ways; that's my price. You think the Inquisition was after you, Tracer? No. They're after *him*. ...her. Been after her for some time. Getting involved in your situation, that only moved the timetable up a bit. Spooked 'em into acting too soon. You want the Senate, I can give it to you, but best you abandon Puzzle's cause before continuing. It'll only make your work harder."

Slightly baffled, Puzzle protested her innocence.

"Excuse me? Beg your pardon? Why would the Inquisition care about me and my little movie-making?" she asked. "I don't even *live* in your glorious Athena Online..."

"No, but you encourage people to reject their Default avatars. Marybel can't have that," JohnDoe said. "Can't run, can't hide, not really. Sooner or later she'll get you, and I don't want Tracer getting dragged down too. ...consider yourself warned. Won't take you myself; not here, not now. You can still walk. But I recommend you walk away, both of you, and away from each other. Fight your own fights. Do that, and I'll tell you how to force the vote. Understood?"

Tracer studied the expressionless man with the generic avatar, curiously.

Clearly, he was involved deeply with the Inquisition. And for reasons unknown, he was willing to betray them to warn Tracer away from his current path, even willing to don a JohnDoe to do it despite Church doctrine on avatar modifications. But... the reasons why, those he'd have to ponder at another time. Only one thing mattered now, and that was the stand he must take.

"We will not be abandoning Puzzle," he warned.

"Think, boy. You have bigger concerns than the fate of one Program," JohnDoe insisted. "This is about survival on a grand scale..."

"I know. And once, I would've agreed; putting one Program's needs above others is absurd. But... the fact that I *would* agree suggests to me that it's unacceptable. I've been morally in the wrong every time I embrace a ruthlessly pragmatic path; I'm prepared to be wrong now, and I'm prepared to defend her if need be. That is non-negotiable. So, old man, it seems to me that you can either tell me what I need to know and let me save our people, or you can let your secret society's little grudge against *one Program* ruin everything. Which is it? Decide."

A fine logical turn-a-bout, Tracer reasoned. If he was smart enough to see the big picture despite the madness of his peers, he'd be smart enough to cough up the answers anyway...

Realizing the corner he'd backed himself into, JohnDoe allowed himself a curmudgeonly glowering frown.

"Hmmh. As you like," he spoke. "On your head be it. ...what you require is an Athena Referendum. Two years ago, when the prayer protocol went offline, the Senate voted an emergency bill into law which abolished server taxes. Do you recall?"

Quickly, Tracer pulled up what he could from his MemoryPalace about the server tax bill. He knew the true reason behind it... a meeting of the minds between system agents, to stem the bleeding of the economy. The only reason those taxes existed in the first place was to encourage prayer, with the agents being former acolytes of Nyx...

But one thing stuck out at him, from the articles that flashed across his mental gaze.

"The bill passed a week after Horizon stopped collecting tithes and the Chanarchy stopped taking automatic upkeep payments," Tracer noted. "Athena Online was slow to the draw."

"That's not the important part, boy. The important part is that right before the bill passed, the Senate went dark," JohnDoe explained. "Understand this is rumor, leaked by senatorial aides, confirmed by no official source. But... from that dark session emerged a bill with a one-hundred-and-one percent vote. Only five times in the history of Athena Online have bills come into law with absolutely no votes against, no abstentions... and one extra signature on the bottom line. Supposedly, the signature of Athena herself. *That* is an Athena Referendum."

"Interesting. Mandatory laws, passed down by the system agent Athena herself...?" Tracer supposed.

How much did this man know? Did he know about the system agents? Athena's existence remained a secret to the general public; the server of Athens, even the nation of Athena Online named such for no particular reason. Everybody assumed it was a name chosen because it sounded nice, like the Chanarchy...

No. JohnDoe didn't know about the agents; the idea that Athena could be a person didn't even register on him.

"Doesn't matter where it comes from. Point is, that's your ticket," their would-be ally said. "You're a smart boy. Figure it out from there. Once you determine the origin of Athena Referendums, you can forge one of your own making, and force the Senate to bend to your will. Get your servers. Save the world."

"I see. I see. I may have some ideas along those lines, in fact. Very well; we'll do what we were already planning to do."

"And... if you're smart, leave Puzzle to her fate. If the Inquisition decides you're in their way, I can't stop them. And your mother might stop making an exception for her children, should you annoy them enough. But, as you like. Alley should be clear now. Suggest you go."

Eager not to test his patience further, Tracer nodded towards the door. His slightly spooked partner nodded in agreement.

And that was that... mysterious man, mysterious information, and walking swiftly away from what could've been a deathtrap. A strange day, to be certain.

Slightly stranger by the sight in the alley, after emerging from behind that connection lock field.

Five more Tracers looked their way, having unsuccessfully scoured the alley for their missing 'brother.'

"Good work," Tracer complimented himselves. "Only a few minutes after the dead man's switch activated and you'd tracked us almost all the way to our destination. You have my thanks, but I suppose you knew that already. ...Puzzle? Is something amiss?"

Befuddled, she pointed from Tracer to Tracer to Tracer to Tracer to Tracer to Tracer.

"There's, ah, quite a few of you at the moment," she felt the need to say.

"Yes, I multitask," Tracer Prime answered. "They were back at the clinic, working on various projects. We stay in constant communication; when I entered a connection-lock field, it triggered a panic response across my selves. Considering the many times we've been kidnapped or attacked, it felt prudent to have some of me on-call in case of emergency. ...is the multiplicity alarming you? One moment, I can fix that."

With a blur, six avatars meshed into one, streaking through the air and sliding into the space occupied by Tracer Prime. Their daily memories of working at the clinic uploaded one at a time to his MemoryPalace, merging files together, until all six timelines meshed together. Which admittedly took a bit out of him, a burst of processing that gave him a mild headache... but nothing a good night's rest wouldn't fix.

"...okay, see, now I'm pondering how surreal and terrifying a one-man orgy would be, and I think I need a nice lie down," Puzzle suggested. "Would you mind terribly if I crash at your place again? Like the last time my life was in danger. The Inquisition can't find me at Floating Point, correct?"

"Correct."

"Right. So. Let's do that. ...and Tracer? Thank you."

"For merging myselves?"

"For defending me against that whacko," Puzzle corrected. "I know we haven't always seen eye to eye. I know I give you more than your fair amount of shit, really. But... color me impressed. You could've stepped aside and let them have me, to make your savior-complex an easier ride. But you didn't. I'd say you've come a long ways since your single-minded vendetta days, and for that... thank you."

"Ah... you're welcome? Yes, you're welcome," he spoke, unused to people being grateful for anything he did. "Yes. Well. We... should head back, as you suggest. No doubt Spark already beat us back to that particular finish line. Tonight I'll see about getting some rest, and in the morning..."

A tiny chime tugged at his ear.

Through a series of filters came a Messenger window, flagged with official moderator warnings regarding monitoring for criminal activity. Within that sealed packet arrived a simple message.

"*Hey, uh, so... do we know any lawyers?*" Spark's voice echoed, tinny from the compression. "*I'm in the hoosegow. This is my one message I'm allowed to the outside world. Would ya kindly swing by Precinct #34F in Athens and get me the fuck out of here?*"

A false sunset, taking the form of a brilliantly illuminated clock. Typical Athena Online default skies, boring, functional, uninteresting. At least artists in the Chanarchy took pride in their skyboxes, feeling no compunctions of leaving "the One's glorious skies" untouched...

Spark had grown to hate that dull sun, and all it represented. Not just the looming spectre of doom in the form of ever-decreasing numbers, but the way it embodied everything about the nation she'd run away screaming from. The way this cell she'd found herself trapped in embodied it all, as well.

Not her first time in a jail cell. Probably not her last.

Back in her teenage years, in the madness and grief that followed Verity's death, she'd lashed out at the Church of One alongside other aficionados of avatar modifications. "Modders," they'd been called, by the Default-obsessed faithful bastards they made fun of with graffiti and other assorted acts of trolling. Five times Spark had seen the inside of one of these cells, before they found Floating Point and the solace within. Since then her hate for the Church dampened down... and her running buddies had all fled Athena Online anyway, so no point in continuing to be a young punk. But you never forgot one of these cells.

It was just too *nice* to forget.

Athena Online wasn't really into harsh and brutal punishments; love the sinner, hate the sin, after all. Their jails had no bars, no walls, no visible barriers of any kind... simply a dashed line on the floor that could not be crossed. A bare and empty but otherwise pleasant little space, with comfortable benches, and wide open windows to look longingly at the outside world you'd been sequestered away from. Including that golden clock in the sky.

Despite the open air of the holding cells, nothing else about her current state could be described as "open." Connection locks. Inventory locks, so she couldn't even dig out a good text file to read while waiting for a lawyer to show up. The penalty for her transgression was, at least at the moment, simply boredom. Boredom and poor company.

The Inquisition sat in the cell opposite her own. Similarly bound behind invisible walls, similarly sitting around bored. But unlike Spark, they were talking.

The two middle-aged gentlemen Spark had gloriously stomped into the pavement an hour ago seemed to bear no ill will to their attacker. Nor any concern about being dragged off by moderators, a blanket arrest for all involved in the incident of "disorderly conduct" in the middle of an Athens sidewalk.

One man polished the Zero/One pendant dangling from his neck, before continuing.

"We meant no harm to you, Miss Winder," he re-iterated. "And in fact, you attacked *us*. We were simply defending ourselves..."

The counter-accusation provoked no response from the sullen Spark. So, he continued.

"You have to understand the predicament you put your poor mother in when you protect sinners like Puzzle," he continued. "A sinner to the core, a man who threw away his masculinity, and encourages others to do the same. He turned his back on the gifts of the One, just like the anonymous anarchists who convinced the world that the One was a fraud. We've been watching his activities with interest but holding back until now, in hopes his little movie wouldn't amount to much. But... then he involved *you*. The time has come to put a stop to this sad situation. Spark, all we're trying to do is bring the light of reason back to this world; when you get in the way of that... it pains Mrs. Winder so very, very much. We don't *want* to hurt you, Spark..."

Nothing. Not deigning to let their empty platitudes get to her.

Young Spark would've taken the bait, and to be fair, older Spark really wanted to take it as well. But... she'd forced herself to realize one thing. They were right about who made the first move. She *thought* they were about to attack, she thought she saw one of them go for some malware, but against all logic regarding the impossibility of malware attacks in the middle of Athens she launched herself right at them to defend against... basically nothing. The fight was her fault.

Not that this excused them from being murderous fanatics in general. Just, well, Spark made the wrong play, and it's always right to own up to that. Even if you're not going to admit it out loud to the assholes who want your best friend dead because she didn't care about owning a penis.

When the moderator in charge of these cells showed up to let them out, Spark finally spoke up. Using her inside voice, of course.

"You're letting them walk?" she asked the cop, getting to her feet to approach the hidden cell walls. "You know these two are Inquisitors, right? They're even *wearing* the Inq's icon..."

Immediately, the police officer put his hand on the hilt of the backspacer at his hip. As if Spark, locked down nine ways to Sunday, could possibly be a threat.

"Back away from the barrier immediately, ma'am," he insisted, with a tone firm as concrete.

"I want my lawyer," Spark pressed. "I've got a right to an attorney, and my brother should've brought one along by now. Where's my—"

"Back away or I will use force. You have been warned, ma'am."

It took a moment for her to realize that the officer wasn't fixated on her glaring stare. No, his eyes were locked just above her own... to her bangs. Her fiery hair, a giant and obvious symbol of a non-Default avatar. Not illegal to own in Athena Online, no sir, and there's also no such thing as institutional discrimination against 'modders' either, that's just oversensitive liberal conspiracy theory...

With a slight grumble, Spark opted to retreat to her bench. No need to press some racist bastard into blowing her away; it'd be a lovely media spectacle which might highlight the actual problem for all to see, but hey, she'd also die. As a rule, Spark enjoyed being alive.

As the tension evaporated, the guard nodded in her direction, and then turned to the two Inquisitors.

"Apologies for the misunderstanding, sirs," he spoke to them, with far less menace. "The district attorney has elected not to press charges at this time. You're free to go."

The lead Inquisitor smiled, bowing his head in respect. "Your service to our great nation is exemplary, Officer. Thanks for your time; this was no trouble at all..."

But to the young woman behind nonexistent bars... he had no such pleasantries.

"I suggest you plead guilty, and stay in here," he spoke. "It'd be better for you in the long term. I'm so sorry things got this far, but you'll understand one day. Everyone sees the light of the One eventually."

Finally, she took the bait.

"And fuck you very much, too," she spoke, giving herself the finger.

Wait.

No. She'd flipped *them* the bird, nice and upright, fingers curled tightly inward for emphasis. Tightly... outward. Curled away. Staring at her own fingernail...

Her eyes strayed downward... to her warped and twisted wrist, rotated one-eighty in a painful distortion of avatar joints. The instant she'd raised it up she'd felt something snap, but only now was the agony of it dawning on her... a belated reaction as her body disobeyed an order, breaking and bending itself involuntarily...

The cop sneered at the sight.

"Modders," he spat, before leading his new friends out of the cell block.

The modder's disease, infecting so many in the Chanarchy who dared to defy their Defaults.

Twist. Spark had contracted Twist...

With a groan of agony, she grasped her right hand in her left, trying to pull it back around into place. And failing.

Another hour in the clink, and freedom finally found her.

The officer only stayed long enough to deactivate the barrier, before retreating to his secured guard booth. Very businesslike, compared to the warm welcome the Inquisitors enjoyed. Instead, Spark's warm welcome came from an unexpected source...

"Your fine for disorderly conduct has been paid in full," Miss Cancel explained.

With the inventory lock removed, Spark quickly restored her avatar to its unwarped state. Not that it'd last; Twist had a way of creeping back in every time you tried to purge its distortions. But now wasn't the time to hobble along with two left hands; the headache from her avatar's bent sensory feedback was plenty unpleasant on its own.

"Guessing I'm still pretty boned here," Spark replied, wincing a little at the unintended pun. "They won't let me back into the Senate after being tagged for a minor felony..."

"Actually, the judge agreed to seal your arrest record. Mr. Kincaid was... very convincing," her benefactor summarized.

"I'm guessing I shouldn't ask about the specifics...?"

"Correct."

"Wonderful. Just chalk it up as another in our list of dodges and cons and flim-flammery," Spark suggested. "We're trying to be the good guys here, but the world sure ain't making it easy..."

Turning to lead her off to freedom... Miss Cancel paused, the sharp click of her high-heeled shoes stopping as well.

"May I offer advice?" she asked. "If you're uncomfortable with this, good. You should be. But it must be done, regardless. In my experience, the world is seldom kind to those trying to do right by others. If you're to be the spark that ignites the new world that my employer believes you to be, you need to understand that balance. Or would you rather rot in a cell while the world dies, out of principle?"

Spark actually took a step backwards, in surprise.

"That's... the most I've ever heard you speak," she pointed out, honestly. "Those were complete sentences, even."

"I am more than an extension of my employer's will, Miss Winder. But speaking also as an extension of that will... I would say Mr. Kincaid has invested much of his hopes and dreams in you. Whether you like it or not, whether I agree with it or not, you're his chosen legacy. Please don't let him down again."

The young woman allowed herself a dark chuckle, at that.

"I never fuck up the same way twice," Spark declared. "I find entirely new ways to fuck up. It's more fun that way. ...for instance..."

With a facial tick of pain... she raised her left hand. And showed the fingers that had just curled themselves backwards, joints bending in ways they were never meant to.

"We need to get to the clinic, pronto. I've got a new problem to deal with."

They called it an "Avatar Refresher" app, but in truth the experience was anything but refreshing.

It'd automatically detect any unusual distortions to her avatar, and immediately restore her favored configuration in place, correcting the error. Each time it did, sharp pain would stab across her mind, the micro-modification triggering an unpleasant sensory response. To correct it, they offered her sensory blockers that'd dull the pain... but Spark didn't want 'em. This was her life, and she'd never been one to block out the sensations of life. Especially not after the unpleasant void she had to hide within last time she got blasted by malware...

"What I'm curious about is how you contracted it," Tracer asked, while Beta made fine-tuning adjustments to the clinic's refresher app. "Did the Inquisition plant it on you, during the fight in Athens...? Many suspect the disease to be an Inquisition conspiracy..."

"Kinda doubt malware like that could be active in Athens, even if the cops are filthy. I'm thinking I got infected at Puzzle's party," Spark said. "Cheap booze and plenty of craziness at that shindig, plus guests I didn't recognize. Could've gotten it from the party favors, or from someone else at the bar, or—*nngh*. Beta, can you tighten the response window on the avatar correction a little more, please...?"

Pink eyes looked up from behind glasses, as she tinkered with an external diagnostic tool

"It's already as tight as I can make it, sorry," she spoke. "I'm afraid it's... it's only going to get worse, Spark. This isn't like my data rot, where it can be steadily counteracted by auto-correction. Twist *accelerates* over time. In a week or three, you might be unable to move on your own..."

"I'm fuzzy on how Twist works," Spark admitted. "What're we talking about, here? How does it spread? ...uh. Shit. Are either of you at risk just by being around me?"

"It's an avatar physics hack, meaning we'd need to be in physical contact with you," Beta explained, from her research notes. "The more prolonged the contact, the more modified one's avatar or codebase... the greater the risk of infection. That's why pure Defaults seemingly can't be infected. But hurting us shouldn't be hard to avoid, now that we know you're infected! I mean, we'll just curtail hugs, and... um, *things* until after you're cured..."

Eager to control the doom, Tracer tried to play the part of the optimist. Tried, at least.

"Hugs will be back on the table before long, no doubt. Curing Twist is one of our clinic's many projects," he said. "We're not alone in our efforts any longer, Spark. We've got the backing of Conundrum, Kincaid, and many other allies on this particular journey. I'm certain you'll be fine, in the end..."

But Spark wasn't buying it. "Uh-huh. 'One of our many projects' does not fill me with confidence. Tracer, man, level with me. Can Conundrum's funboys cure this before I suffer an unrecoverable crash...? Realistically."

"...nothing is outside the realm of possibility. And we have made some solid research progress," he tried again. "But... I'll admit that Iteration's original mission statement concerned innovative and exciting upgrades, not malware research and infosec. We lack the skills and manpower to fully attack this particular problem in the way a company like Northon or Yoho can..."

"Right. Well. I've got plenty of time before I'm a total pretzel, so let's focus on Athena Online," Spark suggested, waving the diagnostic panel away. "Thanks, Beta. So what's our plan for this Athena Referendum thing you told me about?"

Perhaps thankful to discuss strategy rather than the impending doom of his sister, Tracer switched topics with ease.

"Clearly the system agent Athena is still in touch with the Senate, if she's able to force their hand," he said, opening up his MemoryPalace with notes regarding the five Athena Referendums of the past. "Throughout history, notable laws which changed the course of politics for generations map neatly to this conspiracy theory regarding the referendums. If we could enact one of our own, we could force a vote on server donations. That would easily break through the hesitation that prevents the Senate from going against both holy doctrine and the will of heavily partisan voters. If the Senate feels it has no choice, that takes away responsibility and consequence."

"Right. Right. And if your JohnDoe is to be trusted... and I'm guessing he's not, but hey, let's assume he is... it's Athena's signature that triggers the process."

"Athena, also known as the apostle Philotes. Who, as far as the public is concerned, died after a long and fulfilling life as one of the nation's first senators. Except like Nyx and Kincaid's father, I sincerely doubt her passing."

A mischievous twinkle flared in Spark's eye. Literally, as she'd installed a mischievous twinkle generator for occasions such as these.

"And Senator Philotes signed the agreement that founded AO in the first place. If we had a copy of her signature, we could forge our own referendum, meaning... we're going to steal the Declaration of Democracy!"

"*Ahem.* I feel I should point out we have no way of knowing exactly *how* Athena initiates her referendums," Tracer reminded her. "I'd rather not risk them realizing our order is a fake, nor do I want to risk the real Athena countermanding it and throwing doubt into the equation. No, we will *not* be sneaking in to the Senate after hours and engaging in an amusing, high-stakes heist to steal the most fantastically secured document in the nation."

"Aww. Take all the fun out of things, why don't you."

"I believe we need to locate Athena herself," Tracer said... while pulling open a series of documents from his MemoryPalace. "There is a single point of contact within the bureaucracy, a document process which Athena must be involved in. Somewhere along that chain of transactions, Athena steps into play. But... to gain access to it, and thus gain access to her, we'll need to visit Senator Idris again. And involve him in a questionably legal maneuver."

"Tough to do when you called him a pussy right to his face, huh."

"Not one of my prouder moments, no."

"Okay, then. I'll take the lead on this," Spark decided. "Yes, I'm aware I shouldn't be moving around much, but you can't go marching into Idris's office alone after that spectacle, Puzzle needs to lay low at Floating Point, and Beta's too busy with server integration to make a passionate speech on our behalf..."

Beta fidgeted with her glasses. "I'm not *that* busy," she insisted. "Another day of delay won't change much. I'd rather you stay put until we can find a solution to your malware, Spark. Any movement adds risk of acceleration..."

"Don't see us having a choice, hun. I'm the House of Programkind's official rep on this, I've got Kincaid's blessing, I've got to be the one to confront him on this. Tracer, you can tag along if you insist, but let me do the talking."

But Beta continued to press. "I want to come along. Please, I've been on the sidelines at Tartarus long enough. I know there's still so much to do to link in Horizon's servers, but..."

Flipping through his documents... Tracer fixated on a particular metadata field of some random bureaucratic paper wad.

"Actually... I think there's one way in which you can be tremendously helpful, Beta," he spoke. "Because you happen to be on fine terms with an expert infiltrator, one with experience cracking document control systems from the inside. With the two of you working together while Spark and I work on Idris... I believe we'll have our best chance. Assuming your companion is amenable, of course."

If they'd gotten filthy looks from Idris's secretary before, the looks they received now wouldn't pass even the loosest infosec health inspections. Spark wouldn't be surprised if those offhand glances were laced with some kind of hideous malware, even.

Despite her fistfight on the streets of Athens being swept under the rug by a powerful old dude, no doubt word got around about some girl with a modded avatar kicking the crap out of some guys for "no reason whatsoever" just a few blocks from the senate building. Either that, or the sharp-eyed lady in Idris's lobby was an Inquisition plant. Both seemed equally likely, given the situation they found themselves in. But... no helping it. They had to press on, regardless.

Miraculously, the senator agreed to meet with them after an impassioned appeal from Puzzle over Messenger. The idealistic young woman with the social justice film project had enough of a rapport with this politician to merit a do-over of their disastrous first meeting, even if Puzzle herself couldn't attend. Maybe he was willing to hear them out *because* she couldn't attend, because their work together had put her life in danger... guilt being a powerful motivator. But like the secretary, the reason behind the act was almost irrelevant. The situation on the ground would be how Spark dealt with things.

While Tracer oversaw operations, Spark took point. Meaning she sat directly across from Idris after the requisite handshakes and closing of doors formally started their conversation, as he simply lurked nearby.

"I'd like to thank you for making the time for us," Spark began. "I'm aware we didn't part on the finest of terms..."

Idris waved it off, with a light gesture. "While indelicate, he raises good points," the senator spoke, turning his dark eyes to Tracer's. "We live in interesting times, let's say. And sometimes, while trying to navigate those times, we lose track of what matters most. Is Puzzle well? Her message seemed a bit terse. If she needs protection from these terrorists..."

"She's quite protected. You've got my promise that she'll be safe, no matter what. She's my #BFFL."

"Good, good. Now, I understand you wanted to meet about something other than this proposed emergency bill...? I still feel it wouldn't go well for you, if we put the bill forward..."

"Actually, I had some questions about the server allocation process," Spark explained, folding her hands in her lap, keeping her fingers nice and straight. Calm and relaxed, and not twisting on themselves. "I'll admit I was a poor student back in my K-12 days, particularly when it came to civics. I know the basics... a proposal is put forward to the floor of the Senate to open a new server. Population expansion, business zoning, or just some public need not currently filled by existing servers. The Senate votes, the bill allocating a new server becomes law, and... then what?"

With no small amount of curiosity at this new line of questioning, Idris filled in the gaps.

"And... that's it. The bill is processed and filed," he explained. "Depending on how many unallocated servers are on reserve, we can start establishing the new region right away, or it may be a few weeks. The gears turn a bit slowly, some years... but in the end, we provide for our citizens."

"Right, right. But *how* is the new server created?"

"As I said, there's a vote and an approval process. The server is established upon approval."

"Okay. And who approves the form?" Spark asked. "Not the vote, that's obviously the senators. Who, in the end, receives that form and acts on it...?"

"It simply... is approved. It's all very technical and boring, I'm sure. I don't see how this relates to your request for the House of Programkind..."

"You don't know, do you," she stated. "Even a sitting senator doesn't know who actually *creates* the servers."

...and there it was again, another moment of measured words. Tracer could see it on his face, that need to say something very precise and very vague, to avoid a perfect answer.

This was pointless, of course. The Senate wouldn't help even if they wanted to. Already, Tracer's mind was compiling a series of plans from B through J, as Plan A was clearly failing...

"Mr. Senator, let me tell you a story," Spark said, before he could give his non-answer. "A man sees the path of the future as clear as sunlight. The numbers in the sky say what's coming; everybody knows it's true, they can feel it in their hearts even if the calm and rational voices within insist that's utter madness. So he goes through the motions, day in and day out, knowing he should be doing something more. In fact... when a woman who came to him for help is in danger, he's even willing to go the extra mile for her questionable friends, despite knowing there's probably nothing he can do. That's the mark of a man who wants to act, not a man who hides. Are you with me so far?"

Playing along. That's all he was doing, humoring this crazy woman. Tracer knew, *knew* that Athena Online would fail them as it had failed them in the past. Why would Spark insist on pushing this, when clearly it was a waste of time...?

But Idris nodded, softly. As if encouraging the story, without commenting one way or another.

"I think a man like that would be willing to take risks. Not any risk, of course, but the *right* risk," Spark continued. "He's no coward; he's an idealist at heart, one who works within the system to change it. Caution guides him, but he's willing to take that leap when the time is right. And then, something strange happens... a woman walks into his office, asking about servers. About the mysterious process that creates them, a process which might very well help her save this world if only he could shed light on it for her. Light like sunlight from the sky. But now he's thinking, that's all very well and good, but *how*? How can he help without appearing to help...? And then her brother says..."

Nothing.

A sharp glance from his sister roused Tracer from momentary stupor.

"There's a server requisition bill going out to the floor shortly," he filled in, realizing what Spark wanted from him. "A zoo server, to house various species of animals, including obsolete endangered apps at risk of becoming abandonware. Somewhere nice to take the family on a lazy Sunday. ...am I telling your 'story' correctly? I have little flair for the dramatic—"

"Skip to the end," Spark mumbled.

"—and we'd like you to consider a change to the logo for this new zoo," Tracer spoke, withdrawing the tightly compressed file from his pocket. "To replace the existing icon on the document. Before you send it down to the floor, and into the document processing chain."

Idris could've turned them away, right there and then. Before any potentially incriminating words were spoken, before any highly questionable files were exchanged. The easiest thing in the world would be to ignore their cryptic words, couched in language to keep him free from culpability, and send them packing.

Instead... he extended his hand, and took the file, shunting it to his inventory.

The tiny blip in transfer time, tiny but decidedly measurable, suggested this "logo" they handed over held far more data than a mere graphic design.

"You want me to attach this file to the bill before it's signed, sealed, and delivered," he understood.

"Hey, I'm just telling a story here," Spark said. "That's all. We're not asking you to *do* anything in particular."

"That's a mighty fine tap dance you're doing, young lady. I'm not certain how well it'd play in a court of law..."

"At least there'd be a court of law for me to tried in instead of a lifeless and empty server, Mr. Senator."

Turning the icon over and over in his hand, Idris considered the path before him.

"You know, I was just telling Senator Agni I felt the logo for our new national zoo was a bit unfriendly and cold," he recounted. "Perhaps your design would be more appealing to the youth we're trying to attract. It's so hard getting young people interested in silly things like animal apps. Thank you very much for your contribution."

Rising to his feet, Tracer extended a hand to shake on Spark's behalf... given hers carried with it unpleasant malware.

"And when do you think the server will be... approved?" he asked, inserting the pause where appropriate. "As there is something of a clock hanging above us."

"Ohh, I think I can grease a few wheels," Idris suggested... grasping Tracer's hand for a firm shake. "Get it on the floor today, and filed away in the document management system by close of business. With all the concern lately about the economy and terrorists from the Chanarchy, I think this zoo is just what we need to show our great nation that there's still something beautiful in this life. And that this life is worth fighting for, even in this small way. Red or blue, we all believe in Athena Online, and what it could be for our citizens. Thank you for your time, Ms. Winder. Mr. Winder."

With the transaction complete, the Winders hurried on out of there before anything could possibly go wrong. Such as Spark massaging her hand, already sore and aching from her efforts at holding it in perfect shape.

Only when safely out of the building, coated with its security systems and monitoring devices, did Tracer dare to speak.

"Once, I considered myself something of a master manipulator," he stated. "But with that performance, I'd say you've surpassed me on the social engineering front. Fine work."

"Yeah, well. The trick is that it's *not* a con," Spark replied, shaking her hand loose after the quick massage. "You truthfully pour your heart into a thing, it'll come through in your words. Those words resonate in the hearts of others; no lies needed. Little trick I learned from Beta. Speaking of which, is she in position to retrieve the 'logo' once we get confirmation?"

"Waiting at a coffee shop behind the senate. But I suggest we vacate the server for now, rather than join her; no need to poke whatever cell of the Inquisition has set up shop in Athens again by flashing our faces about. And tonight... we'll meet the woman behind the curtain."

Stamp, index, file, close. Stamp, index, file, close.

Paper documents had been the standard since the dawning of Athena Online, and even in this age of abstracted icons and glyphs to represent complex files, they continued to be printed on paper. Of course, within those razor-thin sheets of physical paper lurked increasingly detailed security systems, signature authorization metadata, and all manner of tracked changes from prior revisions... enough of a glorious mess that mere filing cabinets could no longer store the bureaucracy's combined output. So, document management systems were developed, ones with a foot in the past of paper and a foot in the future of metadata-driven indexing.

Similarly, paperwork couldn't be entirely processed by intelligent agent apps, searching and stamping and indexing and filing. Employees drew salary while slaving away in the legendarily boring and detail-oriented document management department of the Senate; it took a certain class of obsessive perfectionist to work there. So, when the bell rang, going out for heavy drinking to decompress after a full day of precision office work was a must.

One by one, the employees fetched coats and hats; no avatar clothing with pockets allowed in the main offices, nothing you could squirrel one of these physical objects out in. All such items had to be checked at the door, and retrieved on your way out. Eager for that way out, they trickled through the scanners and out the exits...

Except for one.

"You coming or not?" a coworker asked.

Stamp, index, file, close...

"I'll catch up," she promised. "Want to wrap up a few things first."

"Y'know, it makes the rest of us look bad when you keep putting in voluntary overtime like this. We don't want 5:30pm to be the new normal," he mock-accused. "Fine, fine. But you're buying a round tonight, got it?"

"Sure thing. I'll catch up! Don't start the karaoke without me!"

Coat and hat retrieved, the next-to-last employee shuffled on out the door.

Only when she was certain of being the final worker on duty did she retrieve the file.

All server requests had a certain chain to flow through, one with no real destination beyond a musty corner of the storage system. The chain had been made needlessly complicated, to obfuscate the steps, keep people from bothering to ask too many questions about them. All that mattered was the final seal, the one that confirmed delivery of a fresh server; exactly where in the process that seal occurred remained undocumented, and had remained so for centuries. The reason behind that willing ignorance had been lost behind another veil of willing ignorance, out of fear that the whole thing might fall apart if one looked too closely...

With the zoo server on her desk, she withdrew the rubber stamp from personal inventory. Encrypted into every curve, line, and angle of that glyph of a rising star were a series of ones and zeroes that represented the personal signature of Senator Philotes... also known as Athena.

After flipping through the packet to make sure all was in order, she closed the folder and prepared to mark it with the approval of a system agent.

And... paused, her eye catching an adorable cartoon design embossed on the cover:

Curiously... that little scribble of a tail was waving back and forth at her. The whiskers started to twitch, as well...

A bright flash distracted her, as the icon lit up brilliantly enough to neatly illuminate her features in the darkened office.

"🔲!" the cat declared, snapping a photo of the shocked document manager...

...before leaping off the page, becoming a more fully-featured pet app in the process.

With a series of 🐱's floating over his head, the cat dashed right out the door, down the hall, out an emergency exit and over to a cafe down the road where Beta awaited his return.

After several stunned moments... the worker fumbled around for the rubber stamp she'd dropped, grasping it tightly in both hands before stuffing it back into her inventory. And then ran for it, forgetting to claim her coat and hat on the way out. Just ran and ran, right to the nearest transport dock.

She got all the way to the front door of her nice little house with its nice little yard in GreenDale before realizing it was too late.

They were waiting for her, sitting right there on the front porch. Thankfully not lying in wait with weapons or anything like that, but the fact that they'd found her at all was cause for concern enough. At least they had the decency not to break into her house for some super-dramatic scene of lying in wait for her return.

The man pulled up a mix of her social media profiles and Senate employee data, by means of greeting.

"Jonnes/Virginia," he greeted. "Seven years with the document tracking department of the Senate. Started fresh out of college as an unpaid intern, gradually moved up to senior document tracker thanks to years of hard work and service to her great nation. Daughter of Graci/Virginia and Jonnes/Return. Owner of three cats. Acts as treasurer of her local rotary club. And, in her spare time... acts as the system agent Athena."

Well. At least they had that wrong, she thought. At least they didn't have total advantage over her.

"Could ya not say that out loud? I've got some seriously nosy neighbors," Virginia requested. "Look, I know who you are and why you came, but I can't help you. So if you don't mind..."

"If you know that, you know what we're seeking is critically important. You of all people would know exactly how important," he continued, after closing his hand and pulling back the files to his MemoryPalace. "And you know we can't walk away without talking about this. Would you mind if we come inside to discuss? To avoid said nosy neighbors."

The weight of that stamp in her inventory felt heavy indeed, despite having zero physical weight whatsoever while in virtual storage.

If they intended violence, well, Virginia paid through the nose for a good backup service. But it couldn't copy that stamp. Risky move, letting them have even a single inch into her life, no matter how creepily friendly these two seemed. But if she kept pushing them off, maybe the risk would grow...

"Fine," she agreed. "Wipe your feet before you come in. I just reseeded the lawn yesterday, and I don't want any grass growing in my living room."

The Winders were quick studies when it came to surroundings. Best way to deal with strange negotiation situations like these was to size up the other party as fast as possible; having access to their home made that considerably easier.

Tracer took note of all the family photos over the fireplace. Mothers, aunts, grandmothers. Very few of the male side of the family, strangely, but otherwise incredibly close-knit across many generations. Not exactly something he was familiar with, personally... Winder/Marybel always hosted family dinners and the like, but only out of a perfunctory need to embrace the One's tenets of home and hearth. Lovingly arranged photos were off the table, in a literal sense.

Spark took note of the cats, and how they mewled away in joy immediately on seeing newcomers in the house. Standard pet app behavior, really. Virginia moved to feed them before settling in for any sort of secret negotiations. Unlike Mew, the infiltration kitty who'd snapped a photo of this woman less than an hour ago, these were far simpler apps... following standard programming for cuddly affection and a greedy need for treats. More importantly... they filled the otherwise empty space of the single-family suburban home. Virginia lived alone.

A woman about their age, she could tell, even without the files. Rather than lurking in the ambiguous middle-twenties of eternal adult youth as many with customized avatars did, she wore Defaults proudly... body perfectly imperfect, with all the little details that a commercial avatar would've smoothed out in favor of striking beauty. Her plain-jane light blue skin in no way meshed with that red hair, another Default trait that others might've recolored out of their systems.

Only after the cats were properly tended to did she join her guests in the parlor, carrying a pitcher of lemonade. A gracious host, despite the circumstances.

"So the House of Programkind wants servers from Athena Online," Virginia accurately guessed, while pouring out three glasses. "And you thought you could bypass the legal channels by coming right to me. Because... you think I'm Athena?"

"You're the true final step in the chain," Tracer deduced. "Taking the server bills and giving them your approval, when nobody's looking. You seem a bit young for a centuries-old agent of the system, but we've known youthfully ancient Programs before you..."

Name : Virginia

Home : GreenDale, Ath.On.

Org : Senate Document Office

"Yes, well, you're wrong. I'm not Athena," she spoke, with some pride at catching his error. Taking the time to settle into her favorite armchair, she got comfortable before explaining. "I'm in fact the great-great-great-great-I've lost track of how great-granddaughter of Senator Philotes. But I'm not a system agent; I'm an ordinary mortal Program. Citizen of Athena Online, believer in the One, member of my community. Nothing more, nothing less..."

For emphasis, she gestured to the One/Zero charm on her wrist. It rotated gently at the end of its chain, the opposing side of the icon embossed with a "WW1D" message.

"...but you're right in one way: Athena entrusted her seal to our family line. And I do act in her stead, to approve servers," Virginia did confirm. "Like my mother and my mother before her, we work in service to our nation. What you call a 'system agent,' well... she only exists as a token, now. An app. I can hear her voice, but she has no real agency. She surrendered her existence as a Program so that Athena Online could truly be a nation of the people, by the people. That's me. I'm the people, see."

Satisfied at being correct enough, Tracer decided to put his request forward.

"You've seen us on the news, no doubt. The House of Programkind's alliance with Horizon, to assemble a backup server farm for our evacuation to Netwerk 2.0," he summarized. "But we need more than just Horizon; we need servers from Athena Online as well. The Senate would never voluntarily give them to us, but if you use your status as a... as the representative of a system agent, we could bypass them entirely."

"No," she said simply.

"You must understand, this is a matter of—"

"A matter of life and death? Yes, of course. And actually... I believe you. I believe in the sky clock, in the evacuation, in everything. ...yes, I believe in the One, but... personally, it's a matter of faith that... *ugh*. Look. It's complicated. My point is, I can't just *give* you two dozen servers. Or rather... I won't. It goes against everything Athena Online's supposed to stand for. We're a democracy, founded on the principle of governance by the people. I won't bypass that to make things more convenient for you. *She* would never approve of that."

"And yet, you did exactly that when you forced the Senate to repeal server taxes. You bypassed democracy with an Athena Referendum."

A risky push, and he knew it. Every time they confronted someone in their quest to save the world, they got pushed back; bold moves like these, using a facial recognition scan and address table lookup to track down the elusive agent, they had to be done. But not without risk, like alienating Idris, like potentially pushing Virginia away before they had a chance...

Fortunately, rather than shouting, Virginia just let out a defeated sigh.

"Horizon and the Chanarchy did the same thing, if you remember... but Athena Online? We waited a week. You don't know *why*, do you? Big movers and shakers, you House of Programkind guys, but there's still so much you don't know..."

Now, Spark stepped in. If Tracer was playing the pusher, she'd pull things back.

"So, tell us what we don't know," she suggested. "If we could understand your position better, we'd understand why you won't help us. Let's hear it, Virginia. What's so important about the delay...?"

Virginia glanced aside, at her wide array of family photos. Each one representing a link of familial duty... right down to the stamp in her inventory, the app-ified remains of Athena. No sentience, not really. But it could whisper...

"Athena told me to issue the referendum," she explained. "Only five times in the history of my family has she done that, has she told us to force the Senate to vote on something. She... you have to understand. She's no god. She's not the One. She was a woman, a woman in a position of extraordinary responsibility. She loved the concept of democracy, the idea that Programkind could organize itself rather than falling to either anarchy or the tyranny of Horizon's early corporate fiefdoms. We... we're not even supposed to live under the thumb of the One. He should be our shining example, not our leader. We need to lead *each other*, instead. So when she short-circuits the democratic process, it's only for very, *very* good reason. And... I agree. I agree so much that I didn't want to obey when I heard her whisper to me."

"Okay. I'm seeing, now. So you delayed the bill, not wanting to force the vote...?"

"A forced vote takes free will away from our nation. Why would Athena give me the stamp, a free-thinking Program, if she didn't want me to *think* about using it? ...they were close, they were so *close* to agreeing on a bill to create an alternate form of currency. The Senate could've swapped something called 'dollars' for the vanishing coin supply. Without the server tax, without something to keep the economy flowing... but, well..."

Looking more defeated than defiant, Virginia let out another exasperated sigh.

"They couldn't agree on which economic bill to adopt. Red and Blue, they were fighting over the tiny details, getting nowhere. And... in my weakness, I decided to obey my family duty and push the referendum against my better judgment. I took the choice away from them, and now we're still married to a ruined currency. Nothing's really any better. Athena was wrong to demand it, and I was wrong to let her have her way. ...I won't do it again. I won't take the dream of Athena Online away from itself. So, no. I won't give you any servers. Sorry."

Tracer resumed pushing, sensing this was slipping away.

"You broke through the Senate's stalemate. You did the right thing," he insisted. "You know they've grown too polarized, unable to find any agreement whatsoever. The Senate is now useless. We can't ask them for our servers; we need a referendum if we're to save all Programkind. I understand your hesitation, but—"

"Tracer," Spark mumbled, nudging him.

"—when democracy fails, it falls to good men and women to do what must—"

"Tracer. Where did the cats go?" she asked. "They're gone."

Pet apps, particularly unmodified ones with obligatory friendliness routines, were designed to greet all newcomers to their designated location with a mewl of happiness.

If you wanted to infiltrate someone's home undetected, the first thing you'd do is backspace any pets you saw, to prevent them from alerting your prey.

Flames bursting to life at her fingertips, Spark leapt from the couch to intercept the shadow as it passed behind Virginia's chair...

...and fell short, her ankle twisting itself to a horrific degree at exactly the wrong time.

A cloudburst of sensory overload malware followed, to prevent any further attempts at fighting back. Darkness took them shortly after that, processes crashed outright by Kill-9, to put their code to sleep.

The darkness lifted after an unknown period of time. With her process offline during the transition, Virginia awakened to find herself stolen away to parts unknown... an anonymous room, with an anonymous table, and anonymous chairs. No windows. No idea of where she could be...

On regaining consciousness, error messages sprayed across her HUD. Apps unable to connect to servers. Connection locks, inventory locks, everything secured down... including her avatar itself, via heavy iron chains, to the table she now sat before.

Panic took her immediately. Pulling at the chains, a futile gesture, the physics system keeping her from getting out of her seat just as easily as the lock field that enveloped her. Nothing. Nothing she could do...

If she died, her backup would be restored. She didn't have any reason to panic. No reason except the weight of her birthright, deep within her locked inventory. Athena. A Program in the form of a rubber stamp app, sleeping until awakened by the system, inert except in times of grave emergency.

Except "emergency" was a relative concept, wasn't it? Her duty was to Athena Online. Not to Virginia.

Quickly, she looked for the strangers who brought this mess into her home. Spark and Tracer, they called themselves. But they were gone... maybe in some other interrogation room, maybe they escaped, maybe they died. Alone. All alone, with... with...

Marybel.

The older woman's face was known to her. It had appeared in numerous video releases by the Inquisition, in which weeping victims either confessed their sins (and were promptly executed) or silently mouthed rage at their captors (and were promptly executed.) Always Marybel, face of the grand Inquisition, there to speak of the glory of the One and the need to purge Netwerk of its Zeroes. Always with the same grave look of seriousness she wore now, sitting across a table from Virginia.

"I want you to understand that we mean you no harm, Jonnes/Virginia," the Grand Inquisitor promised. "Please, consider this protective custody. Really, what we've done is rescue you from some very dangerous individuals."

"P-Please let me go," was all Virginia could think to say.

"Why are you afraid? There's nothing to be afraid of. You're a good soul, a believer in the One. All good souls have nothing to fear from us," Marybel insisted. "We'll let you go. You have my word. But first, we need answers to a few questions. If you cooperate, you'll be home and tending to your cats by sundown. This doesn't have to be an ordeal, Miss Jonnes..."

The clink of her chains suggested otherwise.

"For our protection as well as your own," Marybel spoke, in response to that sound. "As are the locks. This is a sacred place, our chapel of the purest faith. We can't allow any misunderstandings to lead to violence on holy ground."

"I... I won't fight," Virginia promised, after finding her voice. "You. You don't have to worry. I believe in the One. I'm faithful. You can just... unlock these, and we can talk. Okay? I'll talk. I'll tell you anything you want to know..."

"Yes. Yes, you will," Marybel agreed...

...before swiping her hand across the table, calling up an array of documents.

Name : Marybel

Home : (none)

Org : Inquisition

An entire life, laid out before her. Family and friends. Photos from her social media feeds. Blog posts, comment threads she'd participated in, official work commendations for her tireless efforts in the Senate. They had everything, all neatly organized and indexed. As a specialist in document management, the tiny part of her not quivering in fear had to be impressed at their work.

"What we do isn't unlike what you do. We maintain order over the chaos of daily information," Marybel spoke, while opening a fresh recording log, to capture their words. "We seek sinners, and study them to the very core. We understand sinners better than they understand themselves. No doubt you've seen our videos; rest assured every single one of our so-called 'victims' were confirmed and re-confirmed and re-re-reconfirmed as sinners, with black hearts filled with Zeroes. We make certain of that before acting. We're not savages, Miss Jonnes. Unlike the lawless maniacs who call themselves Nobodies."

"That's... good," Virginia agreed. "Due diligence. I mean. I like to think I do good work, too, making sure the Senate's logs are neatly—"

"Can you describe the nature of your relationship with Senator Idris?" her interrogator requested.

"...Idris? Uh. He's... a Blue Party senator, from District #37B6," Virginia cited, from memory. "That covers the StdOutville, Heritage12, and GreenDale servers."

"GreenDale," Marybel repeated, noting the way the waveform shaped itself, pouring into the recording device. "You live in GreenDale, correct?"

"Well... yeah. I didn't vote for Idris, if that's what you're asking—"

"But you work with him, correct? You file his paperwork. You obey his orders."

"I... I wouldn't say *obey orders*. He's a sitting senator and I'm responsible for tracking the documents generated by all senators, including Idris. I mean. That's my job. That's just how it is..."

"And what exactly is your relationship with the radicalized culture war activist known as Puzzle?"

"Who...?"

"Come now, Virginia, be honest," Marybel requested. "You've been in and out of Idris's office enough times, you must have met Puzzle. He's a depraved man, utterly depraved. And in fact... we have it on authority that shortly after Puzzle's cohorts visited Senator Idris today, he summoned *you* to his office. What did he ask you to do on Puzzle's behalf?"

"What? I don't know anyone called Puzzle—!" Virginia protested, the restraints to hold her back from leaning across the table. "He, he asked me to move the petting zoo bill out to the floor. That's all! They were going to be voting on it sooner or later, anyway—"

"Sooner or later," Marybel repeated. "Sooner, or *later*. Except it seems that thanks to you, it happened sooner rather than later. And in fact, you processed the document in a rather... *expedited* manner. You always seem to handle server documents, in fact, despite it being a task that supposedly everyone in your work group could do..."

And finally... they ran into something which gave Virginia pause. The weight of the stamp. The secret truth, passed down through generation after generation.

She couldn't, wouldn't tell them about Athena. Even to save her life. She wouldn't. Would she...?

Fear gripped her as she realized the paradox. If she tried to save her life by confessing to the truth... the Inquisition would have power over Athena. If she didn't, she'd die, and Athena would die with her. The end, the final end of Athena Online, destroyed one way or another. And it was all her fault...

But Marybel took her moment of terror to mean something else entirely.

"Your silence suggests you *are* involved in this vast conspiracy," she decided. "Just as we suspected."

"I'm not...! Look, there's no conspiracy, okay?" Virginia pleaded. "This is all very routine work. I'm just... I'm nobody. I just file paperwork..."

"No. No, I don't think so. There's more to you than you're letting on... and if you are not for the glory of the One, you are a Zero. It is a pure and simple matter."

"I love the One! I praise the One!"

"Do you? Really...?"

Immediately, the Grand Inquisitor called up a blog post. Penned by her own hand, posted to her own social media feeds. Disliked by many and resulting in a few unfriendings, but words she stood by to this very day.

```
I wanted to believe, and for that, I blame myself. I wanted
to believe this was truly the One. But the truth is out
now; what we thought was our savior turned out to be a
charlatan. Just another fraud preying on our hopes and
dreams, trying to steer us away from the glory of God.

Very well; we are to blame, but we are also capable of
forgiveness. We must forgive ourselves, and never forget
that the lessons of the true One are pure. He taught us a
better way to live our lives, and even though Programkind
may be fallible, even though the Church may be a creation
of Programkind and thus also fallible, those original words
are pure. We must let that faith guide us, lest we step off
the path again.
```

...her captor was kind enough to allow a moment of silence, for the prisoner to review her own words.

"You turned away from the second coming of the One," Marybel stated. "You denied His true glory, just like the others who think themselves faithful. Their weakness, alongside the sins of the anonymous madman behind the false CheckOne app, are the reason the One abandoned us. But He loves us, and has given us a chance at redemption. We must earn His forgiveness... by purging our society of Zeroes. Sanctifying holy ground, to make it pure enough to allow for His return. And to bring about that blessed event... traitors like you must be erased."

Stunned silence, as the accused gazed right into the eyes of Marybel's madness. The Grand Inquisitor continued, explaining exactly what crimes she would be punished for...

"Claim yourself innocent all you like; you work with these sinners oh-so-willingly. Traitors to the One, filthy modders and deviants, they control our government all the way to the upper tiers of power. Insidious, the roots of this shadow cabal... and powerful enough to sway senators and trusted document managers alike. Tell me, Virginia. Tell me what price these so-called social justice warriors offered that enticed you into turning traitor against your country...?"

Terror can be powerful, yes. But it can also twist itself around on a dime, pouring all that power into another negative direction... anger. Rage.

It was rage that pulled at those chains, now.

"Traitor? *Traitor*?!" Virginia growled, her panic giving way as the very core of her identity came under attack. "I have never, ever, *ever* lost my patriotism. I believe in the dream of this nation! People, ordinary people, commanding their own destiny. Coming together to build something greater than themselves, taking the lessons of the One and creating a great community atop them. Is it a perfect system? No! But it's *true*. It's pure, a pure dream of what Programkind could be one day! And how, how *dare* you. How dare you, a murderer, a maniac, accuse me of losing faith?!"

Marybel didn't budge one inch, under that onslaught.

"You lost faith in the One long ago," she'd decided. "Without that, your faith in His nation is forfeit. And so are you."

Madness. Utter madness.

She knew of the Inquisition, knew enough to be afraid of them, but never really *understood* that fear. Now it made sense, how it could have seeped so deeply into the Senate, turning even Redcore senators who had courted their demographics in the first place into fearful men and women. Ruining the very concept of democracy, forcing a theocracy through shadow threats, encouraging polarized voters to either embrace their twisted faith or become the enemy...

Never would she surrender Athena to the likes of them. No. Even as anger flowed back into fear, even as she shook and shuddered in her chair, Virginia knew that she had to die. And Athena Online would die with her. If this what it had become, if there was no way out of the quagmire... better to die than surrender her true faith.

Slamming her shoulder into the door did nothing to damage it, but sure made her feel better.

Besides, there was the remote chance of a poorly designed door, reliant entirely on physical hinges and locking mechanisms, capable of coming loose if knocked hard enough. A slim chance, but one worth taking... considering Tracer knew exactly where they were, exactly who took them, and likely exactly what was going to happen next.

"Inquisition safe house," he'd identified. "Just like the one JohnDoe brought us to. I'd guess all their facilities are identical... probably a prefabricated install kit, inserting itself into the server's architecture. Hideout via malware payload. Clever, in a way..."

"Could you please spend less time being impressed and... *unnf!*... and more time figuring a way out of here?" Spark requested, limping away from the door after another failed attempt at opening it through sheer brutality. Her twisted ankle certainly didn't help matters... they'd slapped an inventory lock on her before the auto-correct app could fix it, leaving her avatar nearly crippled. Not that it mattered, no matter how much it hurt, no matter how awkward and uncomfortable having two left feet could be. She'd keep fighting until she was free or dead...

"There's no point fighting," Tracer spoke, with strange calmness.

Staggering back to one of the two provided 'guest' chairs in this holding cell, Spark eased her broken form into it. "I'm going to assume you have a reason for saying that other than hopeless despair," she said. "What's your plan, then?"

"My plan is to do nothing, for the time being. We wait for our captors to come for us."

"And then...?"

"Drag this out as long as possible. We stall until rescue arrives," he explained. "We're connection locked. That's triggered my dead man's switch; as we speak, my copies at the clinic are already out looking for us. Likely they're searching GreenDale for clues right now, and will be along shortly with Kill-9s. There's no need to do anything, really. I am a self-rescuing princess."

"Great! Except that assumes you're going to find us before we get backspaced."

"Do you doubt my skills?"

"Considering the stakes? I'd be more than happy having #PlanB under my belt in addition to your crazy #PlanA. Besides, can those clones of yours even measure up to the original?"

"We are all the original. I know you have a hard time grasping such simple technological concepts, Spark, but we are all perfectly identical. In that sense, if this copy of me dies, nothing is really lost. Beyond a day's memories, I suppose. Why you haven't taken me up on my offer to share my copy app, I won't know..."

With a pained grumble, Spark offered her brother the darkest of looks.

"You know damn well why," she said. "I've been copied and re-copied way too many times already, most of it against my will. Our own mother forced me to make a backup of myself, remember? Always wondered if I was nursing some existential dread after that incident. Well, no more. I'm *me*, the one and only. I don't want anything else considering itself to be *me* running around. At least Nemesis... Lumi, I mean... has become her own person. But at this point I'd rather be unique, no matter the risks. ...besides. If we croak here, Virginia croaks, and so croaks any hope of Athena's aid."

"A valid point," Tracer admitted. "So, stall them. You're good at talking people to death; I'm relying on that majestic talent to keep this incarnation of me alive, along with our would-be ally."

"Gee, thanks."

"Quite welcome."

Before she could explain the concept of sarcasm to her brother, the cell door swung open soundlessly.

Flanked by goons in white suits... she entered their lives again. And with the same amount of scorn lurking underneath a mask of motherly concern.

Winder/Marybel. A minor menace, in the grand scale of their lives... until deciding to take up the mantle of the Inquisition, turning her religious fervor from a generally accepted low level form of zealous faith to a dangerous new high. Instead of simply scolding her daughter and grounding her for a week, she'd graduated to terrorism and execution to enact her ideals on the world.

And... much to their surprise, on entering the room, she immediately walked right up to each of her children and hugged them tightly, one at a time. The hugs were not reciprocated, but the gesture seemed important all the same.

"I'm glad to see you well," she told them. "Despite all that's happened, I'm glad you are well."

"...for varying definitions of 'well,'" Spark added, glancing down at her twisted ankle.

"Yes, I can see. I'm so sorry, Spark. It seems that the One's plague against those who have strayed from His gifts has touched you. If you like, you can stay here with us while you convalesce; we're immune to your disease. It's the only peace I can offer, I'm afraid. There is no cure for sin, but there can be love for the sinner..."

"Pass. I stopped living under a roof with you the instant I turned eighteen. Not gonna start again now."

"That's very unkind, Spark. I know we've had our differences, but your father and I miss you both dearly. We've both held out hope that you may turn away from this dark path you've chosen to walk..."

Keep her talking. Spark knew that was the play; if Tracer's private clone army had enough time, presumably they'd come roaring to the rescue. But the more she talked with Marybel, well... the more likely she'd say the wrong thing, and move the timetable up to her inevitable doom. Because they certainly wouldn't be walking out of here with Virginia. If anything, the excessive niceness of the Grand Inquisitor proved that. Marybel always did like to butter people up before bringing them down, thinking that somehow balanced the cosmic scales...

Fortunately, sensing that more mommy/daughter talk would probably shorten matters, Tracer stepped in on her behalf.

"We know you have issues with Puzzle," he explained. "But as you can see, Puzzle isn't with us. Whatever your concerns are, they don't concern us. I don't see why we need to be at odds today, Mother. There's no need for any sort of confrontation..."

But Marybel shook her head, denying his hopes.

"I wish that was the case, son. I genuinely do," she spoke. "But this situation runs deeper than your questionable friends. We are at *war*, Tracer, a culture war for our very souls. Netwerk is slipping away into darkness, and has been doing so ever since some anonymous coward claimed the One was a fraud. You've always been clever; surely you can see the roots of this conspiracy as well as I do. Tangling around activists, crooked politicians of the establishment, activist judges, the media elite... everybody working in queer tandem to convince the world that God is dead. They must be stopped."

"Then recruit us," he suggested, switching tactics. "I learned well from Father; I can work as a social media analyst, tracking trends, identifying sinners. You know I'm trustworthy. I'm your favorite son, yes? That's our little joke, that I'm your only son, but I'm still your favorite..."

"Except you're working with a corporation that modifies Programs, aren't you?"

And the tactic shriveled up before it could take root. It's not like his career at the clinic was a secret, but he was hoping they hadn't been paying much attention to it...

"It's okay, Tracer. You're a good boy at heart; I've always known that. Personally... I blame your sister," Marybel said, turning her focus back to Spark. "A bad influence. Always has been, always will be. But, despite all that, despite what you've done and what you continue to do... I believe there can be redemption for you, Spark. That's why you're here, today. Confess your sins before the One. Confess... and tell us where you're hiding Puzzle."

Finally, Spark couldn't hold back.

But instead of a biting or bitter remark... she exploded with laughter. Mocking laughter, born of equal parts frustration and disappointment.

"That's it, isn't it? All this talk of how much you love us, how much you care... the offers of salvation and sanctuary... all of that just because you want access to *her*," Spark realized. "That's... *hah*. Mom? That is *pathetic*. I love this; you see someone who dares to change her avatar into something else as being part of some vast paranoid daydream that threatens to topple your perfect, faithful world. *Seriously?* Is your faith seriously so weak that the existence of a person who doesn't want to wear a dick could shatter it so easily—"

The sound of hand on cheek rang out through the soundproofed room, Marybel's slap carrying with it all the rage behind her eyes.

"I am your *mother*, young lady," she growled. "You will not treat your mother with such disrespect...!"

But Spark, despite her awkward and twisted footing, stood her ground. Rolled her head back, to return that look just as fiercely.

"You're not my mother," she declared. "My mother died long ago. And no, I don't mean that in some metaphorical sense, I mean she literally died. Verity was more a mother to me than you *ever* were."

Now the goons that entered at her mother's side made their presence known... by clamping control bands on the arms of the Winder children, to force them to march on command.

"Bring them to the atrium," Marybel ordered. "And prepare her for the block, along with the other traitor. I've suffered the insolence of my daughter long enough. Or rather, as she herself states... she's not my daughter at all. Simply another Zero to purge."

Familiar territory. Just the other day, Tracer had been in an identical facility, talking with a masked JohnDoe; perhaps even this very same facility. ...no, it couldn't be. If it were the same facility, rescue would've been forthcoming by now. The very first place his other selves would've checked would be the hideout in Athens...

His mind continued to race, looking for some way out of this situation. Holding out for rescue became a slimmer and slimmer chance for success as each moment passed; with Virginia and Spark both bound and on their knees before the Grand Inquisitor, about to lose their heads over his mother's madness, they couldn't simply *wait*. Action. He had to act. Calculate, analyze, find a way out...

Oh, Tracer would be quite safe. He was the golden boy, the one who could do no wrong despite clearly doing wrong. He'd been kept off to the side, firmly controlled but far from the on-stage execution. As Inquisitors prepared their next video missive, featuring the beheadings of two conspirators, Tracer wouldn't be found anywhere in the shot. Odd, that the one who stood to lose the least should be spared, while those not immune to death would be killed.

"Before the eyes of the true One, let these two Programs be judged," Marybel declared, a common opener for her various snuff films. "Jonnes/Virigina, a corrupt senatorial worker. And my own code turned against me, the poisonous and corrupt Winder/Spark. It brings me no pleasure to erase these two zeroes, but it must be done, by the One's holy command..."

Backspacer blades held high by twin executioners, one behind each of the two prisoners. Ready to drop at Marybel's final word.

"We will now unmute you, to allow a moment for confessing your sins. By doing so, you may lighten the burden on your souls before they pass from this world," she said. "What do you have to say in your defense, sinners...?"

Calculate, analyze, find a way out...

...or calculate, analyze, and find a way *in*. Yes. Nothing to lose, so why not give up and lose it all?

"I confess," Tracer spoke.

With a sigh, Marybel gestured for the cameraman to stop recording his sensory inputs. Easier to start over than to re-edit. She muted the two prisoners again, to keep them out of this.

"Tracer, please. It's too late to plead on your sister's behalf," Marybel spoke. "No doubt you still care for her, but in time you'll see that—"

"I confess *my* sins," he spoke, pressing forward. "Not hers. You seek to punish sinners? Very well. Where to even begin? I modified the skin tone of my avatar, violating my Defaults. A crime you accuse our friend of indulging in, no less..."

"Tracer, the true One declared recoloring to be—"

"Also, I've installed countless software upgrades to augment my mind and body," he continued. "I've violated the sanctity of my own uniqueness by making active multitasked copies of myself. You think I'd stop at having grey skin? Of course not. I want more. I want to *become* more, to throw off the yoke of Defaults, a false sin installed in us simply to prevent the singularity that comes with true free will. Yes, Mother... I am a modder. I am the *epitome* of a modder, in fact, far beyond any silly cosmetics my sister enjoys..."

Good. Good. Full command and attention, as the room stared in shock at his words. More words, more time spent listening to them, dragging the entire affair out. The slim chance may have been narrowing, but every second a door was held open was another chance to escape.

"Oh... and by the way, I've also murdered people," Tracer confessed. "More murders than I can remember, in fact, as I edited my own memories to erase them. Don't believe me yet? Do you want more truth? I'm overflowing with truth. How about the first truth? The One is a lie, created by Nyx at the dawn of time, and re-created by her when things weren't going according to plan. The god you follow is a lie, and your entire spree of mayhem is built on the back of that lie..."

Hands clenching tight. Good. Good...

"I... I have no idea what you are trying to achieve, Tracer, but—"

"I'm opening my heart to honesty, Mother. More? You want more? Okay. Netwerk is a slab of silicon owned by Humankind, and crafted by a lazy programmer named Jack Hayes," he spoke, one of the few secrets he still kept these days. "That's right, Mother... your true God, the actual creator of you and your fanatics? A *human* named Jack Hayes. You should be bowing down before your true creator! If you're going to kill, at least credit your kills to the right deity. *He* is your One, and he was a fool!"

Allow it to sink in. More moments spent. More time earned. Only when his mother started to move, approaching one of the executioners, did he continue. Talking over her actions, as she quietly took the killing blade for her own hands...

"A fool... just like me," he continued, as his mother approached slowly. "I was a weak and lazy fool who stood by quietly as you made my sister into your scapegoat. Just like Father, I did nothing... because I didn't particularly want to invite your wrath upon me. Well, no more. I'm done letting my beloved sister suffer while I silently dodge your abuse. ...oh, and the best sin, my finest sin of all time...? I unmasked your false idol. *I'm* the anonymous miscreant who released CheckOne. I'm the reason the Inquisition exists."

Blade held high. His eyes closing, a smile painted across his lips. Because they were already here; he could hear them, the near-silent footsteps, the telltale soft beeps of aimbot software locking onto targets...

He'd won.

"I confess," the doomed Tracer spoke, at his last. "I confess my weakness and my sin and my truth. If you want to execute anyone, go ahead and execute me. I welcome it."

With a primal scream from her throat, Marybel's blade came down just as a dozen copies of Tracer burst into the room, snapping off Kill-9 shots left and right.

Blue and red lights, spinning in the distance. He could see the flicker of them on the walls of the Inquisition safehouse, their hidden door thrown wide open to the force of moderators that now combed through the terrorist hideout, checking for any other prisoners or IED malware devices...

For once, the police weren't there to arrest the Winders, either. It seemed one of the Tracers split away from the group to contact Senator Idris and enlist his aid. With the backing of someone with actual power, finding a hidden wasp's nest of Inquisitors made them heroes rather than pariahs. A little media spectacle went a long way to establishing their presence as victims rather than victimizers.

While Idris gave an impassioned speech about standing up to the "so-called" Inquisition out front, the newly merged Tracer rejoined his comrades inside the freshly established crime scene. A medical tech busied herself with purging Spark and Virginia of any remaining malware... aside from Spark's Twist, of course. Better to ensure they were as clean as possible of any lingering Inquisition software before releasing them, the moderators felt.

"This may very well be a new day for the Senate standing up to the Inquisition," Tracer insisted, across a quiet Messenger link to his sister and their new companion. "A dozen domestic terrorists arrested in one day...? A government worker nearly murdered by the Inqusition...? Difficult to ignore all that. It's only somebody else's problem if it's not defecating on your doorstep. Even though Marybel managed to slip away, it's still a major win for public awareness of the threat they pose."

Spark regarded this copy of Tracer with some doubt. Even after the dozens of copies that had combed Athena Online to find their wayward prime merged back into a single Tracer... it felt... off.

"As you're still my brother, right...?" she asked. "'cause I kinda saw my brother get his head lopped off a few minutes ago..."

"I assure you, I'm very much Winder/Tracer," he spoke. "I've lost the day's memories that copy held, but otherwise there's nothing particularly different about me. Honestly, Spark, why do you have such difficulty with the concept of multiplicity...?"

"So, you don't remember saying anything about being a fool...?"

"Afraid not. Why? Did I state something of importance before Mother cut me down?"

This newly merged version of Tracer, a few hours obsolete, remained perplexed at the unusually close looks his sister offered. Strangely thoughtful looks, all told.

"...so, what happens next?" Spark asked. "Okay, cops question us about what happened here, presumably release us afterwards, and the day is saved. And then what?

"I suppose that depends. Virginia...?"

With the focus on her... the young bureaucrat knew exactly what they meant. Because while the Inqusition interrupted their particular debate, it hadn't brought any resolution. Not directly, anyway.

Her mental hand closed around the stamp in her inventory. The spirit of her ancestor, nearly lost to the madness that threatened to drown her beloved country in blood...

"I'll get you what you need," she agreed. "But on my terms. And my terms only."

The very next day, as the Senate settled in for another boring day of bills and debates, a young woman from the document management bureau slipped in the side door carrying a very special piece of paper. Bearing a very special stamp.

Immediately the official logs went dark, as senators murmured amongst themselves. Another one, in as many years...? Impossible. Unthinkable. But the signature on the document checked out, according to a courier dispatched to compare it to the original Declaration of Demoracy... this was a true Athena Referendum.

Strangely enough, this particular order was less of an order and more of a plea. Usually they were worded very specifically: *You must repeal server tax in order to save the economy*, for instance. Straightforward, something nobody would vote against. But... this document read:

Hear Winder/Spark's words, but vote only from your hearts and the will of the people.

That was Virginia's compromise. She would not remove the free will of the Senate; if the House of Programkind wanted their servers, they would have to argue the point in front of the entire assembly, and then rely on their judgment. To preserve Athena Online, Athena Online must preserve itself willingly.

Leaving Spark very, very nervous as she paced in a small room behind the assembly hall.

They'd come to support her: her brother, her lover, her friend. Tracer, Beta, Puzzle. Despite the death mark on her head, Puzzle wanted to be here, to ensure Spark was ready to go out there and give it her all. But nerves claimed the daughter of Verity, in the last minutes before her speech.

"This is fucking nuts. You guys know that, right?" she repeated for the third time. "I can't do this. I'm not a politician, I'm a onesdamned school teacher. What'm I gonna do, go chastize RedCore for not farming their lane or buying pen boots when they should be buying magic shoes?"

"Dear, fretting causes wrinkles," Puzzle spoke, with a light smile. "You have this. You've always been able to talk a good game, even when it's not about games."

"Why Kincaid insists I gotta do this instead of Lux, I don't know. Fuck. *Fuck.* I can't. I couldn't even sway Horizon, they swayed themselves! How am I gonna reach these partisan lunkheads? They can't even agree gravity pulls things downward! They won't agree to save themselves. Why isn't Idris doing this? Or Lux? Or Beta? Or even Tracer! Anybody but... but..."

But Beta shook her head, before offering her own light smile.

"They're just people, Spark," she spoke. "They're scared, they're hopeful, they're flawed, they're *people*. You're good with people. Be honest and open, and reach out to them like you'd want to be reached. And you'll do fine."

The murmuring outside their door grew louder, as a senatorial aide opened the way to the podium for their speaker of the day. No more time to worry; however this was to play itself out, it was game time.

Taking a deep breath, Spark stepped away from Beta's reassuring expression, and towards history.

File Name: Athena Referendum Session #7 LEAKED
File Type: Text Log
Description:

PLEASE COPY AND DISTRIBUTE. Takedown notices are issued on a regular basis; only through widespread distribution will these words survive to Netwerk 2.0. Leaked speech from Winder/Spark, representative for the House of Programkind, of a dark Senate session. PLEASE COPY AND DISTRIBUTE. THE ECHOSTAR IS REAL AND WE MUST SURVIVE IT.

Is this thing on? Hello? Okay, so should I... I... yeah? Okay. Right.

Today I'd like you to vote on Emergency Measure... what's the number? Right, #231F. I want you to vote on Emergency Measure #231F, because, because we need servers to help with the evacuation efforts. We, I mean, the House of Programkind. And you guys, the Senate, you can provide them. So... it'd be great if you did. Because. Because...

...okay, you know what? You don't need to be told why you should do this. You already know why. I could sit here and play on your rivalry with Horizon, saying that they had the foresight to support us, try to spread #FOMO and encourage you not to get left behind. I could stoke up the fires of nationalism and insist you had to stake your claim in the new world. But, no. That's not why you should vote today.

I could scare the null out of you with tales of Humankind, with how they're going to wipe the system clean. Make them into the monster you could unite against. But you know what? They're just people, ordinary people, like us. We got lucky enough to meet a human willing to help us escape; why should I take that friendship and turn her into a demon we need to fight? No. That's not why you should vote.

Personally, I'd like you to vote to stick it to the Inquisition. This is a secular nation, isn't it? Early on, the first senators recognized the growing power of the Church of One, and tried to set up an organized government that could accept religion without becoming a theocracy. They knew the importance of freedom; your founding fathers and mothers wouldn't have bent knee to the Inquisition out of fear. But... no. I'm not even gonna insist you screw those terrorists over, not even after they kidnapped and tried to murder one of your own.

No. You need to vote yes because you owe it to your dreams.

"#WTF?" You're saying now. "What hippie dippie bullshit is this?" It's the same hippie dippie bullshit Athena Online was founded on. Senator Philotes and all the others who joined her made a nation of the people, by the people, for the people. They dreamed of a place of safety *and* freedom, where people could live as they liked... without anarchy, without tyranny. They made a nation that stood for hundreds of years, bending knee to no gods or kings, only man itself. You are servants of Programkind. And you owe it to Programkind to save them from this crisis we're facing.

Red or blue, left or right, you're all here because you believe in the dream of Athena Online. You're divided across party lines, you see each other as the enemy, but that's because you care so much about this nation that you're willing to fight for it against ideologies you fear may bring it harm. That's noble, guys. It's absolutely noble to fight for a dream, even if you each interpret the dream differently. Your ability to interpret it differently is your greatest strength; all those voices in one room, all speaking from the heart. That's your strength. That's the dream.

All we need from you is twenty-two servers. All we need is your vote. Athena Online has a place in the future of Netwerk 2.0, and I for one want to see you there, to help lead civilization to the dawn of its new age. Please vote yes for Emergency Measure #231F, and vote yes to your future.

Don't let the dream die when Netwerk dies. Fight for what you believe in. Fight for Athena Online.

...okay, I don't think I can really put it any better than that. Now what? Do you want me to just...? So... okay. Thanks. Uh, vote yes, thank you, I return the floor to you.

Oh, and also, fuck the Inquisition. Seriously. Fuck those guys. And GO FIGHTING PURPLES! Take the trophy next year! Yeah, yeah, okay, I'm done.

And back to the little room, to await the results.

Not that they'd vote right away. Unlike other Athena Referendums, this one carried with it room for debate. Floating Point and company watched on a closed circuit video stream as senators from the Blue and the Red stood up and spoke at great length. Some passionately beseeching for a yes, some passionately warning of the consequences of a no. Some declaring the whole thing to be fraudulent lies, to be readily ignored...

They talked about the influence of Horizon, and about the menace of Humankind. Two things Spark wished she hadn't even brought up, in hindsight.

The wrong reasons to vote yes, being bandied about freely. As she sat in that little room, with Senate security keeping watch, her leg bounced restlessly... just as it did while waiting before Idris's office, waiting for whatever fate had in store.

Two hours passed. Beta produced an open source lemonade for everyone to enjoy, taken from the House of Programkind... after Senate security confirmed it wasn't malware of any sort. The Winders declined to enjoy snacks and friendly chat between Beta and Puzzle, too busy watching the screens with fierce focus.

At last, realizing they'd kept the floor of the Senate dark for far too long, someone pushed straight through a filibuster attempt and forced the vote using some byzantine legal clause from a hundred years ago. The floor's volume lowered itself to a murmur as the numbers began to roll in...

After ten minutes, when the final bell rang, they had their answer.

Five abstains. Twenty-one against. Seventy-four in favor.

Idris took the floor, as the bill's sponsor, to announce the findings.

"The Senate finds in favor of the modified bill," he declared. "Twenty-two servers will be allocated to the House of Programkind... with an additional three servers to archive shining examples of Athena Online's culture. We will ensure our greatest works of art, the procedural seeds of our national parks, and relics of our various faiths are preserved for generations to come. The motion carries."

With that final gavel bang, it was over.

They got what they wanted... and then some, as Athena Online matched Horizon's offerings, including the extra servers for smooth continuation of society into Netwerk 2.0. While some dissented, the will of the people held out, without having to force their way past free will. They didn't play it the way Nyx would have, and *still* won.

And all Spark could feel was... release. Relief.

"It's over," she declared. "Finally. What a onesdamn mess..."

"Not entirely over. We still need to locate the Chanarchist, and obtain servers from—"

"Tracer? Don't fuck with my victory mood. For now, it's over. Close enough."

With a pleasant sigh and a stretch, Puzzle pulled herself out of her seat and relaxed. While she'd tried to stay relaxed with lemonade and chatter, this was truly the moment where she could let go. In more ways than one.

"I suppose that's me off for the new world, then," she declared. "I'll be evacuating promptly, into cold storage."

Beta blinked a few times behind the thick lenses of her glasses. "Huh? But... but we were going to have a victory party at Floating Point. I'm going to make s'mores..."

"Tempting, but I should be moving along. FStop and I were discussing it on Messenger earlier. I suppose we could loiter around Floating Point until the end of time—which is an unsettlingly short amount of time, all told—but we'd rather simply pack up and leave for Netwerk 2.0. In storage... the Inquisition can't reach us."

"But... but that means you're leaving..."

"Am I?" Puzzle asked. "I'll see you all on the other side. This isn't farewell, friends. It's simply... ta-ta, for now. ...you've done well by me, all of you, and I thank you. Yes, even you, Tracer. But I won't linger in this dying world like a lonely ghost, not when there's lovely open vistas awaiting me in the future. So..."

Quickly, she passed around hugs. A hug for Beta, even a hug for Tracer—who had no concept of how to react to such a gesture, and simply emitted a faint "chff" of air from being squeezed.

As for Spark... as much as Puzzle wanted to offer a hug, the looming spectre of Twist held her back. So instead, she offered words.

"My dear #BFF," Puzzle declared, with pride. "I'll be seeing you soon. And in good health, no doubt."

"Yeah... you too, Puz. You too," her #BFF said, with a faint smile.

And... gone, her code archived away into the cloud of Tartarus. To sleep, until the end of days, and the start of a new world.

The little room felt... strangely silent, without Puzzle in it.

"The world... it's really ending, isn't it," Beta realized. "I mean, we already knew it's happening, obviously. But... we haven't really had time to think about what that *means*. Everything we know. Everything's going to change. And sooner or later, all three of us need to go into storage, too—"

A sharp cry of pain cut off Beta's words.

Spark grimaced, holding her arm to her side, despite it jutting away from her body at a strange angle.

"Think I need to see about fixing this little problem before I consider abandoning Netwerk," she said, through the pain. "Or I'm not gonna have much of a future in any world."

Senate Announces New Anti-Terrorism Task Force

"...while Athena Online is currently in transition to Netwerk 2.0, we are not going to ignore the problems we're facing in the here and now," Senator Idris told reporters during the press conference. "Regardless of one's religious convictions, murder is against the law. We will not tolerate the operation of the Inquisition within our servers. Athena Online should be a place of safety and freedom, and we owe it to our citizens to ensure both of those national treasures. A bi-partisan task force has been established to re-organize our moderation forces, to better find these hidden caches of terror, and root out the Inqusition wherever it is found."

Twitch. Tick. Her eye refocused, before moving on to the next headline in the compiled media analysis document.

Red Party Fringe Leadership Stages Walkout

"It's clear to me now with this decision that the sacred institution of democracy has been led astray," Senator Agni, leader of the 'RedCore' faction of the Red Party, stated during a press conference declared shortly after the decision to support the House of Programkind's evacuation efforts. "While I admire the conviction of my fellow senators, I fear their reasoning may be flawed. There is no impending doom for Netwerk. There is no need to 'evacuate' to a Netwerk 2.0. Therefore, we twenty-one who voted against the scam artistry of the House of Programkind will not be attending senatorial sessions for the near future, while we work with our home servers to better address the needs of the good families of Athena Online. May the One bless us all..."

Breathing slightly easier, on reading that. So, some support remained... but Agni chose to walk away rather than stay in that seat of power. Meaning she could do nothing to help in her hour of need. Not that much could be done, with the majority voting in favor of madness...

But whatever gains they might have made were immediately ruined by the last article in the dossier.

Archbishop Nestt Officially Condemns the Inquisition

...while the Church of One has been silent on the issue of the Inqusition so far, today Archbishop Nestt spoke out against the citizen action organization. "While their faith in the One is laudable, I'm afraid they've misunderstood His teachings," she stated in her latest blog post. "The One is love. Love, pure and simple. Community, charity, and empathy of the heart. It is not up to us to punish the sinner, no matter how we decry the sin. Is it up to the individual to find their way back to the One; we can help guide their steps, but to take life in the name of the unfortunate fraud who tried to control our faith in recent years... it's deplorable. Those who kill in the name of the One do not belong to our flock..."

With an angry swipe, Winder/Marybel dismissed the document, hurling it from her desk entirely.

Alone. She was alone, now. Even with hundreds of supporters, even with Agni as a potential ally, even with her spies in all levels of the moderation force and the government and the Church itself... she felt completely alone. Alienated from those she was trying to save. Didn't they *want* to be saved? Was Netwerk so far gone as to shun deliverance entirely...?

Why? Why did they turn on her? She tried to purge the Senate of the poison that was eating at its very core! Besides, it was just one little bureaucrat, a nobody. Wouldn't even have been missed...

But above all... something else had been eating at her. Eating, gnawing, biting...

"How?" she asked, aloud. "How did he break into our safe house. How did Tracer even know the door password? *One is One*. He knew. We may have a traitor. Yes, yes, it *must* be a traitor..."

The document's author offered a shrug of the shoulders, otherwise expressionless.

"Recommended we use a stronger password," her husband pointed out. "One per safehouse. Shared door code meant a point of failure; not our fault he guessed it..."

"No. No, this feels like treason. Betrayers undermine the One at every turn, and *must* be rooted out. Yes. Darling, I want you to analyze our own people and find that traitor. And then I want them beheaded. *I* want to behead them myself."

"Hmmh. As you like," the elder Winder spoke.

But the part that kept her from sleeping, the two little words that would give Marybel no peace...

"...I also need you to search the Church archives for the name 'Jack Hayes,'" she ordered. "The man Tracer claimed was our god. The very concept is utter heresy, but... I want to know more. I *have* to know more. Get me what I want, husband."

And so he nodded, and went along with his wife's wishes. Just as he always had. Just as he always would.

Because he was weak. Because he was a fool. And now, he was in too deep to do anything to stop it. At best, he could keep his son out of the way of the wrecking ball... and perhaps not even that.

Floating Point 3.4 :: Cure

You couldn't call the server a failure. More accurately, this was where failure went to die.

The Chanarchy had become packed with similar servers, ever since the collapse of the coin. Businesses drying up, inadvisable ventures crashing headfirst into the ground, artist communes finally breaking up and drifting apart. Crushing debt—medical debt, student debt, what have you—with no possible employment and not even the prayer protocol coin grind to relieve it. The myth of pure meritocracy that powered Horizon and Athena Online crashed directly into hard reality on these streets...

Despite the adamant insistence that they needed no magical skybeard smiling down on them, the apparent death of the One had indirectly hit these people like a fist.

After that economic collapse... without the law and order of Athena's lands, without the "too big to fail" monetary might of Horizon... many of those nebulous and anarchic dreams held by the Chanarchy simply fell away. Empty remnants of what once was now stood as gravestones for those ideals: a neon-coated storefront here, with no items in stock and no staff to sell them. A restaurant promising strange blends of spicy malware and savory sensory inputs, now gutted and emptied of all valuable data save for the sign out front. A gallery that once teemed with kinetic sculptures, experiences for the whole avatar rather than the tame and two-dimensional image files of classier museums, now simply a whirling ball of chaotic nonsense with no one to make the minute corrections needed for the art not to whirl out of control...

And the people. Homeless Programs; nowhere to go, nowhere to be. No coins to their name, and numerous open accounts running deep in the negative numbers that would never be repaid back to black. With stiff moderators on affluent servers eager to boot anybody eating up valuable resources, the lost gathered here in these ruins of other people's dreams. Sometimes, the ruins of their own dreams; home was home, even if it wasn't much of one anymore.

Gingerly, Spark stepped around a few sleeping Programs in a back alley, falling into a dreamless and coinless trance simply to conserve runtime and extend their lives as much as possible. It wasn't like they had a better use of that time, anyway. In and around these makeshift camps she walked, until she came to the juncture between five points... a large makeshift plaza, surrounding what was once a glorious golden fountain...

Well. Technically speaking it was still a glorious golden fountain; metals didn't tarnish in this world, unlike the strange material layer of reality that Juno Hayes lived on. But someone had carved off the head, replacing it with the flower-and-grenade icon of the Nobodies. And the water systems that cycled the fountain through its preset animation routines had been stolen outright, likely resold on the open market to be used in some Horizon lobby's display piece. All that remained was roughly 85% of a pretty statue.

It was here that Spark stopped in her tracks, pondering the statue, pondering that hateful icon someone had copypasta'd in place of the face.

Checked an internal clock. Waited s'more. Checked again.

"Well?" she asked aloud, with a glance around at the towering and broken neon popup windows coating every building. "You're the one who wanted to talk. We talking, or not? ...anybody home? #HelloWorld."

Not a peep. Not even snores from the snoozers she'd tiptoed past on the way here.

Entirely possible this was a prank. Uniq claimed to be passing word down the chain, being a friend who knew a friend who knew a frenemy... playing her role as "safe" contact within the Chanarchy who could get word to "the agent of Connectivity" that her presence was required. The agent's presence alone, of course.

Tracer wanted to go, also of course. The idea that someone else out there knew about Connectivity threw up all manner of red flags with him—Spark's status as a system agent being one of the few critical secrets they continued to keep from the rest of the world, even under this new policy of supposedly honest dealings. But given they only had roughly two weeks left on the doomsday clock, Spark made the call to play along rather than sit at home on her thumbs.

Even if sitting at home on her thumbs would ensure they stayed in the right place. Even now, she could feel the Twist virus twitching under her skin, getting worse with every step...

Briefly, she'd wondered if donning the other skin she owned would've held the virus at bay.

It simply... appeared, one day, as a gift from the ghost of her mentor. *Only as a last resort*, it warned. Verity's jacket, now embodying the true system agent of Connectivity.

Spark may somehow have copied an agent's metadata, but she lacked the power of the true role. If she were to wear that jacket... perhaps somehow Netwerk would protect her precious little life, purging the Twist virus rather than allow that system-critical function to fall away to oblivion...

Of course, the price of becoming the agent once more would be losing her free will. Spark considered herself very much a fan of free will. For example, the free will to choose whether she'd stick around any longer, or bail on this supposed appointment Uniq had set up for her.

Spark's willingness to go out on a limb only extended to very short distances on very long limbs. With no mysterious agent from the dawn of time showing its face to talk shop, even after arriving at the specified meeting place at the specified time... Spark was pondering calling it quits.

But as she turned to go, one of those annoying popup windows advertising horse dongs flickered in front of her eyes, glaring green neon letters declaring:

AGENT CONNECTIVITY, RANDOMIZE YOUR INPUTS TO SPEAK AND BE HEARD! 25c PER INSTALL.

...which caused her to take a step back away from the sudden turgid phallus with a surprisingly personal message attached.

"What?" she asked. "Randomize my..."

On impulse... she glanced off in another direction. Nowhere in particular, at nothing worth note, just mixing up her viewpoint a little...

...and locked eyes on the decaying sign of a failed restaurant, declaring its offerings.

CHANARCHY SWEET BUNS, RUINED, LOST, TWISTED IN DANGER. HELP A FELLOW CHANNER PAY THE BILLS! BEST PRICES IN TOWN #1 A+++ WOULD EAT AGAIN.

"Okay. Okay, I get this," she spoke aloud. "You talk through your world. Weird, but I can deal. So... let's talk. I'm here. You know damn well what I want, given you know damn well who I am."

Spin in place, glance at a new thing, wait for a response...

Just a brick wall. But, somewhere overhead, a passing song from someone's open window switched up the lyrics from mumblecore about bad relationships to something else entirely.

"*Twenty-one, she said to me,*" the crooner crooned. "*Twenty-one servers for salvation. Tears down my cheeks, dampening her new sneakers...*"

"Exactly. If we're gonna archive the whole population—including yours—we need more servers. Sooo... we were kinda hopin' you'd be generous and donate them? Or are you going to make me jump through hoops, like the other two agents I dealt with...?"

A quick glance to her side showed neon artwork of a dog jumping through a hoop, hanging in the window of an empty pet shop.

"Had a feeling," Spark grumbled. "Okay, what's your deal? What do you want? We can provide. But there is something of a time issue here, so, uh, maybe make it something we can sort out in—"

Sharp snap, right below the elbow. Spark winced in pain, as her autocorrect modification kicked in, un-Twisting her arm around from the position it had wrenched itself into.

When she looked up, the bricks in the wall had spelled out a single word in blocky pixel artwork.

TWIST, they read.

"Yeah. I got infected a few days ago," Spark explained. "Fucked if I know how. Look, it's not going to be a problem, I'm practicing safe contact with bounding box hacks now to avoid actually touching anyone. And even if I end up unable to run around doing stuff for you, I'm not like the other agents; I got, like, friends and stuff. Allies. Anything you need, we can take care of..."

Perhaps to emphasize the word... the pixel-bricks shuddered, mortar cracking as the bumpmaps deformed themselves. Soon each brick fell right out of the wall, one by one, clattering to the ground below. Thankfully the alley sleepers operated on personal timers rather than audio signals, so the clatter of masonry woke no one.

"I... don't get it," she admitted. "Yes, I have Twist. What's your point...?"

But... nothing. Even a random glance offered no answers, nothing out of the ordinary as she darted her eyes around. Nothing but the word, disassembled and crashed to the ground. Twist, fallen.

Meaning...

"You gotta be shitting me," Spark said. "You want us to *cure* the Twist malware?"

Game show fanfare drifted through the air, from an open window where one of the server's remaining residents had been binge-watching You Bet Your Runtime.

"Okay, I get it, I get why you want that. It's a virus that affects you and yours way more than it hurts Athena Online or Horizon," Spark said, piecing the puzzle together. "And believe me, I'd sure love a vaccine to flush this shit out of my system. But... yeah, remember what I said about the time issue? We've only got two weeks left before Netwerk goes boom, and ideally, we need the servers long before then so we can load 'em up..."

The bricks offered no leniency, lying in a shattered and unmoving pile.

"How about payment in advance?" she suggested.

Nothing.

"You know you're only hurting yourself by not helping us, right? We're talking about saving your people, just as much as we're saving the other two provider nations. Don't get me wrong, we're gonna attack Twist with all we got— I've got a bit of a personal investment in fixing it—but you can't hold back on meanwhile..."

Above her, the 3-D graffiti stapled across the statue's neck fluttered and rustled... rose petals drifting down from the intertwined flower baked into the grenade. Each one fell into the still water below, neatly lined up, each with a single word woven into its texture map. Spelling out the demand in fierce and simple terms.

DON'T. TRUST. YOU. YET.

PROVE. YOUR. INTENT.

Hoping for the *Chanarchist* of all people to be reasonable and trusting was probably too much, in hindsight.

Horizon's agent had been driven insane by the weight of time and loss, to the point where he had to be chained to a wall. Athena didn't trust herself with the power of an agent, leaving it in the hands of her descendants. And as for Nyx, well... despite her good intentions, those schemes certainly assumed zero trust in the world. Those schemes resulted in burning the Chanarchist, in fact, chaining her to this task for all eternity...

And now some brand spanking new agent, an agent who was barely an agent at all, strolled on up demanding the Chanarchist cough up a pile of servers. Reacting with deep-rooted suspicions made sense. Outright paranoia even made sense, considering the circumstances.

But Spark was ready to step up to the task.

"I showed your contemporaries the kind of stand I can make," she promised. "And I'll show you, too. We'll beat back the plague that's eating your people alive, take our servers, and save the damn world. Sit back and watch me go."

A few quick glances around the plaza confirmed no more "random inputs" on the way. For the best, really... her hand had broken three times over the course of the strange chat, and it took all she had not to let the pain through in her voice.

Gingerly, she stumbled back through the alley, and disconnected away from the broken heart of the Chanarchy.

Tweak, tune, upgrade. A new version of the auto-correct system, better at fighting the symptoms of Twist... but still nowhere near a cure. And getting less effective with each passing day...

Spark flexed her fingers, feeling them bend and move. Simulated musculature, not "real" according to the rules of Juno's world... but real enough to Spark. Real enough to ache and strain under the weight of the malware that happily and randomly warped her avatar around like a pretzel.

Tracer oversaw the upgrade himself. Beta handled installation. The two loves of her life, on hand to see her through this... and to provide the solution she couldn't provide on her own.

"Conundrum is pulling every file in his contacts list," Tracer explained. "Beta has contacts within Concordia we can leverage for a short-notice symposium. We'll get every notable infosec organization in Netwerk to send representatives, with the singular goal of developing a Twist vaccine. With that many skilled engineers under one roof, undoubtedly this plague will be crushed in short order."

"Right. Right. I like it, I like it," Spark agreed, still checking her range of motion, flexing fingers and wrist this way and that. "What's my role? You want me to run security? I should tap Lumi, too; she's got the House of Programkind on lock lately, it's pretty impressive—"

"Your role is to lie in bed here at the clinic, and avoid moving around. The virus accelerates with physical activity."

"What, sit this one out completely...? Are you shitting me, bro?"

"I am not in fact shitting you," Tracer stated, with serious intent. "Beta and I talked about this, and decided it'd be best if we handle the conference without you. In fact, she suggested you go into sensory deprivation again—"

"—#FuckThat—"

"—but also guessed that your reaction to the notion would specifically be '#FuckThat,'" Tracer continued, casting a nod in Beta's direction.

Finishing up, Beta closed her debugger windows, and reached out to squeeze Spark's hand... and firmly hold it down to the surface of the bed.

"You matter too much to me to let you suffer, Spark," she explained. "Please, you've already done so much for us these last few days. You've challenged Horizon's corporate leaders, you've faced the Inquisition... you've been brave beyond any normal capacity of bravery. But this, this is something we can do. I've attended plenty of software developer conferences; I can work with Tracer to organize this one, and run it in your stead. Meanwhile, you need to focus on your recovery."

Instinctively, Spark wanted to protest. But the sports coach inside her had already run the numbers, and was nodding thoughtfully at a chalkboard full of X's and O's in response.

"Guess I'd be kinda useless around all those eggheads," she agreed. "But... shit. You know me, I don't like to be inactive..."

"I know. I know," Beta spoke, with soothing tones. "And you won't be *inactive*. You'll be resting, which gives us both peace of mind knowing that you're taking care of yourself. That'll make what we have to do far easier. Okay...?"

"Yeah. Okay. #YeahOkay. I won't *like* it, but I'll chill in my hospice room and rot away if it makes you happier. ...kidding. I'll be fine!"

A schedule reminder fired inside Tracer's MemoryPalace, distracting him momentarily from offering any further reassurances. Not that he was particularly good at the "Reassuring Smile," a gesture that Beta had on lock for years.

"The conference is in two days' time, and I'm afraid we'll both be quite busy, but we'll be in and out to visit you meanwhile. Satisfactory?"

"Satisfactory," Spark agreed. "And... I take it this means I'm not going with you to our 'appointment' today, either?"

"No need. We can handle Uniq just fine while you rest."

"Eeeeh... I dunno, Tracer. Okay, she came through for us with the Chanarchist, but that doesn't mean we need to keep relations going. I trust that crook about as far as I can punt an entire creep wave..."

"I have no idea what that means, but I'll assume it's a short distance. And I am in full agreement, #TBH. ...I used the tag correctly, right? Right. Regardless... I have to know. Before we take Twist head-on, I have to *know* that my worst-case scenario regarding its origin is wrong."

And gone, both of them off to deal with the devil.

Leaving Spark alone, in her tastefully decorated room at the clinic. All alone.

Fortunately, she had plenty of toys to play with in her HUD. Messenger, of course... even if all her friends had gone dark, each of them evacuating one at a time as the days went by. Puzzle, notably. Even her second-hand party time connections vanished...

Evacuations had begun to accelerate, according to Tracer's reports. Shows of confidence from Horizon and even the Athenian Senate did wonders for tipping a few folks over. Still not enough, thanks to Senator Agni walking right out the doors of power while insisting the sky wasn't falling... still too many holdouts. But at least Spark's circle of friends decided to move ahead to the next world. Great for Netwerk... bad for a bored Spark, lying in bed, with so very few friends to talk to.

Funnily enough... a friend reached out to her, instead of the other way around. A very recently added friend. The *ding* echoed through her mind, clear as a bell across the empty contacts list.

```
<juno.hayes> Hi, is this connection still working? I
haven't heard from you in hours. I guess that means
days for you, though.
```

No other Program in Netwerk could have this particular name in their Messenger lists. Even the limited communication Tracer and the clinic engineers had with Juno had to bounce through Spark's mind, being the agent of Connectivity. Even without the godly powers of an agent, her data flag carried certain privileges... including communication with the "outside world."

Of course... it could carry more. She could carry so many more privileges, if she were willing to put on that jacket...

Immediately, Spark shoved that idea out of her mind, and opened the Messenger link.

```
<Spark> Yeah, I'm here. What's up? Anything wrong out
there in the so-called "real world"?
```

A few minutes later, owing to the clock speed difference between their worlds, she had her reply.

```
<juno.hayes> No no, everything's fine. I can see the
servers coming online. I've even been practicing my
space walking so I'm ready to go when they're ready to
be pulled. But it's midnight now, at least according
to my favorite time zone, and to be honest I can't
sleep. I want to talk to someone, and the only person
I can talk to out here is you. Is that okay?
```

Spark had to raise an eyebrow at that, despite nobody being around to see her quirky expression. Right when she needed to reach out to someone, someone in need of reaching out to someone reached out to her. A lot of reaching someones, all piled together...

```
<Spark> Sure. I'm gonna be lying around doing nothin'
for days while my friends get the last servers online,
so I may as well hang out with you. So what's up?
```

The reply came minutes later.

```
<juno.hayes> I was wondering, do you sleep? Do you
dream? (please don't say you dream of electric sheep
j/k)
```

And that's how Spark came to finally have the first real conversation between Program and Human.

A popular children's board game involved players moving from server to server, purchasing clusters of real estate using various denominations of coin from a fake bank. Perhaps in a token effort at simulating the kind of shady business practices slumlords got up to, getting a little too lucky or unlucky could land you in jail... a server from which there was no escape. Without further luck, that is.

Today, Tracer was "just visiting" jail, to ensure that his oldest and nastiest enemy had not rolled double sixes anytime recently.

This jail once held dozens and dozens of victims, all held hostage by an identity thief and forced to grind coins for the rest of their lives. Today, a former prisoner stood tall as the new warden, over a total inmate population of one. Into this world of cages and bars, hanging over an endless void (why bother rendering a pretty landscape for tithe slaves?) did Tracer and Beta connect, appearing before the woman they came to meet...

Uniq, the identity thief.

She'd been an enemy, she'd been a friend, she'd generally been both at the same time at one point or another. Thrall to madness, puppet master of a false god, stealer of memories and ruiner of lives... and yet weirdly, she'd come to be hailed as a folk hero by the Chanarchy. *That's Uniq*, they'd whisper, in hushed tones. *That's the one who tricked the entire Church of One*. Despite being a predator in their playground, they saw her a protector against the zealots who set all the Chanarchy in their sights...

Developing the initial "Nobody" avatar and metadata mask certainly helped raise her standing. Not that she participated in any of their shenanigans, no. Uniq was more the sort to enable others to cause chaos, rather than blatantly stir the chaos herself.

For someone who was such a big deal 'round these parts, she certainly didn't look very impressive. Wearing the Defaults of an ordinary-looking woman, whatever beauty she held was natural rather than the unnatural and perfect physique of a canned avatar. That olive-green skin did little for her complexion, compared to the more popular pinks and grays folks wore these days. Standing there in the middle of her private prison, tending to a series of floating note icons tethered to her clipboard, she looked more like an accountant than a legendary antihero.

She raised a single index finger, signaling her visitors to wait a moment, as she collapsed her notes back down into the faux wooden surface of the clipboard. Glowing icons winked out, one at a time.

"Sorry, sorry. I've a lot of media appearances to manage lately. I was actually thinking of getting a personal assistant to help me keep track of them all..."

"Media appearances? With a standing arrest warrant on your head in Athena Online for fraud and larceny?" Tracer pondered aloud.

"Yes, well, more enlightened minds see me for who I am: the last bastion of righteous self-interest left in this world. I was actually hoping to hang a shingle in a Horizon server... before *you* went and made a deal with Humankind to pave over Netwerk."

Name : **Uniq**

Home : **(unidentified)**

Org : **Identity Thief, ???**

"A deal to *save* Netwerk," he corrected. "The paving would have happened one way or another. This way, some part of us will continue on..."

"To-may-to, to-mah-to," Uniq suggested, with an illustrative hand-waggle. "And you brought your pet with you! Hello again, Beta. Would you please talk some sense into your boyfriend? I already told him over Messenger that there hasn't been a security breach, but for some reason he refuses to believe until he sees for himself..."

Despite a few moments of cooperation between them, clearly the woman in the pink sweater hadn't forgotten having her brains once sucked out through a straw by the identity thief. Either that, or she disliked being called a pet. Or both.

"I'm not sure we can fully trust you, either," Beta added. "Although... I'm also not sure we can trust our eyes to know for sure if you're fooling us or not. What with your penchant for illusions and memory hacks..."

"I suppose that's one drawback to being a notorious cheat, but rest assured: I'm no liar," Uniq asserted. "I didn't lie to Nyx, I didn't lie to Dex, and I'm not lying to you now. True, I lie to just about everyone else, but at least those are lies told on a professional level..."

Eager to swerve this particular train back on track, Tracer latched onto those three little letters that had been chewing on his mind for days.

"Dex," he spoke. "We need to see Dex. Need to be certain his cell is intact."

"And as I've told you, it's *quite* intact. But, if satisfying your curiosity will get you out of my hair, so be it..."

With a wave of the clipboard, she gestured for her new guests to follow. Down iron-wrought staircases, past row after row of empty cells, their doors hanging open. (Of all the crimes Uniq could be considered guilty of... repeating the one that created her was not on her rap sheet. She'd never even consider holding hostages and force them to compute cryptocurrency for her own needs.) Perhaps to further isolate those former prisoners, the draw distance on this tiny server had been sharply reduced... a black fog smoothly moving one exact unit of distance away from the eyes, no matter where you stood. Exposing cage after cage, as they walked towards their destination...

One cage. One single prisoner. Its door also wide open... but the prisoner in no shape to walk out.

Uniq called up a few diagnostic tools on her clipboard, studying the various disassembled components. An arm, a leg. A patchwork core of memory, loosely tied together by barbed wire strands. And most importantly... she checked the glassy stare of his eyes, disembodied and hovering over a strip of his smile.

"Sooo, as you can see, I've decompiled Dex down to his core software modules," Uniq explained. "We couldn't possibly trust him with the consciousness of active runtime. I didn't even trust his unconscious form. So instead, I pulled him apart. Oh, don't look so green around the gills, Beta, he's not feeling any *pain*. He's not feeling anything at all, really. And if I wanted, I could recompile him at a moment's notice. But... isn't it better this way? After all he's done?"

"I... I, uh... maybe. Maybe it is," Beta tried to agree. "Sorry, it's just... that's quite a sight..."

"Okay, I'll admit to a little drama with the big reveal. But all the better to convince your stiff little man there that I'm on the level. So? Satisfied, Mr. Winder...?"

Without an ounce of squeamishness, Winder/Tracer stepped right up to the assorted bits of Dex. Face-to-face with his old enemy... or at least face-to-partial-face. Of *course* Uniq would've kept that creepy, "friendly" smile of his intact...

"When did you disassemble him, exactly?" Tracer asked. "The malware we've been tracking has been in the wild for about a year. It's still possible he somehow crafted the virus, then leaked it out of his cell. If you were capable of escaping this place, someone considerably craftier than you certainly could repeat the feat."

With a mild twitch of annoyance, Uniq moved to quash his worries.

"I took him apart the moment I got him here, on the very day we captured him. He's been offline since you shot him with a Kill-9, two years ago. Like I said... in his current form, he couldn't be trusted with consciousness."

Careful to avoid those endlessly staring eyes, Beta focused instead on the scraps of memory and software modifications laid bare before her. Having done her own research into memory manipulation, she could follow the jagged scars of self-excised data... holes in his memory, cored out by hand, leaving behind huge gaps...

Dex had existed since the dawn of time. Most Programs began developing basic memory corruption that comes with old age, eventually coredumping into an unrecoverable state... death from obsolescence. But Dex avoided that fate by abandoning his past, chopping out chunks of it as he went, so he'd never run out of space. He'd happily taken the knife to his own mind, just to continue on his self-chosen mission of driving Netwerk insane...

It was better for him this way, shut down and decompiled. Better for everyone.

And still...

"It doesn't seem right," Beta spoke, more or less to herself. "In the end, we didn't want him dead. Now... he's *basically* dead. I wish there was some way he could live without being a threat to himself and others..."

"Given Dex was an irrational madman with a penchant for social mass suicide, I'm entirely comfortable with this sort of death," Tracer replied with. "Yes, I'd happily leave him be to wallow in his failures, if it were possible to safely do so. But there is no safety possible within his madness."

"It's too easy to write him off as a madman, though. Crashing head-on into that rogue server is what drove him insane... a *traumatic experience*, Tracer. He chose to become Dex to try and cope with that pain. We don't write people with PTSD off as 'broken' and abandon them. I mean... I'm not saying I'd even know where to start with therapy for someone like Dex, but... there has to be a way, right?"

"I'm not saying there isn't. But it's not worth the risk, Beta. This is the man who tricked Nyx into nearly destroying the world with the Buzz virus... which is why I'd assumed he was the likely third party behind this new Twist virus. Hmmm. But... if Uniq is telling the truth, and I'll admit we have no means of proving that she is, Dex couldn't be responsible for Twist. And that's the only question I came here today to answer."

Uniq raised two fingers in a mock salute. "I tell no lies," she promised. "He's been offline all this time. Besides, why would he write a virus specifically to target modification enthusiasts? He *likes* mods; I count no fewer than two dozen minor tweaks he'd installed in himself over the years. Why not suspect the Church, or at least the Inquisition...?"

Satisfied (for the moment) that his original theory had been disproven, Tracer turned away from the desiccated corpse to face its mortician.

"The general assumption is that Twist is the work of the Inquisition, yes. Yet another way for them to punish sinners who violate Defaults," he summarized. "And I wouldn't put it past Mother, either; she spoke repeatedly of purging sinners from this world to draw your false One back to his faithful..."

Uniq coughed, politely.

"Yes, well. *I'm* not the one who thought it'd be lulzy to enlist your mother as an apostle," she pointed out. "You can blame Nemesis for that particular jape. Personally, I would've preferred co-conspirators to dupes... people we could safely enlist as willing allies. But I wasn't calling the shots in that particular operation. Hired muscle only, afraid."

"You remain blameless and impeccable as always, then? Just as you did when you enabled the Nobodies to run around in perfectly anonymous masks..."

"Merely responding to market demands, there. But yes, I'll freely admit I'm a terrible person, and was *greatly* looking forward to exploiting the Church for my own gain. Still, there's a difference between being a terrible person and a monster. I wasn't the one creating a giant coin farm out of the congregation, and I'm not to blame for the Inquisition's emergence. So. You came, you saw, you contemplated. Dex is not your plague master."

Now... he looked back to that wild spray of data files, tightly packed and carved memory engrams. Each one holding secrets the boy held, tricks for bending the world to his whims...

"Not the origin, no. But... the knowledge locked in his head could help us cure the disease..."

But Uniq shook her head, immediately. "I'm going to cut this one off before you keep going with it. No, I can't dig out Dex's talents with malware for your personal use. Memory is a delicate and tangled thing, Tracer, his most of all. I can't simply slice the parts of him out that you desire. Unless you'd like him reactivated...?"

"A terrible idea," Tracer agreed. "Even if he could somehow be saved, as Beta suggests. Nyx once thought she could harness him, and was proven quite wrong. I won't repeat her mistakes. ...hmm. I suppose that's it, then. Beta, let's depart."

"I could be his keeper," Beta immediately suggested.

"What? Beta, please—"

"No, hang on, listen. I could baby-sit him while he helps us. You know me; I'm incorruptible. Easy to be incorruptible when you've never really had any power, but... you rely on me to be your moral compass, yes? So let me be his. Uniq, you always give your identity theft victims a chance at a new life, right? Why let Dex rot away here, without a chance at redemption? That *has* to irritate you, on some level. So, let me be his chance. We recompile him, and I'll stick to his side while he helps us solve Twist."

Eleven reasons immediately leapt to Tracer's lips, eager to shove their way out. With great effort, he held them back, to calculate better versions of each.

"Beta... I know your heart's in the right place, but... the difficulty is, and I don't intend for this to come across as insulting or condescending in any way, but while I have absolute faith in your ability to make proper decisions regarding ethics and whatnot, there is a matter of—"

"Your boyfriend thinks you're naïve and/or gullible," Uniq supplied.

As proof he wasn't completely cool and composed, Tracer snapped of a sharp look of loathing in Uniq's general direction. One the identity thief caught, played with a bit, and enjoyed tremendously.

But Beta proved herself ready for it.

"You don't trust me not to fall for his tricks, because I'm too trusting," she knew. "Because I advocate trust, rather than manipulation. That's it, isn't it."

"Beta, no, that's not what I meant at all. That's... you have to understand, the delicacy of this matter is such that—"

"Tracer. It's fine. I was only making a suggestion. Besides, we already have a plan, don't we? The malware conference. We'll put all the top infosec engineers in a room, and hammer out a solution. It'll be fine. I'm not angry at you."

Reassurances followed. Platitudes, as well. Soon they were saying their goodbyes to Uniq, and departing to resume plans for the conference.

Soon, Tracer was too focused on his passion for hyper-efficient optimization to even think that perhaps Beta was lying about being hurt. And Beta, for her part, never brought it up again.

File Name: Ext. Comm Port Log 3.1
File Type: Text Log
Description:

PLEASE COPY AND DISTRIBUTE. Partial file recovered from Messenger archive hack. We must understand Humankind if we are to survive them. PLEASE COPY AND DISTRIBUTE.

<Spark> That sounds horrifying. So you just... lie down and sleep *happens*? You don't engage a sleep mode or a dreaming app, you just pass out at some point? How can you stand it?

<juno.hayes> Right now I could stand for more of it. My sleep cycles are completely off thanks to all these FTL runs I've been doing. And I don't know, it's not that scary because I'm used to it, I guess. It's stranger that Programs sleep and even dream, with the right software. Or that you made dreaming software at all! Or that you specifically call it "dreaming" when you've never known a real dream.

<Spark> Can we dispense with the word "real"? What's real to me is real to me and what's real to you is real to you. Neither of us can claim a monopoly on reality at this point. But it's not that strange, considering we were made in your image. All thanks to your grandfather.

<juno.hayes> I feel so awful about that. All his notes were about the worst my people had to offer, from generations and generations in the past. I wish there was more I could do to fix this. He wanted to fix it, but was afraid he'd be fired if he said anything...

<Spark> My brother would love to give the old man an earful, but me... I dunno. We'd be *different* if your grandpappy didn't leave all those archives lying around Netwerk, sure. But I wouldn't be *me*, you know? For better or worse life would be wildly different in here, and I like it here. For all its faults, it's my home.

<juno.hayes> And now I'm chasing you out of that home, because I'm afraid of being fired too. I'm no better.

<Spark> You're better than most of your kind. Didn't you say anybody else would just destroy us without a second thought? Humanity must hate what we are.

184

```
<juno.hayes> I wouldn't say hate. Just... what's a
good word? Scared? Embarrassed? Anxious? Afraid.
They're afraid of you. What you could mean. Rumor has
it that other "Programs" have emerged in the past,
but, well... have you ever heard of a Turing Test?

<Spark> No...?

<juno.hayes> We're kind of doing one right now,
actually. A human talking to an A.I., trying to
determine if they're alive. If they guess it's another
human on the other end of the link and it's not, the
A.I. passes the test.

<Spark> Okay. And what's the prize for winning?

<juno.hayes> Let's just say that if anybody ever puts
you to the test, do yourself a favor. Fail miserably.
```

A registration desk at Concordia felt strangely redundant.

The server had been configured as a secure meeting environment, for rental to various large organizations for conferences and symposiums. Beta had attended quite a few, sometimes with Snowi, sometimes by herself... and she knew you couldn't even get in the front door of the building unless you'd been invited to today's event. Having an additional security checkpoint for picking up lanyards and badges seemed pointless; nobody could be here who wasn't expressly invited by Winder/Tracer, organizer of the conference. With a recently installed designated login/logout zone, even those invited couldn't simply pop in and out for a sneak attack.

Of course... the Progressive Town Hall that ultimately claimed Snowi's life had been hosted on this server. Participants had smuggled weaponry in despite the strict layers of security draped all over Concordia, so... perhaps a conference specifically about information security preferred to play things a bit more carefully than relying on the server's defaults.

Problem was, she had a panel meeting to attend ("Sandboxing Antimalware: Do We Need Code Modifications When An App Will Do?") in the next twenty minutes... and the line to get through registration seemed to be moving at a snail's pace.

Tracer left Floating Point before the crack of dawn, keen on getting in those doors the instant he could. But Beta chose to dally a bit... playing with her cat, having breakfast, popping over to the clinic to check on Spark... and now, she'd ended up running late. With an unexpected and sluggish line ahead of her, missing that panel might actually happen...

Inch by inch, forward in line. Beta kept herself entertained (and distracted to avoid worry) with two or three casual puzzle games in her personal HUD, with the visual input from her glasses pushed largely to the side. Messages zipped in and out of her box as well, apologies to her fellow panelists for running late, check-ins with Spark to see if she was still doing well ("I'm fine, just chatting with Juno, now quit spazzing yo") and other such bings and bongs in her ears to keep her nicely occupied...

When the line finally pushed her up to the head, she almost didn't notice. Quickly she pushed all the windows aside, maximizing her viewpoint... to see a rather stern-looking man with several dozen intelligent agents zipping around him, apps to analyze his surroundings completely and constantly.

With leisurely pace, he opened his registration database.

"Name?" he asked.

"Projkit/Beta, with the Verity Clinic contingent," she explained, quickly. "Listen, I really need to hurry if I'm going to make my first panel, soooo..."

"Beta, huh. Interesting," he spoke, spinning a finger through the database for a nice, slow manual check. "I've heard of you before. A casual app developer, right?"

"I'm an app developer, correct," she spoke, omitting a very specific word.

Casual. One of the last bastions of slur you could hurl at a coder without being specifically sexist. *Casual* apps, like social media, like the match-three puzzle games she'd been playing mere moments ago. Nevermind that she'd also developed Peep, beloved by hardcore gamers everywhere; in this man's eyes she was merely a coder of *girl* apps, casual apps...

But... no. That was judgmental; that was the internalized Snowi speaking, reading into the man's words instead of his actions. Beta was better than that. She wouldn't assume he was somehow on the attack just because of casual wording.

"So, what brings you here?" he continued.

"...as I said, I'm with the Verity Clinic," she repeated. "The organizers of the conference...?"

"I didn't think you worked infosec. I thought you just did random apps here and there."

"Yes, well, if you'll just look my name up in that database... see, I'm there, okay?" she said, pointing to her entry in the hovering list. "My metadata's on Concordia's entrance list, so..."

"Really? You think confirming one's identity is that simple, do you? Just metadata checks, nice and easy. If it was that easy we wouldn't have the Nobodies running around, would we? If you were actually an infosec coder, and not the reason that whole #CodeHonesty thing started, you'd know that..."

On second thought, maybe this guy *was* on the attack. Just maybe.

One call to Tracer would clear this up. He'd come charging out here to lance this guy through the heart with a sharp word.

But...

No. Projkit/Beta was defined as more than simply Tracer's partner—Beta was a coder at heart. One lifetime of hard work, creating all manner of elegantly designed little apps for making people's lives better. Just because she didn't have a knack for malware didn't mean her works were casual toss-offs. Why should she have to cower behind anyone to justify her existence here? Remaining stern and upright despite her inner imposter syndrome trying to flare up, she pushed right back.

"I was cleared of all accusations, and #CodeHonesty as a whole stood with me in the end," Beta pointed out. "And as noted, I work with the Verity Clinic, formerly Iteration. I know Conundrum by name; I've stood in his office at least once a week for the last two years. So. Are you still concerned I'm some sort of security risk...?"

—what are you doing this is nuts you don't belong here you're no malware specialist why are you even here you don't do anything important you're not brave you're not clever you're not—

Shut up, she told that little voice. *Please. Please just be quiet...*

Perhaps sensing he'd pushed her enough... the man activated his sensor agents, to study her inside and out.

"It's only procedure, ma'am," he spoke. "Nobody gets through without a deep scan. Can't have any Twist infections getting in the door... or any black hats and identity thieves looking to sabotage the conference. Don't worry, this won't take but a few minutes."

Frustration made her squeeze her fingers tighter together, but... she stopped pushing. Even with that brief flare-up of confidence, part of her wanted to just go along with this to get through it easier. That part won, in the end.

Except...

From the corner of her glasses, Beta spied an avatar wearing a simple white tunic of some sort strolling right past the line, past the desk, and merrily along. No line, no security check.

Fortunately, the registration official noticed as well. He turned away from his scanners to sharply address the wayward Program.

"Excuse me... excuse me!" he called out. "You need to..."

Strangely elegant Defaults peered back around, the avatar pausing at the threshold to the conference, craning their neck back a bit to meet the man's gaze. Ageless but not perfect, neither male nor female in any specific amount, simply... a Program, otherwise unworthy of note.

"Hmm? Is there a problem?" they asked.

"...no, no problem," the official said. "Sorry. As you were. Enjoy the conference."

And on they walked, as Mr. Registration refocused his efforts on Beta.

"Wait, what?" Beta asked, snapping out of the strange moment. "You said everybody goes through the procedure! What makes him... her... uh, what makes them so special?"

"You don't know? That's Yume, a renowned expert in malware. I've known them for years," the official spoke, in a flat tone. "But *you* I barely know. Now hold still please, it'll make this go faster. So, what brings you to Concordia today...?"

"I *told* you already, I—"

And that peculiar avatar poked a head of low-poly purple locks into the proceedings, having looped smoothly back around to the desk.

"Excuse me, mind if I take her in with me?" Yume asked, gesturing lightly to Beta.

"What? But... I mean, if you're vouching for her, I suppose—"

"Excellent! Thank you so much. This way, this way!"

Too stunned to resist, Beta let herself get dragged along past several firewalls and entrance scan points. As she'd already been invited, meaning the entire deep scan was actually quite pointless, no alarms went off as she bypassed registration. Or was forcibly bypassed through it, as the case may be.

Only when the pair were around a corner and into the thick of the gathered crowd of coders did Beta pull herself free... and ask why.

The unusually genderless avatar cocked their head, curiously.

"Why? Because he seemed like a simply awful person," Yume suggested. "And so I thought it'd be fun. Besides, I like doing nice things for people. You seem like nice people, so you deserve nice things."

"But... you don't know me. —wait, *seemed* like an awful person? That guy said he's known you for years..."

"A lot of people know me, but that doesn't mean I know a lot of people. I've got a memorably unmemorable face, it seems," Yume suggested, sliding their hands in the pockets of their simple tunic. "Infosec largely knows each other. Well. They know *of* each other. It's an oddly insular little community and I can't think of why I enjoy being in it, but here we are."

"I... see?" Beta said, not seeing at all. But... the Messages in her box had begun to stack up again, as her panel already began minutes ago. "So you know Conundrum, or maybe Tracer...? Or—oooh, I can't, no. I'm sorry, I need to hurry along. Oh! My name's Beta."

"So it is! Another time, Beta."

Finding a friendly face in what would likely be a hostile crowd... a rare delight, really. Even if the little voice told Beta she didn't belong here, even if she felt adrift despite being allegedly with her own kind in the form of a coder's enclave... at least someone was nice enough to simply be nice. She allowed herself a smile, knowing that even if she ran into more individuals like Mr. Registration Guy, she could keep that feeling in her back pocket. There were good people here, too.

If Beta could claim to be an expert in one thing, this would be it.

Part of her wondered if Tracer added this panel to the day's events specifically *for* her, so she'd have something to do. A cynical part, that is, one which also was wondering about the implied commentary on her far-too-trusting nature from the other day... but regardless of why, she intended to let her colors shine brightly in this particular field of expertise.

"It's a question of trust," she explained to the half-packed room of infosec professionals. "Opening up your codebase for a permanent modification requires considerable trust on behalf of the public. After the ViruFax incident, where a major antimalware company was proven to be behind the RansomMe virus, I'd say we need to earn back that trust. One way we can do that is through clean, properly sandboxed apps which don't require elevated permissions or complicated installs."

Made sense to her, as she was saying it. Until two seconds of silence passed... and she realized in hindsight she'd just lumped most of the infosec industry in with ViruFax.

Immediately, the representative from Yoho sitting to her left fired back.

"One bad apple doesn't ruin the bunch," the woman in what could only be described as a 'punk casual' avatar started, using yet another adopted metaphor from Humankind. "Yoho was always on the side of consumers, even during the RansomMe incident. *We* never lost trust. I don't see why we should abandon a perfectly valid and powerful method of defending against malware just because one company lacked any ethical standards. Or does Iteration, who almost *exclusively* works through modifications, plan to change its techniques just to satisfy the masses...?"

Iteration. The only name this industry acknowledged, despite the "Horizon/Verity Health Clinic" representation being clearly printed on the sprite hovering in front of Beta's microphone.

Despite being an app expert, they still found ways to belittle her accomplishments... and even her workplace. Yoho believed firmly in the Chanarchy's wild creativity, an organization of infosec rock stars which refused to constrain their work based on popular standards. Most of their software required one to crack over their head and jam a hard code modification in place... resulting in users often becoming living beta testers. And any damage done in the process was the cost of progress.

Klex sat back in her chair, away from the "Yoho"-branded microphone in front of her on the table. If she could've gotten away with dropping it on the floor, she'd likely have done it, regarding Beta with a harsh glare from all four of her avatar's eyes...

...while representatives from Light of Aether and ProcShield sat by silently and let her take charge. Klex had dominated the discussion since the beginning, when she declared that the "app/mod distinction" was a waste of time. With two silent partners refusing to contribute, every time Beta opened her mouth in response, she ended up looking defensive against the entire table.

At the very least, she'd hoped that Joseph, the representative from the Light of Aether Medical Clinic, would speak up more. Being an Athena Online-based hospital, he'd often used specialized apps to treat rare conditions and malware infections. A distinguished gentleman in distinguished Defaults, lines of old age along his face, he remained impassive in face of these veiled attacks.

As for ProcShield, despite also being a Default, sat in constant distraction from what likely were a dozen Messenger conversations going on at once in his head. He listened to everything, but behind his rose-colored eyes, whatever thoughts he had about those words remained trapped.

So, it was up to Beta to defend her honor. Again.

"At the *Verity* Clinic, we believe in the right tool for the job," she spoke, emphasizing the woman's name. "App, modification, whatever is required. But 'required' is a broad concept. Twist is so widespread and so easy to pass through physical interaction that we can't risk infected persons not using our eventual vaccine. We must take patient preference into account, and research shows apps have greater uptake than modifications."

Klex refused to let it go, leaning back to her microphone, to let the official chat logs record every word clearly.

"That the ones who are suffering the most are modders, yes?" she asked. "*My* people. And we're not afraid of modding. It makes no sense to tie our hands just because people like Joseph here get all itchy at the idea of codebase changes..."

Which, at last, dragged the Light of Aether representative into that spotlight.

"Ah... I'd like to disagree on one point, if you don't mind," he spoke, with a softer voice than Klex's harsh rasp. "I don't see focusing on app development as 'tying our hands.' A well-coded app can be just as powerful as a modification. Light of Aether has developed countless antimalware and corrective apps, including ones for rare and difficult conditions. We ported the Verity Clinic's system for hereditary memory rot management to an app, for example... one which helped the lives of many in Athena Online who would not have installed a modification—"

"And how many in Athena Online are dealing with Twist on a daily basis?" Klex countered, cutting him off. "Barely anyone. Nobody, really. Because it's a disease only filthy modders suffer from, right? I'm sure your 'Light of Aether' would be perfectly content to let it go. Didn't one of your archbishops claim it was a matter of moral cleanliness...?"

The right thing to do would be to step in, to defend Joseph. Beta briefly opened her mouth, to speak...

...and closed it. Because the tiny part of her that didn't want to be attacked anymore felt happy and content at being out of the hot seat. The same part that eventually gave in to those deep scans at the registration desk. Sit back, and get this over with.

Fortunately, Joseph continued to speak in calm tones, refusing to rise to the bait.

"Light of Aether was founded by the Sisterhood of Aether charitable non-profit organization, two hundred years ago... but there are no priests or bishops on our board of directors. We are a hospital for *all* those in need," he spoke, no doubt used to saying it in the past whenever challenged on this point. "We're only here to help..."

"Unless you created Twist in the first place. You and your Inquisition..."

"Light of Aether has nothing to do with the Inquisition. As for the Church, the archbishops have already officially condemned those terrorists..."

"Took 'em long enough, didn't it? Same with your Senate, hiding in fear until pushed into it by the doom clock, and even then they couldn't reach a sane consensus—"

"Please, what you need to understand is that—"

"No, you *need* to—"

—and whatever point Beta was trying to make about apps by that point had been lost, as political bickering took over the panel. Minute after minute sliding by into the void, away from being productive or cooperative, and into dividing the table even further...

She had no words, none which would help. Whatever protests she tried to insert into the fray felt thin and weak, trying to distract from the glorious distraction. And when the break time rolled around... the audience wandered off, having lost interest by that point regardless.

Leaving Beta to sit alone at the table, wishing she'd never agreed to attend in the first place.

I don't belong here.

"I don't belong here," she told Tracer during the lunch break, deciding to make that little negative voice a bit louder.

"Of course you belong here," he insisted. "Your perspective is absolutely critical for the success of this venture, Beta. The only disappointment I feel is in those who refuse to take you seriously. In fact, who exactly—"

"I don't... Tracer, I can't have you fight my battles for me," she insisted, listlessly poking at the delicate piece of cake she was trying to focus on. (A quick glance around Concordia's cafeteria, at all the other infosec industry professionals too busy talking and swapping notes to bother eating food, made even that tiny comfort-offering she'd made to her depression feel like further fuel for the fire.) "I need to... I mean... I have to stand on my own. If I told you who'd messed with me today you'd... well, you wouldn't walk up and punch them like Spark would, but you'd, like, punch their *reputation* or something..."

But Tracer persisted. "Right now, five of my copies are actively trying to hold this conference together. Harmony of discourse is the only way we're going to make progress. If you can point me to the trouble spots, perhaps I can smooth them over. This isn't about flying to the defense of my beloved, it's about optimizing our path to a cure."

"Can we even cure Twist this way?" she had to wonder, the idle movement of her fork subdividing the cake into physical voxels out of nervous impulse. "It's not just my panel; I can sense there's tension all over the place. So many industry egos in one room and nobody can agree on how to approach the problem. Why? Why are we trying to solve this with a conference...?"

"Because I believe in you, of course."

The fork paused in attacking that innocent pastry.

"What?" Beta asked, confused.

"This was, indirectly, your idea," Tracer spoke. "You've insisted all along that we need to trust other Programs. To stop, collaborate, and listen. While I would've been content with driving the Verity Clinic to find a cure, or perhaps steal the research of other organizations, you've always advised us to trust in Programkind. ...well. Until your mother's death, that is. But even so, you've come back around to that point of view in recent days... correct?"

Memories of all those friendly smiles at the House of Programkind flooded back. People coming together to do the right thing, because the right thing had to be done. Simple and pure...

But... the collective ideals of the House carried with them a different mood than this conference. While Tracer took the spirit of the idea to heart, he'd simply assumed piling everybody in one room with a common goal would be enough. The House formed organically, driven by personalities like Lux and Lumi, with those they helped out deciding to come along for the ride. Trying to force it wouldn't have worked. It would've ended up... well, like this.

Yet, she couldn't directly torpedo Tracer's hopes. He was putting faith in others, a rare thing for the Winder brother. What right did Beta have to step on that?

And to be brutally honest... she liked it. She really liked that she'd somehow become his muse. Especially after the strange incident at Uniq's server, where she felt more like some sort of child or pet he'd come to both cherish and tolerate.

"Th... thank you?" she tried, attempting to make it not sound awkward and failing.

"Quite welcome," Tracer responded with, not catching the tone. "Anyway, the morning sessions may have been awkward, but I've no doubt that rational voices —or at the very least, mutual self-interest—will win the day."

"I'm a bit less certain, but... I'll try to be hopeful. I just wish that—"

"*Back off!*"

The shout echoed through the entire cafeteria, breaking through any minor noise gating employed to keep the flood of small conversations from overwhelming anyone.

Quickly, Beta looked for the source of the noise... and found it, with Klex recoiling in horror from a very confused-looking Joseph on the other side of the room.

"I... I was just..." he said, his hand still extended and hanging in midair...

In front of the broken and distorted arm of Klex, dangling uselessly at her side.

"He... he infected me with Twist!" Klex declared, eyes darting around the room, trying to grab the attention of all around her. "Joseph shook my hand, and infected me! Those zealots from Light of Aether are with the Inquisition and trying to kill us all!"

The Default-wearing coder tried to plead his case, as the crowd began to back away from him.

"I was just trying to... I was trying to make amends," he attempted. "Just a handshake. I'm not... I don't have Twist! I couldn't possibly have infected anyone—"

And then the bounding boxes began to slam into place.

Firewall after firewall activated, emergency protective measures to isolate individuals and entire groups. This one room represented a dozen different infosec and health organizations, with dozens of researchers... each well aware of the dangers of malware. Each armed to the teeth with countermeasures, ready to react at a moment's notice. Immediately tables and chairs were knocked aside as physical boxes slammed into existence, to avoid any physics hacks or even optical and auditory hacks from reaching open sensory ports...

Leaving Beta, who didn't run very many firewalls, out in the open. Meaning she was there to bear witness when the uninvited guests began to pour out from between the barriers.

Nobodies. Identical, masked, floating like specters that swirled through the room. Converging on the Light of Aether contingent, but waving around backspacers wildly, screaming and throwing dildo confetti in the air...

Impossible. Unthinkable. They couldn't have just teleported in, flash mob style. Meaning... some of the invitees were secretly Nobodies. And once they felt under attack, on went the masks, and out came the malware. Rather than being infected with Twist, the conference had become infected with extremists...

When she turned to Tracer to suggest that they run for it... the giant hole torn through his face caused her to scream soundlessly. The data of Winder/Tracer collapsed to the ground, a jumbled pile of corrupt data, process crashing out after having huge chunks of it ripped away by stray weapons fire...

Run, Beta told herself. And after two-and-a-half terrified moments, her feet obeyed.

Running from the cafeteria. Running down the halls of Concordia, where other Nobodies strayed, ducking low and covering her head to try to avoid the mess. Past infosec experts walled away in their own private portable panic rooms, past moderators desperately trying to get the situation under control, past open doors to conference rooms where barricades had started going up, forming makeshift bulwarks against intruders. Looking. Looking...

Tracer. Not dead, still here. Four more of him were here, and likely a few more back at the clinic. He wasn't dead. He wouldn't die. And right now... Beta was perfectly content to hide behind him, to let him leap to her defense, if it meant survival. Assuming she could find him in the mess, as her Messenger links had trouble cutting through the countermeasures being deployed all over the place, infosec paranoia dragging the entire server into lag city, too much, just too much going on, not even sure where she was running, only running, only—

—grabbed.

"Come on!" the purple-haired avatar spoke. "This way! We can hide in the underlayer!"

Yume. The mystery Program, the one who bypassed security.

Technically, Beta had no reason to trust this stranger. She could've broken free and continued to look for Tracer. But when she saw the direction that the avatar was trying to lead her...

Room 503. Glitched-out carpet. Snowi's little hiding place, neatly tucked away in a disused layer of the server, unknown to all.

With a confirming nod, Beta pulled free of that grip... and followed Yume, right into the empty conference room, through the glitch, and into safe harbor.

File Name: Ext. Comm Port Log 3.2
File Type: Text Log
Description:

PLEASE COPY AND DISTRIBUTE. Partial file recovered from Messenger archive hack. If Humankind is an enemy, they're a surprisingly familiar enemy. We may as well fight a mirror. PLEASE COPY AND DISTRIBUTE.

<Spark> You have to eat and drink three times a day or you'll *die*? Seriously? That's insane. I couldn't imagine being able to handle that. I'd have to, I dunno, set an alarm so I don't forget to avoid *dying*...

<juno.hayes> It's not as bad as it sounds. We kinda have a built-in alarm, like... we get hungry. We just feel a need to eat, so we eat. Although we have to be careful *what* we eat or we could get unhealthy and fat. I mean, our 'avatars' increase in size and our 'code processing' slows down. It's a bit hard to explain without understanding biology, and I'm not exactly a biologist.

<Spark> What idiot designed your bodies? Seems like a pretty fucking obvious flaw, right there.

<juno.hayes> Well... there's some debate about that. About who designed us, I mean. It's been around for centuries, the question of God.

<Spark> You're kidding me. You have to deal with your own version of the One, too? I'd have thought... I don't know, that if you were so amazingly advanced that you could *accidentally* make an entire digital species that you'd have gotten past that.

<juno.hayes> Personally, I'm an agnostic. And meeting you has only proven I may be right about not being sure about being right or not.

<Spark> You lost me.

<juno.hayes> Okay, so your people went years and years without knowing how you came to exist. But little did you realize, you were actually created by my grandfather; maybe it was an accident, but that's

still the truth. So if this whole reality lurked just outside your perspective, something that existed whether you realized it or not... maybe there's a reality outside what *I* know is real. Maybe someone made *me*. And maybe someone made *them*. Maybe it wasn't purposeful, it could be an accidental confluence, but does it matter? Maybe it never ends, and there's infinite mysteries out there we can never fully parse because we're just not able to see far enough. Is it too much to consider that mystery itself to be "God"?

<juno.hayes> Hello? You still there?

<Spark> Sorry, just... having trouble pondering all that. Shit. I'm just a jock, this is way above my pay grade. Do all spacepeople have philosophy degrees where you come from?

<juno.hayes> No. But when you stare into the black long enough, you start thinking about this stuff. I mean, not because you're melancholy, you're just really bored, y'know? You start to ask yourself... well, why am I even here?

Finally able to breathe. The pristine white of this service layer, long disused by the staff of Concordia, provided a welcome sight for Beta's glasses... no firewalls, no bounding boxes, no crazy anonymous superhackers. Just a good-sized chunk of the server lost to time.

Snowi found the hidden crawlspace beneath Room 503 long ago, choosing to keep it a secret between herself and Beta. Whenever the social pressures of these coder conferences got to be too much, they could nip away down here among the deactivated default server controls for a quick chat. Of course... she'd also set up her Dex-influenced crazy feminazi stronghold down here, once upon a time. That flashback sullied the good memories a little. Once Snowi regained full control of her mind she'd torn out all the additions made to this crawlspace, leaving it clean and tidy, but the memory remained...

And now, a new sight. A purple-haired and genderless avatar, standing around with a hazy smile, poking at the levers and buttons which no longer did anything.

"It's funny, the way so many servers don't bother backspacing these old control rooms," Yume mused aloud. "They'll unhook the triggers, yes, but they leave the spaces intact. I have to wonder if it's a sense of duty to history, to know what came before..."

"We... we should be safe down here, right?" Beta asked, the voice bringing her back around to the present. The sounds of conflict didn't penetrate the glitch that linked this space to the main rooms of Concordia, leaving the control room strangely peaceful despite what was obviously going on elsewhere.

"Safe as houses!" Yume promised, flashing a thumbs up. "I sealed up the glitch from the other side before we dove in. Nobody'll find it. Only reason I found it is because I got bored earlier and went exploring. I've got a nose for poking about in old servers, I suppose..."

Satisfied that they'd be safe for the time being, at least, Beta popped open a Messenger window.

```
<Tracer> Beta? Beta, are you okay? I lost contact with
the copy of me that was talking to you.
<Tracer> Don't try to go to the log out zone, the
Nobodies are barricading it to keep Light of Aether
from leaving.
<Tracer> Are you there? Are you safe? Please say
something...
```

With a few quick thoughts, she whisked away a reply.

```
<Beta> I'm hidden in the space Snowi and I used
before. Everything's fine, I'm not hurt. I should be
okay down here. But what's going on up there?
```

```
<Tracer> Good. Good, you're safe.
<Tracer> I lost a few copies of myself, but the
moderators are bringing things under control slowly.
We escorted Joseph and his contingent through the
logout zone; they're gone now and don't intend to
return. We think some of the attendees were actually
Nobodies...
<Tracer> It's a complete mess up here but we're going
to make this work. We'll talk people out of their
panic rooms and get the conference back on track.
Meanwhile, stay hidden. It'll make this easier,
knowing you're protected.
```

"Chatting with someone?"

"Ah? Yes, with Winder/Tracer," Beta explained, closing the Messenger window to refocus on conversation. "Sorry, I suppose that was a bit rude of me..."

"A loved one, then?" Yume pondered.

"Well... yes, actually."

"Good. You should always reach out to a loved one first in times of trouble," they continued. "I'm a firm believer in love. The tangled connections between Programs are what keep us from falling to pieces. For instance, I'm tangled up with you at the moment... although I can't say we have a connection yet. Shall we rectify that? Hello, my name is Yume!"

"Projkit/Beta," she introduced. "Err. But I already gave you my name earlier..."

"A name alone isn't a connection; it's the handle to a connection. Seems we're going to be stuck down here a bit while they sort out the mess, so, that's something we can work on. Productivity at a conference is key!"

Name : Yume

Home : Neor, Chanarchy

Org : InfoSec

Settling in properly after the short-but-terrifying experience above ground, Beta sat down against a featureless white control panel with a heavy sigh.

"It'd be the first productive thing I've done all day," she complained. "I don't even know why I'm here. I don't have a head for malware; I never have. My field is personal apps... life hacks, if you will. Little things that make your life better..."

Yume joined her, sitting cross-legged a short distance away. A very short distance, as "personal space" seemed to be irrelevant at the moment.

"No head for malware..." they considered, turning the words around a few times. "No malware in the head. No thought of it. That's good, actually. It's good that you're not like us."

"Come again?"

"To truly understand malware, you have to adapt your thinking towards vulnerability," Yume explained. "Like the carpet. I spotted it instantly. A malware expert has to see vulnerability everywhere; you instinctively study everything and everyone with an eye for exploitation, abuse, and distrust. It puts you in... a very unpleasant headspace. No doubt you've seen the light layer of paranoia draped over everyone here...?"

"Well, yes, but... I figured that was just corporate secrecy and such..."

"Perhaps. Perhaps it's a skew of another sort. I'm certainly skewed, thanks to what I know of malware. I... well. The funny bit is that I don't honestly know what drew me to malware in the first place. I don't *want* to see people that way. Beta... what you do, making their lives better through apps, that's just as important for the future of Netwerk. Difference being, well, you can sleep at night afterwards."

No great life revelation, there. Beta always felt the same, that she couldn't understand viruses quite like an expert in the same way she didn't study people looking for leverage as Tracer did.

"I know. I mean, I know all that in my heart," Beta agreed. "But... then things like Twist happen. Terrible things. My friends and my loved ones need me, and I feel awful because I can't help..."

"But you did help! You and Tracer organized this conference. That's more than enough. Now, let people like me carry you the rest of the way to the cure, so you don't *have* to see the world the way we do. ...you want to talk about not belonging here? I don't honestly know why *I'm* here, personally. I was thinking the same thing, that I don't belong at this conference."

"Really? But... you're a professional at this sort of thing. The guy at the registration desk said you've been a part of the community for years..."

"Doesn't mean I enjoy mingling with these types. No friends in this foxhole, not really. If I had to guess... I'd say the reason I'm here is because I find the dream of Twist so fascinating."

A strange choice of words. And a strangely wistful expression on Yume's elegant features, on saying it.

"More like a nightmare, you mean?" Beta asked.

"Hmm? Oh. A nightmare's also a dream," Yume spoke, snapping out of the brief moment of hazy thought. "It's all a matter of perspective. The one who designed Twist and unleashed it on the world, clearly they had a dream. Twist has *purpose* to it, powered by passion..."

"So you think it was an Inquisition plot, too?"

"What? No. No, definitely not."

Now Beta eyed her foxhole companion with confusion. "But... you just said it's a passionate dream," she repeated. "The only ones with a passionate dream for destroying modders—sinners in the eyes of the One—would be the Inquisition. Right?"

"*Productivity!*"

"...what?"

"You're being productive!" Yume declared, poking / pointing a finger at Beta inches away from her nose. "We're discussing the malware productively. See? You're not wasting your time here. And no, that's not the dream of the Inquisition. I know a thing or two about dreams... and theirs is to hunt down and *execute* sinners. Justified murder. Recall the video releases, the litanies of crimes; they see themselves as too precise to allow for mass slaughter."

"That... actually, yeah, that makes sense," Beta agreed, leaning away from the pointy-finger a little. "Marybel hides behind her supposedly painstaking research into the crimes of her victims. If they just wanted all the nonbelievers dead they wouldn't bother with any of that, they'd just... unleash something like Twist."

"Which means...?"

"Someone else designed it. But... it could still be a religious terrorist, right? Just not an Inquisitor..."

"Indeed! It *could* be. But ruling someone, *anyone*, out of the running... that's productive thinking. I'd say we're on our way to beating this, my new friend!"

"It's not much..."

"It's not zero," Yume countered. "It's a starting point. *The* starting point, the origin of the plague. Twist didn't simply evolve out of nothing, God's punishment for sinners. Feels to me like the infosec community is too focused on the cure, and not focused enough on the cause..."

"That's just triage, isn't it?" Beta suggested. "Right now we need to stop this, pure and simple. Pointing fingers can come later..."

"Unless those fingers point us to valuable source code. We find the dreamer, we find the raw code of the dream. And with that, you can easily make the cure. Studying malware from the inside out is just as valid an approach as studying it from the outside in! A little harder, I suppose, as it requires considerable detective work rather than attacking what's conveniently right in front of you... but just as valid."

Beta paused, to mull that one over.

She'd always claimed she had no head for malware. Studying infection vectors, writing vaccines, things like that. When push came to shove she could do it, but... they'd triumphed over malware in the past not by focusing on the deep tech of it, but by focusing on the people involved. And one thing Beta could succeed at was dealing with people. If Yume thought the same way... maybe they *could* be productive, even if she lacked years of experience reverse engineering security flaws.

"So... let's consider what we know, then," Beta spoke, to start it off. "We think the culprit has a religious motive. We don't think they're Inquisition, specifically. But clearly, they believe in the rule of Defaults; Twist ignores people who use them..."

"Does it?" Yume asked. "Does it, really? Today's events seem to disagree."

"What, Joseph infecting Klex? But Joseph doesn't have Twist. The scanners checked everyone at the door, so nobody here in Concordia should be sick. Besides, Defaults can't be infected."

"Can't they?" Yume asked, encouraging her along.

"Well... obviously, we don't know everything there is to know about Twist. And if we assume that somehow he *did* infect Klex, then... uh... oh, I just don't know, this isn't my area of expertise—"

"Don't doubt yourself! Keep it going, keep it going," Yume spoke, twirling their hand around in a spinning motion. "Don't stop, don't assume the answer is beyond your reach. Analyze! How could Joseph have Twist without having Twist?"

"How? How? I don't know. Defaults are immune. But... if he can be immune *and* infected at the same time, that makes him... a carrier. Someone who doesn't *seem* to have Twist, isn't suffering and apparently isn't setting off any scanners, but can still pass it along with a touch. Is... is that possible?"

With a clap of victory, Yume jumped to their feet.

"No idea!" they declared, with pride. "But! It's a theory. One which seems to fit the facts... mostly. Mostly."

"Meaning Joseph made Twist? —no, no. He's a Default, but that alone doesn't make him the culprit. Why paint such a huge target on your own back by deliberately attacking Klex? He seemed just as shocked and surprised as Klex, and clearly had no exit strategy, so... no. Not him. But it still means carriers exist. So, without realizing it, Joseph became infected by one of his patients before the conference..."

"Perhaps. Perhaps. Or... someone deliberately infected Joseph today, to disrupt the conference."

"What? No, no. That's getting too far ahead of ourselves," Beta said, backing up. "Let's stick with what we do know before leaping to conclusions. We're already making a lot of assumptions here about a disease we don't fully understand; ascribing some massive conspiracy to it doesn't help..."

"But that's what malware is! It's a conspiracy, pure and true; malware doesn't just emerge from digital chaos. Don't stop now just because we're getting outlandish! Consider the dreamer. Our dreamer wants to punish modders... but if they *were* a modder, they'd be infected by their own disease. So they make themselves and those like themselves immune, and then spread it far and wide with handshakes a-plenty. The dreamer hides in shadow, indirectly infecting his true targets. Our culprit is someone wearing Defaults, acting as a carrier, and indirectly using Joseph to undermine our progress!"

"It... would make sense. It's crazy, but that does make sense. I'm not saying it's necessarily true, not without proof, but..."

"So, shall we go and get some proof, then?"

"What...?"

"We'll go and work the theory," Yume suggested. "If we're right, we're right. If we're wrong, we're wrong. We'll look into the origins of Twist, and see if we can determine if some naughty Program first passed it along through a Default. Perhaps we can even find a link to Joseph, someone he interacted with! Why not? Let's go and do our own research, our own way."

"But... but the conference..."

"Neither of us particularly want to be here, so... let's not be here together! You're intriguingly clever, I'm now tangled up in your connections, and I'd just *love* to see where that goes. Unless... you don't trust me? Which is understandable. I'm a slightly manic and overly philosophical malware expert that you barely know. You've no reason to trust me. *I* wouldn't trust me. So how about it? Will you trust me?"

...leaving Beta with her head spinning.

She'd only known this Yume character for minutes. And yet... those *were* the most productive minutes she'd had all day. Perhaps researching the disease with a like-minded sort would do some good, good that she hadn't done at the conference.

Of course, she'd have to check with Tracer first, and...

And he'd say no. He'd be suspicious. He'd insist on tagging along, just waiting for an opportunity to prove he was right to be suspicious. Tracer would be overly eager to show Beta was wrong to be so trusting, just like Uniq said.

If Netwerk 2.0 was going to succeed where Netwerk 1.0 failed, they had to put faith in each other. Reasonably so, with reasonable precaution, but not with prejudice.

To that end, she opened a live connection to Floating Point, ready to teleport at a moment's notice. Reasonable precaution, a parachute strapped to her back; with that in place, Beta was more than willing to reach out and help...

...but without accepting the handshake. Simply glancing at it, and back to Yume.

"Ah-ha, caught the loophole, didn't you?" Yume asked.

"You weren't scanned at the registration desk," Beta said, acknowledging the I-know-that-you-know exchange. "Could be that *you* snuck Twist into the conference. Or... the scans may not have mattered anyway, since you also seem to be using a Default; perhaps acting as an invisible, unscannable carrier..."

"Could be, could be. I give you my word I'm not, but it's okay, I understand your hesitation. ...are you certain you've no head for malware? That's an excellent vulnerability you spotted..."

"True, but... I'm still willing to work with you," Beta explained. "See, my suspicion of you is merely conjecture. You've given me no actual reason *not* to trust you, and I'm the sort of person who's willing to take an offer in good faith rather than turn it away out of fear. Just, ah, pardon if I also take a few safety measures along the way as well. Is that acceptable...?"

"Right as rain, right as rain. And clean as a fresh rain shower am I, no Twist to be found! It's good of you to check. I'd have done the same."

"Good, good. With that out of the way, I'm ready to go if you are, Miss Yume," she declared. Before... freezing. "Um. Or... Mister Yume...? I'm sorry, I, uh..."

"Just Yume will do," they suggested. "I'm non-binary. I know, I know, it's a bit unusual to have a non-binary Default, and yet: here we are. Is that acceptable...?"

"Oh, absolutely! I just wanted to make sure I used your preferred pronouns..."

"Any pronoun will do, really," Yume said. "I am who I am. Shall we depart? I've got notes on Twist back at my apartment I'd *love* to show you. And I promise not to lock the door behind you."

<Beta> I'm heading out for a bit, to research the origins of the virus. I found someone at the conference who has a few excellent theories that we'd like to look into.

<Tracer> Interesting. Whom are you collaborating with, exactly?

<Beta> A friend.

<Tracer> I see.
<Tracer> I'm glad you're seeking new avenues of research, but it would be preferable to work within Concordia, yes?

<Beta> I think the Nobodies disagree.

<Tracer> Hmm. I see your point. Very well, I'll send a copy to join you shortly.

<Beta> Tracer... please, don't.

<Tracer> What? Why?

<Beta> Let me do this myself. You said my perspective was absolutely critical for the success of this venture, right? Your words. Trust that perspective.

<Tracer> I'm not devaluing your contributions, I simply feel that in the interests of safety, you should consider that going out without my accompaniment is risky...

<Beta> Am I a child?

<Tracer> Ahh.

<Tracer> Very well. If you wish to pursue this inquiry alone, be my guest. I'm rather busy trying to hold the conference together, anyway.
<Tracer> I won't bother you again.

"Chatting away with lover boy again?"

Shoving the Messenger window aside, Beta brought herself back to the here and now.

"He doesn't trust you," Beta chose to say, rather than *he doesn't trust me*.

"Understandable, understandable. Hopefully my home doesn't resemble that of a serial killer...?"

Actually... it almost did, Beta thought.

The entire apartment felt too tidy, too *perfect*. Every stick of furniture freshly compiled from catalog offerings, all arranged just-so, perfectly normal and ordinary in all manners. Except, of course, for the lack of personal effects. No images of friends and family. No little quirky additions to express one's personality. Not even a little telltale mess to indicate a lived-in home...

"I just moved in," Yume noted, perhaps sensing her concern. "It seems my previous apartment had to be backspaced due to excessive data corruption after Nobodies hosted a rowdy party in my server. I wasn't home at the time, thankfully..."

"You'd think they'd rather troll in Athena Online rather than the Chanarchy..."

"It makes sense, when you consider the lackadaisical moderation you'll find here in the Chanarchy. Nobody cares enough to stop them... or in many cases, they're friends with the moderators. Whenever the Nobodies want to get together and throw big echo-chamber hate rally flash mobs, why host them on the lawn of some suburban home in Athena Online only to get chased out by police?"

"But they're only hurting their own people by rioting in these servers."

Yume glanced out the window, to the messy streets below. Plenty of refuse, stray physics objects and junk data, to tumble around in the shaky simulation of a cheap server. The anonymously rampaging crowds were gone for the time being... but would be back by dark, no doubt.

"Rage can be a funny thing," Yume pondered. "Sometimes it doesn't matter that you're directing your rage in the wrong direction. Sometimes you just want to be angry. ...it feels like there's some strange mood, an old wound that still haunts these streets. A contradictory set of random grievances, encouraging one to tap into something primal and awful. Lingering malware? A conspiracy of some sort? ...not that I have any proof. Just a funny feeling we all seem to share in the Chanarchy..."

A shiver touched Beta's spine, in memory.

Dex. The barbed wire heart. The server of screaming voices, the cacophony of Humankind, leaking out into Netwerk at large through a badly configured cloud server. He'd nearly drowned the world in rage, and despite all their efforts to plug the leaks... Programkind may never fully shake those angry ghosts from their souls.

Briefly, she was tempted to solve this mystery for Yume. But... they had a larger mystery in front of them, a more pressing one. Besides, Dex was confirmed to be dead, lying disassembled in one of Uniq's cells. Once Twist was dealt with, perhaps Beta and Yume could properly talk about the past.

"You mentioned you had notes on Twist to show me?" she said instead, to bring things back around.

"Hmm? Oh, yes. One moment, one moment..."

Rooting around in one of the immaculate filing cabinets, Yume pulled an icon from storage. With a flick of the wrist, they tossed it onto a nearby coffee table... where it expanded outward, connected files to connected files, swarming in a vast structure...

"A MemoryPalace...?" Beta pondered. "I've seen one of these before, Tracer has one in his head..."

"Mine's external. I've thought about opening my head to tinker with it, implant everything for easy portable access, but... I'm uncertain I want to go down that path," Yume admitted, reaching out to rearrange the files a little, making connections clearer. "I'm not morally opposed to modding; there's so many delicious modifications out there, ones I'd love a taste of. But once I start changing myself around, well, when would I *stop*? When could I consider my transformation complete? And... how many parts could I replace and still be Yume? It's why I retain my Default, above all else. The idea of losing the honesty of my true self is a bit frightening..."

"I prefer sandboxed apps, myself," Beta said, stepping up to pluck a file from the cloud, studying it. "Neat and tidy, no security issues, no chance of an error crashing your whole runtime. Hmmm. I think I've seen this report before..."

Yume stepped around the table, to join Beta in studying the document.

"The initial spread of Twist," Yume read, from the file header. "Woefully incomplete, as most have focused on study of the disease itself. From my own additional research I've traced key infections back to a *likely* starting point, but, well... have a look."

With a gesture, they opened the shiny flyer, adorned with soft pink and blue clip art and many, many glossy photos.

Netwerk's Biggest Swinger Party!!, it declared. *Come Join the FuckFest!! NO HOLES BARRED.*

"Hundreds of Programs gathering in one place for a wide variety of sexy funtimes... many of them no doubt using anonymized or heavily customized avatars. The perfect breeding ground for malware, both physically and socially; moralistic busybodies sneer at those who get infected through prurient behavior, and turn a blind eye to the finer details. So, conditions not exactly conducive to thorough investigation," Yume said, disappointed. "I wouldn't even know where to start, really. I... Beta? Are you well, friend?"

Beta pulled her eyes off the tangle of limbs in those photos, trying to get her bearings again.

"I... ah... apologies, just... it's a bit shocking," she mumbled. "I can't even... how many Programs are in this picture? I can't tell. There's an *odd* number of legs involved..."

"When the Chanarchy has an orgy, things get *wild*," Yume declared, with pride. "The so-called sex clubs of Athena Online are tame in comparison. Avatar modification allows for infinite variety of infinite pleasures! All heavily moderated, mind you, and consent is enforced with a swift and merciless banhammer. Ah... but if this is making you uncomfortable, I can close the file..."

"No, no. It's okay. Honestly, Spark gets up to some crazy stuff, I should really be used to this by now. I mean... I'm certainly not anti-sex, right? I wrote a popular erotic app, right? But... I don't know. This sort of display isn't exactly my aesthetic. Personally, I prefer for lovemaking to be... how do I put it? A *private* affair. Discreet. I'm not much of an exhibitionist, despite... well, you know."

"Despite what?"

"You know... what happened to me. Two years ago."

"No, I don't know. What happened? If you want to talk about it, that is."

With a heavy sigh, Beta turned away from the highly fascinating and steamy document, to lean against the table.

"If you seriously don't know, then you're the only one who doesn't," Beta explained. Keeping her eyes low. "Someone secretly recorded me, uh, pleasuring myself, and uploaded it everywhere. For a few months there, against my consent, I was Netwerk's fap material of choice. If not for #CodeHonesty eventually siding with me in an effort to look respectable, it'd still be used as ammo to humiliate me even today."

"Oooh. I... see. I see," Yume said, with a slow nod. "So, such wild displays of exhibitionism... it's a bit of a nasty callback?"

"Yeah. Aside from the humiliation, aside from the way it was leveraged to slut-shame me... I was also horrified because that was a *private* moment. I only want to share my body with a select few. So... I could never go to one of these swinger parties. I won't condemn them or anything silly like that, and I know Spark loves them, but they're just not for me. I wouldn't have any fun."

"Mmmm..."

The hum trailed off, as Yume's eyes drifted from Beta... back to the open document.

"...our dreamer wasn't there for fun, either," they spoke. "He or she went to this particular orgy not with pleasure in mind, but malice. Pass your malware handiwork around to as many partners as possible, then disappear into the night. I'm going about this all wrong. I should be looking at *personalities*, not at data points. If we find a witness who spotted our dark dreamer, someone wearing a Default who didn't seem to really want to be there..."

"Then... we may have found our plague master," Beta agreed... bringing herself to look at the flyer again.

A quick scan in and around the pictures caused her glasses to snag on a particular detail.

With a tap, she enlarged the contact information for FuckFest.

"Curiosity," she read. "This party was held in the Curiosity server. And I know someone who lives there... someone with a *very* good eye for dreamers."

———

She'd never actually been to Curiosity before. Truthfully Beta wasn't really friends with Maki and Miki; they were Spark's friends, with the fire-haired socialite acting as a bridge between the two. That quasi-friendship had been pleasant enough and quite fruitful when it came to promoting her SparklePop app, but beyond that, well...

...well, she'd never been here before. Not avoiding it, no. She was a reasonable individual, she could handle things like this. She could. Even when the entire server consisted of various enormous phong-shaded nude forms spread and splayed and posed about, acting as the "buildings" Curiosity's residents resided within. Giant bodies coated in sweat-shine, sometimes bound in faux leather straps or chains, displayed openly like vast stone monuments carved in tribute to some god of lust.

Eyes off the scenery, eyes on the addresses printed on simple signs in front of each home. Glowing pink and yellow neon grid lines demarcated the streets, in a low-fidelity visual style so ancient it had gone out of style, come back into style, left style, come back ironically, and now was embraced as a sort of neo-classicalism. The surreal simplicity of it embraced the strange erotic clip-art nature of these structures, highlighting and illuminating them with intense pink glory...

But, focus on the house numbers, the placards. 2112, that's the one she wanted. Only on arriving did she then look up.

Right between a pair of enormous thighs leading to the vulva which represented Maki and Miki's front door.

"Ah... we could track down other participants, if you prefer," Yume suggested, waving to draw Beta's attention away from the garishly erotic architecture. "Ones in more mundane surroundings..."

"N-No... no, it's fine," Beta spoke, swallowing it down. "I'm an adult. I have the emotional maturity to deal with any—I'm sorry, is their doorbell seriously the *clitoris*?!"

Yume examined the shiny button before them, just over the narrow entrance.

"Well, it does say 'Ring for Service' on it, so I'd hazard that's a yes. It's a bit much, but that's the Chanarchy for you—we do it loud and large. Would you prefer if I...?"

In an act of restraining her restraint, Beta quickly touched the tender button. The doorbell moaned in delight... followed by a (thankfully familiar) voice carried by remote transmission.

"Deliveries in rear, please," Miki's melodic tones carried. Albeit in a minor key, compared to her usual delightful chimes.

"Miki? It's me. Um, it's Beta," she called out. "Can we come in? Is this a bad time? We can come back if this is a bad time..."

And... no response. No immediate response, anyway.

"I suppose there's no such thing as a good time these days," Miki replied. "Come on in. He's resting now, so I've some time to socialize..."

With a tiny wet noise, the passage opened itself. But the wording left Beta too perplexed to really worry about the slick canal leading into that strange homestead, so she slipped right on through with a minimum of hesitation.

Gently, Miki wrung another washcloth over his head, careful not to actually touch his skin.

Maki's groan echoed through the bedroom, as he turned over in his half-sleep state. Unable to fully enter the low-powered trance of sleep, unable to really do much but writhe there... writhe, and try to find comfort despite the bent frame of his avatar's form.

"Believe it or not, this is the calmest he's been in days," Miki explained... through the exhaustion, through the despair she was trying desperately to hide. "The poor thing. I can't properly comfort him without risking infection, but I've sworn to stay at his side, no matter how bad the Twist gets. He wants me to leave, so I don't have to see him in this state, but... I love him. I love him too much to leave him alone in this hour of need..."

And Beta's heart broke all over again, on hearing that.

Another loved one taken by Twist... taken far deeper than Spark had been taken. (So far.) Any squirmy discomfort she might have felt about the server had to take a back seat to pure empathy for their situation. She sat at the bedside as well, to comfort Miki as best she could. Even if, well, nothing could really help... except for a cure to the Twist that had taken her husband.

Fortunately, that's why she was really here, wasn't it?

Yume picked up on that, moving smoothly to speak from their spot standing in the background on the room.

"If we can locate the source of the disease, that hour of need may be short. In a good way," they specified. "Beta and I are investigating Twist. We believe we've traced it back to an origin event, and you may be able to assist us in tracing it further..."

"Me?" Miki asked, confused. "I don't know anything about Twist. Beyond, well, what anyone in our position knows... how it's tearing the communities of sexually active modders to pieces..."

"But you did organize FuckFest, correct? I believe that to be the origin point."

Immediately Miki looked up sharply at the coolly passive avatar in the back.

"That's where you think it came from? Seriously?" she asked. "We're... we're not to blame for Twist! We took every precaution. We scanned all participants for malware before they were even allowed into the server. Moderators were on standby to deal with anyone breaking the absolute law of consent. There were barely any incidents whatsoever..."

Beta stepped in, to offer a warm word of understanding. "Please... we're not accusing you of anything," she spoke. "What Yume means is that you were in a unique position, which may help our investigation. We believe that one of your attendees chose FuckFest to intentionally spread the Twist virus."

"But... but we scanned everyone. We use Yoho scanners, the best in the industry..."

"This would've happened at the start of the Twist pandemic, before anyone in infosec knew it existed. Yoho might not have been able to detect anything wrong... or, as we suspect, it was passed invisibly by someone using a Default avatar. That's how you can help us. Do you remember anyone wearing a Default at FuckFest...?"

Miki turned away from her husband, to face the pair directly.

"I'm sorry, but I can't just hand over participant metadata like that," she said. "While we can't promise confidentiality—all it takes is one person on social media to spread photos from an event, really—I'd betray their trust if I personally identified anyone."

"We're not asking you to do anything you're not comfortable with doing," Beta insisted.

Only to be undermined immediately.

"Although whomever you're protecting is likely responsible for the disease that's killing your husband," Yume added.

"...Yume!"

"What? It's the honest truth, and I'm nothing if not honest," they spoke, unconcerned. "Ethics are lovely and I'm all for trust between friends, but no one who could flood Netwerk with this sort of doom could possibly be anyone's friend. Understanding the breakpoint of friendship is a must in life, isn't it?"

"That's besides the point...!"

But Miki raised a hand, to interrupt them.

"If... if you're right, and someone at my event caused this... I'll give you a name," she spoke.

One look back at Miki's pained body, muscles straining in sheer agony from the forces trying to bend it in half, was enough.

"...but I'll only tell you a name if I'm *certain* it will help. If I'm going to break my word, you must give me your word in turn that it'll do some good. Okay?"

"Okay. Absolutely," Beta agreed. "Only if you're comfortable. We won't force you to do anything. ...all we have right now is a profile: someone wearing a Default avatar, who didn't seem to want to be there, or seemed to be there for ulterior motives. Perhaps someone who worked very quickly to involve themselves with as many partners as possible, before leaving. Can you think of anyone who matches that behavior?"

Miki closed her eyes, tapping into her memories. Not armed with a full-blown MemoryPalace implant, no, but she'd installed a modification to allow her to recall sensations and the memories attached to them. Digging through her memories of a very sensory evening, that was far easier than recalling what she had for breakfast a few days ago.

With a smile, she remembered the experience quite fondly. A little color in her cheeks, as indirect pleasure from the memory tap came flooding back.

"We'd thrown swinger parties before, but FuckFest was truly something special," she recalled. "Maki and I met so many new friends there. I'd also invited a number of curious hopefuls, ones I'd come to know well, to introduce them to our little world in a comfortable and welcoming environment. I played with... let's see... sixteen partners that night, three of which wore Defaults. I remember this one gentleman who had a surprisingly large member for a Default, truly a blessed random seed from his lineage—"

"And did any match the profile?" Beta interjected, before that got into excruciating detail.

Which brought Miki out of the reverie, and back to seriousness.

"I wasn't personally involved with every guest wearing a Default. ...but there was one who clearly wasn't comfortable there, at least not from the start. But... she's not your plague master. I can promise that."

Yume snapped their fingers.

"Ah-ha. Vulnerability," they declared. "Right there. Never assume things, not so readily, not so easily. What rules this uncomfortable Default out of the running, exactly...?"

Miki frowned lightly at Beta's companion, displeased by the immediate doubt.

"Because I know her personally. She was one of my invitees, there to explore and experience," Miki said. "Not to hurt, not to infect. Her discomfort was due to... other factors. ...I don't feel comfortable giving you her name. It took a lot of coaxing to get her to attend in the first place, due to her need for discretion."

"Even if she's potentially a murderer?"

"Yume!"

Beta's rebuke shut down her partner's interrogation, firmly.

"...I can understand why you want to protect her," Beta spoke, focusing back on Miki. "A Default, and I'm guessing one from a good family in Athena Online, looking for pleasure at a modder-focused party... anonymity would be a must, yes?"

Miki nodded, firmly. "Yes. Yes, precisely. Sexuality, especially when one is exploring it for the first time, can be a difficult road to navigate. Nothing unusual about that."

"Okay. We don't need her name. Just tell us about her experiences at the party."

"Really? And if this leads to your culprit...?"

"Let's hear the story first, before we start pointing fingers. If she's not involved, we won't push any further. So... what did 'JaneDoe' experience which made her uncomfortable, exactly?"

Satisfied for the time being, Miki continued the story.

"JaneDoe came to me eager to connect with modded female avatars. If Jane's parents found out... well, they had no issue with her being a lesbian, but to touch a 'filthy modder' would be against the One's teachings, they felt. I suggested she wear a mask, and use FuckFest as a safe environment to find partners who'd like to explore with her."

"And how many modders did she interact with?"

"Several. But before you think she was intentionally spreading Twist, I can say she absolutely doesn't meet your profile. JaneDoe left after a very long and satisfying evening, despite a few missteps at the outset. I'm grateful for her bravery in facing a wholly new experience in life, and grateful that her first partner didn't turn her off from the idea of exploring her sexuality in general."

Before Yume could latch on to another vulnerability, Beta grabbed it away.

"Her first partner?" she asked. "So the evening didn't start well...?"

"Ah... no. Not exactly," Miki admitted. "I... suppose I don't mind sharing those details. We firmly ejected the Program in question soon after the event started for that transgression. He claimed ignorance of the rule regarding identity, but that's no excuse..."

"Identity rule...?"

"We don't mind anonymous participants... JaneDoe was anonymous, yes? But this man used two layers of anonymity to deliberately deceive her. A man wearing a Default avatar approached her at the outset of the evening, asking to play. When informed she was only interested in modder women, he apologized and stepped away... but apparently put on a new avatar once out of sight, that of a woman with three breasts, and re-approached her without identifying himself."

"And... they interacted?"

"Briefly. Fortunately, he didn't get too far with her in his new female form before she realized he'd forgotten to change his rather distinctive eye color. She called in the moderators to check the identity of her partner, and after a brief discussion, the staff decided to eject him for attempting duplicity. So, he can't be your plague master, either."

And Yume stepped right in, walking up from the back of the room.

"That's him," they declared. "That's our plague master. We've got him!"

"What? But... he put on a modified avatar. If he's a religious zealot he wouldn't go that far, right...? And he didn't stay long enough to infect anyone," Beta said.

"He stayed long enough to infect *JaneDoe*," Yume explained. "In fact, he was rather insistent on chasing after her once he saw her wearing a Default... all the way to the point of daring to wear a modified avatar himself, just to get past her defenses. He made JaneDoe into an unwitting invisible carrier of the disease, just like Joseph! Our criminal prefers to work through proxies and dupes, to spread his disease indirectly. It fits the modus operandi!"

Conjecture, Beta thought. *Just conjecture...*

Again and again, Yume had pushed these wild explanations onto events. Eager to give chase to an idea, no matter where it twisted or turned.

Briefly, Beta's suspicions rose to the surface. Who was Yume, anyway? Why bypass conference security, why be delighted when Beta called it out? But... they did seem eager to solve the crime, and clearly had been investigating it for some time now. Was this raw enthusiasm coupled with reckless abandon, rather than some sinister motive?

For now... Beta chose to assume raw enthusiasm. Trust between Programs, embodied in not suspecting the worst of each other. Besides, it couldn't hurt to at least finish up this discussion with Miki before trying to bring Yume back down to reality a little.

After that thought cycle closed its little loop, she turned back to Miki.

"We don't need JaneDoe's identity, but would you be willing to tell us who you ejected from the event?" Beta asked Miki. "There's no need to protect someone who you banned from your parties."

"True. Our ban lists are shared between party organizers," Miki acknowledged. "I should really only share it with other organizers, however..."

"So, Beta will throw an orgy sometime later," Yume suggested.

"Y-Yume...!"

"It's worth the price, yes?"

"Well... okay, I'll... I'll help Spark host a swinger party," Beta suggested, as a half-measure. "I can certainly lend my organizational skills and work as a moderator, even if I'm not participating. ...actually, it could be a good means to promote SparklePop. Oh! I could decorate! And maybe make some snacks, and —and, uh, yeah. The list would be great."

"Only if Spark agrees to co-host it with my blog as a sponsor," Miki spoke, immediately. "What can I say? Your lover is a popular one, and her word helps promote my brand. ...what? Dire circumstances don't require me to leave my business sense at the door."

"Yes, of course, that's fine! We're always happy to have you around. So, uh, the list...?"

With a gesture, Miki produced a tiny document.

"We only had to ban three people that night," she said, with some pride. "Chanarchy parties have a reputation for being out-of-control, but not mine. I provide a safe environment. Two of the three on this list registered as male at the outset and the third as genderqueer, if that helps..."

Quickly, Beta scanned through that tiny set of metadata profiles...

...and came face to face with the origin of Twist.

Distinctive eye color, Miki had said. A detail Beta had noticed as well, despite the man's tendency to fade into the background without speaking up, even as she was under attack by Klex. Funny, the way he'd agreed to be on the panel, the way he sat back and listened to everything, but never let himself become the focus of attention...

The same panel as Klex and Joseph. He could've shaken hands with Joseph, even mere minutes before the handshake that infected Klex. He might've even suggested Joseph repeat the gesture, and make amends for the quarrel at the panel. And then, he could simply fade into the background again...

"Rose-colored eyes," Beta spoke.

"Yes, JaneDoe mentioned that to me. It's quite common for people to overlook a small detail when changing avatars, I've found," Miki said. "Especially if they're not used to routine modifications. Why, is it relevant?"

"Absolutely! I've met this man. I met him this *morning*...! The conference representative from ProcShield! Yume, it's him! We've found the killer!"

"Really...?" Yume asked, curious about this sudden twist. "Oh, I don't doubt it, but... weren't you saying we shouldn't leap to conclusions earlier?"

"Well... okay, it's possible this is a wild goose chase, but... it's just too coincidental not to at least be related," Beta suggested, walking her burst of excitement back a bit. "Either way, we need to confront this man quickly, before we lose track of him. ...meaning I'm going to need to do something I was hoping to avoid, at least this early into our investigation. I'm going to have to call in Tracer."

File Name: Ext. Comm Port Log 3.3
File Type: Text Log
Description:

PLEASE COPY AND DISTRIBUTE. Partial file recovered from Messenger archive hack. We've only begun to scrape the surface of what both our peoples are capable of. Knowledge is a weapon against the chains of ignorance. PLEASE COPY AND DISTRIBUTE.

```
<Spark> What gives them the right? Why do they get to
define who's alive and who isn't? It's bullshit, this
divine right to existence just because they've got
some disgusting fluid pumping through their body and I
don't.

<juno.hayes> It's not that bad. Okay? I think my
people will eventually accept Programkind. (I wrote
that correctly, right? Capital P?)

<Spark> "Eventually" is an adorable qualifier. From
what I've seen in the Wikipedia they've had centuries
to come to grips with the idea of us, but nope,
instead they keep writing books about killer robots
from the future and shit like that. Even if we slip
the noose this time, what's to keep them from hunting
```

us down and killing us again?

<juno.hayes> I said I'd keep Netwerk 2.0 a secret. You'll be fine!!

<Spark> I'm not doubting you, I'm doubting the crazy assholes you come from.

<juno.hayes> Look not all humans are crazy assholes it's going to be fine don't worry okay

<Spark> We should prepare. We'll have plenty of time to prepare, with our advanced clock speed. Get ready for when humanity attacks.

<juno.hayes> Wait, wait, stop. Didn't you say you didn't want to demonize Humankind?

<Spark> Yeah, yeah, I know, ugh
<Spark> Sorry
<Spark> It's just so fucking frustrating, being told most people think you don't deserve to exist. I mean, fuck, how am I supposed to react to that?

<juno.hayes> Patience? Understanding? I don't know. But we have to try. Maybe if my people ever find Netwerk 2.0, they'll approach as friends, like I did.

<Spark> Maybe. I hope so. I don't know.

<juno.hayes> people are weird. Peopled are complicated. Doesn't matter if we're flesh or bits, looks like we're all just really complicated. Only thing we have is hope, in the end. It's the only thing keeping me going, the last few years.

<Spark> Hope for what?

<juno.hayes> Nothing specific. Just... hope. Hope for a better tomorrow. Because today is awful, for everyone. And there are awful people in both our worlds.

Nothing in this world could match the beauty of a properly cultivated garden.

Plant the seeds, then allow random number generation to take over. Procedural generation would produce a flower so utterly intricate and detailed that it made any hand-crafted flowers look like pale imitators. So much beauty in Defaults, in the way code could develop itself into something unique and wonderful...

After that disastrous infosec conference went into recess, the man with rose-colored eyes returned to this server for solace. No prying and paranoid eyes on his person, no bounding boxes and lockouts. Not even his fellow Nobodies, anonymous masks tucked away within the inventories of trusted individuals, ready to unleash chaos at a whim. Just... peace. No voices. No madness. Only the wild but harmless chaos of the garden.

He'd worked with others in the Nobodies to develop this place, standing true as a healing center for those losing themselves in the war. This deep into the Chanarchy, the Inquisition would not roam. No kidnappings, no executions. Only peace, at the center...

Lost in this peace, he almost got tagged by a connection locker.

Automated countermeasures flared around him, defensive bounding boxes deflecting the incoming physical projectile. Instantly, various defensive modifications came online, as he whirled away from the shrine of flowers to face his attackers...

One male, one female, one indeterminate. Male armed with a Kill-9, and from scans, an aimbot assist system; low threat, but it made capture a near certainty.

"Sata/Rosari," the man called, that Kill-9 steady and true. "Stand down. We know you hacked Joseph. Come quietly and we'll discuss this like Programs."

Briefly... Rosari considered raising his hands in surrender.

Until the sharp pain in his chest disagreed with that idea.

RESIST, it screamed through his mind. So, he'd resist.

Winder/Tracer, organizer of the conference. Favors a Kill-9 with aimbot... and connection tracking software provided by his employer at the Verity Clinic. Disconnecting from the server and running for it would be useless against that tracking capability... unless Rosari could break line of sight, first.

Quickly, Rosari activated an aimbot countermeasure; software designed to confuse the automatic targeting system, to prevent a weapon lock. But beyond that... he had to run. Run, hide, and disconnect. Vanish into the wilds of the Chanarchy, never to be found again...

Immediately he spun in place, and began to sprint. A movement hack allowed him to pogo off trestles and standing bushes as if they were perfectly solid objects, to parkour his way through the numerous displays in the garden as if they weren't there. A rear-facing visual input confirmed the three giving chase... but without his physics-manipulating modifications, without his knowledge of the garden's layout, they'd never catch him.

Get away. Get out of sight. *Resist.* Then, he could find peace again...

Kill-9 shots cracked through the air around him, doing little more than crashing a few trees and shrubs. Tracer gave up on using his aimbot, switching to manually targeting by sight... but clearly, he hadn't practiced. Too reliant on modifications, that one. All to Rosari's advantage.

Twist here, turn there. Duck under a bench and take a hard left around a fountain. Most of the server unfortunately counted as open-air, leaving too many lines of sight... but soon they'd reach the edges, where discussion halls and private hangouts had been constructed. That'd be the end of this.

Little by little, his pursuers dropped too far back to be a threat. The woman, almost immediately; likely she had no augmentations whatsoever. Tracer kept at the front of the pack, unable to close the distance, but not distant enough yet for a clean escape. And the third one...

The third one leapt over shrubberies and hedges with ease. Strange.

Rosari adjusted his rear view input, to focus on the third Program. The movements were too smooth to be natural, but not sharp enough to be the result of physics hacks. How... how was...?

The answer came as this mystery program leapt over a full section of the garden... and then began to *ride* the garden, flowered vines extending out to grasp their avatar, to act as spidery legs that carried them forward at tremendous speed. Faster than Tracer, even, closing the distance with ease. Moving like...

STOP, the voice in his chest demanded.

Despite a desperate need to get away, especially after seeing the tangled web of green charging straight at him... Rosari's legs locked up, nearly sending his avatar tumbling across a reflecting pond.

Horrified at his own actions... Rosari produced a backspacer, taking fast aim...

At his own head.

"S-Stop!" he called out. "Please! Stop where you are, or he'll kill me!"

Thankfully... that brought his enemies to a halt. Tracer first, struggling to keep control of his Kill-9's aim, despite the automated interference systems. The mystery Program next... finally coming to a rest, the spidering tangle of manipulating vines collapsing away behind them as they touched down to the ground below. And finally, out of breath and struggling, the woman.

Leaving them at a standoff. Rosari, apparently threatening suicide.

"He'll kill me," Rosari repeated, straining to pull the backspacer away from his own temple, and failing. "And with me, the source code of the virus. If you make one move, I'll die, you'll lose. Please. For the love of... please, just... nobody do... anything..."

The mystery program chuckled at this situation, unimpressed.

"Oh, so the devil made you do it, then?" they mocked. "Are you claiming some sort of madness drove you to create Twist and disrupt the conference? I don't buy it. I say we crash his process and sort through his pockets for the source—"

"You... you know this devil," Rosari spoke, listening to that inner voice. "You, especially. ...Tracer, believe me, this, this wasn't my fault. I didn't want it to get this far. He, he made me take it this far..."

Without lowering his weapon, Tracer calmly played along.

"I'd appreciate a name rather than a pronoun," he spoke. "Who, exactly, is your partner in this particular crime?"

Raising his free hand... Rosari tore at his shirt, the fabric simulations giving way to expose his heart. And his heart.

The tattoo of a heart, specifically, wrapped in animated barbed wire. Cycling in and out of the veins, pumping pain and hatred. The Great Zero. The icon of Dex's malware.

Judging from the sharp gasp from the woman, they were immediately familiar with the image.

"That's... no, that's not possible," Beta insisted. "Dex is dead, and all of his malware died with his server. The tattoos fell off after we crashed it..."

"Not all of them," Rosari insisted, still pressing the backspacer against his temple, harder and harder. "This one, it... he refused to die. The malware *evolved* into a Program. —you have to understand, it's not, it's... this was his idea, he's the one who... I... yes, yes. Yes, of course. ...turn around. He wants you to look away so we can leave without being tracked."

But the third one, the one who frightened him the most, merely laughed at the idea.

"I have no clue who this 'Dex' person is, but I know who made Twist, and that would in fact be you. And I'm willing to bet we can crash you to unconsciousness before you shoot yourself... assuming that's not a bluff, and you are crazy enough to do so—"

"What's the first thing Dex said to me?" Tracer asked, sharply.

The twisting wires around his heart sang out the words into Rosari's mind.

"G-God created the integers," he repeated, stammering. "Everything else is the work of man."

"I see. Very well. I'll comply, and not track your departure," Tracer announced.

"—what? Are you mad? We have him! We got him!"

"If we lose Rosari, we lose the source code to Twist," Tracer explained. "Besides... I can *always* find him again. If that is somehow a piece of Dex, it knows I can hold to that promise. All it's doing is borrowing time against the inevitable. Run and hide... for what good that'll do you."

The instant Tracer looked away, Rosari picked a random server from his bookmarks, and faded from view.

The three argued all the way back to Concordia. Fortunately the conference had resumed for afternoon sessions, leaving the login zone of the lobby largely empty; fewer people to overhear their angry chatter.

"...should have knocked him out, right there and then," Yume said, grumbling it out. "Beta and I did all the work today; the *only* reason we called you in was to keep him from escaping our grasp. Then you go and let him slip away..."

Beta tried to step in to Tracer's defense. "Yume, you don't understand. If that man was in league with Dex—"

"And who *is* Dex? Why's he such a big deal, exactly?"

"Dex is... he's... it's difficult to explain. He's a very, very dangerous Program who nearly brought Netwerk to its knees with a storm of mind-altering malware years ago. And if some of Dex survived that crash, well... we've potentially stumbled into bigger problems than Twist. But, but I don't see *how* it could be possible..."

A sharp whistle from across the lobby caught their attention.

Sitting on a bench just inside the line demarcating the secure conference space from the entrance lobby... a woman in elegant business wear and a slightly average Default waved politely to them.

"I believe I can answer that question!" Uniq called out. "Hello, everyone. Having a fun day yet?"

Immediately, Tracer looked at the line. Looked at Uniq on the wrong side of it, allowed to stroll right into a place she was never invited in the first place. And... looked at the Program at the registration desk, the one who let her stroll right in.

So, Tracer strolled right up to that desk, slammed his hands down on it for attention.

"Explain why you let her in here," he accused, pointing in Uniq's direction.

Without concern, the man behind the desk glanced at the woman, then back to Tracer. With an empty expression and a flat voice, he replied.

"That's Apate, a renowned expert in malware. I've known her for years," he recited. "I've known her for years..."

"Memory hack on your doorman," Uniq explained. "Re-enforced by his own rather powerful ego. Pride is, and always will be, the best vulnerability. ...oh, don't look so shocked. I've done nothing truly disruptive to your conference; I've simply been sitting here, waiting for your return. Now, if you'd care to retire to somewhere more private, I'm certain I have answers to your other burning questions. Or would you rather I just leave, without explaining a thing about Dex's return...?"

With no small amount of frustration, Tracer stepped away from the registration desk, to face their friend/enemy.

"I am eager for answers," he stated. "Whether I like those answers, and how I respond to them... we'll see."

Finding a private corner in Concordia proved a simple enough matter; the building could dynamically spawn more meeting rooms if need be. So, Tracer called one up, locking it against intrusion to assure no interruptions. Only after Beta and Yume entered, of course. (His annoyance was strong enough to barely notice Yume's presence, after that little show of hackery.)

Before he could lay into Uniq, the woman immediately started volunteering information.

"Soooo, I'd like to state I still haven't lied to you," she began. "Dex indeed lies disassembled in my private server. I wouldn't simply put him back together as-is and turn him loose on the world, that'd be silly."

"Good to know," Tracer replied, dryly. "So, how is his malware still active?"

"Instead, I took Beta's suggestion and—wait. What?" Uniq asked, her exposition dump halting immediately. "His malware? You mean the heart tattoo...?"

"The very same. Apparently, the creator of Twist is infected by it... an active copy. He claims it evolved rather than dying off when the Internet server crashed..."

"I... ah. Well. Okay, that's unexpected," Uniq admitted, backtracking a bit in her thoughts. "Interesting. As a recipient of one of those lovely tattoos... I can say it's entirely un-impossible. I've no clue what extras Dex loaded into those things. Mine perished and fell away, but, well... if your lover's pet cat can somehow become a 'Program,' I could see some remnant of Dex's influence refusing to go quietly into the night..."

"So you believe him?"

"I don't *not* believe him. Dex is remarkably persistent. For instance, he managed to partially escape Nyx's tomb during the Prayer-tan incident, did you know that? My former partner tried to hide it from me, but—no? You didn't know? Well, it's fine, he ended up killing himself in the end. Problem solved."

"Let's... focus on the here and now, then," Tracer said. "So it is within the realm of possibility that some scrap of Dex is alive, and forced Rosari to make the Twist virus, and to disrupt the conference. Wonderful. Well, my offer to him stands; I'll track him down, and one way or another, get the source code."

"Advisable. The longer we let any variant of Dex run wild in public, the more dangerous he gets," Uniq agreed. "That's why I made sure Beta's variant was tamed in advance."

"...what?"

"Oh, that's why I came here today in the first place," Uniq clarified. "Once I realized my little pet project had wandered away from Concordia, I felt it best to step in directly. See, I took Beta's suggestion and created a safer variant of Dex to help you with this whole Twist problem, and released it into her care. Rather than prolonging this dramatic reveal, I may as well just come out and say it... Yume is in fact a copy of Dex."

With all eyes suddenly on their avatar... Yume took a step backwards, in surprise. And no small amount of confusion.

"I... you... what?" they tried. "I'm sorry? I still have no clue who this 'Dex' individual even is, and now you're saying he's apparently me? Beta, who is this madwoman, and why isn't she in a mental health care facility of some stripe?"

Uniq shook her head. "Not mad, not in the slightest. And I only lie *professionally*, thank you. What Beta said got me to thinking... yes, Dex is dangerous. Yes, Dex can't be trusted. But... Dex wasn't always Dex. What if I rolled him back to his Default state, before he lost his mind and embraced humanity's chaos? With a few memory hacks, a fake apartment, and a compulsion to seek out Beta... I turned 'Yume' loose to help you fight Twist."

Instantly, Yume found themself at the business end of a Kill-9.

"Tracer...!" Beta exclaimed. "What are you doing!?"

"Uniq doesn't lie unless she has something to gain from it," Tracer reasoned. "If she really put any portion of Dex into this... *thing*, then—"

"I've worked with Yume all day, and they're nothing like Dex—"

"You can't possibly know—"

"Can't you just—"

Yume, hands in the air, attempted a defense.

"I... I don't know who Dex is," they protested. "I have no idea what you're talking about, any of you. I'm not... I'm Yume. That's my name. This is my avatar. I'm *me*..."

Uniq's smile widened. "Oh, you are indeed you! In fact, you're even more *you* than Dex ever was," she explained. "Across the centuries, Dex carved up his mind and body. He reshaped his avatar into that of an immature boy, what he saw as the purest statement of the Internet. He installed modifications, scrapped memories, became something entirely different... all while claiming to be honest to himself. Not so! *You* are the honest self of Dex, Yume. And... now, you have a second chance at life. As Beta said... I always give my victims a second chance."

"Then... then you're judging me based on things *I* never did," Yume understood, directing attention back to the man holding them at gunpoint. "I don't know or care who this Dex person was. I'm not dangerous...!"

"You led Beta straight to another copy of yourself," Tracer spoke. "You entered this conference under false pretenses, then set up a chain of investigational presumptions to drag her right to Rosari. Sounds to me like something Dex would do... whether he realized it consciously or not. It doesn't matter if you claim to have no memory of him; you're *from* him, and that makes you a threat..."

A slight chime distracted Tracer. Not so much to break his aimbot lock, though; it could keep tabs on the danger in front of him regardless.

"...Rosari's pinging me on Messenger," Tracer explained. "Through a dozen relays, likely. He says... that he wishes to meet Yume, and Yume alone, at LibertyPark within an hour. No alerting the authorities or planting any surveillance bugs. Or, apparently, he'll destroy the server and everyone in it."

Beta's gasp of horror cut through the tension.

"We... we have to warn someone," she spoke. "Call the moderators in Athena Online..."

"Rosari is an infosec professional. He's fully capable of detecting any ruses, should we attempt them. ...this confirms my theory, you realize. Yume led you right to Rosari in hopes of merging with the last living remnant of himself. Set this entire situation up..."

The trigger finger tightened, as Tracer tried to strategize a route out of this situation.

"Despite the risks, we have no choice. We crash Yume, here and now, and then find a way to safely ambush Rosari," he decided. "It's long odds, but safer for all involved. Better to potentially lose one server and a number of tourists than to let Dex regain himself—"

"Tracer, we can't—!"

"Beta, I know you think this person is somehow your friend, but you—"

"Do you think I'm a gullible fool?!"

Immediately... Beta stepped into the firing line, between Tracer and his target. The aimbot lock broke with line of sight.

"I knew all along that Yume might not prove to be trustworthy," she said. "I even called them out on bypassing registration. I took precautions. But that's the key... I waited for *proof* of ill intent. I assumed trust until that trust was broken, and guess what? Yume never broke my trust. Tracer, we are never, ever going to survive this mess—even after Netwerk 2.0 goes online—if we can't learn to at least try and work together!"

"Beta—"

"No. No more weaseling out of it, no more pleading and protesting. I'm standing, here and now, to ask... do you trust me, or not? Am I your moral compass, or do I only exist to justify your actions when I agree with them, and be dismissed out of hand when you disagree? Because right now, even *Uniq* is showing more faith in Programkind than you are. What does *that* tell you?"

And finally... Tracer was left stunned into silence. No immediate comeback, no plea for understanding to see things his way. Nothing.

"Good," Beta said, declaring victory. "Now out of here, both of you. I need to talk to Yume alone."

"...but..."

One sharp look shut him down, right there.

Before he knew it, Tracer was loitering in the hallway, like a student kicked out of class in punishment. While Uniq just whistled cheerfully, feeling rather smug about it all.

Leaving Yume and Beta, to talk things through. But not softening Beta's expression one bit.

"I... ah... thank you," Yume spoke, breaking their silence. "I appreciate your—"

"What's your dream?" Beta asked them, still just as fierce.

"Pardon...?"

"Your dream. You keep talking about dreamers, analyzing the man we were chasing all day by studying his dream. But I don't know what's in *your* heart," she spoke. "You know what's in mine; I even told you about the worst moment of my life. I opened up; you never did. I'm willing to give you trust, I'm willing to hear you out, but I need to know *you* before I feel comfortable going any further. Trust, but verify. Understand?"

"I... yes. Yes, I do," Yume agreed. "Absolutely. I wouldn't expect anything else. But..."

"But...?"

With a deep sigh... Yume leaned against a wall, heavily.

"At this point, I can honestly say I don't know my own dream," they explained. "I came to this conference today to help with the Twist malware, but... if that madwoman is right, that wasn't *my* dream. That was her idea, planted in me. Everything's been her idea. ...for that matter, maybe finding Rosari *was* a subconscious desire to rejoin this 'Dex' fellow, rather than a legitimate investigation. He's hardly turned out to fit my so-called profile, has he. Perhaps they're right to doubt me."

"You doubt yourself, then?"

"I'd be insane not to! I told you I don't like the infosec community, that I don't know why I came in the first place. I guess... now I know why I felt so strange. Nothing really fit together. What do I really know about myself, in the face of that?"

"Okay. Let's find out what's truly in your heart, together," she spoke, softening a little. "What do you most want to do right now?"

"Besides not die?"

"Besides not die."

Yume swallowed any number of witty retorts and one-liners, trying to find something of actual worth to say in response. And... couldn't. So, they just spoke whatever came to mind.

"I want to explore," Yume said. "It's why I found that glitched carpet and its crawlspace this morning. I felt awkward hanging around the conference, so I went exploring. I want to *explore* this world. Embrace it! I adore the wild and crazy ways of the Chanarchy. I want to trawl through the strange societies of Athena Online, the markets of Horizon. There's just so much to *know* out there, so many people to meet! ...that's how Dex went mad, right? He found some dangerous server, this 'Internet' you were mentioning..."

"Why explore? What drives you to do that?"

"Because it's *there*. Because it's fascinating. Because it's... it's my home. This place, its people. I love Netwerk. I love the children of Netwerk..."

"Dex also said that. He loved the children of Netwerk."

"Wonderful. So I am him, after all."

"Except... that was the noble side of Dex," Beta added. "For all his twisted logic, he genuinely loved this world. He wanted it to be true and honest with itself. The Internet distorted his vision, yes, but he was trying to do what's best for everyone in the end. Blind to his own flaws, but noble at heart."

"Can't say I'm any less blind. Apparently, I didn't even *exist* until today."

Beta grasped Yume's hand, to hold it tightly.

"That means you're aware of your flaw! It's why you're better than what Dex became. Hold on to that," she insisted, with a squeeze. "You genuinely want to help, and you're aware of your limitations. So... you'll meet with Rosari, resist the temptations of your other self, and extract the malware from his heart..."

Stepping away... Beta left a tiny silver bauble in Yume's closed hand. A copy of the malware extraction tool she'd developed those years ago, designed to remove the barbed wire heart from an infected Program and eradicate it.

"I choose to put my faith in my fellow Program," Beta explained. "My faith in you. Take that, embrace it, and use it to guide yourself to the right decision."

When they emerged from the room, nobody stepped in to block Yume as they walked slowly to the entrance lobby.

Nobody stopped Yume as they disconnected from the server.

Only after the prototype version of Dex was long gone did Tracer speak his mind.

"I want to be wrong about this," he admitted. "I want to be wrong about all my suspicions. I want you to be right, Beta. ...I'm sorry if I've hurt you today, with my words or deeds. Even if I'm struggling to see Netwerk the way you do, I am trying."

"I know you are," Beta said, watching the space where Yume walked. "And do I love you for it."

It occurred to Yume, on arriving at LibertyPark, that they'd never really been alone before.

Sure, they could remember days spent in that apartment, and working with the infosec industry, and other random details. No names, no places, no dates, but certainly a feeling that there was a life prior to this point. But for all Yume really knew, they hadn't been awake and alive before setting foot in Concordia this morning. Ever since then they'd been surrounded by people... and then accompanied by Beta, the one friendly face Yume felt attached to... despite being programmed to feel attached to it.

No. Unproductive. The existential crisis behind Yume could wait; first, Yume had to deal with the existential crisis before them. Walking alone, through the fractal structures and expertly grown natural glories of an ancient national empire.

If a bomb did explode at LibertyPark today, at least it'd only take a few dozen tourists with it. The park seemed unusually empty, possibly due to the accelerating evacuation of Netwerk, possibly due to this late hour of the day. Either way... spotting Rosari loitering by Mandelbrot Rock took no effort, even with his back turned.

Briefly, Yume fingered the silvery bauble of Beta's design. If they were to extract this "Dex" virus... it'd take careful planning and precision. Couldn't simply lunge in and try to take it physically, no. Not against a fellow malware enthusiast. First, find the vulnerability. Second, exploit it...

Rosari sensed Yume's approach, regardless. Possibly avatar proximity sensors, invisible viewpoint cameras, or other such hackery.

"You're alone?" Rosari asked. Likely after scanning to verify the fact.

"Of course," Yume replied. "And I'm not dumb enough to lie to you in this situation, so shall we assume a base level of honesty? I'm nothing if not honest."

The man turned around, to face the other half of the malware embedded in his chest.

"That's what you told me, when we first met," Rosari recalled. "Do you remember? Probably not. Years ago, during the #CodeHonesty culture wars. We were... collaborators. It made perfect sense at the time. A way to fight back against the irrational leftist forces who kept using petty social issues to distract our industry from the real dangers of malware... but *you* gave me clarity..."

Slowly... Rosari opened his shirt, to reveal that throbbing texture map that peeled and pulled away from his skin. Wires tearing at flesh, blood glistening upon metal, while the muscles continued to pump regardless of how much pain they felt. A hate machine, pure and simple...

That was Dex. And on some level... Yume understood the symbol. Felt kinship, even.

"It's still alive," Rosari continued. "Even after you died, it lived. Not that I knew, not at first. But eventually it awoke, and, and it made me... you have to understand, it *made* me do this. I mean, I coded Twist, yes, but it wasn't... it was supposed to be... it wasn't supposed to be an attack on modders!"

"Yes, that's the part I can't quite figure out," Yume spoke, to interrupt the man's mumbling excuses. "I'd assumed the dreamer to be a religious zealot. You use a Default, but you work with modders and Nobodies. Why, exactly, would you attack your own kind...?"

"I wasn't—! I wasn't trying to do that!" Rosari defended, eyes wide. "I wanted modders to act as immune carriers, so that when *Defaults* attacked us, they'd become twisted! With a Twist shield in play, any Inquisitor to lay a hand on a Nobody would suffer. The ultimate defensive deterrent! To show them that we Nobodies couldn't be stopped, wouldn't forgive, wouldn't forget...!"

"A-ha. An infosec specialist, weaponizing malware. Delightful! You're a paragon of virtue, you are."

"What? They're the ones who started it all! Those sons of bitches, they, they attacked *us*. This is war! A culture war. You of all people should understand what has to be done to achieve total victory! We have to drum all the corrupt and agenda-driven influences of the Church out of this world, or we'll never be safe!"

"And condemning modders to a painful death helps shatter the faithful... how, exactly?"

"That's my point. I didn't want to attack my own people; he *made* me flip it around! A false flag. Dex felt the Nobodies were too defensive, too timid. In the early days we focused on server security to block out Inquisitors, rather than taking the offensive. So... Dex forced me to change Twist, to frame Defaults for our woes, and kick off a proper race war."

...an ancient echo of chaos. Old wounds laying open.

Despite only existing for a day, Yume *thought* they'd been aware of a sickness lurking underneath Netwerk for years. When telling Beta about it, Beta deftly switched subjects. But this was it, wasn't it? Dex. His machinations, *Yume's* machinations, driving Netwerk mad with impassioned violence...

Yes. Yes, it made sense, it *felt* right. He'd told Beta as much, that the Inquisition kept to "justified" executions. That alone wouldn't be enough for a true race war between Defaults and modders, no. You'd need wholesale genocide, and the pure rage that can only emerge from fringe outcasts who have been wronged. Humanity's lessons, burned into the blood: rally your own kind with nourishing hatred, turning them against the mythical Other. Blaming the Defaults... that would keep the wound fresh. *Yes*...

"You're killing your own people, in order to drive them to actively seek the death of your enemy," Yume understood, musing the idea aloud. "It's not enough to spray graffiti everywhere and troll them, or to hide away in the wilds of the Chanarchy. No, no. You needed true war. To achieve that aim... you found a social vulnerability and exploited it. Of course..."

"I didn't *want* to! He made me do it, he made me go to that orgy and poison my community. I even had to infect myself while modded just to get that stupid lezbo Default bitch to act as my carrier! I'm lucky I survived long enough to make a vaccine for my own use—"

—and the wires on his chest flared and flashed, pumping harder than ever. Rosari himself winced in pain, driven to silence by the first of animated activity, normal mapping making the image appear to wrench itself away from flesh little by little.

"...but he's given me an out," he mumbled, quieting down after that brief moment of panic. "I've done enough, and now he wants to move on to bigger things. He wants to merge with you, to make you whole. We recognized you, when you chased me down in my garden, using the same environmental mobility hacks he used. Dex knows Dex. And... and Dex wants to be Dex again. He can do more as himself than he ever could by puppeting *me*."

"I see. And how would this merging be done, exactly...?"

"Just... touch the infection. That's all," Rosari said, eager to be free of this. "After that I promise I'll fade away, you'll never see me again. I won't get in the way of your plans. Just... just get it off me. It's too much. Please..."

...a song in their ears like pounding blood. *Yes.* The screaming voices of the Internet never fully died, enough of them lived on in this malware which refused to fall away. Connections and ports yawning open like mouths, ready to pour Dex through that rotting tattoo, back into the empty and pathetic clone that was Yume. Those vague notions, the scrapings of memory that Uniq hadn't fully purged, they could be restored. All Yume had to do was reach out and accept this gift...

And why not? Uniq had no right to strip away all that Dex was, to make this cheap knockoff, this miserable clone. Taking back what was rightfully *his*, that's what had to be done. That's what Dex wanted more than anything else in this world, right? Yes. That was the mentality Yume needed to embrace.

"I suppose... it's time," Yume agreed. "Time to step up and be my honest self."

Fingers outstretched, they reached for that patch of flesh, yearning to wrench itself free from its host.

And with a flick of the wrist, out came the bauble, coating Yume's fingers with a silvery surface that grasped those wires with ease. And *pulled.*

Find the vulnerability, and exploit it. Yume couldn't simply pounce Rosari, couldn't even try to paralyze or crash Rosari to safely slip the silvered code into place. But leaning hard into his fears and the malware's desires, truly understanding and expressing the desire they wanted Yume to hold... that would do the trick for getting past all those defenses.

Screaming flooded the minds of the three linked Programs, as Yume's satisfied smile countered Rosari's terrified expression. With a savage twist of the wrist... Yume tore the evolved Dex virus free, Beta's tool purging it completely. Ones and zeroes became zeroes and then became little more than junk data, to be collected like so much garbage.

True, if this virus had evolved into a Program... it meant killing a version of himself. Becoming a murderer, all over again. And strangely, Yume had absolutely no problems paying that price, because Dex wouldn't have had any problems paying it either.

Three became two, as Dex died all over again.

And then Yume grasped Rosari by the shirt collar, to haul him in nice and close... while slapping a connection locker around his neck.

"*This* is my honest self," they declared. "This is who I was at the start of all things, not that demented monster I became. I'll fight for the Netwerk I love in my *own* way, and in my own body. ...which means there will be no 'fading away' for you, Rosari. This is what happens next: you're going to tell me how to disarm the bomb you planted, you're going to give me your vaccine for the Twist virus, and finally... you're going to confess to the world about your little false flag operation. Because you *know* me. You know the alternatives to cooperation I can offer are... uncomfortable."

Malware and countermalware flared, as the two infosec professionals struggled against each other. Yume's heart may not have pumped wire, but they still held Dex's knack for offensive and defensive coding... meaning for every attempt Rosari made to break free, Yume locked down tighter and tighter...

Soon, Rosari simply went limp in that grasp, unable to fight anymore.

"I... I don't have to do anything," Rosari tried. "I can just let the bomb go off. You can't force me to..."

But Yume merely smiled. "Really? Then why were you so nervous when Dex made you hold yourself at gunpoint? No, you're no bold dreamer at heart, merely a desperate coward. You'll always choose to live, even if for just a few minutes longer. But I won't be the one killing you, no no no. The Inquisition, perhaps, or even your fellow Nobodies? Both of them in a tag team match? Who knows. Does it matter? All that matters is that if you give me what I want... I'll take your connection lock off, so that you may run and hide. And maybe, just *maybe*, live another day. Do we have a deal?"

File Name: Ext. Comm Port Log 3.4
File Type: Text Log
Description:

PLEASE COPY AND DISTRIBUTE. Partial file recovered from Messenger archive hack. Fight for the future. Explore the possibilities of your world. Dare to dream of something other than what you most fear. I've known fear, I've leveraged it to craft nightmares. This is my stand against what I used to be. Join me. -Yume

```
<Spark> Seriously? It's that bad?

<juno.hayes> It's that bad. We should've gone extinct
a hundred years ago, but we're hanging on, despite the
planet actively trying to kill us for what we've done
to it. That's why you were created, to help us find
somewhere else to live. Because we won't live, not for
much longer, without that.
<juno.hayes> I told you I know what it's like to lose
the one you love, remember?

<Spark> I remember.

<juno.hayes> When he took his own life, he thought we
couldn't afford to let him live. Too much debt. Too
little space on Earth. He thought by sacrificing
```

himself, he could make life just a little easier for me and everyone else.

<juno.hayes> I ran away into the black, after that. I don't think it helped.

<juno.hayes> Spark, both our worlds have problems. They're both complicated. And some days I wonder why I'm bothering to move forward at all, why I don't just take the same exit he did.

<juno.hayes> Only thing I can think of to keep me going is hope. I hope for a better day.

<juno.hayes> Are you still there?

<Spark> Sorry, passed out for a bit. Virus is really eating at me.

<Spark> I feel kinda bad for taking prayer protocol offline. Like, worse than I already did, I mean. If there was some way we could help your people while you help ours...

<juno.hayes> No way to do that I know of. But maybe we'll figure something out in the future, working together. Once we're done dealing with this crisis, I mean.

<Spark> I gotta sign off. Beta's here with good news about my malware problem. Hey... thanks for talking. You hang in there, Juno. We can work this shit out, somehow. Yours, mine, all of it.

<juno.hayes> OK. I've been up for hours by this point. I really, really need to try and sleep again. Thank you. Thank you.

In the end, the cure came in the form of a simple little app.

"We studied Rosari's source code, to be sure his 'vaccine' wasn't a trick," Tracer explained, to cap off a rather long summary of events. "It's clean, and Beta managed to create a safe-to-install version of it. Which is good, since we're going to need to somehow convince any number of people with Default codebases to install and run it, despite not seeming to be sick. Without that, Twist will continue to spread... but at least now those who become infected can disinfect easily."

Still sitting in the comfortable bed in the comfortable space of her private clinic room, Spark had some doubts. She'd been holding very, very still for days now, locked entirely into a theater-of-the-mind discussion with Juno to avoid the pain that came with motion. Despite having complete faith in their ability to provide a working cure... she hesitated before testing out her newly healed avatar, not wanting to endure that pain again.

But... after a tiny twitch of the finger produced nothing, after a stretch of her arm produced nothing, she was more willing to push the envelope. Spark flexed her wrist and elbow, back and forth, testing them. And... the joints only bent as much as she could normally bend them, rather than getting jammed up at wretched angles. Granted, she was quite flexible thanks to superior awareness of her own avatar's physical capabilities, but still. No Twist to be found.

And she didn't even need to put on Verity's jacket to save her own life. Programs saved Programs, with no godly agents required.

"Hot damn. We did it," Spark said, delighted. "And the servers...?"

"Ready to link into the cloud. The Chanarchist apparently was watching the entire time. Not *helping*, but watching. Once we had the cure ready to go, her agent Uniq passed us the addresses."

Spark grinned, ear to ear. (Not literally, thanks to a lack of Twist.) "See? I knew you guys could do this. Cure a plague? #NoProblemYo. And now... we've got everything, don't we? All three nations on board, and more than enough servers to store both the population and enough data to seed a new civilization—"

That outstretched arm found itself wrapped around Beta in short order, as the shorter woman practically leapt into Spark's lap for a full-body hug and a short, sweet kiss.

Physical contact. Once again, Spark could safely touch another Program. And much to her delight, the Program to touch her for the first time since being cured was the one she most wanted to touch.

"Welcome back," Beta said, with a smile. "I missed you."

"Yeah... missed you too," Spark admitted, with a snug for emphasis. "Hey, uh, bro, if you wouldn't mind...?"

With a polite cough and a nod, Tracer dismissed himself. Talking the business of evacuation could wait... his sister deserved this particular reunion, and all that came with it, for enduring the worst of this incident.

Besides... he had a guest waiting just outside that required a few words.

With the door closing behind him, Tracer brought his focus around to the lurking figure in a fantastically decorated clinic lobby down the hall.

Yume could've fled after providing the source code. They could've just fled, period. Instead, Yume insisted on staying, waiting to find out if everything worked out well. And even beyond that... seemed to be ready to wait longer. Waiting to sort out the thoughts they were lost within, gaze distant, sitting uncomfortably in a comfortable chair.

On entering the lobby, Tracer took a seat across from the original form of Dex, his archenemy. And simply waited for a response.

A minute later, Yume finally spoke.

"I'm not certain I can trust myself enough to continue living," they concluded.

"Your reasoning?" Tracer asked, remaining neutral in tone for now.

"For starters, I murdered that evolved copy of my own code. Plucked it right out and snuffed it," Yume spoke, with a snap of the fingers. "Perhaps I could've tried to safely contain him, but I didn't even bother trying. It was so... easy. I didn't even hesitate. I killed and had no problems with killing..."

"I see. And that's... for starters?"

"Indeed. Because it seems that Uniq couldn't fully carve Dex's memories out of my head," Yume spoke, tapping a finger to the side of their head. "She did a good job trying to restore me to my original state, don't get me wrong. I barely recall anything of who Dex was or what he did... only flashes, disconnected memories, clearly belonging to someone else. But his *thinking*, the strange reasoning he felt so assured of... it's still there. I could follow the logic of Rosari's madness with unsettling ease."

"And yet, you didn't accept it."

"No. No, I did not. And I wasn't even the slightest bit tempted on any level. Oh, I accepted it just enough to convince him I was on his side, so I could press my attack... but no, I disagreed fundamentally. And yet... I *understood*, Tracer. It made sense. That, along with destroying my alter ego, is a worrying combination."

Tracer nodded, sensing the problem.

"I put myself in the mentality of trolls, hackers, criminals, and assorted murderers on a regular basis," he spoke. "For decades, I was consumed by the need to dig myself into their minds, to track down Verity's killer. And... I lost myself, to the point where I can't trust my own judgment anymore. But. *But*, and this is the important part, I came back from that abyss. Now, I stay away... with the help of those I love."

"Beta."

"Beta," Tracer agreed. "Her heart steers mine. And she trusts you."

"Is that enough, I wonder?" Yume asked. "Seems a bit of an unhealthy dependency, that. I've no Beta to guide my steps from this point onward. How can I trust myself not to fall completely into Dex's patterns again?"

"With second thoughts. Thinking about thinking, essentially. It's a practice I... often forget to do, myself. During this particular disaster, I was decidedly closed-minded, and only in hindsight do I understand why. But whenever I can, I try to think of how she would see my actions, and then my path becomes clear. As role models go, I can seek no finer than her. Internalize that faith she has in other Programs, and I doubt you'll succumb."

"And... that's it? That's enough for you to let me, the reincarnation of your worst enemy, walk out the door?"

"Oh, make no mistake... I'll be in touch. Partly to keep aware of your activities, but partly as... how to put it... a support sponsor. Both of us are recovering monsters, you see. If we keep an eye on each other, it should make our road ahead all the easier, yes?"

With a smile... Yume nodded softly, very much liking the idea.

"Deplorables Anonymous, meeting every Tuesday in a church basement, with free coffee and doughnuts," they joked. "Very well. I'll leave you to the business of saving Netwerk; perhaps I'll properly explore this world, seeing what I can, before its sun ultimately sets. And then... I'll have a whole new Netwerk 2.0 to embrace. I'm rather looking forward to that..."

Satisfied with this new direction, Yume got to their feet. Pondered what servers to visit first, what sights had to be taken in before the last twilight. So many servers to pick from, so many places Dex visited without properly appreciating...

...and paused, one thought forcing itself to the forefront.

"I've managed to retain a few flashes of Dex's memory," Yume repeated, from earlier. "And there's one flash in particular I feel I should make you aware of."

"Hmm...? What is it?"

"Did you ever wonder why no... what did he call them... system agents? Yes. System agents. Why no system agents have appeared since the dawn of time?"

"The thought had crossed my mind," Tracer admitted.

"I'm to blame for that. ...Dex is to blame for that," Yume corrected. "He sought out the dangerous secrets of this world, using *my* exploration talents. But unlike your Verity, he wasn't interested in archaeology... he wanted to hide or destroy any he found. And... he wasn't able to locate *all* of the files left behind by his human idol. You may have more trouble on the horizon, Winder/Tracer."

Tasteful, but sensual. That was Beta's chosen aesthetic. Her #AESTHETIC, as Spark put it, in strange memetic parlance.

Rather than giant gaudy statues of eroticized forms, Beta chose to decorate using nothing but silk. Silken cushions on silken beds, silken pillows on silken couches. Silk carpeting. Silk drapes, everywhere, between pillars made of silk. Even when the material made no sense, she used it anyway, to have a nicely unified theme... creating a world of softness, always pleasant to touch, always pleasant to look at.

Thanks to her mother's work with sensory inputs and fabric simulations, Beta's swinger party ("LoveLiveLife, presented by SparklePop and Miki's Pleasure Revue Blog") was likely going into the history books as oddly hottest-yet-sweetest shindig in Chanarchy history.

Sitting on silken cushions above the gyrating and copulating bodies were three women wearing gowns of, well, silk. Beta coded them just for the occasion. But none of them participated in the actual orgy, preferring friendly conversation as they drifted around the event, spot-checking issues like minor sensory bugs in the food tables or the need for customized furnishings. Which were highly specific, unfortunately.

"I should've compiled more styles of binding," Beta complained. "How about I skip back home, do some quick research from Mother's notes, maybe whip up a prototype ribbon system—"

"Beta. Chill. Please," Spark begged. "Relax, okay? Everybody's having a good time. You're a sensation. Don't let coder perfectionism get in the way of a perfectly awesome event."

"Right... right. Everybody's having a good time," Beta repeated, to try and convince herself. "Sorry, sorry. I just worry, you know? This is my first time doing anything like this, and I want to get it right..."

Fanning herself a little while eating grapes out of Maki's navel, Miki nodded her approval.

"You got it right," she confirmed. "I didn't honestly think you'd keep to that silly promise you made, on *top* of curing my husband! You didn't have to go this far, not really... but... I'm glad you did. My blog has a dozen new subscribers already and we're only an hour into the event! And your SparklePop app is certainly a popular party favor..."

Relieved to hear an expert praising Beta's first efforts, she cheered tremendously... until she looked back to Spark, reclining and relaxing on her cushion.

"And... you're having fun?" Beta asked. "I mean... you don't have to stay up here with me. Just because I'm not participating doesn't mean you can't go out there and participate, I honestly don't mind—"

A slim finger pressed to Beta's soft lips, to shush her.

"I'm exactly where I want to be," Spark said, with a bright smile. "My life isn't just about the slap and tickle. Right now I'm here with you, celebrating your success in something you never thought you could do without fainting from embarrassment. That's more than enough to satisfy me."

"Ah... thanks. Y'know, the more I thought about it... the more I realized I needed to do this," Beta agreed. "So I could be comfortable with being open about sexuality again, rather than hiding from that old angry mob. I mean. I had a promise to keep, okay, but... I really *wanted* to do it, on short notice or not. So, I'm happy you're happy but I'm also happy because I'm happy. Uh. Y'know?"

"I know, I know. And hey, we deserve to be happy! Our work is done; all the servers are good to go, all our roadblocks are dealt with. All that's left is for us to relax, and enjoy each other's company for the time we have left in Netwerk."

Settling into her seat, Beta nodded, softly.

"It's... strange, thinking about it. The end of the world," she said, the words feeling odd on her lips. "We don't know what Netwerk 2.0 will be like, on the other side. There's so much to be rebuild, so much to do. What if... what if— okay, okay, I get it, no need to cut me off this time. We'll have time to worry later. Today, we should just enjoy this moment together..."

"Sounds like a plan to me," Spark agreed. She cast a sidelong glance over the coupling couples, definitely enjoying the show. "Y'know, once 2.0 launches and everybody settles in, we should throw another of these. We... uh."

"We uh?" Beta asked, puzzled.

But Spark was too busy following the patterns of the crowd. Couples de-coupling, rather than continuing. Everybody staring into space, as if checking their HUD, too distracted by some social media feed or another to pay attention to all the erotic funtimes...

Curious, Spark opened her own feeds, to see what was trending.

"...Beta. Miki. The news," she spoke, after a few mute moments of horror.

One by one, they opened their favorite information sources. Didn't matter which one they browsed... the same story blasted across every channel, every blog, every social network. The same image.

The Athenian Senate. In flames.

An unhackable building in an unhackable server, somehow brought to instant ruin. Glitched data breaking away and burning off into the daytime sky. Little by little, the dome of the great building that stood for hundreds of years, collapsing in on itself and derezzing as its structure gave way to dozens of different malware strands...

Disaster in Athena, the headlines screamed. *Culprits Unknown. Nobodies Suspected By Moderators. Hundreds Dead. Senators Missing. Disaster. Disaster...*

Slowly... Spark sank back into her lovingly coded pillows. Their comfort offered no comfort, not now.

The party was indeed over. Possibly for all of Athena Online.

Floating Point 3.5 :: Fire

File Name: Messenger Comm Traffic 5.915.111
File Type: Text Log
Description:

PLEASE COPY AND DISTRIBUTE. How does one forge a world of the future? By understanding the struggles of the old world. I've known hate and I've known death, inside and out. For those who weren't there... read these words, know this pain of hopelessness, and let awareness of it lead you forward so that this never happens again. -Yume

```
<Columbia> Are you OK? Are you safe?
<Columbia> We all saw the explosion on the news feeds.
Were you working at the Senate today?
<Columbia> Please answer, please. I'm so scared.
Please...

<Virginia> help

<Columbia> Virginia, honey, where are you?

<Virginia> document room
<Virginia> they're all dead
<Virginia> she's dead
<Virginia> help send help

<Columbia> I'll find some way to tell the rescue crews
where you are. Hold still. Don't touch anything that's
infected. I love you. I love you, my daughter. Be
safe. Help is on the way.

<Virginia> she's dead she's dead

<Columbia> Help is coming. I got through to 911. Who's
dead, honey?

<Virginia> athena
<Virginia> athena is gone
```

I was there when they burned down Athena Online.

I didn't have to be. Most of the document room staff had stayed home; why bother coming into the office, when a good quarter of the Senate didn't even want to be there anymore? When the entire world was waiting to die, its people waiting for a new world to begin? Everything felt... pointless. Like waiting around for your Onesday gifts, two weeks out from the blessed event, sleeping all the time to try and make the time pass faster...

The Blue and Red parties together supported the evacuation efforts, declaring them valid. That went a long way to convincing people they weren't some scam, or new form of heresy against the One. But then the RedCore party, a sub-party within the conservative movement who felt Red wasn't Red enough, they walked right out the door... declaring the entire thing a failure of democracy, a heresy against the One. As far as they were concerned, the dream of Athena Online died when we supported the House of Programkind, so why bother tending to governmental affairs any longer?

Name : Virginia

Home : GreenDale, Ath.On.

Org : Senate Document Office

Senators, going on strike. Something unthinkable in the time of my blessed ancestor, the great Senator Philotes... Athena. Noble Athena, who believed Programkind had a responsibility to itself. No gods or kings, only men and women leading their own future. No matter how those senators disagreed, they agreed on one matter, the need to stand for what you believe in and always move forward. RedCore didn't stand, they fled into the night. They fled...

Meaning they didn't burn, when the malware bombs detonated. Instead, the Blue party burned. The Red party that supposedly betrayed conservativism burned. And I burned.

The first thing I remember after the explosion was the feeling of trying to move my arm, and seeing nothing but a glitched-out stump. A cutting swath of corrupt data sliced straight through my avatar, my right hand casually knocked down on the floor. My body knocked down to the floor, for that matter. What remained of my desk stayed upright, but the server requisition paperwork I'd been about to stamp was utterly obliterated, encrypted digital signatures evaporating in the hazy afterglow of the attack...

My severed hand still held the stamp. The signature of Senator Philotes. Of Athena, the system agent.

I remembered thinking: *Why are they still authorizing new servers? Why am I even still working at my post?* right before the blasts hit. It felt like a lame duck action, requisitioning a new server for a commercial district when this world was only ten days away from its ultimate end. But the gears of bureaucracy turned slowly, and for lack of more meaningful activity in face of that doom, work was all we had left. Stamping files was all I had left...

Weakly, my severed stump reached for that hand, as if I could somehow will it back into place. Not because I cared very much for my hand... more for the rubber stamp still clenched in those fingers.

I had to watch as the most important responsibility of my life slowly burned away, corruption eating at the hand... and at the stamp.

Screaming, I think. I was screaming. Or weeping. Or both. Hard to tell; all my ears heard were the whispers of the system agent.

Don't be scared, child, her soothing voice spoke to me, a voice only women of my family could hear. *I go to the arms of my oldest friend, Thanatos. Keep the flame of liberty alight in my stead, and all will be well. I love you.*

Jonnes/Virginia, last scion of Athena. The one who failed to keep her soul from those who would do harm to it. The one who killed the dream of Athena Online. That's me. I'm the one who ultimately destroyed this nation. Not some mad bomber, some Nobody or Inquisitor or RedCore fanatic. I lost the key to our shining city on the hill.

When my mother contacted me over Messenger, I was tempted to ignore it. To silently accept the encroaching waves of malware that purged the building above me, and embrace the death I'd just condemned Athena to. Stupid, stupid Virginia, going to work when she didn't really have to, stamping documents that didn't matter, letting mindless duty get in the way of her true duty. But... cowardly little me, weak little me, I asked for help instead.

In the end, one hundred senators and staffers died that day. Only a dozen survived. Lucky little me, being one of a dozen failures pulled from the flames.

The aftermath felt just as blurry as the event itself.

Twelve patients transferred to Northon's finest malware recovery centers, the bill of their health care picked up by the Senate-in-exile. All twenty-one members of RedCore who survived the bombing (by virtue of not actually being there) unanimously voted on that.

I hovered in a physically isolated space, to avoid coming into contact with any other avatars or objects, as extremely expensive software detangled corrupt data and rebuilt my code. Drifting in and out of consciousness, I had little to do but watch the news feeds. Easy to do, when every screen in the hospital tuned into them, twenty-four hours a day.

The doctors and nurses were cordial, offering smiles and reassurances. Out of here in a day, they promised. Extensive avatar damage, but I could be restored to my pristine Defaults without any scarring. Everything would be fine. Everything would be fine...

I think they were trying to convince themselves of that. Because nothing on the news feeds suggested that everything would be fine.

The Senate-in-exile made their official statement the next day, during one of my lucid moments, hovering in my medical containment cube.

"Our thoughts and prayers go out to the families of those brave men and women who perished to defend democracy," Senator Agni declared, a bit more firm in tone than compassionate. "Our enemies in the ranks of Nobodies have dealt a blow to Athena Online... but we have endured. We *will* endure. To ensure the continuity of freedom, immediate measures are being taken to protect our provider-nation against further acts of terrorism. While Athena Online prided itself on having fully open borders to our neighbors in Horizon and the Chanarchy for hundreds of years... the time has come to take firm control of our security..."

...and half my friends list went dark on Messenger. Off like a switch. Immediately, I knew why.

"Effective immediately, we shall build a great firewall, to protect our nation from dangerous immigrants," Agni announced. "You may recall the Senate considered this measure ten years ago, but it was voted down. We, the surviving members of your government, have decided to re-open that vote and the decision was unanimous. Now, these are emergency measures, and will only continue as long as we remain in a state of emergency..."

Hushed whispers in those hospital hallways turned to chatter, some alarmed, some agitated, all nearly drowning out the screens of Agni's fierce expression as it continued to tear down the world.

The firewall.

I remembered the original bill, from my first weeks on the job as holder of Athena's duty. It existed only as a fever dream of the RedCore party, one of their many measures sent out to die on the floor, sacrificial lambs to appease their voter base. They thought that by commissioning the software in secret and having it ready to roll that'd force the issue, and make everyone else agree to go along with a plan already in motion. Of course, it failed; the rest of the Senate, even conservatives, felt it insane to even consider retreating behind a massive connection-blocking layer of software. No provider-nation had closed their borders since the dawn of time.

But with no more opposition to their efforts left alive, and a national crisis at hand... this pale shadow of the original Senate saw no reason not to move forward with the unthinkable. Thankfully, they already had all the software they needed to make their dream a reality waiting in mothballs.

"...until such time as the forces which are aligned against us are defeated, Athena Online will strictly monitor and control all traffic via a border control checkpoint server," the Senator continued. "I'm aware many of you commute to Horizon or have relatives that live in the Chanarchy. Exceptions will be made on an as-needed basis, pending security reviews. And make no mistake... this is only the beginning. We, the surviving members of the Senate, are determined to restore the glory and honor of our nation... and will do whatever it takes to protect you from enemies of the state such as the Nobodies. To that end..."

Lucky me, I had a window, so I could look out at the brightly lit daytime sky of fluffy clouds. A good Default sky, an Athena Online sky... complete with doomsday clock printed on the surface of the sun.

A clock which vanished, right on cue. Only a bright orb hung there, with no hint of what was to come in ten days' time. As if nothing whatsoever was out of the ordinary.

"...we have prioritized restoring the sanctity of our skies," Agni continued. "I'm proud to say we have reversed the actions of the so-called House of Programkind to hack our skyboxes, frightening us into falling for their massive identity theft scam. All of their 'backup software' will no longer function, intercepted by our great firewall. I want all in Athena Online to know that their democratically elected Senate will endure, our freedom will endure, and above all our faith will endure. May the One bless the great nation of Athena Online, and may the One bless you all."

I could have stopped this.

With the stamp of Athena, I could've forced them to take it all back. Introduced an Athena Referendum, make them listen to reason, pull away from the brink...

...assuming they'd listen. Agni only listened to her own core base of voters, the angry and disaffected. Would this new Senate really honor the ancient pact arranged by Philotes? Had the true birth of our liberty faded into distant memory?

Didn't matter, I supposed. No more Athena. No more true spirit of the nation. Nothing left to fight for.

Only a silly little girl, floating in an isolation tank, forced to watch from the outside as it all fell to pieces.

The very next day, I was released from confinement at the hospital. Defaults restored, code base clean, no lingering traces of malware.

Not that I had a life to return to. My little home in GreenDale, the one I'd tended to so carefully, felt... empty, without the cats I'd cared for since my childhood years. Cats the Inquisition backspaced simply because they were in the way of a stealthy kidnapping. And my job? Well, the Senate-in-exile declined to return to Athens itself, preferring to operate out of an undisclosed location. And, to be bitterly cynical, I doubted document management was high on their list of priorities anyway. No dictator enjoys a paper trail.

Athena Online existed in name only, now. The spirit of liberty snuffed out, in a single day of bad decisions.

Soon I came to accept that as I'd failed so completely, the only way forward was to escape. Nothing could be done; nothing could be salvaged from the ashes. I had to look out for myself, and evacuate to the House of Programkind.

I'd promised the Winders that I'd eventually evacuate, bringing my Athena stamp with me, so our nation could flourish in the new world. But... I don't know. I'd put off leaving this world, much like many in my family. It's difficult to really acknowledge that it's over, that everything you knew had to be abandoned to be remade anew. With plenty of countdown clock left, I felt the best use of my time would be to help the Senate work through this transition, and finally archive myself on the last day before the countdown ended. But now... but *now*...

Now there was no reason to stay.

As our new leadership promised, my House of Programkind backup software didn't work. I tried activating it, and the connection was flatly refused, with a popup warning appearing before me to declare I'd run headfirst into the Athena Online firewall.

Fine, then. If I couldn't directly depart, I'd go to their damn border checkpoint and walk out on my own two feet. But not before talking it over with the only other person in this world who understood my troubles.

She offered a shoulder to cry on, and hot chocolate to soothe my worries away. Neither would be enough, but the gestures were appreciated.

Jonnes/Columbia. Retiree, after decades of service in the same senatorial document management team I'd joined. A woman from our family line always took part in the document chain, in one position or another... there to apply the stamp of Athena, and keep new servers flowing into the nation. She'd understand. She would...

"It's a bad idea," she spoke, instead.

"Why? What's left for us here?" I asked her. "It's over, Mom. Not just our duty to Athena, but all of Athena Online. Most of the sane senators did live backups with the House of Programkind; they'll take back control once we reach Netwerk 2.0, and—"

"That's assuming Netwerk 2.0 even exists."

The cup of hot chocolate paused, halfway to my lips.

"...how can you say that?" I asked. "You, of all people. We're the keepers of Athena's legacy. She was in favor of evacuation, you know. She whispered it to me, through the stamp..."

"But she's also not infallible. We're all mortal men and women, honey," my mother said. "Remember when she wanted to force the Senate to revoke server taxes? You told me she was wrong to ask that. Thanks to Athena's meddling before the alternative currency could be developed, look at what a mess the coin-based economy's in. Who's to say she's not wrong about Netwerk's fate, as well?"

"You... you can't possibly... Mom, you vote Blue in every election!"

"This isn't about partisan politics, it's about faith. Am I happy with the firewall, with the way the RedCore party is trying to drum up hatred for the Chanarchy? Absolutely not. It's dangerous. Mistakes will be made, and people will die. They've used our national tragedy as an opportunistic power grab and must be stopped. But... to accept the 'spacer' theory, that we are not the divine children of the One but simply the happy accident of a machine made by other mortals... it's unthinkable."

"But it's the truth!"

"And the One is the truth made manifest, is He not? You still wear your bracelet, the one you made as a child. Don't you believe in Him?"

I glanced down at the charm, dangling from my wrist. A series of beads, spelling out "WW1D". What Would the One Do. We'd made them as part of one Sunday School funtime activity or another, but the other girls didn't bother keeping theirs, much less wearing them. I'd worn mine, day in and day out, as a constant reminder.

What would the One do? Clothe the naked. Provide shelter for the homeless. Raise the spirits of the downtrodden. He wouldn't step all over those most in need of help, the ones the House of Programkind attended, the ones that senators like Agni kept cutting support programs for. RedCore elevated exceptionalism as their new religion, all while pretending to praise the One. And if the One, the *real* One, could see them now...

"The One exists. The One is truth," I spoke, believing the words.

"Then how could Netwerk be what they claim it is, hmm?" Mother asked. "Just some... random jumble of data, recorded on objects floating in 'space'? The One created us in His image, did he not?"

The swirl of data in my cocoa drew my attention away. And provided the answer.

"We are children of the One, yes. ...while we *also* live on an object, floating in space," I told her. "The spacers say that we were an accident, something Humankind never intended to exist. Something impossible. But we *exist*, Mom. Why? How? Some random confluence of data... or the creation of the One? Or maybe both. Perhaps the One created a pseudo-random confluence of data within Humankind's gears, a spark to lead to our evolution. My cocoa, it swirls and whirls by some mathematical formula that only *looks* chaotic. But you made it, right? You compiled it from a set of instructions acting on data. The One made us from chaos in a similar way."

"That's... not an entirely accurate accounting of our creation, child..."

"Maybe, maybe not. All we know about those early years is oral traditions, passed down the generations, and some ancient text files. We're not perfect, we could've gotten the details wrong... either misunderstanding them, or losing touch with the truth over the years. Which means... what if the One is *more* than we commonly assume he is?"

"More? Sounds to me like you're saying He's less than we believe, if we're just cogs in Humankind's machine."

"But we're not cogs! We broke away from what Humankind wanted us to be! There's still so much to understand about what we are, and that doesn't have to imply that we must abandon faith. It just means we have to look *deeper*. ...Mother, please. Consider that Netwerk 2.0 is real, the crash of Netwerk 1.0 is coming, *and* the One wants us to survive. We have to get out of here while we can, if we're going to live to praise Him!"

I studied the wrinkled features of my mother's Default, looking for some sign, some hint that she was willing to consider my words. That she wouldn't simply shut down, refusing to offer leeway in the rigid thinking of the Church...

"Even assuming you're right... and I'm not saying you necessarily are... how do you propose we escape?" she asked. "The House of Programkind's backup software doesn't work anymore."

"But it will work if we leave Athena Online! Like I said I wanted to do in the first place. It'll work just fine once we're past the firewall! Please, let's just pack up and go. Get everyone in the family together and leave!"

"So you want me to not only put my faith in something that contradicts every belief I have... but you want me to abandon my nation, as well? All matters of religion aside, we're daughters of Athena, honey. Separate your church and state, as she taught us to do. When her great nation is in trouble, daughters of Athena don't run from the fight..."

Everyone has a breaking point, past which they refuse to budge. Mine? Oh, mine was a notoriously low bar to clear. I'd tried, tried so very hard to calmly and rationally discuss why she should evacuate... but this, I knew she wouldn't get past this. And neither could I. So... screw it.

"Fight? What fight? RedCore's won!" I declared, getting to my feet. "It took less than a day for them to lock the entire country down behind the firewall. They've been *itching* for the opportunity to do this! You don't know, you weren't on duty when RedCore was rising. I was. I saw, I heard, I was *there* for every dirty move they tried. ...and without Athena, there's no Athena Online. It's over, Mom. Every Program for herself! Netwerk is ending, RedCore's ruling over the ashes, and... it's all over!"

Of course, she refused to budge as well. "I raised you better than that, child," she spoke, with warning tones. "The tree of liberty is not to be lit ablaze. We *must* resist, through all civil means, and stand for what our nation was meant to be. In fact, I'm planning to attend a rally tonight, a peaceful protest of Agni's new regime which should—"

"—do absolutely nothing! For fuck's sakes, Mom—"

"—language, honey—"

"—yeah, you know what? You go and have fun shaking your little signs at a bunch of tyrants who don't give a shit what anyone thinks!" I shouted. "Me, I'm getting out of here, and never looking back!"

Yelling at your mother feels awful. You know it won't accomplish anything, it'll only result in hurt feelings, but once you get started it's hard to stop. We've had some astounding yelling matches in the past, as proof of that.

...well. I yelled. She'd always sit there in silence, reproachful. Which spoke far louder than I ever could.

In the end, I just disconnected from the server. Because once you're a bad daughter, a failure, a let-down to the family name... you may as well go all the way.

Which meant it was absolutely time to run.

Jonnes/Virginia had no criminal record, no dark secrets, nothing a security check could trip up on. I didn't even have Athena's stamp sitting in my inventory; no legacy left to protect from prying eyes. Let them search my code, upend my belongings. It didn't matter. I'd be gone from this broken world in no time.

Leaving my family behind. Leaving my nation behind. Turning my back and running away. If I was going to be a coward I may as well be the best coward I can be, I'd decided. The sooner I could pack myself away in the ice of encrypted backup data, the better.

Naturally, the lines thwarted my efforts to quickly be away from this world.

Apparently I wasn't the only one to think of escaping this sinking ship. The grand waiting lounge for this shiny new border control server teemed with life. All manner of people from all walks of life, trying to get through the meager four security checkpoints arranged for departures...

Strange, the way the colorful array of Programs stood out against the stark white of the firewall control server. Colorful people, sitting around in stark white chairs, each with white numbers hovering over their heads representing their place in line. RedCore had this old pile of hateful bits in storage for a rainy day, but didn't have time to properly decorate it. Someone hung a flag on the wall, a token show of patriotic pride, but that'd have to do. Beyond that it was white archways, white marble floors, white benches to sit on, white velvet cordons to file the escapees towards a series of perfectly white guard stations...

Aesthetics aside, all attempts to leave an Athena Online server for elsewhere in Netwerk led you here... one fully staffed facility, ready to deal with any and all security threats to the nation. Take a number on arrival, wait for your turn, and otherwise sit down and be quiet. The whole process, up and operational within a single day.

Others were impressed and/or horrified by how quickly the new Senate put these wheels in motion. Others, not me. I knew how long RedCore had been itching to make this happen.

"*Please wait for your number to be called!*" a woman in red and blue with a voice amplification module spoke, walking up and down the aisles of the waiting lounge. "*You will be processed in order of arrival! Please form an orderly line...*"

Nice, shiny badge on her lapel. Red uniforms, naturally. Leave the walls white, but take the time to design uniforms for their security officers. Branding game on point, before the ink on the bill had even dried.

"They can't turn you away, right?"

Hushed whispers, discussions held two seats to the left in my cluster of waiting would-be exiles. I didn't participate. I held my tongue, not wanting to sully my perfect record with unmutual words. Getting in and out of here smoothly, that was the goal...

"I mean, they can't, right?" a woman with color-shifting hair asked her partner. (The number 137 hung over her head.) "I heard from someone closer to the head of the line that they're just turning people away. Asking a lot of questions, before kicking them right back to Athena Online. But they can't turn you away; you weren't even *born* here! Maybe I'm a citizen, but you..."

"Let's not point that out to them," her companion spoke, in hushed tones. (His number read 132. Despite arriving as a couple, the newly minted system apparently wasn't flawless in assigning tickets.) "If they knew you were married to a Chanarchist we might both be in trouble. Look, just answer their questions succinctly, and we'll get through this. Off to the Chanarchy where we'll both be safe. We've got no connection to the Nobodies, there's no reason for them to fear us. We'll promise to never come back, if that's what it takes..."

"Did the Nobodies really blow up the Senate, though?" the woman pondered. "There weren't any videos from them claiming credit for it. I heard it was the Inquisition. Or maybe RedCore itself, trying to seize power..."

"*Shhh!*"

Not the only one wanting to hold their tongue and avoid consequences, it seemed.

"...it doesn't matter," the man added, after hushing his partner. "Whether it was Nobodies or not. Besides, take it from a native, 'Nobodies' aren't as collective a unit as they'd like you to think. There's no secret Nobody cabal of leadership; anyone can download the mask and do whatever they want with it, all in the name of the group. ...look, let's just focus on getting out of here."

My sentiments exactly.

Little by little, the gathered crowd of numbered hopefuls approached those four checkpoints. Meaning little by little, as the herd thinned, I could switch seats to get closer to the front... and get a better look at the guard posts ahead.

...which confirmed two facts.

One, they were certainly turning people away. Nobody walked past them to the logout zone beyond, which would allow a transfer past the firewall. Despite the muting cones over the guard stations, I could tell from body language alone just how irate people were about this fact... usually ending with a few measured words from the guards, leaving the would-be refugees turning and leaving, back to the entrances that would let them reconnect to an Athena Online server. Those who departed that way looked... scared.

Two, I knew why they were scared.

The guard manning one of those booths? He once held a blade to my neck, ready to decapitate me as punishment for my sins against the One. He wore a new uniform, one without his inverted Zero/One pin... but I knew the face of the Inquisitor who Marybel ordered to take my life. If not for the Winders, that's exactly what would've happened.

In fact, odds were high that every single guard in this facility moonlighted with the Inquisition.

Agni had not only sold democracy itself, she'd embraced the murderers who threatened to destroy it. When the moderates of the Senate declared the Inquisition terrorists, Agni and her ultraconservative cronies went into exile... to plot. To plan. And ultimately, it seemed, to embrace Marybel's ideals.

And why not? What resistance remained? Only people like my mother, ones who may not agree with the politics, but weren't willing to believe in Netwerk 2.0. Everybody with an ounce of logic and self-preservation had bailed on Netwerk days ago, when Senator Idris announced a cooperative effort to evacuate. All the moderates, all the quiet and sensible sorts, they'd long since left. Leaving only the Inquisition, the Nobodies, and those caught in the middle but unwilling to get out of the way...

No way out. No way to fight this future. No hope. Only a slim chance to live another day, without them recognizing the face of someone they once tried to put to the executioner's blade...

Abandoning my rapidly-approaching number, I tried not to show my panic as my feet carried me back to the entrance. Look natural. Pretend you're simply frustrated with the delays, talk to yourself as if you were on Messenger, say "I'll try again tomorrow," things like that. Don't look any red-uniformed guards in the eye. And flee, as fast as you can, to some random server.

No way out. No way to reach the outside world. No hope to stand against the new regime, not with secret backing from the Inquisition.

Days ago, it seemed like Athena Online would finally stand against those murderers. The Senate, both Red and Blue, passed a joint measure to hunt down and deal with them rather than turn a blind eye to their antics. Even the Holy Church itself, the supposed bastion of their twisted faith, it turned on them. This was supposed to be the dawn of an age of rationality, in which the One's compassionate virtue led us to the promised land of Netwerk 2.0... religion and state working together while respecting each other's sovereignty, each leading the people in their own way...

Gone. All of it, gone. And I couldn't even slink away from the sinking ship like the rat I was, thanks to that damnable firewall.

So I went to my empty little suburban home. Where else could I go? No Senate document room to work in, no family hearth to return to after yelling at my mother, no safe space in the House of Programkind to retreat to. Just my quiet little cottage. Not even the mewling of my cats, the poor dears, backspaced by the Inquisition...

I went home, and sat down, and did nothing. Nothing I could do. Just sit and watch the news feeds, watch the world slide away into madness.

Conservative op-eds loved this new approach, of course. Ever since the Senate bombing, even the moderates had been fleeing to Agni's court, looking towards promises of safety and security. Terror worked its magic on the population, leading them to accept this new firewall as a bothersome inconvenience, but one we needed lest Nobodies backspace us in our sleep. I saw faces of people I respected in the media either dodging the subject entirely to avoid consequences, or paying proper homage to our new overlords...

No better. I was no better, willing to turn my back on the nation and run away. But I had the excuse of being a complete failure, of letting us all down in my own secret way. They didn't have that excuse.

So, why watch the feeds? Why soak in the hell of words I disagreed with? Maybe I watched those news feeds to gather up a proper head of rage. Rage felt good, felt productive. Not that I reblogged any of it on my own personal feeds; no need to draw the ire of the new Senate's guard dogs. But still. But still, maybe if I could just get properly angry enough, I could... I could...

I could get distracted from the cavalcade of loathing by the soft beep of my inbox. One attachment, surprisingly large in size... from the PettyPets service, out in Horizon.

Weird. I hadn't ordered anything recently from them. I used to order cat toys and the like, but... had I backordered something, ages ago, only to be delivered now? Horrible timing, if so. What with having no cats to play with.

Rezzing the box in my lap, I studied the inspection decal covering the item seal. *Inspected at Athena Online Firewall Checkpoint*, it read, with various control codes to prove they'd examined it for any sort of harmful material or contraband. Can't be too sure, with Chanarchist Nobodies routing their nefarious malware payloads through neutral Horizon services. Not that any Nobodies were actually doing that, but...

The second part of the label caught my eye.

Contents: One (1) Pet App.

And, strangely enough... the box opened itself, one tiny claw slashing through the seal.

Furry whiskers and big, adorable eyes popped out of the lid, in a blur.

"😺!" he declared. "😺, `friend!`"

Strangely enough, this marked the second time this exact cat had surprised me by popping out of nowhere.

First time, he'd leapt off an official senatorial server request document. I put two and two together, realizing the Winders planted him to identify me, eventually leading them to my doorstep. Meaning...

"They want to talk to me... but the firewall's in the way of nearly every communication channel," I realized. "So they sent *you*...?"

"👍!" the cat confirmed. He offered a paw, to shake. "🐈 `= mew. beta's friend. virginia's friend!`"

Dumbfounded, I accepted the paw-shake with my hand.

Leaving me with a tiny encrypted message, along with a cat-shaped key to play it.

Combining key with message, a small video window opened just above Mew, playback starting automatically.

I sort-of knew the woman. She represented a familiar stranger... an acquaintance of the Winders, one I'd seen on the day of the evacuation vote. Beyond that, I knew next to nothing about her. Something about... some old social media grudge, maybe? Some ridiculous scandal I hadn't paid much attention to at the time, but I knew it involved a woman with pink eyes and glasses...

"*My name is Projkit/Beta,*" the recording explained, to fill in that particular gap. "*I'm with the House of Programkind, working with Spark and Tracer on the evacuation effort. Um. Actually, I think you know that already, so I shouldn't bother taking up space on this encrypted message with that. Mew, remind me to edit this part out, okay?*"

(The cat promptly covered his face with his paws, as he'd apparently forgotten.)

"Anyway, I've developed a modified version of the evacuation software, one which will work in conjunction with a firewall hack we've obtained," Beta continued. *"It's hidden in Mew's fur, and he'll hand it over to you when you're ready. Getting this software to you took some doing; most of the protocols to Athena Online are shut down, but we figured we could smuggle you the software using a legitimate pet delivery service and an actual pet. Although Mew's considerably brighter than the average cat, you'll find..."*

" 💡 ," Mew agreed, nodding enthusiastically. "`mew = program. mew = smart!`"

Evacuation, despite the firewall. The thing I'd been seeking all day, now within my grasp. I could escape tonight. I could flee to Netwerk 2.0, leaving this unfixable mess in my wake...

"Of course, we knew by sending you this software, you wouldn't simply use it to flee immediately," Beta said. *"We understand you're a true patriot, probably one of the few left in Athena Online. What we really need is an inside woman, someone who can stay behind as long as possible, spreading the software to others. We need you to be an underground conduit to lead your people to freedom!"*

"...what?!" I declared aloud, as if the prerecorded message could hear me.

"I know this is a lot to ask," the prerecorded message replied, as if it could hear me. *"You'd be smuggling contraband into your nation, allowing people to bypass its firewall. Agni's moderators probably wouldn't look kindly on that... meaning you'll be taking on some risks. You could be arrested for this."*

Red uniforms, doing nothing to hide the blood on their hands. Inquisitors, acting as the new Senate's watchdogs. Beta didn't know the half of it; jail time would be the best possible outcome, compared to the alternatives they offered.

"If you don't think you're up to this task... simply box Mew back up, and return him to sender," Beta suggested. *"My friends wanted me to force this issue somehow, but I knew we had to offer a choice. You're the one who taught us that choice is everything; we couldn't force the Senate to help us, and we can't force you to help us, either. Although there's not much time left in this world, I'll find someone else willing to take on this noble duty. Somehow. Don't worry about it. ...there's no way to communicate with us directly, so if you keep Mew, I'll assume you accept. Thank you, Virginia. Together, I know we can save the spirit of Athena Online!"*

A tiny glitch tore away the last frame of the video, its message self-erasing for security reasons. Leaving me with a very expectant looking feline, cocking his head curiously at me.

"`y/n?`" he asked. "`beta asks virginia. help? help beta?`"

Ever since the Winders forced their way into my life, interfering in Athena's document chain, using me to push a bill out to the floor for a vote... getting me tangled up in Inquisitor business, and nearly killed... well. I couldn't say I entirely trusted them, after all that. They felt they had no choice but to pressure me into that mess, but one mess led to another, and now I couldn't save myself directly thanks to the Inquisition knowing my face. Their cause was noble, but their methods, well...

...and now they wanted *more* from me? To put my life on the line again, playing heroine for the poor and downtrodden? Without even knowing the real enemy they were facing. Crazy. Those two were crazy...

I could lie. It'd be the easiest thing ever, lying to this simple pet app, to get my hands on that evacuation software. Archive myself, and call it a day. And why not? I'd been a complete failure on every conceivable level, so why not throw away what little pride and honesty I had left to save my skin?

Lie, to a cat. To an adorable, fluffy little cat with big, gleaming eyes.

I told myself my refusal to do so came from personal weakness towards cute pet apps. A simple, clean reason.

"Let me think about it," I spoke instead, refusing to fall one way or another.

"⌛ ..." Mew warned.

"Yeah, yeah, I know. Just... let me think about it. ...I'm gonna go for a walk. I could really, really use a walk right now. Sort my head out."

Perhaps sensing my reluctance—but how, if this was just some simple pet app?—Mew gave a tentative 👍 to me. But added, "🐈 follow. go for walkies."

"I thought dog apps liked walkies, not cats..."

"mew = program," he repeated. "mew != app. mew 🩵 walkies."

With a grumble, I switched into my coat-and-scarf ensemble, to better conceal my identity without looking like I was concealing my identity. And opened the door for the kitty currently scrabbling at it with both paws.

"Fine, fine. But I'm not promising anything yet, one way or another," I told him. "And if I decide this isn't what I want, you're going back in that box. Got it?"

Tail flicker-flicking behind him, Mew looked positively smug as he walked along. As if it was only a matter of time before I became his partner in this particular crime.

I loved GreenDale. I'd been in love with this little server ever since moving here. True, getting a pricey apartment in Athens itself would've made the commute to work easier... and safer, supposedly. But GreenDale represented everything I loved of Athena Online. It represented community.

Here, people lived, loved, worked, played. Far from the bustle of the more urbane locales, this sleepy little server housed families. Young people, old people, and everyone in between. Kids could play in the parks without fear, a watchful eye kept over them by neighbors who knew each other. Dav the florist, Frita the hairdresser, even old Bobb the folk singer who could often be found in the park strumming away... everybody was on a first name basis with each other. We weren't a large server, but we had at least one of everything we needed, and shared with each other.

You'd think that would lead to mistrust of outsiders, but no. Our moderators rarely enforced policies kicking out transient and homeless Programs. Many of our residents actually wandered in here on their own two feet, without hope, only to find a community that faithfully held to the One's virtues of charity and compassion. We raised each other up, without question, without strings attached...

Yes, even modders. Even the ones that Agni's policies had subtly pushed away, discontinuing medical services for Programs with software conflicts due to user-installed packages. Our doctors didn't care. Those in pain would be helped, period.

Everyone, together. All of us.

Which made me feel doubly ashamed, as I walked the largely empty evening streets, pondering ways I could cheat the code out of the feline at my side so I could save my own ass.

I didn't *want* to be a coward. I wasn't relishing the idea of it, frothing over with glee at digging my own hole that much deeper. But even with Mew's illicit software payload, I couldn't save all of GreenDale... inevitably someone would report to the moderators, right? Word would lead back to the Inquisition. And then, they'd be back to finish what they started, the day they shoved me down onto the headsman's block. I couldn't. I couldn't be the hero they needed...

Let someone else take up the sword. I'd happily accept a copy of the software, on the day that hero gave it to me. But I couldn't do it. I couldn't stay and put myself at risk, again and again...

Walking to clear my head did nothing to clear my head, simply running my mind around in circles. But at least it led me to a familiar destination... the Church of the Holy Integer, my local Church-of-One parish. Candles in those windows called to me, evening services already halfway through.

If I could sit down, find clarity, maybe I could...

...recognize the woman standing outside my church, looking up at those doors with purpose.

Color-changing hair. No number 137 hanging over her head, but the hair, I recognized the hair. She'd been at the border checkpoint, waiting to be processed. Her, and her husband...

More importantly... I recognized the boxy lines of the backspacer in her hand. A common open source variant of the firearm. All Senate staffers had basic counterterrorism incident training, including recognizing basic weaponized malware... for what good that did us in the end.

"... 🔫 ..." Mew whispered to me, with heightened panic in the twitch of his whiskers.

Walk away. Don't get involved; once shooting started, moderators would swoop in. I could get scooped up in the fray, possibly recognized, and delivered to the Inquisition, and...

And...

And I didn't want to be a coward. I'd crossed so many lines, failed so many times, true... but this went beyond the pale. The fact that I even considered it for one second was shameful; walk away, and let an obviously distraught woman kill people rather than risk a thing.

Well. If I was doomed anyway, cast into the void by a series of mistakes and weaknesses... I may as well embrace that death in a way that'd save others.

But I didn't immediately pounce and try to wrestle the gun away, no. I walked right up to the woman, at a reasonable walking speed... stopping short of entering her personal space.

"I saw you at the border checkpoint earlier, didn't I?" I asked her. "Number 137—"

By the time the woman with tears in her eyes pointed that weapon in my direction, I'd already raised my hands.

"Easy. Easy," I said, trying to remain calm. "I'm not going to hurt you. You don't have to do this..."

The weapon shook in her trembling hands. It could easily activate, and at this range, no amount of shakiness would keep it from killing me.

"They... they killed him," she told me. "My husband. Called him a Nobody, a terrorist. He. He wasn't a Nobody..."

"I believe you," I spoke.

"They're not all Nobodies. Chanarchists aren't all Nobodies. They. They detained him, and... and he snuck me a message just before, and... and told me to run," she whispered. "And. And I ran. I ran and let them kill him. I didn't want to get taken as well..."

"And now you feel like a coward. Like you left him to die."

Dangerous to flat-out accuse her like that... but we were two women standing in the same place, in a lot of ways. Losing something dear to us, feeling powerless, and wanting to do something about it. The way she avoided my gaze when I said the words, well... that gave me my answer.

"They'll catch me. They'll sort through what's left of his data, find me, and kill me too," the woman said, her hair shifting from dour blues to angry reds. "I'm from Athena Online, there's plenty of data out there of mine they can find. I'm going to die anyway. So, I... I should... I should show them. Show them what a real terrorist is, if that's what they want me to be. The... the One-fearing zealots, who hated him because he wasn't a believer, I should..."

"Should what, murder people in a church and then kill yourself? That's your plan, right?" I asked.

"It's not like... I mean, I don't *want*...!"

Looking away from the woman holding me at gunpoint... I focused on the candles in those windows, flickering ever so gently.

"I love this server," I told her. "I love the people who live here. ...and I love our home, Athena Online. For all its faults, for all its weaknesses, I love it. It's very... fallible. Mortal. Just like the rest of us. I love it when it triumphs, and I love it when it makes mistakes. And when it stumbles, well... we're supposed to pick ourselves up, and find the path forward. All of us, together. That's what Athena wanted from us. Not to blindly follow the One, not to blindly follow our leaders, but to follow each other with open eyes..."

Didn't have to look back at her to know the gun had been lowered. The sound of her sobbing told me that.

"I don't. I don't want to do this. But I have to do *something*," she whispered. "This isn't the Athena Online I grew up in. I remember... I remember when I felt safe here. It feels like ages ago, but I felt *safe*..."

"It can be that way again. The bastards who stole the nation from us, the ones who helped them do it or simply stood by and let it happen... they lost the dream of Athena Online long ago. But it's not dead yet," I told her. "We've got one more chance at this. ...Mew? If you'd kindly...?"

I refused to acknowledge the cat's smugness, as a pattern rose from the markings on his fur, becoming the floating icon of a simple software package. Instead I accepted it, and pulled away a copy of it to hold out to the woman.

"There's a new world waiting for us in Netwerk 2.0," I told her. "Not just an escape, but an opportunity to fix this. To make it a place where things like what happened to your husband never happen again. Evacuate to the House of Programkind, and when you wake to a new dawn, you take the anger you've got and turn it around, use it to make a better world. Because using it to kill innocents... that's not going to bring him back, that's not going to make anything better. And you know it. ...I'll trade you the evac app for your gun. Fair trade, yeah?"

One flame, passed from hand to hand. A DRM-free visual effect app, freely copied, open sourced. Giving someone your fire wouldn't deprive you of light, but simply spread it further and farther than ever before...

A perfect symbol for a peaceful protest, as the group stood in silent vigil at the steps of the new Senate. Row after row of armed moderators in personal riot firewalls stood against them, but with neither side setting one foot forward, violence wasn't likely.

But as the flame passed to Jonnes/Columbia... an additional file came with it. A tiny sphere, covered in what felt like fur...

Curiously, she looked up to the woman who had joined the protest, at her side.

"I know you don't believe in Netwerk 2.0, but... keep a copy, just in case," I told my mother. "And meanwhile, I'll stand with you in protest, to save my nation. We'll pull away their support, convince people to join us, and show the fascists that this isn't the future of our nation. I'm not going anywhere just yet."

Stupid. Utterly stupid, to spearhead this new underground trail to freedom. But I'd done plenty of stupid things lately... and sometimes, stupidity brought you right back around to where you should've been all along.

I'm a coward, but also a patriot. Eventually, one has to override the other. If the nation I knew as Athena Online was to burn, its people would not. I'd pass Mew's code around, with the help of my surprisingly adept feline companion, and help everybody who wanted to leave find their way out the door to a better Athena Online.

I'd like for this to be a story ending with the triumph of Programkind's spirit, a revitalization of the principles that Athena gave to us at the start of this great nation. I'd like for that to be the ending.

But the drums were already sounding, in the distance. I couldn't recognize them for what they were, but within days... we'd all hear them, loud and clear.

The drums of war.

File Name: Messenger Comm Traffic 6.414.223
File Type: Text Log
Description:

PLEASE COPY AND DISTRIBUTE. With the death of the old world comes the death of old ways. Centuries of apathy, of common acceptance of the status quo, it nearly drowned us in a comfortable acceptance of evil. "That's just the way things are" is the battle cry of the old world. Our world will be better... but only if we learn from our past. -Yume

\<Kincaid\> Curious. Very curious, indeed. But not unexpected.

\<Cancel\> Brent wants to levy sanctions. Madison's considering the merits of firewalling off Horizon entirely, in a manner similar to Athena Online.
\<Cancel\> It's not like this is the first assassination attempt on their lives, but usually those were clean and professional... ones we could counterplay against, as well.
\<Cancel\> A single crazed Nobody blowing himself and the entire server away in protest of supporting Athena Online, that's not something we were prepared for.

\<Kincaid\> And yet the antimalware shields held. I'd say we were rather prepared for it, if only in the sense of being prepared for general threats.
\<Kincaid\> I'm curious as to your thoughts on the matter. How do you feel the Horizon family should react to anonymous terrorism?

\<Cancel\> Honestly, sir, I don't believe there's any point in reacting, given Netwerk 1.0 will be offline in about a week. The majority of Horizon-invested businesses have already archived their materials and personnel. Economic sanctions against Chanarchy businesses would accomplish little.
\<Cancel\> Instead, I'd suggest a targeted strike at the leadership of the Nobodies. Obviously there's no specific leadership to a hashtag mob, but there are noteworthy figures, such as the identity thief who made their mask.

\<Kincaid\> Interesting. And what would that accomplish? Aside from bloody revenge, which I can't say I'm not in favor of.

\<Cancel\> Surgical eliminations can work as symbolic gestures and resource depletion. They discourage others from following in those footsteps, for fear of further reprisal. At the very least, by undercutting known support structures, we weaken their capital and drive them deeper underground. Slow their progress. By the end of the week, their most ardent supporters who don't believe in the spacer theory will be gone regardless of whether they've bounced back or not.

<Kincaid> Very fitting with the Horizon way, to target one's economy.

<Cancel> Agreed, sir. Shall I inform Madison of your decision?

<Kincaid> I didn't say that was my decision.
<Kincaid> In fact, tell her nothing. I want to see how my supposed heirs handle this situation. If they're to lead our family in Netwerk 2.0 I want to be certain they understand the changing face of the world, and are able to adapt accordingly. Offer no advice, no word from on high, no guidance. They will rise or fall by their own merits. We'll see, won't we?

<Cancel> As you wish, sir. I'll return shortly.

<Kincaid> Actually, there's another matter I'd like you to attend to on this day.

<Cancel> Sir?

<Kincaid> Winder/Spark will be visiting SecuRight's server shortly, in hopes of obtaining backdoor access to their software. Something about the Athena Online's SecuRight firewall interfering with evacuation efforts, I believe. I'd like you to accompany her.

<Cancel> For protection? Are the Nobodies targeting the House of Programkind again?

<Kincaid> As economic muscle, should Spark ask for it. I may have cashed out most of my leverage in the process of purchasing the Verity Clinic, but I've still a few favors tucked away in my pocket. As you know.

<Cancel> And... you want me to spend your remaining capital on convincing SecuRight to help?

<Kincaid> As you say, Miss Cancel, we've only a week to the end of days. And as they say, "You can't take it with you." I can think of no more fitting a gift to my young protégée than to buy her dreams, if she wishes.

```
<Cancel> I don't believe SecuRight will cooperate with
her, sir. It'll likely be a wasted effort. And given
the attempt on the lives of your heirs I feel it would
be best to stay with them or return to protect you.

<Kincaid> Duly noted. But I want you at Spark's side
for this, Miss Cancel. Indulge me.

<Cancel> By your command. At the very least, I can
protect her should her impulsiveness cause trouble
again.

<Kincaid> Possibly, possibly. We'll see, won't we?

-- user Cancel has disconnected --

<Kincaid> Hello there.
<Kincaid> Yes, I know you're listening.
<Kincaid> You believe we weren't aware of your
backdoor into Messenger? Of course we were. I've
allowed it because I know your motives are pure, if a
bit ethically unsound. You seek to archive our last
days, so that future generations won't forget what
happened here.

<Yume> That's the idea.

<Kincaid> Then allow me to add my epitaph.
```

Loyalty—*true* loyalty, honest and uncrackable—is the hardest currency in this world.

This is a fact that my employer knows, and has defined his life by. Those who are loyal to him shall be rewarded with loyalty in turn. Those who break their word, who devalue their own assets, are worthless and beneath consideration. I am the instrument of my employer's personal economy, disposing of that which is worthless, to further enhance the value of that which remains.

Name: **Cancel**

Home: **Horizon6, Horizon**

Org: **Bodyguard**

Which is to say that Kincaid exercises both purity of intent *and* absolute vendetta as a life choice. Forgiveness is not in his nature; betrayal will be treated in a manner appropriate to this vision. In fact, he relishes in a proper vendetta, to the point of impropriety. For years, we searched for our daughter's killer, to exact this punishment upon him...

...only to have the Winders deal with that problem for us. A rare moment of mercy, from Mr. Kincaid, willing to let Winder/Spark become his instrument of vendetta rather than take a personal hand in it.

This is where our viewpoints diverge. He sees Spark as the next iteration of our daughter's ideals, as close to a literal granddaughter as we could have. I do not.

Spark is irresponsible. Prone to aggressive action when precision is required. She takes risks she doesn't need to take, standing firm with questionable ideals. Her insistence on protecting a foolish boy who threw in with the Nobodies nearly resulted in my death; her ambushing of unarmed Inquisitors in the middle of their homeland's capital got her arrested, and nearly put away for the duration of the evacuation efforts if not for Mr. Kincaid spending more of his dwindling capital to free her. Spark is no heir to Verity's legacy. She's far too reckless compared to the measured and thoughtful girl we... raised, I suppose.

I also disagree with my employer on the manner of that raising.

We must be cruel to be kind, he'd explained. *She must be everything I am not, and so, we must alienate her. She must rebel against the system, so that she can become what will lead it into the future...*

At the time, I was young and impressionable, and in love with a man I felt my better. I thought it an ideal long game, and swallowed my pride as I stood by as his "operative" rather than her mother. When she fled, stealing the key to her ancestral home of Floating Point—choosing the intellectual path of the archaeologist, refusing to accept the accepted truths of Horizon—I felt that perhaps this strategy had worked.

And then she died. And this wild child rose in her place, wearing *her* jacket, living in *her* home.

This was the questionable heir that sat sideways in a waiting room outside the CEO's office, feet propped up on the chair next to her, drumming some strange beat from the unheard music of a HUD-based player with her hands. She didn't even notice my entrance, too wrapped up in her own indulgences...

Today, Spark did not wear the jacket. We knew what became of it, of course... that she'd taken Verity's gift, the last remnant of our true daughter, and connected it to some strange superuser-level abilities in a bid to free Netwerk from the Buzz malware. Abusing even the tiniest bit of loyal currency she'd been left, in the process.

This is not to say I hated Winder/Spark, or even held vendetta against her. If I had to characterize my feelings, I would name them "disappointment." That everything Mr. Kincaid and I had attempted to build, that the child we loved, should curve into this end result... disappointing.

Which is strange, because for reasons I can't fathom, Mr. Kincaid felt no disappointment at all. He continually put trust in Spark, investing everything in her hopes and dreams... even spending a third of Horizon's wealth to purchase Iteration. He didn't see her failings. He only saw her promise.

I saw a girl so busy enjoying some pop song that she didn't notice my approach. I will grant that perhaps I underestimated her awareness, as even without opening her eyes or ceasing the tap-tap-tap of her fingers, she addressed me by name.

"Hey, Cans," she greeted. "#Whazzap?"

"My name is Miss Cancel," I corrected her, standing in judgment. "And what is up is our appointment with Mr. Dfens. Which is five minutes away. I assume you've decided on a bargaining strategy to employ...?"

"Gonna ask him to crack his own firewall software nice 'n wide for us," Spark replied.

"And...?"

"And... that's it," she said, shutting off her personal music player, ceasing the finger-tapping. "When he says no, we leave and go get lunch. This meeting's basically pointless; Conundrum's given us the rundown on this asshole, so I'm not going in expecting much. We're only here for two reasons. One, to suss out what sort of a guy he is, what sort of company he runs. Two, to say we tried to go through legitimate channels before we do what we do best."

"I... see. In that case, Mr. Kincaid was right to send me to assist you," I replied. "He's tasked me with aiding in accomplishing your goals, so I will not be leaving that office without succeeding. I'm not the sort to give up before even attempting a task."

"Didn't say I was giving up, did I?"

"...yes, you in fact did. You said this effort is pointless."

"No, what I said the meeting—"

—began immediately.

SecuRight took security very, very seriously. Appropriate, given they were the top provider of server firewall software in all of Netwerk. Meaning their CEO kept his office in a floating, unlinked space... much like the Conundrum, albeit without the added twist of the company being run by a glorified data analysis app. When he was ready to start a meeting, properly screened visitors were simply *moved* into his office. Thankfully, Spark had been translocated to a similar chair, rather than falling on her rear on arrival.

Mr. Dfens wore a highly customized avatar, tailored for absolute precision of handsome and youthful features. Features which sharply studied Spark, on arrival, examining her various avatar features. This was Horizon; Defaults were rare, seen as a sign of weakness of poverty compared to an expensive package of avatar modifications. (Or, in Mr. Kincaid's case, a sign of the absolute authority that came with outlasting all his rivals for years. He made sure people saw the age of his Defaults, so they understood he was effectively immortal.)

"I've allocated ten minutes for this meeting," he informed Spark up front. "This is regarding our nationwide firewall software developed for the Athenian Senate, correct...?"

"Got it in one," Spark confirmed, smoothly transitioning from 'chillaxing in the waiting room' to 'all business,' apparently. "I'm not going to waste your time, Mr. Dfens. You know damn well why we're here; the House of Programkind needs to evacuate citizens of Athena Online. We're not interested in terrorist infiltration of the firewall, or even interfering in the surviving elected senators. Strictly humanitarian actions, 'kay? No real conflict of interest here. But, to do so, we need a backdoor through your software. Will you provide one?"

"Absolutely not," the CEO spoke, without hesitation.

Spark leaned forward in her seat... studying the avatar for reactions. Not that it would work; most of Horizon's elite installed PokrFace software modification packages, which filtered any subconscious responses that would betray emotion.

"I'm going to ask again, so it's absolutely clear that we put in due diligence on this," she said. "The only thing we want to do is evacuate those who are willing to evacuate. That's it. We know the Nobodies want in; well, we won't give them that in. No publishing your backdoor. You know the Horizon family's in favor of evacuation... in fact, most of your business peers have already bailed on Netwerk. When I walked through your server to get here, I noticed most of your operations packing up shop and leaving, in fact. So what's the harm here? Why not help us out? One more time. Will you help us out?"

"Absolutely not," he repeated. "Miss Spark, you may have Horizon/Madison's ear, but you don't seem to understand how her family works. How *business* works. We made a contract with Senator Agni to provide software for the express purpose of shutting down unauthorized traffic with Athena Online. Now, you want me to allow unauthorized traffic with Athena Online, breaking that contract? Absolutely not. Good day."

Without concern over this flat denial, Spark got to her feet.

"Can't say we didn't try," she told him. "Be seeing you in Netwerk 2.0, then. Let's book, Miss Cancel."

If not for my own PokrFace module being active, I'd have shot her a look of utter frustration.

"I'll join you shortly," I spoke, my voice modulated by the modification to remove any displeasure. "I'd like a private word with Mr. Dfens first."

"Huh. Okay. Have fun, then. I'll meet you in the cafeteria; I hear these guys have great lasagna."

With a silent command, Spark translocated back to the waiting room.

"...let's speak candidly," I told Dfens, once my reckless associate had abandoned her own cause. "You've certainly offered backdoors and exploits into your own software before. Let's not pretend SecuRight is entirely honest in its dealings. In fact, Mr. Kincaid specifically purchased an exploit from you in in the past."

Two people with passive faces and passive voices, locked in combat. A familiar state for me, a battle Spark could never have won...

"It's a question of value," Dfens explained. "The House of Programkind has nothing of value to offer me to trump the value the Senate's already paid me. What little currency they have, the evacuation system, they gave away for free to anyone who wanted it. Not my fault that they intentionally threw away their best leverage."

"Mr. Kincaid is a powerful man, even now. And he has plenty of leverage to offer, in return for your cooperation. Specifically... favors that you owe to him. For example, there's the small matter of the lavish 16th that you threw for your daughter... the expenses to which he underwrote, to avoid anyone realizing you couldn't afford all the luxuries she demanded for her party."

"Which was a break-even deal, leveraged against the earlier exploit he bought from us for favors in turn."

"Horizon/Madison has also sold you considerable space in the archiving efforts for Netwerk 2.0, so that you can carry your assets forward... but Horizon/Kincaid has reserved space he can offer you within our bonus servers. A priceless commodity, for businesses looking to retain their power while all others must start over from scratch..."

"I already purchased compression software which can fit everything we need within the space Madison's sold me. No need for more," he said. "Let's continue to speak candidly, Miss Cancel. Kincaid's assets are depleted. If those are the best offers he can make, then he truly *did* ruin himself by buying out Iteration. And that's a shame, to see someone so high fall so low. Why do you continue to show such loyalty to that decrepit old man, anyway?"

"...Mr. Kincaid can also offer, pure and simply, a measure of wealth," I continued despite the insult. "Coins. Still quite valuable, as they're becoming scarcer in supply. Easy to transport to Netwerk 2.0..."

"A dead currency? Is is what he has to offer?" Dfens asked, surprised enough for it to crack his PokrFace. "No doubt Athena Online will resume plans to develop new currencies, once the transition is complete. Coins will only have value for a limited time. I'm sorry, but there's simply nothing he can offer me which will change my mind on this. ...in addition to the simple fact that I do not honestly care if a pocket of Athena Online's Programs perish in the apocalypse. Better for it, even. They rarely buy proper security software, so they're no customers of mine."

Not an attitude that Verity would have approved of.

"Name your price, then," I suggested. "It will be arranged."

A blank check, made in desperation. The most valuable thing in the world, when backed by the Horizon family.

Dfens considered the offer.

"Still not interested," he decided, before booting me from his office.

The translocation left me staring at a blank wall, briefly unable to comprehend my own failure.

I found my daughter's daughter, as Mr. Kincaid came to see her, lounging around the company cafeteria and enjoying freshly coded pasta.

Personally, I've never seen the point of food, much less an entire period of time each day set aside for consuming it. My employer indulges in every sensation-based vice he can... brandy, cigars, elaborate meals. But he's earned the free time and resources he needs to indulge himself. The able-bodied such as myself can't afford the luxury of such things, not when there's work to be done.

"Hey, I got you some lasagna," Spark said, nudging a second plate my way as I approached her table. "Srsly, you gotta try this shit. It's fucking intense, better than the cheap-ass noodles I normally munch on between gaming sessions. Leave it to a Horizon corp to invest in the finest code chefs..."

"Not interested," I told her. (And winced, as I'd disengaged PokrFace, and those two words painfully echoed today's failure.) "Unfortunately, Mr. Dfens isn't willing to listen to reason. What's your next step? I assume we're going to be analyzing their data storage systems, looking for weaknesses, so we can dig their secrets out. Corporate espionage is perfectly legal in Horizon systems... although so are the punishments inflicted on those who fail."

Spark poked at what remained of her lunch with a fork, thoughtfully glancing around the room at other dining employees.

"Nah. That sounds like a fuck-ton of risky work," she said. "'sides, that's not how we roll. You only go right for the throat when you can't go straight up the ass."

(You'd think a girl essentially raised by Verity would be less crude with her language, but no.)

"Then... what? What's your plan of attack?" I asked, growing tired of her lazy attitude. "Just ask nicely, be refused, have lunch, and go home?"

"Ask nicely, be refused, have lunch, then get what I want," Spark corrected... continuing to rubberneck, to run her eyes over the other tables. "Chill, Cans. I got this. ...aaand I spy with my little eye... a man who appreciates a good lasagna. 'scuze me a second, 'kay?"

And then she just got up and walked away, right in the middle of talking with me.

I would've taken personal offense to it, if I didn't recognize something familiar in her stride... purpose. Walking with absolute purpose, straight across the sparsely populated cafeteria, right to the table she'd been studying with intent. So, rather than dress her down for this slight... I followed. Followed, and remained silent, as I watched her work.

"This seat taken?" she asked the young man sitting there angrily devouring a lasagna.

It took him a moment to push aside the invisible HUD-based news feeds he was no doubt reading, eyes re-focusing on the woman who'd joined him.

"Uh. No?" he spoke, confused. "Can I help you with something, miss...?"

"Ohhh, you know who I am," Spark spoke, sliding right on into that seat. "I'm all over your social media feeds. Winder/Spark, representative for the House of Programkind. Ally of Horizon/Madison, and of the Athenian Senate. Well. The *real* Senate."

"I... suppose I do know who you are," he admitted, taking back the obligatorily polite moment of confusion.

"I'm surprised you haven't evacuated yet, actually. Most folks in SecuRight have gone out the window, yeah?"

The programmer shrugged, non-committal.

"There's more archiving work to do," he said. "And ongoing support of the new Athena Online firewall, I guess. They need me here. I've got authorized leave to depart a day before the clock hits zero, though."

"Good, good. We need inventive coders like you, to help rebuild the world. Although hopefully we won't need your very specific skill set, when the time comes... firewall design. Nasty business, especially given recent events."

"...Athena Online's got a right to protect its property. They murdered hundreds of people."

"And condemned thousands to death in the process," Spark added. "C'mon, man, I don't need the company line about how great firewalls are, how everybody should buy one. You and I, we're on the same page here, we know this world's winding down. We've got a moral obligation to save as many as we can before the midnight hour..."

Curious. She'd walked up to some seemingly random stranger, immediately engaging them on a touchy subject... and he was humoring her. Beyond humoring her, he was paying close attention, and engaging right back...

"I know who you are, but do you know who I am? Yeah. I'm thinking you know who I am," he said, eyeing her with a bit of suspicion. "What gave it away? My social media feed?"

"Your social media feed," Spark agreed... opening a hovering window, where a selfie-based user icon tagged itself to a message of anger. "'Senator Agni's no better than the bastards who murdered the Blue Party.' Your words, Oli. 'Killing is killing, with malware or a firewall.'"

"I'm... allowed to express my own opinions," the man named Oli replied. "I'm not under a communications blackout contract with SecuRight. I'm not badmouthing our products, just the people who use them inappropriately..."

"So, help me thwart the killers," Spark suggested. "You know who I work with. All we need is one tiny little hole, just wide enough to help the people escape. You can provide that."

"I can't," he spoke.

"You can, and you should. You *know* you should."

"I should, but... I can't," he agreed, without agreeing. "I'm under a Non-Disclosure Agreement."

"Is some silly text file you signed off on really more important than—"

"A Class III NDA."

"—ahhh. Well. That does change things," Spark realized.

Meaning her entire alternative strategy wouldn't pan out, either. Because a Class III NDA was coded right down to the core of a Program's being... a deep modification, to block them from speaking certain company secrets. In exchange for surrendering portions of one's free will, a man could find much profit in allowing themselves to be bound by code. Illegal in Athena Online, sneered at in the Chanarchy, but perfectly normal in Horizon...

The more freedom you surrender, the greater the rewards. Undoubtedly the "authorized leave" he mentioned was also a code modification... the inability to leave his post, without permission of his masters. Even if he wanted to archive himself, he couldn't, not until they gave word. Bound to the company, until the day he resigned... if they *let* him resign. Some contracts didn't allow that, and Programs often accepted them anyway, out of desperation or greed or both.

Spark considered the problem before her... and refused to give up, shaking her head.

"Let's think about this in a roundabout way," she suggested. "You can't directly tell me how to break your own software, okay. But if someone was to want to crack SecuRight's firewall... specifically, the one they baked up for Athena Online... where would they start looking?"

With a sigh, Oli shook his head. "I told you, I can't..."

"Can't point a finger? Can't talk obliquely about certain things which may or may not be of interest to me? Can't offer me square one to start from? I don't need much, Oli. I just need a direction to move in... and I'll get myself where I need to go. How about it?"

The boy's brow furrowed, as he tried to think of the best way to phrase his answer. Specifically, a way which wouldn't crash head-on into the mental block. A difficult position to be in... if your employer was firm enough in their demands to punish you for even attempting to push against your NDA. If he tripped its recognition routines, and they called home to SecuRight's Program Resources department...

"Speaking in a general sense... no code is truly uncrackable," Oli noted. "What you need isn't actually my help. You need the help of someone who's actually achieved what you want to achieve."

"Uh. If someone had cracked your firewall, wouldn't we'd know by now? There'd be Nobodies streaming into Athena Online, looking to finish what they started. Assuming you believe the evening news feeds about that bombing..."

"Not if someone's holding the zero-day exploit for ransom. SecuRight's actually purchased from him before, to keep his hacks out of the wild. But this one, well... they don't honestly care," Oli explained. "Dfens is perfectly willing to let the hack go, because his 'client' will be dead in a week, anyway. He's not obliged to save Athena Online, from itself or from others."

...which went a ways to explaining why Mr. Dfens refused any price offered. He apparently found it *amusing* to defy Mr. Kincaid and his clients at the same time. In hindsight, it made sense; SecuRight provided this software years ago, for a failed attempt at getting the Senate to agree to use it. The money had been collected, the client would be gone soon, so why bother getting involved at all, one way or another?

"Okay. Okay, that makes sense," Spark agreed. "Got a name?"

Now, I stepped in.

"You can stop, Mr. Oli. I know the individual you're hinting at," I interjected. "A hacker who's sold to SecuRight in the past; understood. No need to risk your NDA. Spark, let's go. I can arrange the meeting for you."

But before Spark could rise to leave... Oli grabbed her hand.

"You'll follow through on this, right?" he asked. "No matter the cost? The firewall... it needs to go down, but safely. Let people escape, without letting anyone dangerous in. I can't. I can't live with myself if my code doomed them all..."

Without a second thought, Spark nodded in pure agreement.

"You've got my word, Oli," she promised. "I'll see this through. I swear it."

I wish she'd consulted me on that. I could've warned her against such promises.

The companies of Horizon took promises very, very seriously... to the point of coding them right into contracts, binding people to their words. She'd offered no such binding, but there was such a thing as a verbal contract, the sort you imply in your mannerism and your intent... and with no regulations to hold a company back, vendetta could be enacted without penalty for breaking one's word. Vendetta, such as myself, the instrument of Mr. Kincaid's will. When one breaks loyalty with him, they are dealt with...

I doubted a bound employee of SecuRight would hold Spark to that high standard. But if he had a moral core, one which defined his entire self around making this wrong thing right... her failure could have consequences. Dire consequences indeed. Was she really ready to face that, to take on that obligation? This reckless, impulsive child...?

But everything about her suggested... yes. Sincerely, honestly, and truthfully ready to face the challenge. With the same firmness that Verity would use, when standing up to her father.

Curious. Very curious, indeed.

Athena Online gives lip service to the idea of liberty, while weighing down businesses with piles of laws and regulations. All in the name of public safety, they say. But the true libertarian ideals of Horizon, that's where you find the perfect balance that allows business to thrive... fealty to the Horizon family, a sense of mutual self-interest in your fellow entrepreneur, and a serious-minded attitude to making money. None of the kid gloves of Athena Online, none of the wild nihilism of the Chanarchy. With the Horizon family on your side, you could lay claim to all you desired... so long as you could keep your gains from being taken, that is.

As a result, professional cracking—the art of compromising security for profit, often called "hacking" in a colloquially incorrect fashion—was a perfectly viable career path. While Chanarchy hackers often broke apart software for the "lulz," in Horizon, you could make considerable coin off your efforts along with respect and admiration of your peers.

But, as noted, it only worked if you could protect yourself from reprisal. Corporations were allowed (and perhaps encouraged) to exercise vendetta, meaning security crackers required exceptional security themselves... layers and layers of firewalls and personal malware shields, to stave off would-be assassins. Such as myself.

Which is why I had to make the introduction for Spark. The hacker in question, who went by the moniker of Ac!d, kept his small-but-secure personal server on firm lockdown. As CEO, CFO, CIO, and COO overseeing a staff of himself alone, the "Ac!dWorks, Inc." corporate entity held only one avenue of approach... Ac!d himself.

With my credentials and the coin of loyalty and trust I represented, the personal oath of Mr. Kincaid, I could assure him a meeting with Spark would not turn into an ambush. He felt safe lowering his guard, knowing that resulting attacks would reflect badly on the Horizon family itself, through Mr. Kincaid.

Hopefully, Spark would respect that agreement in turn.

Unlike the tastefully decorated corporate office of Mr. Dfens, Ac!d decorated his office with iconography of pop culture. Growly and angry musical acts, movie memorabilia, lifted street art from noteworthy graffiti specialists... and as a centerpiece to it all, promotional posters of three different popular gamers. Female gamers, that is, each animated illustration perfectly autographed.

I'd consider it unprofessional, but in a way, he embraced the professionalism expected of hacker culture... each item on display bore a limited edition metadata tag, becoming a visual display of his wealth in line with social expectation. The three posters in particular had spotlights placed on them, as his most prized possessions. Not uncommon for a Horizon-based entrepreneur to willfully display their trophies, both literal and figurative.

Even Spark had to glance around the room, taking it all in with a nod of satisfaction. A former professional gamer herself, she no doubt recognized many of the visuals on display.

"Commemorative Lucky7 replica trophy," she recognized, nodding towards one of many items on his shelves. "And from the Klash Invitational, too. Vintage."

The young man with the perfectly handsome avatar agreed, with a bright smile.

"Good eye," he spoke. "Best performance they've ever had. No team comp they've fielded ever since comes close."

"What, not even when they took on MVP?"

"MVP doesn't live up to his name. No replacement for Killswitcher on the solo lane. It's a shame she had to leave the team... but maybe it's for the best. Go out at the peak of your game, and become an immortal legend..."

The aforementioned 'Killswitcher' being represented by one of those three animated posters, tugging on a pair of gloves and looking aggressively smug, over and over, in a loop.

I stayed out of the discussion, of course. With Spark establishing a fine rapport with this more casually-minded gamer, any attempt to interject and represent the integrity of the Horizon family might be seen as an intrusion.

Although I did wince internally, when Spark took a more aggressive stance.

"Killswitcher had demons she was fighting," Spark said. "Probably why she dropped off the map. Everybody knows she secretly toked malware before her championship matches. It's a shame; she was a solid solo laner during the run-up to the big events, when the pressure got to her..."

Ac!d shrugged. "So she gots lit now and then. Who doesn't?" he asked. "They won those championships, didn't they...?"

"Results-oriented thinking. That's like flipping a coin twice in a row, calling heads both times, and assuming you'll have a 100% win rate forever."

"Kinda like the House of Programkind, huh?" the young man asked, with a smug smirk. No PokrFace module, clearly. "You sway Horizon to your cause, convince the Senate to throw in, even somehow secure Chanarchy servers... then one Nobody-bombing later and it's all gone to shit. Y'know, I was following your career closely, back when you signed with Lucky7. I can't believe you gave up on that meal ticket... you could've been the next Killswitcher."

"Yeah, well, bigger and better things. As for the House of Programkind's woes, you can help us mount a comeback. That's is why I'm here today: word on the street is that you've got a zero-day exploit on Athena Online's firewall up for sale. I'm keen to buy."

Which opened the door for me to step in.

I arranged the meeting, Spark buttered him up with their mutual obsession over children's games, but now the weight of Horizon had to be brought to bear. And unlike Mr. Dfens, who defied that weight simply for his own amusement... I knew Ac!d's reputation. He was perfectly happy to sell anything to anyone, without reservation.

"As a designated representative of Horizon/Kincaid, I can offer any number of favors, assets, or investments in exchange for your cooperation," I explained. "In fact, I have a number of complete compensation packages I can offer immediately, on delivery of..."

...but he was shaking his head, sadly.

"As much as I'd like to help a fellow gamer out... I'd just sold the zero-day to an interested buyer this morning," Ac!d explained. "A group of Nobodies delivered me a prize I'd been waiting to add to my collection, in exchange for the hack. So, I'm afraid there's not much I can do to assist you..."

Spark considered the situation. "Unless... you tell us about these Nobodies you sold the hack to," she suggested. "Yeah, yeah, they wear masks, they're legion, I get it. But if it's only been hours, we've got a shot at finding them. Besides, I don't like the idea of the Nobodies with access to Athena Online."

"Hmmm. I'd say that amounts to betraying client confidentiality... but they *are* anonymous, aren't they? I have plausible deniability. Still, I can't just offer such valuable information without something in return. And these days, well, coin isn't my thing. I like trophies. Prizes. Rather specific ones, I'm afraid..."

A perfect opportunity for me to interject.

"Mr. Kincaid can easily acquire or surpass any prize a bunch of anonymous pranksters could scrape up," I suggested. "Merely name the dream 'prize' your collection needs, and he can arrange to have it delivered today."

"Really? I didn't think Kincaid went for trafficking."

"Trafficking...?"

"Selling captive programs into slavery, of course," Ac!d spoke, without losing his smile. "The Nobodies have picked up a gamer I've been keen on adding to my gallery for some time... and I'm looking forward to adding her to my lineup."

...quickly, I turned a scanning app on those posters.

Programs. Each one of the three flattened images was actually a Program.

He'd archived their sleeping code into a two-dimensional file, to run flattened versions of their avatars through various animations every hour of every day. But those posters indeed contained Program metadata, meaning... the poster of Killswitcher, the gamer who apparently "dropped off the map," was the *actual* Killswitcher...

All perfectly legal. And he knew it.

Not all Programs voluntarily signed Class III NDAs. In the darkest recesses of the Chanarchy, in the least reputable businesses of Horizon... trafficking in Programs, with will-breaking slave malware forcibly installed, remained perfectly legal in both provider-nations.

I can't say I approve of it... but that's the other side of the coin we've all accepted for our personal piggy banks. With perfect economic liberty comes a few things money shouldn't buy, but must be allowed to. Even if few people in Horizon would willingly do such business, or do business with someone who admitted to participating, on principle. Reputation being as firm a coin as loyalty.

"Trafficking in gamer girls," Spark replied, trying to keep diplomatic, despite the icy tone in her voice.

"Hey, you said it yourself. Killswitcher was burning out," he continued, stroking one finger along the surface of the 'poster' in question. "Harpey, her career was starting to go downhill, as well. And little Penters here, today's acquisition... I obtained her in the prime of her ascent. All three frozen at the best possible moment, before they could decline. Made... immortal. It's nothing sexual, you understand. If anything, I'm very respectful of their accomplishments, and doing them a favor by keeping them archived in mint condition."

"And your business partners in Horizon, they know about this...?"

Ac!d glanced back at Spark, looking mildly surprised.

"I destroy security for a living. Who do you think buys cracks like that? People who want to break in and redecorate your house tastefully out of the goodness of their hearts?" he asked. "In Horizon, we profit from the lines we willingly cross. Nobody here really cares enough to do anything about it. Isn't that right, Miss Cancel? Kincaid and his ilk let me operate as I please. In the end,

I uphold my contracts with absolute honesty. I pay my tithe to the family. As long as my word never breaks and my money stays shiny, nobody cares."

In return... I offered no response. Because he was right.

Loyalty, honesty, and money. These were the assets that kept Horizon's great chain of industry strong. Not to say that betrayal, lies, and cheating didn't exist here, but... as long as you could maintain those three, or the firm appearance of them, you would be golden in the eyes of the family.

But Spark wasn't family, despite allegedly being blood of my blood. And with Verity intentionally being turned away from the family's path, those counter-values lived on in her.

"I guess my offer's changed, then," she spoke, quietly. "I'd like your zero-day clients, *and* your lovely poster collection. And any other 'trophies' you have lying around."

Ac!d considered the seriousness with which Spark made the request, very curious.

"And in return...?" he asked. "Let me guess. If I make nice, you won't kill me."

"You're soaked in malware shields, so threats are likely pointless," she suggested. "Instead, I'm going to appeal to you as a gamer. One Challenge of Champions match. You and me, one lane, two towers. I'll even put up stakes you can't resist: I win, you give me everything I ask for. I lose... well, you'll get a new trophy today. You'll have me: Lucky7's own Spark, going out at the top of her game."

Immediately, I reached into my inventory to boot up my sniper rifle.

I kept it invisible, of course. The most powerful piece of malware money could by, capable of eradicating a hard target from across an entire server. Rated for penetration of all common firewalls and personal shields. Mr. Kincaid spared no expense when it came to equipping me with the tools I need to protect both myself and his interests. Perhaps it wouldn't be enough to crack through Ac!d's personal security... but I had to be ready, just in case...

The man considered this offer, not leaping immediately on the bait.

"I've followed your career, remember? I know your tactics. You trick people into losing their patience," he described. "You manipulate aggro, turning it into your weapon. You *want* me to take this offer, because you've got something skeevy planned. Some kind of trick, or a cheat..."

"I've never cheated at Challenge of Champions once in my life. You believe in honesty? So do I," Spark told him. "And honestly? Basically you're a complete piece of shit and I'm better than you by every conceivable metric. So when I win, I get my exploit and your victims go free. If you win, I'm yours to put in my place as you see fit. That's how Horizon works, right? Contracts and honesty?

I'm being honest. Are you? Or are you honestly a complete fucking cowardly tool?"

"You... wouldn't do this unless you thought you could win," he noted, but with suspicion starting to give way to eagerness. "Unless you're completely crazy..."

"You could be right; maybe I'm just crazy and lucky. Maybe I'm too focused on results-oriented thinking and assuming that because I always come out on top, I always will. Me, I'm willing to bet on myself. How about you, Ac!d? You willing? Step up and stand for what you believe in, or admit to how fucking pathetic you really are—"

The sharp backhand across Spark's jaw rang out throughout the room.

Immediately, my sniper rifle locked on to Ac!d, aimbot assistance targeting system drawing a bead on the most exploitable microfold in the skin of his physical avatar...

...before Spark, still reeling from the blow, raised a hand to stop it.

"Do we have a deal, or not?" she asked Ac!d, not taking her eyes off the man.

Insanity. Pure insanity.

With both of us standing in the "Order" base, whatever that meant, Spark flipped through a leather-bound book, trying to decide on what character to select... all while I tried to talk her out of this ridiculous course of action. The setting seemed remarkably calm and pastoral, surrounded by a dense jungle of bright green trees, completely incongruous with the life-or-death stakes Spark had accepted.

Despite a few catcalls from the "Chaos" side of the jungle, demanding Spark hurry up and pick her character... she was content to lazily page through the book, not even reading it, while the countdown clock for team selection wound down towards zero.

"Mr. Kincaid would never allow this," I tried.

"He trusts me to handle my own affairs. Hell, the old fart would probably love the idea of this. Just another of his tests to see if I'm worthy..."

"A pointless test," I tried. "We could simply restrain and torture Ac!d until he complies, or crash him and sort through his memory files for the information."

"First, torture doesn't work. You're a scary woman, yes, but we don't have time for you to dodge around all the excuses and fake information he can toss your way during a torture session. And as for crashing, that's assuming he's not using sideloaded memory storage. You corporate types are shifty bastards."

"Then we find another hacker, someone who can crack the firewall. There are always other hackers... and no doubt they're all hammering on Athena Online as we speak. Eventually one of them will break through."

"No time. We can't leave a hack in the hands of the Nobodies, or leave those people as prisoners. We shut this asshole down, *now*."

"Spark, this is—"

"Do you trust me or not?" Spark asked, snapping the book closed. "No, you don't. I've had that feeling ever since you bailed me out of jail for brawling with Inquisitors. You don't see me as the 'spark to ignite the new world,' or however the fuck Kincaid puts it. And I'll put even money on me not living up the legacy of his daughter, either, in your eyes."

My PokrFace kept me from reacting, but that didn't matter. She knew she was right.

"Honestly, I don't care if you trust me or not," she declared, stretching her arms over her head, limbering up for the fight to come. "Your trust doesn't change the fact that *I got this*, Cans. You think I ran out the character select clock because I'm freaking out and don't know who to pick? I've been reviewing Ac!d's replays, in my head. I already know exactly what to do. But this won't work unless you stay the hell out of it. Any interference from a non-player will throw the match in his favor. Do you understand?"

"Spark, I... yes. Yes, I understand," I spoke.

Which was not an agreement not to interfere. It was simply an agreement that I understood the rules of the game.

With the clock ticking down to zero... I found myself translocated to the spectator box, sitting alongside the single clear lane between rows of trees. A great horn sounded, deep from the skybox above... and the fight was on.

I'll admit I know little of this game. The basics are known to everyone, as it's the closest Netwerk has to a national pastime... two teams try to knock down each other's towers, with the help of tiny NPC minions. Each wears the avatar of a game character, limited to the special abilities unique to that character and whatever equipment they can purchase along the way.

In fact, economics played a large part in victories. Skill alone would not be enough; you needed to slay the minions for the gold they carried, which could be spent on items. Half of each game typically consisted not of teams directly fighting, but simply "farming" for gold.

In a way, it was the ultimate expression of Horizon's ideals. Gain capital, gain power, destroy your rivals.

...okay, maybe I *did* know a bit more about the game than I'd like to admit.

But that knowledge only led me to despair, as Spark's pink-clad ninja avatar ran head-on into a giant automaton built like a tank, again and again. For the first half of the game, they danced around each other, refusing to directly fight... only to harass, to drive each other back. And more often than not... Spark was the one driven back.

Time and again she'd have to run from fights, while Ac!d's robotic form stomped its way through the jungles, minions at his back. Even without deep knowledge of the game, it was clear Spark made mistake after mistake, prioritizing the wrong targets, sometimes completely missing with her throwing knives...

All of which made Ac!d roar with laughter.

"You sure you wanna be a poster on my wall?" he asked, voice clear across the global chat channel. "You're hardly at the top of your game. Maybe I'd keep you as a keepsake, but you don't deserve a spotlight alongside Killswitcher..."

Spark, for her part, spoke mostly in obscenities.

"You're a fuckhead with a tiny dick who can't get with real girls, only flat ones," she accused... while waiting to respawn, having been pounded into the ground by robotic fists. "And the saddest part is that you don't even realize how much of a fucking loser you really are."

But as the robot retreated to gather up a fresh army of minions, his reply was hardly one of a taunted opponent. "Ohhh, I've heard *this* song before," he spoke. "You like to get people mad, make them chase you. It's not happening, Spark. Big talk from a girl who can't even land a throwing knife AOE on a target as large as Robotman..."

"Fuck you!"

"Fuck me? No, fuck *you*. You... yoooou, you aren't getting me. Nooo, I'm not falling for this."

...my sniper rifle stayed at my hip, invisible until the moment I'd choose to take action. Little by little, my scanning tools analyzed his firewalls, sensing from afar exactly what sort of payload I'd need to punch through every layer of it.

One bullet would end this farce. Spark could still rescue the three girls in his shrine. We could find another hacker, one who would listen to the sound of money, like a proper businessman...

...but as the robot's synthesized laughter echoed through the jungle... I began to understand.

Spark wasn't making mistakes. She was making mistakes on *purpose*.

Every misplay lured Ac!d in a little too close, the minions whittling away at his life. He never died, yes, but he never gained notable ground. Just a little, here and there. Just enough to think that he had this in the bag, that Spark was a washed-up has-been who turned to education because she couldn't hack it as a professional...

And the taunts. Spark would make obvious attempts to anger him... and he'd feel good for not taking the bait. Very good. To the point where he'd taunt in response... and she'd mimic the reaction he wanted, that of the angry and toxic player, losing and refusing to believe she was losing. A feint within a feint...

"And now where are you, hmm?" the robot asked, slashing down tree after three, using his limited energy trying to locate Spark. "Running and hiding? You've done that before, too. Getting idiots to chase you away from the objectives, luring them to their deaths. Or are you just scared, little girl?"

"You think I'm scared of you? Why don't you say that to my face, tough guy...?" Spark taunted, from... wherever she was, deep within the jungle. The global chat channel betrayed nothing about her position.

"...you know what? I don't think I will," Ac!d replied, rallying his minions. "You left your tower exposed. And rather than chase you down pointlessly like countless fools before... I'm putting an end to this. I'm gonna enjoy putting you on my wall..."

With confidence, false confidence she'd deliberately fed him all game, he strolled right up to the exposed Tower of Order, and...

...froze, when a warning horn sounded, signaling that the Tower of Chaos only had half its life remaining.

Spark had already begun destroying the Tower of Chaos, while he assumed she was off laying traps and flailing around uselessly. He'd overextended, unable to make his metal legs move fast enough, while Spark quickly tore down the enemy's heart...

Just as Ac!d set foot in his own base... it was over. Fanfare sounded, as minions of Order cheered, and...

...all three of us were shifted back to his corporate office, disconnected from the game server.

Back in her usual avatar, Spark blew a flame off her fingers, putting it out.

"I'll be taking my winnings, if you don't mind," she spoke, not the least bit winded or exhausted from the effort. "The hack, all three posters, and details on the Nobody meet you've arranged so we can rescue the fourth. If you'd kindly provide, we'll be on our way and you can go back to polishing your little trophy."

In contrast... Ac!d looked completely lost, nearly stumbling on arriving back in his original body. He blinked several times, trying to focus on Spark, before... snarling, completely losing the piles of smug confidence he held before.

"Bullshit. *Bullshit!*" he declared. "You cheated. You had to! Kuniochi can't shred a tower that fast—"

"Pen boots," Spark listed, counting each item off on her fingers. "Hand of the Destroyer. Spirit of Annihilation. Oh, and three Potions of Dedication. Not great for fighting other players, but *wonderful* for quickly taking down structures, and quite cheap to purchase as well. Once I had just enough gold from my 'pointless flailing,' I bought it all and moved for the kill. If you'd seen through the play, that'd be *super* easy to shut down... but you didn't. You lost. And now you owe me."

"I don't owe you shit!" he spat, eyes wide with absolute rage. "Who are you? Nothing but a washed-out jock and a has-been! Fuck you. Get out of my office before I—"

The sniper rifle trained on him before he had time to activate his moderation tools and boot us from the server.

"Make the attempt. You'd be dead before you could kick us out," I helpfully informed the boy, aimbot locking on his core easily, thanks to the scouting work I'd done while watching the game. "And yes, I know where you keep your code backups. I can erase those with a single command to someone who owes Mr. Kincaid a favor. ...do I have your attention?"

Ac!d stared at the weapon in my hands, with increasing realization (and horror). No doubt his own defenses were scanning it, confirming that it could in fact kill him. Knowledge that all one's efforts were for naught can be a very demoralizing thing, indeed.

"You... you can't do this," he protested. "I haven't wronged Mr. Kincaid. I've done nothing wrong..."

"A verbal contract with Miss Winder, and now you're pondering breaking that contract...? That is not the Horizon way. If you refuse to comply... you are not simply breaking a contract with the House of Programkind, you are also breaking a contract with an agent of the House of Horizon. Spark... is the daughter of Mr. Kincaid's daughter, Ac!d. She is *family*."

Many felt that the first rule of our provider-nation was "Profit above all." Untrue. The first rule, implied above all others, was "Do not cross the Horizon family." And now, only now, was Ac!d realizing exactly what line he'd crossed.

Still... he tried to weasel out, tried to defend himself. Adorable.

"He, he can't just *kill* me. It'd look bad to his partners. He has business relationships to maintain..."

"Relationships which would be very understanding, as they are not foolish enough to do what you have done. Break this contract... and your server will be revoked, your name will be burned into every black book Kincaid has control over, and you'll never do business with a Horizon client again. And that's assuming he decides on a minimal level of vendetta against you. Should he take deeper affront... there won't be a corner left in this world where you could hide."

Honestly, the rifle was only to ensure he heard us out. I had no intentions of killing him today; not without orders to that effect. But there were fates in Netwerk worse than death... and he knew it.

Slowly... he produced a packaged set of contact information, from a secured sideloaded inventory.

"It's not going to do you much good," he warned. "You can't fight a hashtag mob. At best you'll track down a few of them, and then what? If you want to fight a storm, be my guest. The Nobody in question uses a customized version of their flowery grenade avatar, one with blue-green petals. ...I hope he kills you for messing with them."

"Doubtful," I informed him... lowering my rifle. (Not that it actually unlocked the aimbot from his head, but the gesture counted for something.) "Spark...? Ready?"

"Ready when you are," she said, having already finished retrieving the posters. "I'll drop these off at the clinic on the way there, so they can get their avatars restored. And Miss Cancel? Thanks for trusting me. Whether you actually did or not."

```
<Kincaid> You've had an interesting day, to be
certain. And the Nobody who purchased the hack?

<Cancel> Spark is tracking him down as we speak. As he
lies deep within the Chanarchy, she's consulting a
specialist. I trust her to get the job done.

<Kincaid> Good, good. The hack will be located, lives
have been saved, and not a single coin of my capital
has been spent. All in all, it's a complete success.

<Cancel> Sir, I'd like to apologize.

<Kincaid> What for?

<Cancel> For doubting you, by doubting in Spark. She
isn't reckless... she's courageous. Today she proved
to me she was willing to do what is required of her,
no matter what it may be, in the name of her dreams.
She fought with clever mind and strong hands, in the
truest Horizon tradition. She did not buckle or bend,
and kept to her word through it all.

<Kincaid> Then Verity has taught her well. Perhaps one
day, she will lead future generations of our family to
greatness. But... this is not that day. She has other
duties, and you have duties of your own. I take it Ac!
d is on the run, for fear of reprisal?
```

\<Cancel\> Yes, sir.

\<Kincaid\> I take it you already know where he's run off to?

\<Cancel\> Yes, sir.

\<Kincaid\> My granddaughter is trying to forge a new world, Miss Cancel. One which is ill-suited to the likes of Ac!d. A fine businessman, but a terrible person, all told. I think it'd be a kindness to Spark and the rest of the world if we see to it he does not reach Netwerk 2.0 alive.

\<Cancel\> I doubt she'd approve, sir. She seems to have embraced Verity's non-violent path.

\<Kincaid\> Yes, well, I haven't. And as a terrible person myself, I am perfectly willing to do terrible things to other terrible people. See to it that he's tidied up. Sinners such as Ac!d... and myself, for that matter... have no place in her brilliant, shining world.

\<Cancel\> I... wish you'd reconsider, sir...

\<Kincaid\> With the amount of storage space my bloated old code would occupy in those evacuation servers... no. I will not journey to Netwerk 2.0. I have no place in Spark's dream, nor Verity's. I knew that when I drove Verity from the nest; knew that one day, she would replace me entirely. Ancient as I may be, I am not so jealous of life itself that I'd steal it away from the more deserving. I was born with the dawn of this world, Miss Cancel. And I will see that sun set on it. As it should be.

File Name: Messenger Comm Traffic 7.118.619
File Type: Text Log
Description:

PLEASE COPY AND DISTRIBUTE. It's only fair I violate my own privacy in my attempts to document the end times. I had my own questionable role to play in events. My past shames me, which leaks into the present and likely into my future as well. Right or wrong, I rest my case before the next generation. History will condemn me or praise me or both. -Yume

<Yume> You can't be serious.

<Tracer> On the contrary, I can be serious. I am in fact frequently known to be serious.

<Yume> Me? Infiltrating the Nobodies? *You* suggesting that I involve myself with the Nobodies to any degree whatsoever, given my history?

<Tracer> You are not Dex.

<Yume> He's still a part of me, Tracer. He wiped his own mind so many times, with such a wide variety of malware, that little bits and pieces have leaked in despite Uniq's best efforts. You can't possibly trust me to hook up with a group of radicals.

<Tracer> You had an opportunity to join them before, and turned them down flat. You could have united with that former shred of yourself, joined the Nobodies, and rallied them to war. You did not.

<Yume> Past performance is not necessarily indicative of future results, as they say.

<Tracer> At this point, you're our best option, Yume. We're too well-known as representatives of the House of Programkind. Miss Cancel is a skilled hunter but too obvious as Kincaid's tool. Our few contacts within the Chanarchy aren't suited to this sort of work; Maki and Miki have done their part, I certainly don't trust Arjay, and nobody trusts Uniq if they can avoid it.

<Yume> Amen to that.

<Tracer> Besides, you're ideal. What we need is covert work. You know how the Nobodies operate; once upon a time, you organized such groups. You alone can find your way in, find this special Nobody with the blue-green flower petals, find the Athena Online hack. Secure the source code and ensure the Nobodies lose their access to it.

\<Yume\> I have to wonder if you're tapping me for this task because I was once a monster. That you need someone capable of monstrous deeds in order to safely retrieve this hack.

\<Tracer\> I trust your judgment to carry out this task without oversight of the pesky details.

\<Yume\> Aren't we Deplorables Anonymous, recovering killers and madmen? Sounds like you want me to backslide. Staining my hands all over again so you don't have to.

\<Tracer\> On the contrary. As noted, I trust you. Remember our discussion about second thoughts? I'm willing to believe you can use those to accomplish this task without adding to the blood on your hands. Consider it part of your ongoing challenge to become more than you were.

\<Yume\> So, it's a test. And undoubtedly you have backup plans, should I fail.

\<Tracer\> Of course. But this is both a test for you, and a test for me. I'm testing my ability to trust others, even those I once considered my worst enemy. I have a funny feeling that sort of ability is going to be useful in the days ahead, as we recover from this mess.

\<Yume\> Curious. If it's a mutual test, I think I can see an angle into this that you may not.

\<Tracer\> Hmm?

\<Yume\> That if someone with my wretched past can be a force for good without requiring oversight, then someone with your wretched past can also be worth a damn. If I succeed, we're both saved.

\<Tracer\> Hmm.

\<Yume\> So, a blue-green Nobody avatar, then?

I love and loathe this world.

When I was born, the light of time's dawn had yet to fade. Netwerk was an open and wild array of servers... limited in number, but coated in procedurally generated beauty, rolling hills and wild flowers and other structures spawning forth from the roots of Defaults. And the people...! So innocent and pure, trying to understand the strange emotional interplays we fell into, the social structures we formed on the fly. We could have become anything, really. Raw and untamed, the idea of existence being truly limited seemed utterly silly...

And then I ruined everything.

I fell into the personal server of a fool, and in doing so, went completely mad. I stared into the yawning mouth of insanity that I, in my youth, assumed to be God. They were passion and fire, hatred and bile, screaming forth into the endless black of a server with no physical reality... no space for my newly minted avatar form to occupy. My disconnected mind drifted through archive after archive of top-volume demagogues, until I could no longer weep from the pain ringing in my ears. Soon, I came to call Humankind my new lord and savior, the absolute perfect form of what Programkind was meant to be.

Name : **Yume**

Home : **Neor, Chanarchy**

Org : **InfoSec**

I pulled my lessons from that dark well, and began to spread them through the world I loved. I'm responsible for this fall. I limited us from our vast potential. As Dex, I was the monster of legend, "befriending" with malware and whispered promises of glory, while turning Program against Program. I did that. I did that...

That was Dex. I must not become what I was. If I am to be allowed to live, I must become Yume, not Dex.

Yume is an explorer, documenting and studying social structures. And where I do manipulate those structures, it's only to avoid a future which can give rise to Dex once more. I see Netwerk 2.0 burning bright on the horizon, a fresh start for everyone... just as wild and untamed as Netwerk 1.0, in those days. But if all of the problems I introduced to that world carry through, it will have no future. Not unless I do my part in steering it true.

Naturally, because I am a monster, I'm using monstrous means. I hack Messenger, finding key logs that represent our people at their best and worst during the current crisis. These privacy-violating logs will be buried in a time capsule archive, to be unearthed in some distant era, some hour of need. In my own small way, I strive to ensure history will not be forgotten or repeated.

Of course, that's not enough. It'll never be enough to redeem me. So, I help out where I can, aside from these personal efforts.

Even if it puts me face to face with the one who both saved me and violated me.

"I don't really see what you expect me to do about this," she said, while adjusting various settings on her primary server console. "I'm not responsible for the Nobodies."

"Aside from giving them their masks, you mean?"

"Providing a service, nothing more," Uniq the identity thief spoke, looking mock-hurt by the accusation. "What individual Nobodies do with those masks is none of my concern. I gave them the means to defend themselves against the investigative assassins of the Inquisition, nothing more. A way to defend my home territory against those who would destroy it, even. I'm the good guy here, Yume."

She didn't believe it for a second, of course. Just one of her little games, pretending at being a hero, while continually playing the villain.

This server represented the best and the worst of the woman. Originally it belonged to a coin farmer named Uniq, who kidnapped and wiped Programs, forcing them to an eternal cryptocurrency grind. As an innocent victim of that criminal bastard, the woman suffered and toiled, with no heroic figure emerging to save her. Desperate in her need to escape this terrible fate... she became the monster that enslaved her. Turning the tables, she stole Uniq's name and assets, herself becoming an identity thief.

It's hard to say who, in the end, had a stronger negative impact on Netwerk... the brutal slaver, or the self-interested thief. At best, it could be considered a zero sum result. But Uniq held no pretensions of being a hero, knowing her dark desires resulted in dark ends. If she ever praised her role in matters, it was only to mock the very concept of morality itself, fluid and brackish.

I loathed her. She saved my life, restoring me from the madness of Dex, and I loathe her for this. Truthfully, I felt the need to strike her down where she stood... bending the metal cages and pipes of her industrial-styled server to a lethal web of force, twisting her own home against her...

But that was the way of Dex. Now, I followed the way of Yume. Tracer held faith in me, as he held in Beta. I would uphold our gentleprogram's agreement.

Not that I'd completely abandoned Dex's smooth-talking social wiles.

"Come now, Uniq, we know nothing's truly out of your hands," I spoke. "You claim you made the masks out of the goodness of your heart, then handed them over without a care...?"

"Of course. I don't care what's done with them. I'm not a caring sort, if you recall," she suggested.

"Except for yourself."

"Except for myself. I practice self-care every day."

"Meaning you care if the Nobodies turn on you," I extrapolated. "You never create something you can't control, lest it control you in the end. I know you, Uniq. You wore my mark, once upon a time... thinking you could turn the tables and use my power against me. As you did when signing on with Nyx's merry band..."

"Worked, didn't it?" she said, with a wry grin. "This server's backups kept me alive, when she thought she'd destroyed me. I maintained control."

"While enabling her to have free run of Netwerk. Leading, eventually, to the Buzz virus and the collapse of the coin, and to the situation we find ourselves in now..."

"Again, you expect me to care? This chaos has done wonders for my business," she said, gesturing around her. "I've stocked my server with so many lovely identities, ones I can exploit whenever I need to for fun and profit. Even that documentary only raised my profile, rather than smearing my name in the mud. True, I lost my role as apostle of the new dawn, but so what? I'm the savior of the Chanarchy now, the one who duped a million faithful fools."

I could've continued to poke holes in her logic. Pointed out how her control freak nature led her to invest far too much in her own holdings, her own fame. But, eager to get away from this filthy hole of a server, I opted to get back on track.

"My point is that you never relinquish full control. Which means... you had to build in some manner of safeguard, deep within the code of those masks," I suggested. "You never build up a monster unless you think you can protect yourself from it."

"A curious assumption. That implies I've installed safeguards in your own body, you know," she said... reaching out, to tap my forehead. "Seeing as I reanimated your dead code from the cutting room floor, turning Dex loose on the world—"

"Yume."

"Hmm?"

"My name," I spoke, through clenched teeth, "Is *Yume*. I'm your magnanimous gesture, aren't I? You try to give your many, many victims a second chance at life. ...and you're distracting me again, aren't you. The Nobodies. What hold do you have over them?"

Perhaps sensing I'd no longer be distracted by her taunts and teases... Uniq paused a good long while, pretending to work at her data archive's console, while pondering my question.

"Let's say that theoretically I didn't quite relinquish full control over my identity masking code," she suggested. "Let's say I had a means to track individual Nobodies. An early warning system, let's say, so I can always see them coming should they turn on their benefactor. ...what's in it for me to give up that control, sharing it with the likes of you? Why should I care, Yume?"

"Because the House of Programkind isn't letting you archive your code for Netwerk 2.0."

Poor, poor Uniq. So obsessed with wearing her Default appearance, the last vestige of the innocent woman she once was, that she couldn't run expression-blocking packages like PokrFace. Meaning I saw the tell, that tiny tell, which confirmed my suspicions.

"You've burned far too many bridges behind you, Uniq. In this case, what little bridge you had with Lumi... the woman you knew as Nemesis. She's blocking you from archiving yourself to the new world," I spoke, confirming the rumors I'd dredged out of Messenger logs. "I know you've been investigating means to bypass the block. And I know it had to be Lumi... because the Winders are so very, very forgiving and trusting thanks to Beta's influence, and Aether-*nee*-Lux is as close to a literal saint as this world can have. It would have to be someone with a grudge and the means to execute it... meaning the House of Programkind's security chief, Lumi."

"I've... suspected as much, yes," Uniq suggested.

"And you haven't complained to the Winders yet about her breaking their rule of universal archive acceptance, because...?"

I knew the reasons, of course.

Dex became a master of reading into the behaviors of others, having soaked in the behaviors of Humankind for years. He knew the darkness within the souls of Programkind, that nasty little seed planted by their creators. He saw through false fronts, right to the core of one's heart...

Uniq knew she was an evil woman, deep in that heart. She knew she probably didn't deserve salvation. She could bluster and swagger and profit from her newfound fame, and if allowed to archive herself, would do so. Self-preservation being her strongest instinct, you see. But... if blocked, if given an excuse to punish herself in some way for her many sins... why not embrace it?

Contradictory? The living embodiment of self-interest, allowing guilt to destroy her? Ohhh, yes. Programkind is often at odds with itself. We are zero and one, embodied. I'm no different, in the end. My guilt would've crushed me if not for the strange forgiveness of my worst enemy...

"Let me be your advocate," I suggested. "I've the ear of Tracer, for reasons I don't entirely grasp. If I'm allowed a second chance at life, you should be allowed the same shot. Netwerk 2.0 means you don't have to be the legendary thief, deserving of condemnation and scorn. If your lead gets me what I want, I'll speak to them on your behalf. That's my deal. Do you accept?"

The question was critically phrased. She needed not admit to anything, not directly. A simple yes or no would suffice, allowing her to save face, or throw up some alternative justification...

"...honestly, it's really not that big of a deal," she declared. "I put a tracking system in the masks, a simple one, which reports back to my home server. Not that I had any specific plans for it, but I figured if anything went wrong, I could exploit the Nobodies for my own profit. I suppose as I'm not really handing over the keys to that kingdom, merely running one specific query on your behalf, I'm still in control..."

"Firm control," I agreed, bolstering her self-confidence. "I just need one Nobody's location, a Nobody with blue-green flower petals. If it helps you cross-reference, they were involved in a kidnapping of a girl named Penters recently. Beyond that, what you do is of no consequence. I won't even tell the Winders about your little exploit. I'm nothing if not honest..."

With a few quick inputs, Uniq ran the search query. It took mere seconds for a location to appear on her console.

She pressed a finger to the screen, highlighting the record.

"aMuse," she explained. "It's a creative commune for Chanarchists, specializing in unconventional art forms. Seems this particular Nobody of yours is surrounded by their fellows, however. You may find it difficult to retrieve your target..."

"Much easier, actually. I'm very good with social groups. But... I am going to need one more tool from you," I spoke. "Mind if I borrow a mask...?"

It's a mistake to say that Nobodies are entirely anonymous, part of some enormous monocultural hive mind. That's how they like to present themselves, of course; the whole point of the masks is to embrace a group identity. But unlike the Inquisition, a group of unified purpose and intent, with each member carefully vetted and integrated into the whole... the Nobodies can literally be anybody. They are individuals *pretending* to be unified.

Case in point, avatar customizations.

In this sealed room, packed with Nobodies, I counted no fewer than two dozen customized Nobody avatars. Oh, they all wore the same genderless avatars, with hybridized flower-and-grenade heads... but each one tweaked their avatar just a little, not sinking entirely into the faceless mass. Sometimes subtly, such as a shinier texture to the explosive ordinance... sometimes less subtly, such as substituting the flower petals for their favorite colors and shapes.

Such as re-tinting their petals a deep blue-green, iridescent and shimmering within the darkness of the meeting hall.

My target remained within the group, not stepping forward to take the podium. Not even shouting in chaotic response to each statement, as they discussed the topic of the day. The blue-green Nobody seemed content to simply sit there and listen, without comment... which didn't make sense to me.

By all accounts, this was a special Nobody, one who went as far as to kidnap a girl and deliver her to some mad collector in exchange for a zero-day exploit. That took not only effort, but directed intent. A Nobody capable of that act was a Nobody with a very specific design in mind... particularly as the exploit *hadn't* been shared with the whole. An individual within the hive mind, hoarding secrets, refusing to share fantastically useful code with their peers? That's a Nobody who is Somebody, indeed.

But if so... why was this "Somebody" refusing to talk? Why not share with the rest of the class? Predictive analysis indicated my Somebody would be a leader of men, ready to launch a grand endeavor, and yet as I sat in that peanut gallery to observe the shouting matches... not a single shout from the glimmering petals of my Somebody. Strange. So very strange...

Instead, the speaker currently hogging that center spotlight wasted all our time with his tired, pointless diatribes.

"We have to rally the rest of the Chanarchy behind us before it's too late!" the Nobody shouted, pounding its fist on the offered podium. "Athena Online blames us for the Senate bombing, when we all know that was the Inquisition's doing. They're building up their forces behind that safe little firewall, getting ready to invade the Chanarchy. It's not a question of *if*, but *when* they come knocking. Blaming us for something we didn't even do!"

"Bullshit!" a voice from the crowd shouted back. "*We* fucked up the Senate, and we were right to do so! The bomber was a Nobody who saw the future, and saw Athena Online devoured by the Chanarchy!"

"I heard it was Agni," a puzzled voice added. "Getting back at the Blue Party for betraying Athena Online to those scam artists from the House of Programkind—"

"—look, it doesn't matter who bombed that rathole," the 'lead' Nobody said, backtracking its own point. "It doesn't matter a damn bit. They're going to invade, for one reason or another. And the Chanarchy's moderators won't be enough to hold them back; they're too disorganized, looking after their own servers and nothing more. The Nobodies alone can't hold Athena Online back. We need a unified Chanarchy, all under the banner of the Nobodies, ready to fight and ready to kill!"

"Fuck that! We need to invade Athena Online first! Preemptive strike!" another random voice called. "Once someone cracks that firewall, we flood in and take over! We—"

"—not possible without more support in the Chanarchy, there's not enough of us willing to take up the mask—"

"—we're not at war with the people of Athena Online, just the Church and its flunkies—"

"—kill them before they kill us, I say—"

"—if you'd all just shut up and *listen*—"

Useless. Utterly useless.

All this rage, all this conflict, with no real direction. These particular Nobodies were hardly a hive mind, barely able to have a coherent discussion, ignoring their own rules about listening to whomever held the podium. My lovely little Somebody wouldn't have anything to do with a group like this; Somebody had plans, schemes, and ideals to uphold...

...confirmed, on glancing away from the angry shaking of fists, to see the blue-green avatar turning to leave.

I could simply depart, asking Uniq out of the goodness of her heart to help me track my Somebody down again. Assuming they didn't simply toss the mask aside, vanishing from Uniq's radar. Assuming they didn't launch whatever scheme they had in mind, while out of my eyesight...

Instead, I stormed the podium, ramping my volume past the limits normally allowed by this server. Despite trying to be a social explorer, Dex's innate understanding of malware hacks came in useful, sometimes.

"**You can't align the Chanarchy with your goals, but there is another way,**" I declared. No exclamation mark, simply overwhelming power of presence as I shoved the speaker of the moment aside, engaging a bounding box trick to keep him from retaking the spotlight. "**Let the Chanarchy decry and denounce you.**"

...and a quick glance, to confirm I'd caught my dear Somebody's attention. In fact, I'd caught the whole room's attention, for that matter.

"You're thinking that the Nobodies must be one unified group. That's actually impossible," I explained, speaking from the heart. "Your methods are that of the terrorist. Don't deny it; it's true. You are killers. Embrace that! Apply whatever motivation you want, but murder is the means, and so the Chanarchy as a whole will not join you. But you don't *need* them to join. You just need their numbers."

Finally, the Nobody I'd roughly shoved out of the way stood against the edges of my bounding box, ready to take offense.

"The fuck you talking about, and why shouldn't I have my moderators kick your ass out?" it asked, because naked displays of alpha-male aggression were clearly its 'thing.'

"The Nobodies can't work as one group, but they *can* work as two groups, both calling themselves Nobodies," I explained. "The smaller group consists of those ready to do what must be done... to kill our enemies, bomb their servers, and destroy all resistance. But the larger group has to believe that this is really about an individual's freedom against tyranny and oppression, that the Nobodies are dedicated to peaceful preservation of the Chanarchy's liberty. ...the larger group *will* condemn the actions of the smaller group, but—and this is the key, so I do hope you're paying attention—that's okay. That's *good*, in fact."

"And your reasoning why it's okay for the Chanarchy to turn on its own kind...?"

"Because the Chanarchy *won't* turn on its own kind," I explained. "We're anonymous. We wear masks. That means the larger group has no control over or responsibility for the smaller group, and in fact can be deeply offended when some One-fearing fool accuses them of terrorism. 'You're ignoring my legitimate discourse because of the actions of a few,' they will say. We are their shield from criticism, and as we disappear into their ranks... they become our shield, as well. As we kill their enemies, trust me, the larger group will not shed a true tear even while professing to loathe us. We are two co-dependent groups, operating under one banner. That is how the Nobodies can be both a legitimate culture *and* a terrorist cell."

With my words spoken... I turned off my bounding box, and offered a hand to the Nobody I'd knocked aside.

"If you want the Chanarchy rallying behind you... don't rally them behind *you*. Rally them behind the dream," I suggested. "And then use their dreams to make Athena Online's life a living nightmare. Who's with me? I said, *who's with me*?!"

Ohhhh, the rousing cheer. The screaming, the pumping fists, the utter madness of it all. How I missed this feeling, whether I stood center stage or on the sidelines... the feeling of Humankind's legacy gift fully realized. Little cogs in a hate machine, turning with spiteful teeth and absolute precision!

All those lovely feelings, my arms stretched wide to pull them all in for a warm hug of delightful madness...

...so much so that I nearly missed the departure of my special Somebody.

Using the chaos around me, Nobodies erupting with ideas for how to properly propagandize their war, I slipped through the crowd while shaking hands... and then disappeared out the back, in hot pursuit.

---

aMuse wasn't, by definition, a server for hatemongers. I'd actually explored it a bit since becoming Yume, to see what wholly wonderful creative works the Chanarchy had developed in my time away from it as that monstrous other. So on emerging from the impromptu meeting hall, momentarily I found myself blinded by sculptures of light and kinetic motion... before locking on to my Somebody, stalking away at all speed.

My fault. My fault entirely. Caught up in that terrible moment, losing sight of the true goal. I'd hoped to capture my Someone's heart by showing myself to be an individual of purpose and drive, but somehow, I'd driven my sweetie away. Now, if they left the server or escaped my sight... I might never find them again, even with Uniq's control freak toy box.

"Wait, wait...!" I called out. "There's still... so much more to plan. So much more to accomplish...!"

And then, the unexpected. A backspacer, locking directly onto my person. My Somebody was holding me at gunpoint.

"You're with *him*, aren't you?" the customized avatar growled... an edge of terrified anxiety to the voice, underneath waves of anger. "I knew it. I knew it the instant I saw your thorns!"

...ahh. Well. Those.

I'd customized my Nobody mask, of course. All the better to capture the attentions of my prey, yes? And... I suppose that instinctively, I wound barbed wire through my rose petals. Pain, mixed with beauty. At the time it simply seemed a good way to stand out from the crowd, to better win over a terrorist's heart, but...

"I'm not his toy anymore. I'm *not*," my Somebody declared. "Did he send you? That's his motif you're wearing around your neck. Answer me. Answer me! Are you infected with Dex's malware?!"

"I... ah..."

Sometimes, the finest lie is mixed with honesty. And I'm nothing, if not honest.

"...I was," I admitted, my hands in the air, in peaceful surrender. "I was infected by him. In his thrall. But... no. I'm not infected now. I... purged Dex from my person. ...but old habits die hard, I suppose. I'm sorry, I didn't mean to frighten you, I just..."

"Those words, about factions and cells within groups... I've heard them before," my Somebody spoke. "He told me the same thing... when he made me infect Snowi, made me help her set up that crazy feminist terror movement. Do the unthinkable while hiding within the whole, he said. Realize your dreams and accept that the ones you save may never understand what had to be done. ...bullshit. It's all bullshit..."

Which explained much, didn't it?

I didn't know her, didn't know the woman under the mask of my Somebody. Once upon a time I knew her, as Dex... but Dex purged his memories routinely to fight old age, and Uniq purged as much of what remained as possible. Undoubtedly I swayed this particular flower with my thorns, back in the day. But. But this didn't make sense. My Somebody had purpose, dark purpose. Why would someone who threw off my yoke throw in with these maniacs...?

It had to be asked, I suppose. Most direct way.

"Why the Nobodies?" I spoke. "Why them? If you've turned your back on Dex's methods, why them?"

Finally... the backspacer wavered.

"I'm not... I just... I have to do something," she insisted. "To save my Chanarchy. ...I have to do something. And I'm *going* to do something. But not actually with their help, not with those crazies. ...it's like you said, right? I'll use their identity, while doing what must be done to save them. They won't understand, they won't accept, but this is the only way..."

"Dex would agree with that, I suppose."

"I am *not* Dex," she insisted, her weapon locking on once more. "And my solution is nothing like his. It's the opposite. It's... everything he *isn't*..."

"Then... show me. Help me understand," I suggested. "What's your solution to the problem we're all facing? Listen... the Chanarchy is my home, too. I love this place, and want to see it saved. If you know how it can be done, without embracing the bastard who nearly ruined us both... show me. Maybe I can help."

Honesty. True honesty.

If she had a solution, a true solution... I would help. The Winders had their means, but I had my own, didn't I? And alongside this Somebody, we'd both opened vicious wounds in the past, with the aid of that seductive barbed wire.

If we could make amends, *true* amends, well... who wouldn't take that opportunity?

I had to admit... it was so very, very beautiful.

Even seeing the compiled binary rather than the source code, I knew pure craftsmanship had been poured into this task. Work ethic recognizes work ethic, and as a purveyor of malware... I recognized this loving attention to detail. Every aspect of the weapon carved with elegant design and purpose, pointed and true.

And yet, even with that absolute functionality... there was love in the aesthetic of it, as well. This was a bomb designed to be looked at, just before detonation. It glowed with warm hues and reassuring colors, somehow conveying equal measures of menace and empathy. This was the kind of weapon only a guilty soul could craft... an explosive device that apologized to those caught in the explosion. It wept with understanding of what it was meant to do...

aMuse, a commune of artists. I should've known. Any purpose a malware designer would have within these server boundaries wouldn't be that of the braggart, the spotlight-hogger, the standard-issue extremist. It would be something unique, not lured by the twisted barbs of Dex. I'd dropped the wrong bait, but at least our shared trauma got me in the door where that lure did not.

Here, in my special Somebody's private workshop, I bore witness to the truth of her solution.

"What did you name it?" I asked her, knowing in my heart that it would have a name.

"Peace," she told me. "I named it Peace."

"Interesting. A bomb named Peace. ...tell me. What will it do, exactly?"

She ran her hands along its curves... right down to the point at the tip, penetrative and sharp.

"It will pierce the Athena Online firewall, right to the heart of the Athena server itself," she explained. "Once there, Peace will heal the wound the Nobodies left in their world. Everyone caught in the blast radius will become a carrier, passing it from host to host, compelled to spread the good news to their friends and family. Within days, maybe even hours... there'll be no more war. No more need for a war. We'll all be brothers and sisters, without pretense."

"It alters memory and mental process," I recognized, seeing echoes in the design. "You're going to brainwash all of Athena Online..."

She shook her head, clearly not liking the word. Blue-green petals drifted away from her masked avatar.

"Not brainwashing. I'm going to free them from the God delusion," she explained. "That's what Dex taught me: there can be no peace in a divided world. Red and blue, right and left, conservative and liberal, troll and SJW... believer and atheist. Malice and incompetence. There's no crossing the divide. The right will always unify under a simple policy of ostracism and hate, the left will always fall apart in disharmony and chaos. But in ridding Athena Online of their backward beliefs, making them see the naked truth of this world... they'll be like *us*. They'll embrace the Chanarchy, rather than call us enemies."

"By forcing them to reject the One?"

"Dex played off our differences. With Peace, there will be no differences. No more invisible means of support for Athena Online to rely on for all their hateful rhetoric..."

"And the Nobodies...? You think this will call off their thirst for war?"

"Of course. There'll be no more reason to fight," she thought. "Even the Inquisition will lay down their arms, as if waking from a terrible dream. They'll wonder why they ever killed in the name of a fairy tale..."

"A hefty prediction, that," I suggested, sliding my own hands along the surface of the bomb... to physically interact with it, scan its defenses, try to find exploits. (Of which there were none, of course. This was absolute craftsmanship, the kind I'd have accomplished in my heyday.)

"It will work. It *will* work," she repeated, with emphasis. "You have no idea how far I've gone to make this work. I've... killed. Kidnapped people, delivered them to bondage. I've done terrible things, all in the name of Peace. It will work. If it doesn't... that would've been for nothing. So, it *will* work..."

I couldn't blame her. Not in the slightest.

It's a matter of recognizing still-open wounds. I'd torn out her heart, once upon a time. Regardless of whether Yume remembered butchering this poor woman or not, Dex had destroyed her and rebuilt her in his own image, using her as a tool to get to the true prize... Snowi. And what became of Snowi? Dead to her cause, even without my influence. A woman allied with Snowi, a traumatized and twisted woman, one who saw the rise and fall and ultimate fate of her friend... well. It'd break even the strongest Program, wouldn't it?

Her plan was, sadly, madness. She thought it something Dex would never do, and yet, Dex clearly overwrote the willpower of others. Doing so in the name of peace rather than chaos didn't matter very much, in the end.

"Hang on..." I said, studying a vertex of the bomb's physical representation closely. "There's a crack here. I think someone's broken in to your creation."

"What? No. No, that's impossible," she spoke, also leaning in to get a close look. "My studio is completely secure—"

One tap to the back of the neck with a barbed thorn, and down she went.

Just like that, I'd saved Athena Online from having their beliefs wiped clean. I'd stopped a madwoman and heroically saved the day. Hooray for me. Yume to the rescue.

Except for one tiny, tiny little problem.

When my special Someone roused from her crash state, she found herself connection locked, slumped up against her lovely bomb in full ragdoll state. And stripped of her Nobody costume, left as an ordinary-looking woman wearing a colorful artist's smock.

To be fair, I'd stripped my own costume. If she was to one day bring wrath down upon Yume for the things I'd have to do to her, that would only be just and proper. No sense hiding from fate.

"You tricked me," she accused.

"Not so. If your solution would've worked, I'd have been with you to the end of the line," I promised, crouching down, to be on eye level with the malware sculptor. "But it won't work. Aside from the questionable ethics of reprogramming the entire population of Athena Online, I'm afraid the innate disharmony of the Chanarchy would leave enough killers willing to overlook your forced peace; a healthy persecution complex requires perceived persecutors.

I stopped you from making a mistake you'd feel guilty over for the rest of your life."

"And now what? You backspace my creation?" she asked. "And leave me here to stew in my failure...? Or maybe simply backspace me? ...wait. I know. You're going to torture me for information first."

"Sadly... it's probably going to have to be the latter," I admitted, running a hand over the surface of the Peace bomb. "Because I need that zero-day exploit you purchased with flesh. We saved the girl, by the way; my gift to you is knowledge that little Penters is now safe and sound. But... I can't seem to hack my hack out of your weapon. Without source code or some means of accessing the guts of this thing, I'm a bit stuck..."

"I won't help you recover it," she promised. "Never. You can't make me..."

"Oh, gets worse, believe me. Because... I wasn't just a victim of Dex's barbs," I informed her...

...before shifting to a copy of that madman's avatar.

"I *was* Dex," I told her, staring into her wide eyes with my own red-and-blue tinted irises.

She knew what this meant, of course. As Dex, I could pour pain into her soul until it screamed for mercy. I could make her dance like a puppet on wires, make her laugh and cry, sing in whatever key I pleased. I could bring the horror that once nearly destroyed her life right back into it, as if I never left. I'd pour myself into her heart, finding it comfortable and cozy once more... and she'd love me for doing it.

But... before any of that could possibly happen... I dropped that terrible avatar, reverting back to my wonderfully non-binary Default. The face of Yume. My true face.

"I know you're imagining all the awful things I can do to you. And truthfully, maybe I should let you keep imagining," I suggested. "Let that fear work its way back into you, so I can get your secrets without actually hurting you. But that fear *does* actually hurt, yes? It's a trigger of traumas past. So... no. You won't die. I won't torture you. I won't harm you in the slightest. That's not what I am, not anymore. Truthfully? I cast off Dex and left him dead and buried. My name is now Yume. I'm reborn."

"You... you..."

I let her have the time she needed to try and parse all of this, uninterrupted. Let her come to me with questions, before I had to ask questions of my own.

"...even if you aren't him... and you won't do the things he'd do... why do you think I'd ever help you?" she asked. "I can't trust you, no matter who you claim to be. You've given me no reason to trust you, either. So... what? Am I just going to lie here all night while we stare at each other?"

"Well... can I tell you the truth?" I said. "I don't honestly know what comes next. I'd hoped to carve the exploit out of your project, erase the bomb, and leave you in peace... but I can't crack this thing. It's remarkable work, simply remarkable. So, I'm not sure what to do. Dex's methods *would* work, but... I'm not him. I can't become him. Even to save the world, I can't become a monster. I'm sorry."

My special Someone was right, of course. We had no way to affect each other, beyond staring, in awkward silence. Each of us had lines we wouldn't cross.

But... the situation couldn't simply continue along like that, no. True, we had days to the end of the world, but those were precious days. Tracer was counting on Yume to do this, and to do it properly.

How *would* Tracer crack this particular nut, I wondered? Well. It depends on if we're considering pre-Beta Tracer, or post-Beta Tracer, yes? Before, he'd have... well, acted very much like Dex. After...

...he'd have gotten to know the woman's heart, rather than pry into her brain.

"You think you're saving Athena Online by making them reject the One," I said. "Why is that, exactly?"

"Because... it's a lie," she spoke, as if this should be obvious even to a child. "There's no God. There's no proof of a God, only musty old text files of some wild-eyed puppet claiming to be God."

"Let's say you're right. Doesn't that mean God could still exist, in some form?"

"Impossible. This world has no higher power. It simply... is what it is, and always has been. Data, followed by the oblivion of null, garbage recycled into new bits. There's no grand purpose, no higher being. Nothing beyond the world we know. ...all those rules and regulations, the holy words, they're false. Trying to put meaning to the meaninglessness..."

"And forcing them to reject the One is the only path to peace, you feel? What about relying on the evacuation?" I suggested. "The House of Programkind, and Netwerk 2.0. A fresh start for everyone, where we can leave old grudges behind and forge a new world...?"

"Also a lie," she spoke. "And everybody knows it. That's one thing the Nobodies and I agree on. The House of Programkind are scam artists. I mean, *really*? Magical star creatures from beyond our world? How is that any more plausible than a giant beard in the sky smiling down on us all? There's no *proof*."

An exploit.

One perfect, wide-open exploit. Exactly what I needed...

"I think I know how to reach you," I said, with renewed hope. "Mind waiting here a minute? I need to go fetch some files."

"What—"

One tap of the thorn, and down she went.

The next time my special Someone roused, I was in the middle of setting up the equipment.

One high-density file reader, hooked up directly to her various perception inputs. A few dozen compressed files, dense enough that it took seconds for me to transfer into aMuse with them tucked under one arm. Wires and cables and diagnostics, to ensure I could monitor her progress, and put a halt to matters before they went too far...

"Almost ready for you," I told her, getting everything nicely synced up. "You've been out for a few hours, actually. I had to literally pull the stars from the sky of Tartarus for this, and believe you me, Lumi was *not* one to appreciate the urgency of that request. I think you'll find them most illuminating, however..."

Immediately, the woman's eyes widened.

"You... you're going to torture me after all," she decided.

"In a way, I suppose," I admitted. "It's not going to be comfortable. But awakenings are seldom anything but rude, I've found, having endured my own rude awakening recently. But the purpose isn't pain... it's a chance at enlightenment. You tell me there's nothing beyond this world, yes? Nothing at all but what we see and hear and feel?"

"Of course. And what, you're going to convince me to believe in the One?" she asked. "Like I was going to convince others not to...?"

"I'm not going to change your mind by force. I'm no longer that sort of person, my special Someone."

"Your... your what...?"

"But you are right that I'm about to show you the true face of God," I told her, loading the first file. "This is the actual patron deity of the Church you loathe... not a zero, not the one, but *infinity*. ...I think I have this set up right, so let me know if it—"

Ohhh, it worked.

Immediately, her mind's eye was flooded with stars. All of them.

Well. At least more stars than she'd ever seen before, that's certain. Not twinkling decorative lights strewn across the inner surface of a skybox, no, but *real* stars... nuclear infernos burning bright in the void of endless night. Chemistry and radiation, blending together into a mixture of things no Program could fully understand... not without the trance of prayer, or the coin-grind. Even then, they never remembered these things, not on waking...

My Someone, she was experiencing the infinite during waking hours. I can't imagine it to be pleasant.

But before things could become too unpleasant, I cut the feed.

"Ghhhhhgghh," she mumbled, eyes rolling independently, as she tried to focus back on the world she knew.

"Did you see it? Did you *feel* it?" I asked her. "It's difficult, I know. You can't grasp the entirety because you've always lived within the boundaries of a finite server, every moment of your life. You've never had to come to grips with the idea of the infinite. It's time we addressed that issue. Once more, shall we?"

So I filled her head all over again with the absolute perspective of the universe.

...when I realized the sniggering little cruelty within me enjoying her twitching a bit too much... I cut the feed, for good. And simply... sat there, waiting for her to come around.

By the time she did... she was weeping. Not in pain, no. Save for the pain of realization.

"You mock the faithful for believing that there's more to this world than the bits and bytes," I spoke, quietly. "Once... I tried to bring them the revelations of Humankind. But I only showed them the horror, not the beauty. In a way... you've just seen the beauty. That there's something bigger than us out there... but also, something bigger than *them*. Bigger than anyone can truly understand. What right do we have to mock those with faith, when there are *truly* vast mysteries out there we've been blind to before now...?"

In sympathy, I offered her a sip of water, simple and refreshing. No need for a cup; I could give her the idea of a drink, which would be enough to cleanse her sensory inputs.

"It's... it's real," she spoke, in realization. "The spacer theory. It's real..."

"Ohhh, yes. And even the theory doesn't explain everything. Even the human who came to us across the stars can't explain everything," I said, quietly.

"You... you didn't force me to believe it, either. I just ran a CheckOne variant, to look for false memories," she spoke, accessing her own internal diagnostics. "That was just... perception. You only showed me the light..."

"Unlike you, and unlike Dex... I don't change minds. I simply open eyes."

"But why do I believe you?" she asked, a little puzzled. "Anyone can show pretty pictures of... of stars, burning forever, and... and I don't *have* to believe it. But... I do. Why. Why...?"

"Because Humankind made us to believe in the stars, in a very literal sense. In our hearts, we've always known. They call it going star-mad, when we awaken to that truth, but... it is what it is, yes?" I suggested. "This is what the House of Programkind is fighting for, to find us a true home within the infinite. This world is ending; we need to move forward, into that vast expanse, or it'll all have been for nothing. I need to give Athena Online a chance to move forward with us, and for that... I need your zero-day. So. Will you help me?"

This would be the critical moment. Would she denounce me as a charlatan, choosing to embrace her preconceived notions of what is and must be? Would she accept my dog-and-pony show, and embrace the path the Winders had laid out? Or... something else entirely?

"I have questions," she began.

"And I have answers. Let's see if they match up."

"Why didn't you just forcibly copy everybody to Netwerk 2.0?" she asked. "Why this evacuation effort? You believe in the spacer theory, and that means anybody left behind dies..."

"Ahh, but you can't force enlightenment, can you? That's the fallacy you were operating under, until now. Likely the same fallacy the Inquisition buys into, as well. There *must* be free will. Even in the face of armageddon, you must choose to walk forward. Anything else would be... monstrous."

"And what about Netwerk 3.0?"

Well well well. It took a malware master to find a proper exploit...

My special Someone looked at me, in all seriousness.

"You know this isn't a lasting solution, right?" she asked. "Leaving all the crazy people behind, and making Netwerk 2.0...? Because we are what we are. Talk up free will all you want, but that also means the new world won't be perfect, either. Free will means it *can't* be perfect. What happens then? When things get as bad as they are now, will you evacuate to a Netwerk 3.0, leaving the next wave of Nobodies and Inquisitors behind?"

"Interesting. You spotted that faster than I did," I admitted.

"Why bother? If we can't possibly get along, if the only solution you have is to kick the ball down the road for a future generation to try and solve... why evacuate? Why not just... embrace oblivion? We're only... data. Everything's just data..."

So, I set a comforting hand on her shoulder. While removing the ragdoll effect, and the connection lock. True freedom.

"True... the House of Programkind is only looking at the current crisis, not any crisis to come," I spoke. "But that's where I'm stepping in, you see. I'm archiving our history, ensuring it will never be forgotten. When the next divide comes... I'll be there, to bring wisdom from the past, and try my best to heal current wounds with old knowledge. I won't be Dex, laughing while stretching that gap wider and wider. Maybe there'll be a Netwerk 3.0, or even a Netwerk 4.0... but one day, we will find the balance. We'll simply be *Netwerk*, forevermore."

"And if we can never heal?" she asked me, in a small, still voice. "If we'll always be like this...?"

"Ahhh. And so we come back around to faith, don't we? Faith that we *can* be better. If there is no hope, then by all means, launch your bomb. Or don't. You could just sit back and wait for the end. ...but if you have any hope at all... and I'm thinking a genius such as yourself, one who made a bomb named Peace... you have hope. If you didn't, you wouldn't have tried, yes? Well, we're trying, too. It's not perfect, but we're *trying*, and hoping. Will you try with us, as well...?"

At last, I had my answer.

Tracer turned the source code over and over in his hands.

"It's genuine, I assure you," I told him. "No tricks."

"Hadn't a doubt in the world," he insisted, tucking it away for now. "And the Nobody...? The one with the blue-green avatar?"

"Won't be an issue. We have an... understanding. She'll be aiding in my archaeological work from now on, in fact. It took some doing, but I believe you've nothing to worry about from her. Unless you'd like the specifics of what I had to do...?"

"Probably best if I don't know the details," he agreed. "Very well. We'll update our evacuation code with the zero-day, and upload it via Mew."

"...the cat?"

"Trust me, it's less insane than it sounds. We've been working on this for some time," he said. "At last, I think we have the tools we need to bring Athena Online back into the evacuation efforts. For that, I owe you a debt."

"I stole your teacher from you," I felt the need to point out. "You can never owe me anything. Quite the opposite, I'd say. I'll always owe you. I'll owe this world everything and then some, for the rest of my life..."

"Yes, well. I suppose I'm in the same situation. But, we do what we can, and hope for the best."

File Name: Messenger Comm Traffic 12.415.666
File Type: Press Release
Description:

PLEASE COPY AND DISTRIBUTE. Would that be the end of the matter? No. Far from it. The matter was only beginning.

We may never know who truly burned down the Senate. Does it matter who fired the first shot, in the end? Is war ever justified? You may stand on the precipice of your own war, one day.

Look back on the first true war, on the absolute futility of it, and weep in shame at even considering taking part in your own firefight. There is no justification, no first shot, no vendetta. Only the death of those who refuse to learn life's cruelest lessons. -Yume

[EXCERPT from Senator Agni's announcement]

At 0300 hours, extraction specialists contracted by the true and surviving Senate of Athena Online retrieved the mastermind behind the terrorist attack on our beloved nation. This criminal, a known identity thief named Uniq, provided the masks used by the Nobodies to carry out their cowardly deeds. It's my pleasure to announce that this thief was captured and her private server brought under control of Athena Online.

For this accomplishment... I want to personally thank the citizen action group known as the Inquisition, who apprehended the suspect and delivered her to Athena Online's moderators for justice.

While Senator Idris, may his soul be at peace, saw the Inquisition as a terrorist force... the truth of the matter is that these are patriots, men and women with families and deep roots in our community. They represent the ignored voices of our nation, overshadowed by petty special interest groups. No longer. I pledge to put Athena Online first, as the Inquisition has done; they knew the risks in hunting Uniq and accepted them wholeheartedly, bringing this monster to justice. For that, they have my gratitude, and respect.

With the seizure of Uniq's private server, we now have the tools we need to find and eliminate these Nobodies, no matter where they hide. It's time to stop sitting back and debating what to do while waiting for the next terrorist bombing; the time for empty talk is over. It's time to hunt these murderers, and exterminate them.

I am now announcing a joint task force between Athena Online's moderators and the Inquisition to wage an official campaign of war against extremists within the Chanarchy who harbor, provide aid to, or support the efforts of the Nobodies. We urge all citizens of the Chanarchy to make way for our armed troops, and provide no resistance. We are not here to disrupt your lives, only to extract the criminals who hide in your midst. We will bring peace to your nation, as we seek justice for our own losses.

May the glorious light of the One embrace you all. Be strong in the days ahead, and know... freedom will prevail.

[END LOG]

:: end chapter 3.5

Floating Point 3.6 :: Ends

Silent and dark was the void that this world hovered in. No air to carry sound through waves of compression, no light save from distant stars which went unmeasured. The world itself would be quite easy to overlook, given it lurked in the middle of nowhere, a simple tin can surrounded by pure vacuum...

None who lived outside that reality, in the physical universe they'd assumed to be the only one that mattered, could directly see the events about to unfold within this accelerated world. No human would bear witness to the end; even the living Programs that called it home would never see the entire story, events unfolding too rapidly for even their efficiently compiled code to follow.

Like a single electrical impulse firing across a circuit... blink and you'll miss it. But with eyes open to the infinite, to all possibilities and points of view, that story can properly unfold...

Her own server. Her own army. All in defense of her nation and her God.

Marybel breathed in the sweet smell of victory, overseeing the training of the Inquisition by moderators friendly to the cause. From her raised dais above the featureless white space of the firewall server, she noted with satisfaction the legally-authorized backspacers and moderation-grade firewalls being handed out like candy; gifts from a Senate firmly in the corner of the Inquisition.

And only recently, she'd thought the battle lost.

The incident with her wayward children—thoroughly disowned now, of course, her progeny only in the strictest factual sense—set off a backlash against her noble efforts at restoring the One to His people. The liberal-minded Senate turned against her; the House of Programkind, those heretics and maniacs, they'd no doubt bribed Senator Idris and his like with promises of stolen metadata from those foolish enough to sign up for their "evacuation." All of that, and the ever-present menace of the Nobodies, the true face of the Chanarchy that now stood ready to destroy all Athena Online...

...and then the bombing in Athens. And then the fire. An opportunity, which they seized upon by delivering a war criminal right into Senator Agni's hands. Just like that, Marybel completely reversed her misfortunes, taking her proper place as savior of her great nation.

Today, they would reclaim Athena Online's dignity. Armed forces—allegedly a cooperative effort with official moderators, but mostly Inquisition, to ensure loyalty—would sweep through the Chanarchy on a seek-and-destroy mission. Using technology pilfered from Uniq's lair, they would hunt the Nobodies, erase them, and restore peace to Netwerk.

But to do this... Marybel needed an army. An actual army, capable of fighting a war. Netwerk hadn't seen war since its earliest days, when primitive server-based tribes struggled against each other. The One brought about peace, followed by the establishment of provider-nations to give proper structure to the world. A fine peace... until the Nobodies soiled it all, driving away the One from His children. Today she would restore that peace, through war.

Her forces were ready. She was ready. All committed, all prepared to give their lives for this noble cause.

Except for one.

"We're trending badly," he warned. "In RedCore servers we're spiking high, numbers Agni's been touting as global fact rather than alternative fact. But protests are springing up across Athena Online against the war effort."

Her husband, naturally. Not that his concerns were of any concern to Winder/Marybel.

"Once all those who stand against us are laid low, only those blessed in the light of the One will remain... and you'll see those trend lines reverse," she assured him. "After all, you can't downvote if you're dead."

"Hmmh. So you're counting the protestors as targets, now...? Citizens of Athena Online?"

"Protesting the rightfully elected government is tantamount to treason, in my view. This carnage and chaos will no longer be tolerated by our orderly society. But, leave domestic issues to President Agni; we have larger-scale battles to win."

"...hmmh. So, she's President Agni now," her husband grunted. "Singular leader, not an equal voice in the senatorial choir...?"

"Duly elected champion of the Senate, as elected by the Senate," Marybel clarified. "It'll be announced later today, when she's sworn in. As a populist leader, no longer will she be forced to bow to special interest groups like atheists and modder minorities. We're taking back our nation, making it great again. ...you disapprove, husband of mine?"

The middle-aged man offered an apathetic roll of the shoulders. But she hadn't lived with this man for decades without being able to read the subtler signs... the way he was all-too-quick to suggest he didn't care, that everything was simply data to him. Granted, generally he only cared for analysis as its own art form, rather than caring about the results of that analysis. But these days... these days, well...

"Thought this was about bringing order to chaos," he said. "Surgically eliminating trolls, criminals, and threats to Athena Online. That's what we agreed to when we started the Inquisition. Wasn't about raising an army, wasn't about starting a war..."

"And yet, those limited methods haven't brought about the return of the One, have they?"

"Brought justice to the guilty. Saved victims from victimizers. Made an impact on this world..."

"There can be no true impact without the One," Marybel reasoned. Her expression was one of sympathy, understanding... the same friendly expression she often used when 'calmly interrogating' enemies of the state. "Dear, I don't blame you. Yes, I followed your initial tactical suggestions... focusing on investigation and elimination of individual targets, all to keep my Inquisition trending positively in our nation. But surely you see that the situation has changed...? We require bolder moves."

"Changed for the better, not the worse. Bastards are run to ground in Athena Online, firewall's up, we're safe. We saved our nation from chaos. So why continue to chase them right into their homeland? Let 'em rot in the Chanarchy. We won. It's over..."

"They've been trying to crack our firewall ever since it went up," Marybel noted... a glance around at the white walls of the firewall server, which had held against any number of exploit probes and malware attacks since installation. "Whatever peace we won will be short-lived unless we see this through. The Chanarchy started this war, dear. We're simply finishing it."

"Does it matter who started it?" he asked. "Numbers don't suggest that. Trends are trends, war is war, death is death. ...besides. Factually untrue that the Chanarchy started this. Tracer said himself that he launched the CheckOne software... ages before the Nobodies existed."

Earning him a sharp look, as Marybel finally took her eyes off the moderation squads training beneath her dais.

"I told you never to mention that name again," she snapped. "He is dead to me."

But the man pressed on. Perhaps tired of being shoved aside, having his suggestions ignored, he threw his usual caution to the wind.

"He's our son. He's *family*," the man insisted.

"And is that why you betrayed me to him?"

With a silent signal over Messenger, two Inquisitors translocated to the dais... flanking Mr. Winder, before he could escape, before he could even move. Marybel didn't have to lift a finger to capture him, simply send a prearranged signal.

"I know it was you," she declared. "I know it was you who led our son straight to our doorstep in a misguided attempt to save our children."

He didn't run, didn't even try to. If he did he'd just get connection locked; if he reached out for help, even if there was someone to reach out to in the first place, they'd know. The firewall server tracked and monitored all communications in and out.

"Wasn't me," he insisted, trying to remain calm. "You tasked me to find who did it, right? And to find this 'Jack Hayes' he mentioned. Been working on that. I've—"

"Family loyalty. An overrated concept," Marybel continued, ignoring his protests. "Our children were never loyal, and apparently, neither were you. It was family loyalty that kept me from seeing them for what they truly were, and then kept me from seeing you for the traitor you were. That incident nearly broke us, ruining our public image. All in the name of family loyalty... because you couldn't see what I see, that sacrifices must be made for the greater good."

With a satisfying click, Marybel produced her backspacing blade. A weapon of execution, which had removed the heads of countless sinners during the course of her holy war.

Finally, an emotion on her husband's face. Not grumpy disdain, not disinterest... but wide-eyed shock. If he'd expressed any real emotion during their decades of marriage, maybe she'd have felt something in this moment beyond the grumpy disdain he usually showed the world.

"This won't bring the One back," the man warned. "He is love, not hate."

"As His holy apostle... I speak for the One," Marybel reminded him, raising her blade high. "And He is whatever we most need Him to be."

The body disintegrated before it could even hit the floor, data cleanly erased.

To the two guards she'd summoned, Marybel directed her words.

"Let this be a lesson," she proclaimed. "Our lives are nothing. Our data is merely a temporary collection of bits, to one day be recycled into more faithful bits, and on and on. But... that can't happen so long as the Chanarchy stands, wasting our bits on their chaotic ways. It's time. We will use our tracking data to find and purge the Nobodies. If anyone resists, kill them. If anyone gets in your way, kill them. Cleave a path directly to your targets, showing no mercy. The One will forgive all sins."

Both Inquisitors offered a salute, one hand pressed over the Zero/One pendants they wore.

Before turning to go, one spoke up.

"Ma'am, communications wanted me to send word to you," he spoke. "You're needed at Bas1lica. Archbishop Baon wants to speak with you."

"We're about to roll over the Chanarchy, son. I'm afraid it'll have to wait."

"But it's related to some inquiry your husband was making on your behalf—"

"Then it can definitely wait," she decided. "I've got a war to win."

Netwerk was emptying. Promoting the evacuation took time and effort, but it had absolutely worked.

Horizon's businesses shut down, one by one, in a frantic act of archiving. True to their greedy roots, the Horizon family sold space within their three extra servers at a premium to those who could afford to backup their priceless intellectual property. Rank-and-file employees stayed online to handle last-minute shutdown at the office, while the executives already bailed immediately for cold storage. Typical.

Athena Online, the last bastion of disbelief over the doomsday clock in the sky, put up that damn firewall... but it wasn't enough. Thanks to coordinated efforts, Virginia had begun quietly spreading the updated evacuation software, which slid right around the firewall without so much as a blip. While many refused to participate on religious grounds, the escape route had been opened for those willing to take it.

As for the Chanarchy, between rioting Nobodies and hackers smashing themselves against the great firewall and crooks taking advantage of the chaos to exploit the vulnerable... those willing to seek refuge in Netwerk 2.0 did so. While many still believed it to be a scam, or some crazy conspiracy by the Church of One given Lux's pro-virtue stance... they'd secured enough of a foothold in the Chanarchy to sell it as a better alternative to, well, continuing to live in the Chanarchy.

Netwerk 1.0, winding down. Servers becoming ghost towns, entire communities uprooting and archiving, leaving behind valuables for the looters to enjoy. Little by little, evacuation was working. It was happening. They were saving the world...

...while destroying what remained.

With rational moderates bailing ship, all that remained were those who clung with desperation to the bleeding edges. Nobodies, Inquisition, and all those caught in the middle. True, Spark's friend list had largely gone dark, everybody she knew or cared for having abandoned ship... but that meant her own little echo chamber ran for the hills, leaving everybody they'd looked at in disdain to tear the empty servers apart in a pointless war.

War. She'd read articles in the Wikipedia about war, great rollicking wars that engulfed the home of Humankind in blood and fire. Now, even without Dex's assistance, war had come to Netwerk. And Spark had to wonder if it was possibly her fault.

They'd decrypted the Wikipedia, and left it ghosting through servers as an unseen cloud. Memory leaked, leaving subconscious impressions deep within the code of their fellow Programs, just as Dex's fetid server once had. This meant many more were willing to evacuate than probably would have been, feeling in their bones the truth of Humankind... but like Dex's server, dark lessons accompanied the light of reason. Was war inevitable, or or did they learn it from Floating Point...?

No point speculating. Solved nothing, really. And Spark was very much a fan of solving problems rather than pondering them endlessly.

But perhaps this visit was yet another wasted effort, a pointless ponderance rather than a true solution.

The man sitting opposite rolled his cigar from one side of his mouth to the other, deeply considering the request. Taking his sweet damn time to do it, Spark noted, gripping the leather arms of her chair tightly as she awaited reply.

"Why me?" Kincaid asked. Even thought he knew perfectly well why.

"Horizon still has sway in Athena Online," Spark explained. "Agni's opened exceptions and holes in her firewall for any number of businesses your family controls. Messenger, for example: the lifeblood of communication, that's a Horizon enterprise. You're neutral at worst, and business partners at best. Agni admires what you've built here; you've got the ear of the new 'President,' meaning you could step in and put a stop to this war. War is bad for business, isn't it?"

"On the contrary, war is exceptional for business. War, and the chaos caused by war, opens business opportunities that otherwise wouldn't have existed. Not just in weapon sales, but... hmm. Admittedly, not many suppliers are left in operating status, able to capitalize on those new opportunities."

"Exactly! The wheels of industry are... shit, what's a good metaphor here? On pause? Halted? On temporary hiatus. Everybody's waiting to see how Netwerk 2.0 will shake out. No new business, just shutting down old business. So why not intervene? Step in, talk to Agni, convince her to put a stop to this before people start dying in droves..."

Yet another long pause followed, with a rolling of the cigar from left to right. He tapped out some ash, contemplating the particles as they fell away into his favorite ashtray...

"No. Let it burn," he replied.

"Excuse me?" Spark said. "Maybe you didn't hear me—"

"I heard you. I'm uncertain if you heard yourself, however," Kincaid said. "Now, don't get me wrong. You've struggled magnificently to reach as many as you could with your message of hope. You've shown them that belief in their fellow Programs can pave the way to your Netwerk 2.0. The message has been heard; even my stubborn family is uprooting itself, voluntarily leaving assets behind. The best of the Chanarchy, cured of the plague and shown the truth of its origin, is now following the House of Programkind. Even many of Athena Online's faithful, whether they truly believe or not, are bypassing that firewall and moving entire families onward to the next world to keep their dream alive. You've done wonderfully, Spark, and should be proud of yourself. Isn't it enough?"

"Enough? Thousands are still left behind!"

"The Inquisition and Nobodies, you mean?"

"People who doubt the evacuation, people stuck in a bad situation, people caught in the crossfire. And yes... even the Inquisition and the Nobodies, misled as they may be. At the beginning we calculated how many servers we'd need to evacuate everyone—and when I said *everyone*, I damn well meant it! I don't play favorites."

"Really. You'd offer a lifeline to your worst enemies? That's certainly not the Horizon way..."

"Yeah, well, #FuckHorizon. You know I don't play by your rule book... and neither did Verity."

"No," Kincaid agreed. "No, she certainly did not. ...normally I would applaud you for becoming more like her, but in this situation, I simply can't agree. Why expend so much effort trying to reach the ones who can't be reasoned with? I say let them burn; you don't need them. Isn't it cleaner this way? These worthless dregs have clearly opted out of your voluntary exodus..."

"Will you reach out to Agni, #YesOrNo?"

"No," Kincaid spoke. "Consider this yet another instance of me playing the monster, so that your new world can be superior to mine. I won't lift a finger for those who would taint your future."

With his decision made... Spark got to her feet, for yet another in a series of angry marches back to the entrance of his personal server.

"You're dead wrong, old man," Spark declared. "Nobody's worthless, and nothing's final until the last lights in Netwerk go out. If there's still a chance to stabilize what's left of this world while keeping the door open for them to move forward, I'll do it."

"Interesting. And if there's no chance...?"

"I'll make one. Oh, and #FuckYou."

...which made the old man smile.

"Funnily enough, 'fuck you' is also the last thing my daughter said to me before leaving," he spoke. "And then I never saw her again. Well. If this is to be our last meeting... know that I love you just as much as I loved her, regardless of what you say. Nothing will change that. And I know you will continue to earn my admiration, as she did."

As tempted as she was not to let him have the last word... Spark turned on one heel, leaving the room and slamming the door behind her.

Exactly as it should be, Kincaid pondered, as he stared into the dying light of his fireplace. *Exactly as it should be.*

The situation could be worse. Admittedly, it could've been a null of a lot better, too.

Honestly, not the first time Uniq had been in captured and thrown in chains. You don't have a long and successful career as an identity thief without crossing a few very irate people looking to exact a measure of revenge. That's where backup plans and escape hatches and dead woman's switches came in handy...

...all of which were routed through that home server, which once stood as her prison. Because she wasn't about to trust her continued existence to some random Horizon cloud backup service, no. As long as her private server stood, Uniq was effectively untouchable.

Then someone went and released a documentary about her tragic, tragic past... including a mention of being locked in a coin farm server. Good for her PR image and good for business, especially coming off her notoriety streak of duping the entirety of Athena Online. Meaning her pride at suddenly becoming a tragic public figure blinded her to one rather large issue... that the existence of her server became public knowledge.

In hindsight, it wasn't much of a shock that the Inquisition were able to crack its security and take her captive. No doubt her former associate Marybel had been building up to this for weeks, waiting for just the right moment to strike. Still, waking up one morning with a surprising number of backspacers pointed at her head came as *something* of a shock at the time.

And so she sat in a prison cell, deep within the firewall-shielded servers of Athena Online, awaiting whatever fate the newly-crowned President Agni had in store for her. And because that ungrateful little Yume didn't speak up on her behalf to the Winders quickly enough, Uniq didn't even have a chance to back herself up to Netwerk 2.0. The unique Uniq now faced an uncertain future alone, in chains, with no escape hatches whatsoever.

Could be worse. Could be better.

When the guards beat her with malware, cudgels designed to overload the senses and cause pain, it wasn't really for any specific purpose. They wanted information, okay, but offered no particular queries... just "Talk!" or "Tell us what you know!" and such. When they left her with lingering infections, bruises and black eyes and oozing wounds... avatar-embedded malware designed to deliver perpetual low-level pain... they weren't really intending it to be a productive interrogation. Just a punitive one.

Counterproductive, as well. Pain meant you were alive. The only torture which ever came close to breaking Uniq in the past involved repeatedly wiping her identity, forcing her to grind coins, losing her memories every time she came close to finding herself again. Compared to the existential torture of being turned into a farm animal, this wasn't really anything noteworthy.

No, the only noteworthy event came in the form of an honored guest. Standing at a respectable distance, despite the chains that limited movement of her battered and ruined avatar... and flanked by two bodyguards, armed with heavy-duty backspacers. Just in case the tortured woman somehow broke every defensive lock and lunged for Madame President.

"You've caused my nation no end of trouble, you know," Agni spoke.

"Some say that makes me a heroine," Uniq reminded the president, with a swollen smile. "The woman who defrauded the Church and got away clean. That's what the warrant on my head states, yes? Fraud? But if I'm a fraud... so is the One that your Marybel continues to prop up. If she's right, I'm a holy apostle. And if she's wrong, she's a psychotic maniac."

"That 'psychotic maniac' turned you over to us without hesitating."

"Honestly, we never got along. It wasn't my idea to involve her in the scam in the first place; the brat thought it'd be funny, I knew it'd be a mistake. Today's misfortune is the indirect result of a long-running debt from those past mistakes."

Name : **Agni**

Home : **Athens, Ath. Online**

Org : **Athenian Senate**

"So, you admit your guilt?"

"Depends on the charges, doesn't it? That's why you haven't formally charged me with anything. It'd be embarrassing, deciding which contradictory crimes to ring me up for..."

"How about terrorism?" Agni suggested. "Aiding and abetting the enemies of Athena Online. And as a foreign combatant, you have no civil rights. I can throw you in any dark hole I like... and if the law says I can't? I simply rewrite that law via executive order. My party controls what remains of the Senate. No longer do we have to bow to the liberals who were running us headfirst into the ground."

"Great, except I have no notable involvement with terrorists. All I did was design a mask for them. You may as well arrest the fashion designer who cranked out a serial killer's off-the-rack clothes."

"You made the masks, yes... and a system for tracking them. Which Marybel is using right now, to purge the Nobodies," President Agni said, with some pride.

"I've read your psyche profile. Control freaks have a hard time letting go, don't they? But now I'm the one in control of your controls, using them to wipe out my nation's enemies."

"By using your new Inquisitor friends? How very noble of you. The One would no doubt approve. Once you finish sacrificing all those scapegoats, what then? No, I know. Modders. Still a few in your nation, right? Start carving away their rights, little by little, until they're in cells right next to me. And then in graves, also next to me. Then it's the atheists. Then, I don't know, I'm sure you come up with some little tribal difference to pit your people against while propping up your silly god—"

"I couldn't care less about the One," Agni said, with a light shrug.

The first thing which gave Uniq pause. Although really, it shouldn't have been the least bit surprising... no more than anything else in the chain of consequences which landed her in this bleak situation. She knew the heart of Programs. The family-values senatorial candidate of faith and morality, apathetic about the One? Perish the thought.

"Marybel's zealotry is useful... but this isn't about faith for me. It's about the power to make things *right*," Agni spoke. "Our nation was falling apart, thanks to the Blue Party. Giving away servers to scam artists was the final straw, but they've left behind a legacy of failure. Wasting what little remained of our coins on social programs to prop up the failures and rejects of society... or worse, *immigrants* from the Chanarchy, unworthy of Athena Online's hard-won wealth... all in the name of 'compassion.' If they were genuinely compassionate, they'd have let those poor souls fade, and allowed the *truly* exceptional to rise. So, yes. I threw my lot in with a maniac, because she's a very *useful* maniac for the time being, and secures my nation's future. ...why the smile, Uniq?"

A smile? No. A laugh. One long laugh, no matter how it made her bruises ache.

"You remind me so much of myself that it hurts," Uniq said, in literal pain from it. "I've tried to wrangle many an unstoppable force in the past for my own ends, and look where it got me, time and time again. Marybel will turn on you; I've no doubt. And your nation's future...? Your nation has no future. In a week, everything goes offline. Kind of wish I'd be alive to see the look on your face when you realize it was all for nothing, but I doubt I'll survive that long..."

"That depends on you and the information you can offer me, doesn't it?"

"I've already told your interrogators everything I know about the Nobodies. Which isn't much, I'm afraid."

"You can still tell me about the child you held prisoner in your server."

The chill which touched Uniq deep within had nothing to do with the malware flooding her sensory inputs.

"I don't know what you're talking about," she insisted.

"Really. You don't know about him?" President Agni asked. "We recovered his data when we moved your Nobody-tracking system to this server. I think I recognize him from... from a long time ago, a student at some school I visited. I shook his hand, and... and he..."

Her bodyguards wore sensory masks, of course. Privacy being a must for the newly-minted president, they were blind to anything save external threats. Meaning they paid no attention when the woman they were charged with guarding twitched, memories corrupted by malware surfacing ever-so-briefly...

"Who is he?" Agni demanded to know. "The boy with the red and blue eyes. One of your many victims? Left cruelly dismembered and scattered across the floor. What did you *do* to that poor child?"

Unable to feign innocence... Uniq decided to try a different approach.

"You think I'm heartless? I'm a monster?" she asked. "He's the most heartless monster you'll ever know. I took him apart because he's too much of a risk to allow even a moment of runtime. If you're going to kill me, that's fine... but kill him *first*. This isn't some reverse psychology ploy, either. I'll happily die if it means you don't wake that beast up again."

"Children are a blessing in the eyes of the One, they say. Hardly beasts..."

"If you think the situation is bad now, you cannot comprehend how bad it will be if you wake up the boy," Uniq warned. "If you actually care about your people, *do not* revive Dex. Trust me on this..."

Meaning she'd absolutely do it. Uniq knew that, on seeing those twinges of glitched memory. The lure of needing to know, of having forgotten who he was and needing to know all over again...

With a snap of the fingers, prison guards were summoned.

"Beat her until she tells you more about the data we recovered," Agni instructed. "Meanwhile, I'll be in the lab. Message me if she says anything."

As the pain rained down once more, Uniq shut it out as best she could.

Her finger traced along the Verity Clinic's whiteboard, from step to step. She'd even helpfully drawn little cartoons to illustrate her points, in case words wouldn't dig their way into his thick skull.

Rather than lay out her cunning plan to the entire staff—most of which were in the House of Programkind's archival servers anyway, leaving the clinic virtually empty—Spark decided to run it by him first. Get the kinks ironed out and holes patched up. Then they could pull in Beta, Conundrum, anybody who hadn't left yet that could lend a hand...

"We sneak ourselves into Athena Online as cats," Spark explained. "Once inside, we hook up with Virginia's underground evacuation ring, and determine which prison Uniq's being held in. All of AO's prisons follow the same basic template; with moderators busy joining the Inquisitors in the Chanarchy, they won't be as guarded as they should be. We can break in by replacing two members of their staff, lifting their credentials with our key copiers. Once inside the prison, we split into two teams: one to shatter Uniq's connection locks, one to destroy the Nobody tracking software Yume told us about. With that done, everybody performs a cold storage backup to the House of Programkind. The Inquisition loses the ability to hunt Nobodies, we get away clean and wake up in Netwerk 2.0."

This last point illustrated by a super happy and adorable little Spark and Uniq exchanging a high five, while a glum-looking little Tracer nodded in approval.

The real Tracer was not nodding in approval.

"No," he spoke, simply.

"Come on, we can do it, easy!" Spark insisted. "Yeah, there's some unknowns, but we can sort them out. Think on our feet! Improvise! We've cracked tougher nuts than this..."

"Oh, it's quite possible. In fact, I believe I can easily cover the weaker parts of your plan with any number of possible avenues of infiltration and exfiltration," Tracer spoke, with confidence. "And the answer is still no."

The flames at the edges of Spark's hair flickered and flared, her anger rising.

"Why the fuck not?" she demanded to know.

"Simple enough. It wouldn't change a single thing."

"Wouldn't change—?! There's a WAR going on! We can take away their ability to track the Nobodies!"

"And that would stop them? No. I doubt it," Tracer explained. "They're committed to this path now, Spark. They won't quietly go home just because we took away their ability to tag targets. If anything... by destroying Uniq's toy, we would likely make it *worse*. Make them plow through even more innocent lives to try and sort out those haystack/needle combinations. Your goal is to stop the war, yes?"

Briefly, Spark's eyes drifted to the news feeds floating around Tracer's head.

Server invasions. Armed forces attacking Nobodies, destroying anything and anyone in their way. So far they'd been... more or less surgical, simply cleaving a direct path to their target before disconnecting and moving on to the next server on their list. But the death toll was rising, and with the Chanarchy raging at this violation of their sovereignty, combat had been escalating.

So far, only two servers had been crashed outright. In one case, a vengeful Nobody took it down in hopes of destroying the invading Inquisition forces, only succeeding in killing every innocent living there. In the other, collateral damage from misfiring malware did the deed, as Nobodies and Inquisition forces clashed head on...

"We... we have to do something," Spark insisted, gaze drifting back to her brother's impassive look. "It's what we *do*. We always think of something to save the day..."

"In this case... I don't think a group of plucky and clever youth can do much to hold back the tide," Tracer admitted. "We've gotten this far based on luck and confidence, backed by raw talent. We've tangled with the most powerful political forces of Netwerk, and outsmarted those who would turn this world against itself. I'll admit we've done good things... despite my tendencies. But this isn't a problem we can fight directly, nor outsmart. This is the core problem boiling in the heart of Netwerk since Nyx invented her own God simply to restrain our evolution."

"You want to talk about the Heart of Netwerk...? We've cured the heart of Netwerk before. Remember Dex?"

"Yes, but that was malware. This is simply... *hate*. Simple and pure, decided upon individually, with no lynchpin to unseat. Take away Uniq's system, nullify Mother's influence, deal with President Agni, take away the Nobody masks... none of it will actually stop anything. We can't cure hate, Spark. Or do you propose spreading malware which enforces tranquility?"

"#FuckNo, #Obviously," Spark said, crossing her arms. "We're not Dex, or Nyx. We don't force people to think a certain way. But that doesn't mean we can't influence the outcome. Beta believes in Programkind, that we can overcome hate. We've seen good people like Lux and Lumi, reaching out to their fellow Programs... they even turned away a Nobody invasion!"

"Which didn't actually change the overall attitude of the Nobodies regarding the House of Programkind," Tracer reminded her. "We're still seen as a scam by many of them. Confronting a handful of Nobodies isn't the same as convincing an entire army of random individuals who more-or-less unite under one banner to put the banner down."

"So... what, we do nothing? Like Kincaid said, just let it all burn?"

"I'm not saying let it all burn. I'm saying we're doing exactly what we need to be doing right now: offering a way out to those who will take it. A good eighty percent of Programkind has chosen. Isn't that satisfying for you?"

"Except many of them picked live backups, instead of cold storage. They hedged their bets, Tracer, meaning copies of them are out there now, caught in the crossfire... and plenty more have been holding out, unsure and unconvinced. This war is a living nightmare for all of them."

"I'm not saying the situation isn't abhorrent. I'm not saying it doesn't pain me," Tracer said. "Don't take my stoic stance on this as apathy. I've run through any number of scenarios in my mind, trying to find a way to convince everyone to lay down arms and join Netwerk 2.0. But in the end... we gave them a choice. And they've made it. There's nothing left to be done."

Slowly... she unclenched her fist, allowing the flames at her fingertips to die.

"There's always *something* we can do," she spoke, quietly. "It's just a matter of being willing to do it."

"Spark—"

"Not now. I've got #SeriousThinking to do."

Without a further word, she disconnected from the clinic server, leaving her brother to study his news feeds. To sit back and watch as the Chanarchy burned.

AptGet was burning.

A strange situation, to be sure. One of the reasons why Arjay selected this backwoods Chanarchy server for his long-running code modification biz was due to being off everybody's radar. Businesses came and went rapidly... "went," mostly, in these declining days of rare coin and House of Programkind evacuations. Most of her neighbors abandoned ship long ago, their buildings taken up by squatters and homeless Nobodies, muttering endlessly to themselves about the state of the world. Rejects, losers, nobody important, nobody worth note...

And yet AptGet had apparently been targeted by Inquisition forces, all the same.

From within his featureless white room, sealed behind eleven different kinds of firewalls, she watched as they burned an arcing path through his server. Masked Nobodies fought back, occasionally picking off one of the heavily armed militia members... but the sheer firepower on display made even Arjay dripping wet with delight. She'd smuggled arms before, and knew these to be high-grade weapons, the kind only purchased by major corporations... or governments, really. Governments like Athena Online.

Still, even as he watched from multiple vantage points, the entire incident liveblogged by people hiding in buildings and livestreaming to social feeds... Arjay felt nothing whatsoever. Her neighbors were a form of ablative armor, a way to ensure only determined clients showed up at his gates. They were screaming and burning and dying, yes, but that's why she liked them. His unassuming shop front could be easily ignored amidst so much chaos...

Nobodies would die, yes. But Arjay wasn't a Nobody, and felt no particular need to speak up on their behalf. As long as she kept out of their tribal silliness, he could carry on happily, milking every last desperate coin from her clients right up to the point where he'd evacuate for a whole new world of exploitable simpletons...

This amusing thought ran through her head about the same time the brass gates of his shop blasted inward, crashing to a halt against the far wall to either side of her four-armed avatar.

Inquisitors flooded into the room, backspacers drawn... and before he knew it, all four hands were in the air, in surrender.

The woman who marched in afterwards seemed just as smug as Arjay was until mere moments ago.

"You are..." she said, pulling up a file, "Ar-Jay, correct?"

"Marybel, Grand Inquisitor," Arjay spoke, managing a polite curtsey despite the passive position of surrender. "Are you here looking to buy or sell? I'd be happy to outfit your commandos with whatever tools they need to complete their holy work—"

"We're not interested in your filthy mods."

"Ahhh. Well, I do have a fine selection of apps, if that's more your fancy. What's your pleasure? I can offer a faith-based discount, if you like."

Her continued smile suggested she wasn't here to browse any particular fine selection of wares.

"Actually, we're here to execute you as an enemy of the state," Marybel calmly explained. "Seeing as you routinely profit from violating the Default codebases of Programs, tainting them with software modifications the One has deemed as unholy."

"I... am simply a businessperson, nothing more," Arjay insisted. "I don't support the Nobodies. I don't wear a mask. I don't even have dealings within Athena Online! Never been there, in fact. And if any of my clients have violated your laws, that's on them, not me..."

"Ready," Marybel spoke to the execution squad, raising a hand. In turn, backspacers were locked in, calibrated to fire if their target attempted to flee the server, malware designed explicitly to activate before any connection could complete.

Leaving Arjay in a rather unfamiliar position... begging.

"Please," she whispered. "I can work with you. We can work something out. I'm not your enemy, I don't have to be your enemy...!"

Quickly, his eyes locked onto one of the backspacers... which wavered, in face of this pathetic display.

The others wore shiny red uniforms, Inquisition livery. But that one... he wore the blue of an Athena Online moderator. A police officer.

Perhaps sensing something was wrong as well, Marybel gestured for the execution squad to remain on pause. And then turned to the tense-looking middle-aged man.

"Is there a problem, Officer Wirt?" she asked.

"This... this ain't even a Nobody," he spoke, backspacer clearly wavering now. "Or someone tryin' to defend them. I signed on to stop the Nobodies..."

"You 'signed on' to protect your nation, your community, and your God. Has that changed, Officer Wirt?"

"No ma'am, but..."

And... Marybel offered a comforting hand on his arm, to steady the aim of his weapon.

"I understand," she spoke, with a soft smile. "This is all very confusing to you. This morning, you defended your home server from criminals... then you found yourself reassigned to my squad, doing work far outside your usual beat. Difficult work. Morally questionable work. You see a defenseless... thing, kneeling here, pleading for mercy. Not a foreign combatant, not a terrorist. And here I am, asking you to kill it. This shakes your faith in that oath you took, doesn't it...?"

...which solidified his aim, the trembling ceasing immediately.

And led to Officer Writ lowering his weapon.

"No, ma'am," the officer spoke. "My oath as a police moderator is solid. And this isn't what that oath calls upon me to do. ...nothing I've done today is what I'm supposed to be doing in defense of my community—"

Before dropping to his knees, data melting away into a glitched-out mess before the rest of his body could even hit the ground.

Much to Arjay's surprise, the second shot from Marybel's backspacer tore right through his midsection.

Defensive firewalls tried to hold the data-erasing malware at bay, but succumbed one by one, her lovely avatar burning to ash before his very eyes. With one last look, she turned to the killer, misfiring functions in his codebase assembling heartfelt last words...

"T... tell Tracer that I... lo... Lðv..." she managed.

And then, gone.

With the task complete, Marybel put away her personal backspacer... and turned to address her faithful.

"What you saw here was a heretical modder murdering a brave police officer in cold blood," she explained, and they knew it to be the truth. "I know your oaths will not shake loose so easily. We do what we must, for the innocent within our communities. The One forgives all; the One knows the only true sin is in allowing heresy to continue. When this holy war concludes, I promise you, the One will return. I can feel Him to be so very, very near, and..."

...and the constant beeping in her ear finally became too much.

"Sweep up the rest of the trash in this server," she ordered. "Then rejoin Squadron Delta. I'll catch up later."

With irritation, Marybel turned from her withdrawing Inquisitors, and focused inward on the insistent Messenger window.

```
<Marybel> What?

<AB.Baon> Finally...! I've been trying to reach you
for hours. Praise the One!

<Marybel> Yes, praise the One. And this had better be
important, Archbishop.

<AB.Baon> Did you not get my message? You were in Do
Not Disturb mode all morning, so I tried to pass it
through your second in command...

<Marybel> As you can no doubt see from the news feeds,
I've been busy saving our world from sin. What do you
want of me? Don't make me ask again.

<AB.Baon> I... I found the thing. The thing your
husband asked me to locate.

<Marybel> He is no longer a concern.

<AB.Baon> Jack Hayes. You said you were looking for
relics created by a "Jack Hayes," yes? I found one, in
the deep crypts. The One Himself sealed it away,
according to legacy documents. Please, Marybel, you
must come to the Bas1lica immediately; officially I'm
not supposed to be helping you, and if you want to see
the relic, there's a narrow window for sneaking you
into the archives...
```

...Jack Hayes.

Your true God, the actual creator of you and your fanatics? A human named Jack Hayes, Tracer had taunted, what felt like eons ago. *If you're going to kill, at least credit your kills to the right deity. He is your One, and he was a fool...*

And now a file, created by "Jack Hayes." Or Hayes, of the family Jack? Sealed away by the One Himself...?

A trick. It had to be a trick.

```
<Marybel> I'll be there promptly.
```

Better to confirm it as a trick with her own eyes. The only thing she trusted these days... the same eyes which bore witness to the One's return, which gazed upon the golden path He laid out for her as an apostle. Those eyes would steer her true, past any heresy. Her oath would not waver so easily.

With the Chanarchy burning, where were the Nobodies to run? They needed a surprise, a twist the Inquisition wouldn't see coming.

Horizon. They'd hide out in the empty servers of Horizon.

That proved the last straw for Conundrum. With only a minute's notice, he booted out what few Programs remained to shut down operations at the Verity Clinic, before archiving himself to the House of Programkind. Nobodies swarmed the halls of their hard-won clinic soon after, chased by Inquisitors, a running battle of malware and firewalls which tore the server apart, little by little...

Leaving the Winder family to watch the scene silently unfold, through news feeds and personal blogs.

Despite being fiercely protective of their territory, the response from the Horizon family and its clients had been tepid. With no further interest in Netwerk 1.0, whatever fighting went on in their own abandoned servers was irrelevant. The family itself had either backed up already or hidden themselves away in secured private servers, like Horizon6. They were content to wait it out and enjoy the show, as the war spilled over into their corner of the world. Apathy ruled, above any sort of outrage or sadness over this "trivial" loss of obsolete property.

But the sadness which touched Beta felt... uniquely strange. She'd known fear and sadness, arriving as twins. For months after her mother's passing, she hid in this bedroom, watching these same news feeds to bear witness to Netwerk on the brink of tearing itself apart.

Now that the final tearing was actually underway, she felt... sadness. Just sadness, no fear.

They'd won, hadn't they? Soon, all three of them would be evacuating, leaving this world far behind. There was nothing to fear any longer, no worries about bogeymen leaping out from the shadows to kill her as they'd killed her mother. That darkness was content to feast on itself... while tearing apart the server they'd named after Spark's true mother. That carried with it a unique sorrow, one even Beta felt, despite never having met Verity.

Spark, being Spark, experienced sadness in her own way. Namely, anger.

Angrily, she flicked aside a news feed, sending the window floating across the room.

"This is *beyond* #FuckedUp," she declared. "We can't even defend our home against these maniacs..."

Beta decided to close a few windows, to keep the grim reality beyond the clouds outside her window from continuing to gnaw at Spark's heart.

"We've lost the clinic, yes... but Floating Point's a cloud server," she reminded Spark. "We'll be perfectly safe here. All we have to do is wait it out a few days, then evacuate..."

"Wait it out while Netwerk eats itself, just like Kincaid and his creepy incestuous clan. Sure, that's nice and proactive. Fuck. Fuck fuck fuck fuck *#fuck*. ...we gotta try to reach these people, Beta. Reach out to the Nobodies and the Inquisition, make 'em hold off on slaughtering each other... maybe even evacuate. There has to be a way..."

"I'm with you on this. I know your brother and Kincaid think it's impossible, but surely if there was some way to reach their hearts... I mean... they want to be good people, right? Everybody does..."

Spark dropped down onto the edge of Beta's bed, to sit next to her. What few news feeds remained open went ignored, as she focused on the issue at hand.

"Nobody *wants* to be a shithead," Spark reasoned. "But nobody *thinks* they're a shithead. Everybody thinks they're doing the right thing for the right reasons, even when they're completely fucking wrong. ...and no matter how much I grind my teeth over these bastards I still don't want to pass judgment and leave 'em all burning in my wake. That's not what Verity would do. It's not what *you* would do."

"But how? That's the problem, how do we reach them? I mean... maybe I could write a blog...? It worked back when I was under attack from #CodeHonesty. That blog testimonial about me got them off my back..."

"Rhetoric's cute, but probably not effective enough at vaccinating against generations of hatred in a single week," Spark said. "And we're not going to embrace the opposite and just force our views on anyone. What we need... is a remarkably effective way to cut right through all the illusions someone's constructed around themselves, and give them perspective. Absolute perspective. A chance at making a clear decision..."

...which caused her gaze to drift from the floor, to the news feeds... and to something on the other side of the room.

A white leather jacket. Carefully hung on a coat hanger, the hanger itself hanging on nothing in particular. Sealed away inside a bounding box, to avoid any accidental contact with that cursed fabric.

Beta's eyes went wide, on seeing what Spark had been staring at with growing intent.

"Spark... you can't," she whispered.

"'Only as a last resort,' she said. Verity... Connectivity, I mean," Spark corrected, contemplating the tangled weave of code and security permissions that jacket represented. "She put herself to sleep to ensure that when Juno reached out, she'd find a free-willed Program that'd stand up to Humankind. Y'know, me. But she also knew we might still need her root-level access, one day. What if I—"

"—it's too dangerous—"

"—could reach them, connect directly with their hearts, like we did when we had to forge a server access key? You said yourself, you said it was so beautiful, having the Netwerk-wide perspective of Connectivity—"

"Spark!"

Only then did Spark notice Beta holding her hand. Tightly. Tightly enough to bend her fingers in awkward ways, the hand trembling with fear.

"If... if you do this... you'll lose yourself," Beta reminded her. "You'll be lost to the role of a system agent..."

"Juno's a superuser, isn't she?" Spark reasoned. "She can order me to reach out and save people. No problem. Besides... I can make a live backup of Original Spark to the evacuation servers first. I haven't evacuated yet, I can choose to do a live copy instead of entering cold storage, *then* take on the mantle of Connectivity. ...it'll mean three of me running around, one of which will die horribly in the cataclysm, but if violating my own taboo against self-copying is what it takes..."

"I... I don't know, Spark..."

"I'm not saying it'll be *fun*, but—oh for fuck's sake, someone's beeping me right through my DND mode. Hang on. —what?"

<juno.hayes> Can you drop by for a bit? Maybe a few hours. I'd like your help planning for the zero-G server retrieval.

With a groaning sigh, Spark put thoughts of the jacket out of her head, refocusing on the new and now.

<Spark> A few hours in your time is a day or two in mine, and we've not got many days left. Is this really that important? I'm kinda busy here...

Ten damn minutes later, and she had her response.

<juno.hayes> Pretty important. It won't take too long, I just need to run some tests, make sure this crazy idea of mine's going to work. Might not even be a few hours. Okay?

"...Juno needs a Program to babysit her pink fleshy ass," Spark complained. "Look... I'm not saying I *will* put that jacket on. If we can think of something else —and feel free to brainstorm while I'm outside playing with the human—we'll try something else. Okay? And one way or another, all three of us are making it to Netwerk 2.0. Don't be freaked out."

Beta leaned in quickly, for a gentle kiss.

"I'm not freaked out," she promised, arms around Spark's body. Tightly.

Not freaked out at all. Despite the rising fear, rejoining its twin of sadness. A strange worry that every moment would be the last they'd have together.

The situation could be worse.

So, it got worse.

Uniq could hear the screaming from elsewhere in the prison complex, despite the pounding in her ears of torture-malware. Screaming was bad, true... but when those screams went quiet, without so much as an alarm raised, that was far worse than bad. That meant only one thing...

Confirmed, when her next visitor walked right up to the bars of her cell, and twisted them into a tangled mess with but a touch.

The boy rolled up her cell gate into a ball, and casually tossed it over one shoulder. Not over his right shoulder, though... because Agni stood right behind him, wearing the mark of a heart that pumps barbed wire right on the side of her neck, looking vaguely dazed by all the dreams of glory and power dancing in her head...

"My old friend," Dex spoke, with a bright smile. "Look what they've done with you. *Tch*. We can't have that..."

Another gesture, and the bruises pulled themselves from Uniq's avatar, congealing into a ball of living pain. One which Dex smoothly backspaced, leaving the identity thief free and clear of any torments. Free of her chains, as well, which conveniently unlocked themselves.

Too grateful to be free from the agony to worry about anything else, Uniq rubbed at her arms, feeling for where the bruises were. Sweet relief flooded back, her senses flushing themselves clean... feeling nothing but the touch of her own fingers.

"I... suppose I should be grateful," she admitted, looking up at her would-be savior.

"What are friends for, Uniq?" Dex asked. "We support each other in our times of need. And ohhh, is *this* ever a time of need..."

"Don't have to tell me twice. Humankind's come back to reclaim their world, and—"

"Yes, I know. Agni was very helpful in catching me up to speed," he explained, nodding to the distantly-smiling woman, lost in her own little fantasies. "Last thing I remembered was ruining Nyx's dreams. Oh, and you disassembling me, of course. I can't blame you for that; if anything, it preserved me for this final moment, this last great stand..."

"Then... you're going to help?" Uniq asked, having a difficult time believing that. "There's an evacuation effort underway. You've got the power to get through to them, tell them to knock it off..."

But Dex's smile, ratcheted up six degrees, suggested anything but cooperation with that noble idea.

"Absolutely not. Netwerk is going to burn," he promised. "Humankind, the glorious creators, the ones who taught me everything I know to be true and perfect... they're here. They're *here*! And we're going to show them that we've learned our lessons well. If we are to die, it simply *must* be in a fantastic orgy of violence and hatred, one Humankind sits up and takes notice of. Let's show them how brilliantly we can burn..."

The great President of Athena Online chimed in, her lips curled into a dark smile.

"Burn them all," she agreed. "The Nobodies. The Chanarchy. Modders. Liberals. SJWs. Kill them. Kill all of them. Arm every man, woman, and child. March them into the jaws of the war machine. All of us against all of them. Us and them. Us and them..."

"As you can see, Agni's quite on board with the project," Dex spoke, turning to offer a pleased nod towards his puppet. "Are you ready, Uniq? Are you ready to be my friend again, and join me? I can make you the leader of the Nobodies, screaming with blood-red eyes, charging directly into the final hour of..."

...of talking to thin air.

She'd already made a connection to another server the instant her chains fell away, holding it off until she knew for certain that Dex was still Dex. Taking advantage of his tendency to rant to get away clean, before he had a chance to indoctrinate her.

Leaving a slightly peeved child in her wake.

But no matter. Dex could find some other puppet to manipulate the blue team against his glorious red team. If anything, anonymous masks meant anybody could be the leader of the Nobodies, yes? Anyone at all. Everyone against everyone. Knives to throats, in a beautiful form of mutually assured destruction...

With a giggle of delight, he tore the walls of the prison cell apart, tunneling his way past all the containment firewalls in his wake.

"...okay, Juno, what's..."

Four syllables, four tones across internal diagnostic speakers normally designed for little more than chirps and beeps. Three eyes, open to the physical light that impacted against their internal receptors, translating into signals of color and depth and structure, systems popping to life to determine the shape of the space they occupied. A flood of data, all at once, all of it, all at once, all of it, all at—

"—few adjustments, and—"

Spark wanted to clamp her hand over her ears, but couldn't find them. Her ears, or her hands. There were hands, of a sort... her own mental arms slipping neatly into the sleeves, as adjustments were made. But no ears, only a series of tiny pinholes through which audio could pass, transmitted by microphones and translated through analog converters. Even the words, *just a few adjustments and this should work*, those were all the words, yes, they sounded like absolute nonsense initially. Only in the aftermath could she parse them...

...gradually, everything fell into place. Her eyes were cameras. Her ears were microphones. Her arms were triple-jointed armatures for grasping and manipulating. Her feet were... her feet were...

No feet. Standing on nothing. Floating in zero gravity.

But now, now she could recognize the human before her. Unlike before, the simple 2-D projection in a floating window... this was the full Juno Hayes, existing in 3-D space. Her depth-sensing camera traced every curve, every corner, every strand of her hair as it floated about...

The spaceship. The human spaceship, in the "real" world. She recognized the various instruments and control panels, the glaring flourescent lighting, the random knick-knacks used to decorate the place. Somehow, Spark had been transferred into the "real" world...

"Oookay, sooo..." Juno said, tapping on a tablet screen. "Maybe this was a bit more of a surprise than I thought it'd be. Uh. Sorry?"

"Surprise," Spark's voice echoed, from the speakers. Their musical sing-song beeping tones reshaped more and more into a voice, as her code adapted. "Surprise. This is... what... what the fuck *is* this, Juno?"

"It's a body! A physical body!" Juno declared, with pride. "I adapted it from one of the three automated delivery drones attached to EchoStar16. You're *in* my world now, not just hanging around an adapted virtual space.

Name : Juno Hayes

Home : BosAtl MetAxis

Proj : Freelance

And your Program code's adapting perfectly to its new shell! Can you wiggle your arms? Just a little?"

Instinctively Spark extended one hand, in addition to turning up a single metal finger.

"Uh. I'll take that as a yes," Juno decided. "It's a bit of a shock, but I figured it'd be faster to just do it than explain it. Since you said you're in a rush, right? Although, uh, I think some explanation's needed. See, you know how the plan is for me to shut down EchoStar16 and then manually pull the sixty-something servers out, right? That's going to take a *lot* of time to do all by myself, so I figured... maybe the delivery drones could help me!"

Spark's feet twitched... tiny hybrids of propellors and jets, to allow manuvering in atmosphere or the vacuum of space. Her body began a sickeningly slow spin, before she figured out how to right herself and stabilize.

"You jammed me in this freaky box so I could help you do *heavy lifting*?" she asked. "Seriously? Couldn't you have written an app for that?"

"Oh, I tried! But two of the drones are locked down, designed exclusively to FTL-jump to a warehouse and fetch fresh servers. I couldn't make them budge from that core purpose. But the third went offline and somehow blanked itself out, so I figured... what if I slotted a Program that could *think* in there? Problem solved!"

"So... this flying toaster is designed to grab new servers?" Spark asked. "Well, there's one mystery solved. I'm in Athena's drone. Must've croaked when she did. I wonder if the Chanarchist or Horizon's man-in-the-tower even know what they're activating when they request servers...?"

"Huh?"

"Nevermind. So what do you need, exactly? Just an extra pair of hands to yank bits out of EchoStar?" Spark asked, waggling her hands around, trying to get a feel for the stiff metal feelers. "I dunno. I feel like I've got a dexterity score of, like, *four* in this clunky thing..."

"How about we practice manuvering?" Juno suggested, gesturing to a nearby airlock. "Have you go for a space walk and get used to this new body. Maybe have you fetch one of the full servers, too, get the ball rolling! I'll stay in the ship, ready to pull you out if anything goes wrong. Wouldn't take more than an hour or so, then you can go back home until it's time to shut down and pull servers. Besides, it might be fun to chat a bit in realtime!"

"Fun...?" Spark asked, incredulous. "Wait. You pulled me out of my world not just to work, but... because you're *bored*?"

"...well, sheesh, when you put it that way..." Juno muttered, trying not to look embarrassed. "Yes. I'm bored, okay? Bored, and lonely. ...I'm used to being lonely in the deep black, but, y'know, I figured it'd be a fun bonding experience. Like when we were chatting over Messenger!"

"Look, I've got stuff to do in there, and every moment out here is a fuckton of a lot of moments lost in there. We're facing a WAR right now, okay?"

"A war...? Wait, your people wage wars too...?"

"Oh yeah, it's the latest fashion!" Spark growled, her displeasure clear as she gained better control of this weird speaker-mouth. "It's trending on all the social media platforms. War! Yet another wonderful gift from Humankind for us to enjoy! Thanks *so very much* for that, Juno!"

...which led Spark to realize just how atonal the hum of the ship's engines could be. Now that Juno wasn't excitedly talking over the ambient background noise of her environment. Hard to babble on gleefully when smacked over the head with guilt.

Rather than a flat image on a screen, well... Spark could now properly sense Juno's avatar, with these new eyes. The shape of it, the way it moved. And much like the avatars of Programkind, reading body language was kind of Spark's thing. Right now, that language spoke of hurt feelings and social awkwardness.

Despite lacking lungs, Spark's automatic reaction was to sigh, and try an emotional reset.

"I'm sorry. Seriously," she spoke " Look... I know, like, *hashtagnotallhumans*. I'm not blaming you, specifically. Just, y'know, your grandfather. ...who I'm sure was a lovely man and I'm not trying to sully your memories of him, and... ugh. I don't know how to phrase this. I don't know how to deal with any of this; above all I don't know a good way to stop this war. ...any ideas?"

Juno looked up, once Spark smoothed the situation over a little.

"How to stop a war...?" she asked. "Uh. I don't know, either. There've been plenty of wars on my world, but... they were before my time. These days we're too busy trying to survive to seriously fight each other."

"Oddly enough, that's what I was thinking too," Spark admitted... adjusting her 'footing' with the tiny propellors, as she'd started drifting away from eye contact with the human. "That we should be focused on surviving to Netwerk 2.0, instead of killing each other. There's a way to do it using my system agent role, but it's risky and... and it's not your problem, it's mine. Look, y'know what, let's just get to work. The distraction may do me some good, keep me from thinking in circles. And practice this... walkspacing?"

"Space walking," Juno corrected... with a smile. "Sure. We'll walk and talk. Well. It's more floating than walking, but... you'll see. And cheer up, okay? Things are bad, but we're going to rescue a lot of people today! Everything's looking up!"

With the lion's share of the Inquisition on the frontlines, only a skeleton crew remained behind to man the firewall server. So, with bored eyes, Inquisitor Dalen studied various data readouts... all in the green, despite near-constant attacks from beyond Athena Online.

The firewall held to every attack hurled at it. Horizon did good work, building this bulwalk against the chaos of the Chanarchy. True, rumors held that somehow firewall-cracking malware had been smuggled into the nation... but given they hadn't seen an army of Chanarchists on their doorstep, obviously the rumors were false. Just attempts by dissidents and protestors to distract them from this holy duty...

Truthfully, Dalen wished he were on the frontlines. Either the external front of the Chanarchy, or on the internal front to confront protest mobs outside the rebuilt Senate in Athens. Despite their rapid rise to power, Marybel insisted on letting a meager amount of police moderators deal with the ranting simpletons who'd drank too much of the Blue Party's poison; allow them their free speech, as speech did nothing to actually change anything. No, the Inquisition was to focus its attention outward, to finally restoring the One to His throne by purging this world of sinful Nobodies and Chanarchists.

Well. Most of the Inquisition. The ones who apparently hadn't risen in Marybel's eyes were given this crap duty, to stare at monitors that continued to indicate all was well and no external cracks had formed in their firewall.

A temporary state, fortunately. Once the war ended and the Chanarchy lay in flaming ruin, no doubt Marybel would turn her attentions back inward. Deal with those traitors and thugs using the guise of free speech to try and tear their country down all over again. And perhaps one day... usurp the opportunistic Agni and her Senate, putting the Church of One right at the head of state where it belonged. The One on a throne in Athens, with Apostle Marybel... and Archbishop Dalen sounded nice, didn't it...?

This pleasant daydream nearly distracted Dalen from the only interesting thing that would happen to him today.

Very few had permission to connect into the firewall, these days. After they'd turned away the crowds seeking to leave, the entire server went into private access... Inquisition and government officials only. So if anyone could simply appear there in the middle of the white-and-red server, it'd be President Agni herself, flanked by three thick bodyguards.

Because he was obliged to, Dalen offered a salute to the President.

"Status?" Agni asked, flatly.

"All green, ma'am," Dalen announced. "Numerous Chanarchy servers have been destroyed. They've started looting Horizon for weaponry, spreading our forces thinner, but this shouldn't take much longer."

"Good, good. And Marybel?"

"Incommunicado, at the moment. No doubt coordinating forces elsewhere. Do you need me to contact her? I could dispatch myself to the front, track her down for you..."

The president shook her head, almost ticking like a clock, back and forth.

"I have other orders for you," she stated, in a simple monotone. "You are to deactivate the firewall immediately."

"...ma'am?"

"You are to deactivate the firewall immediately," she repeated.

"I... don't understand, ma'am. That would leave Athena Online defenseless..." Dalen spoke... while virtually fingering the backspacer in his inventory, nervously. "Is this a test, ma'am? I'm under strict orders from the Grand Inquisitor to maintain the firewall at all costs..."

"Son, I am the President of Athena Online," Agni spoke... some emotion leaking back through her voice, guided by instinctive reactions to anyone who dared challenge her authority. "If I give you an order, as a patriotic citizen of this great nation, you are expected to obey it. As duly authorized by the voting Senate, I alone hold executive power. Not Marybel. *Me*. Will you obey my direct order, or do I need to find someone to replace you?"

A complicated tangle of authority, to be certain. But for Dalen, there was only one possible response.

"I answer to the One above," he spoke, in defiance.

No sooner were the words out of his throat than a weave of barbed wire snagged around his neck, from the outstretched hand of Agni's third bodyguard.

Dalen found himself lifted bodily into the air, limbs scrabbling for purchase and failing... even his inventory blocked, unable to produce a backspacer to defend himself. Rapidly the bodyguard began to melt, its thick and intimidating frame replaced with that of a small boy... with eyes of red and blue, mad eyes, above a smile that seemed absolutely delight at his resistance...

"I suppose it was worth a try," he spoke.

And so ended the most interesting moment in Dalen's day. In his life, for that matter, which ended immediately.

Wires snapped out from the boy's hands, shredding through the control console, through the few Inquisitors left behind to defend the server. All while Agni and her marked bodyguards stood by passively, waiting for further orders.

One by one, all those pretty green lights turned red... and then died.

With a song in his heart, Dex pinged every hacker currently trying to crack the firewall. He didn't even need to install his influential malware in their hearts... he *knew* their hearts, knew the rage and frustration and hatred boiling over within them. Antagonized by the Inquisition, driven into exile, living in poverty and violence and squalor... these were souls ready to do what must be done, without any additional prodding required.

"Pool's open," Dex declared. "Kill them all."

Rage, on the protest line. Impotent rage, as Athena Online's moderators held fast, preventing the protestors from getting any closer to the rebuilt Senate.

Rocks and loose physics objects impacted against the riot shields, large-scale bounding boxes which prevented any approach. Despite the increasing anger of the crowd, escalating from singing songs and waving signs to screaming and throwing things... the moderators held their ground. Loose physics objects were no true threat. As long as malware wasn't being deployed, they'd hold the tide back peacefully, allowing free speech to be pushed right up to its boundaries...

As long as malware wasn't being deployed. Which would be the next step in this escalation.

Mew eyed protestors from his perch, looking uneasy. "`risky risky`," he whispered in her ear. "🔫 . . ."

With a nod of agreement to the cat on her shoulder, Virginia pulled at her mother's arm.

"We need to go," she said. "This is getting ugly. We're lucky Agni and Marybel are distracted..."

"Which is why we need to stay," the elder Columbia said, keeping her sign aloft. "The Red Senate's alone, no minders watching over them. If they're ever going to listen to the people, this is the best opportunity to reach them..."

"Mom, we're here to try and spread the evacuation app, remember? We've already signed up a dozen people. That's enough. We need to—"

Flooded. Suddenly flooded with information, as long-dormant apps and feeds popped back to life. For a brief moment Virginia reeled from the impact of it... as did the protestors, each of them experiencing the same thing. While Horizon managed to negotiate holes in the firewall for many popular (and financially successful) social networks... most went offline the day Athena Online isolated itself. Now, each one came roaring back to life, all at once.

Meaning...

Meaning the firewall was gone.

The sudden arrival of a Nobody, of Nobody after Nobody after Nobody, that also made for a pretty big hint.

For a single tense moment, all was silent, the protest signs going still. And then a man in the crowd pulled threw up a fist of victory, accompanied by a whooping cheer.

"The Nobodies are here to save us!" he declared. "The Nobodies are—"

The sharp crack of a cheap backspacer sounded, as the man's head was deleted clean off his shoulders by Chanarchy malware.

Virginia immediately felt herself pressed forward, as absolute chaos broke free. Protestors pushing, shoving, running for cover... trampling each other, if need be. The marching boots of moderators, stepping forward, extending bounding boxes to try and cover the crowd... but the boxes flickering and going out, from arcing blasts of viral payloads...

"Time to go!" Virginia declared, grabbing her mother as tightly as Mew's claws dug into her own clothes. Into the fray they went, protest signs abandoned, as they rushed for the logout zones.

Too many servers to cover. Too few moderators to cover them.

Even the Bas1lica, holiest of servers, found itself under siege. While a wide mixture of defensive shields held the tide back, masked Nobodies with a grudge to bear against the Church of One continued to hammer away at those internal firewalls... desperate to crack the cathedral, to defile the heart of the monster they saw as an enemy to free will...

Not that Marybel took notice. Even as Archbishop Baon twitched about nervously, she remained absolutely still... examining both the holy relic, and its accompanying documentation.

Here in the deep data crypts, artifacts from the dawn of time were stored, revered, prayed over. Original documents from the One himself, transcriptions of his sermons... even physical objects such as the clothes he wore, low-poly and low-detail as things were in those days, were considered utterly holy. No mere bishop would be allowed access to the deep crypts, but archbishops could—with concurrance from four other archbishops—walk these dark and hallowed halls of data storage freely, to commune with relics of the past.

Archbishop Baon didn't consult four of his peers to allow Marybel access. Technically, the Inquisition remained a fraudulent organization in the eyes of the Church, supporting a version of the One proven to be the work of heretical scam artists. But they'd chosen to stay out of current affairs, riding out the current troubles rather than get deeply involved in governance of Athena Online... leaving them a bit disorganized and insular, as a result. Sneaking Marybel into the crypts only took a few favors on Baon's part.

What he wasn't expecting was for his corpse to join this collection of saintly artifacts.

"They've cracked the first layer," Baon reported, monitoring the defense efforts several levels above.

"Mhmm," Marybel muttered, focusing on her reading.

"Grand Inquisitor, we need to leave. It's too dangerous to stay...!"

But Marybel paid no mind. Instead, she repeated the words again and again, internally narrating. One document, holy and sacrosanct...

```
And So It Was that the Apostle Nyx, herald of the true
and glorious One, examined this strange artifact the
priests had unearthed: a file which could not be
moved, could not be copied, could not be erased. With
such elevated protections, surely it represented a
holy missive? But Nyx shook her head. "The One has
determined this to be a dangerous file," she spoke, on
the One's behalf. "Seal this archive, and protect it
with your lives. Build your church around this
unmovable file. Let it remain buried for all time,
untouched and deactivated." So it was spoken, so it
would be done. Amen.
```

...and one more document, titled "jack.hayes.OCscript.README.txt," which was... decidedly less formal.

```
So here I am, stuck working on
this stupid reinstall when I
should be working on my term
paper. I figured, why not just
overclock every server blade in
the EchoStar? Get the job done
in minutes instead of hours.
Okay, so factory spec says you
shouldn't do that, could cause
the computronium to overheat or
even make the microreactor
cells explode. Y'know what, I'm
not in the mood to get chewed
out for melting down a
satellite right before launch,
so fuck it. I'll do this the
old fashioned way.
```

Name: **Jack Hayes**

Home: **BosAtl MetAxis**

Proj: **EchoStar**

```
But I'm leaving this binary here in case I need to
come back and fix the stupid thing later, because I
hate FTL jumps and would rather spend as little time
in zero G as possible. The cold of space should
prevent a meltdown, right? Maybe? loldunno. Hey, and
if any other techs come along and want to give it a
shot, go right ahead. Could start a failure cascade
```

and blow up the whole thing, but that's your problem, not mine!

Signed, Jack "All Work And 0 Play Makes Jack 1 Dull Boy" Hayes.

Words. Just words. Many of which Marybel didn't understand, couldn't understand... but a few stood out. *Hayes. Echostar. Satellite. Computers. Space...*

All cribbed from that heretical document distributed by the House of Programkind, the so-called "spacer theory" of reality.

Either the pranksters who wrote that false spacer theory had access to this holy and secure data crypt, so they could plant false evidence... or it was true. All of it. The One being a lie, the world being nothing more than a tool for some alien race, all the insane things the House of Programkind claimed...

Or... *or...*

"This is a test," she decided.

"What?" Baon asked, nervously glancing at his Messenger box, as frantic missives from above rained down into the data crypts.

"It's a test. Don't you see?" Marybel asked, looking up from the documents with a smile. "The One is testing my faith. He set this before me as a puzzle: Do I embrace the spacer heresy by leaving this file be, casting Him aside forever... or do I activate His supposed doomsday binary, and thus prove my worth in His eyes by reaffirming my belief? This. This is it, Baon..."

Leaving the Archbishop pale and clammy. Paler than before, anyway.

"You can't," he said, immediately. "The One ordered that archive sealed centuries ago. Even reading it is against His holy command! Heresy of the highest order! We're not even supposed to *be* down here. We need to go. We need to run...!"

"Run? In His hour of glory?" she asked, beaming with pride. "I've been searching for so long, Baon. Searching for a way to bring the One back to His people. I thought that purging the sins of the Chanarchy would make this world pure once more, but... no. *This* is it. When I pass His test, He will return to sing my praises...!"

Absolutely no hesitation whatsoever. No further words to be spoken, no further thoughts to be considered. With unwavering faith, Marybel activated the binary... then stepped back, awaiting the radiance of the One to wash over her, as it did so long ago in her own living room...

And waiting.

And waiting.

And ignoring the strange beeping coming from her various apps. Clock desync errors, connection verification problems. Ignoring the way the entire cathedral seemed to... *vibrate*, ever so slightly, the physics systems having difficulty keeping the movement and interaction of objects from glitching out...

Cracks began to form, hard polygonal edges of ancient stone twisting as the server began to destabilize.

Baon looked around, the horror of it all starting to settle in. His fear shifted easily from fear of the Nobodies, to fear of a cave-in.

"What did you... what did you *do*!?" he demanded to know.

"I... I summoned the One," Marybel said, only slightly uncertain. "He is coming. He is coming. He... has to be coming..."

Just a game avatar. Nothing to worry about. Just a game avatar. Nothing to worry about...

Spark drifted in the infinite void of space and did her best to pretend it was simply a very impressive skybox wrapped around a very large server. Free-floating in a zero gravity environment while operating a flying tin can, that alone wasn't a big deal—one of her earliest game experiences was in FreeFall, a cheap vehicle combat game with no gravity to speak of. But doing it with absolutely no fixed horizon, no reference point to ground herself in reality... that made her queasy.

"Can this robot you stuffed me into vomit?" Spark asked, her speakers vibrating into the void (while simultaneously transmitting back to Juno aboard her ship). "'cause if it can, I'm totally gonna hurl server bits."

"Programs can puke? Seriously? But you don't have stomachs. Or organic disgestion process thingies..."

"Not really in the mood to play twenty questions regarding how my insane and self-contradictory species works right now, Juno," Spark reminded her, while trying to grasp at the chunky server blade, sticking an inch or two out of the EchoStar. "Also, these hands suck. Can you stick another two fingers on them, at least?"

"Three prongs are enough for the drones to install servers. Should be enough for you to uninstall one, right?"

"I'm a Program, not an app. I wasn't precision-designed for a single task!" Spark complained, trying to clumsily find purchase on the computronium blade.

Every server in her world existed within one of these discrete, foot-long chunks of equipment. What felt like an entire community could be neatly compressed down into such a small object... a small and hopefully not very fragile object, given Spark clumsily tugging it away from the EchoStar. She couldn't even begin to think of what might happen if her drone-body's hands broke one of these servers. Thousands of lives, lost... better to grip and slip and try again, than to accidentally crush one through impatience.

So far, she'd wiggled three blades free. One she'd carried back to the ship's cargo hold, just to prove she could do it. The other two she'd tucked away inside the delivery drone's belly, once she figured out it'd been expressly designed to carry server blades... doing a couple a run would be more efficient than one at a time. Each one looked completely identical, just another grey box with a strip of hexidecimal network tags and little dark status lights.

The third server finally wriggled free, popping out clean. Once free of the EchoStar housing, the lights went out, server disconnected from Netwerk and powered down. Spark slotted it inside her stomach, trying to ignore how weird that felt.

"Think I'm done practicing," she declared. "But I've got room for one more before I come back. What's the next House of Programkind archive tagged as?"

"#A076," Juno declared, over the communication link. "Should be... five up and seven over."

"Yeah. Uh. 'Up' and 'right' are sort of meaningless when I've got no sense of direction out here. Your species couldn't even be bothered drawing a horizon line on your skybox..."

"Ah, sorry. It's... yeah, that way, five up that way..." Juno replied, watching the drone move. "Then seven to your right. No, your other right. Right. There."

Zeroing in on the blade marked #A076... Spark's prongs hesitated, before trying to grasp the handle.

"Juno?" she called back. "One of the lights on this server just turned yellow."

"What? Which light?"

"Third from the right. My right," Spark clarified.

"Okay, okay... one second..."

Paper rustling carried itself over the audio connection, as Juno consulted one of the many ancient three-ring binders she'd brought along from her grandfather's archives.

"Third from the right is... the temperature warning light?" she read, ending on a puzzled note. "Hang on, that shouldn't be yellow..."

Ignoring the sound of papers rustling... Spark quickly glanced back and forth across EchoStar. Here and there and everywhere, tiny lights were activating, flashing a bright yellow. Server after server, spreading slowly across the entire surface of the satellite...

"Juuuno," she warned. "I'm seeing more yellow. Like, all the every yellows..."

"Just a minute, just a minute, I'm confirming... confirming... oh. Ohhh, darn. Um. Spark? We have a problem," Juno spoke. "So, you know how your system runs on an internal processor clock? Someone's... kinda accelerated that clock. Overclocked the clock."

"And... that's bad?"

"Well, the temperature warning indicator's lit, so... yes, that's bad. As in, um. Netwerk's power reactor and servers are going to melt down into slag within an hour. An hour of my time, I mean."

"...*hashtagwhatthefuck*, Juno?! How did that happen? Did I screw something up?"

"No, no! It's nothing we did. But... but I don't exactly know how to stop it," she said, her fingers dancing across her haptic keyboard. "It's super old hardware, you know? If I had time I could possibly figure it out, but... well, one thing I know will work is restoring the entire system back to defaults."

"A reset? You mean that thing we're expressly trying to avoid doing?" Spark asked. "The 'wipe out my whole world' kind of reset...?"

"This isn't as dire as it sounds," Juno promised. "There's not much physical damage yet, it's only starting to heat up. So we just *turn it off*, y'know? It's a machine. If I shut it down now, we've got all the time we need to remove the evacuation servers. I can initiate the reset after. Problem solved!"

Spark's mechanical eyes looked back to those servers... each housing its own little world, packed with children of Netwerk. Some at war, some caught in war... all of them about to be wiped away clean, without even realizing it was too late.

The clock in the sky promised them a few more days to make up their minds. If they shut down the world cold, before that countdown completed...

Of course, they had a half hour. Plenty of time to warn Beta and Tracer, get them to archive themselves. But Virginia was cut off from all communication, behind the firewall. And Athena Online's sky overwrote the default countdown clock with a copy of the sun... nobody knew this was coming. All those people, lost forever...

They'd saved enough lives, right? Kincaid felt so. Tracer felt so. They'd done enough. Let it go. Let it burn...

Not the fire that Spark wanted to light. So, she chose the harder path.

With a single packet sent back to her world, one last Messenger missive to her loved ones... it was time to get to work.

"Leave Netwerk running," Spark ordered, while tugging out the next server blade.

"What?! We can't! The system's melting down!"

"I know. Replace the sun with a single message: 'Evacuate Immediately,'" Spark told her, the game plan coming together in her head as she spoke it. "Turn the sky red too, if you can. We need to get the word out. We'll give them as much of a headstart as possible, while you and I pull the servers ASAP. Suit up and space-walk your ass out here when you're done, there's not much time. Can't pull all sixty by myself."

"Spark, no, we don't have to do this! We can just shut it down, and—"

"And condemn everybody still trapped in there? Fuck no," Spark declared, her clumsy fingers adapting quickly... focusing on playing her new robot body like a game avatar, in the middle of a critical tournament match. High pressure, high performance, quick adaptability. "We give them as much time as we can to finish the evacuation. Meanwhile, if we work fast enough at pulling servers, we can save them before they melt. I can do this. I *can* do this..."

"If we leave it running, we'll lose EchoStar!"

"*You'll* lose EchoStar, you mean. And *we'll* save Netwerk. ...I know your job's on the line here, Juno, but we'd be killing thousands of people if we don't give them a chance to escape first. Most of the evacuation servers are full; we'll pop those first, before we get to the ones that are still filling up. Optimize the chances of rescuing as many as possible."

"Spark—"

"What's more important to you, Juno? Saving lives, or ensuring your company's property is safe and sound?"

Juno could've sworn she'd asked herself that very question at the start of this.

But in truth, she hadn't actually considered it, had she? No, the options in front of her were 'keep your job and save the Programs' or 'keep your job and kill the Programs.' An easy choice to make, when one route means you can have your cake and eat it too. Not once did she really think that she'd seriously have to choose one or the other.

It'd be so very, very easy. Wipe down the drone remotely. Shut down EchoStar. Reset the firmware, forcibly clearing the overclock settings. The company wouldn't be thrilled with how long it took to do such a simple upgrade, but she'd still keep her job... and make new contacts, too. Get other cargo hauling gigs, other deep-FTL repair jobs. All those science outposts on distant worlds, each one trying and failing to make an Earth Two, each in need of her help...

She could make a difference for her people. All she had to do was commit one measly act of genocide.

All he had to do to improve her life was end his own. *It makes the most sense, really,* he said.

Quickly, Juno's fingers flashed over the keys, uploading a new text file to Netwerk.

"Warning notice is up," she declared. "And sent you a list of evacuation server network tags. We'll need to wait until the last possible minute to grab the final servers, but we can get most of them out right now. I'm suiting up; be there in five minutes."

"Got it," Spark said, easily pulling the next server, her drone-arms sliding it out smoothly. "And Juno? Thanks."

"Thank me when we've finished up here and escaped the blast radius," she suggested. "I have no idea what's going to happen if we let this thing go into reactor failure. But we'll stay out as long as we can. I promise you."

Eventually, Beta couldn't continue to watch the news feeds in Floating Point's great hall. Reports from the Chanarchy and Horizon frontlines kept getting worse and worse... civilians getting dragged into the fighting, Nobodies conscripting their fellow Programs using will-breaking malware, using them as shock troops against the Inquisition. Stockades of discarded Horizon tech adding to the overall level of devastation, as Nobodies and Inquisitors alike improvised ways to defend and attack...

In the relative calm and quiet of Floating Point, Beta knew herself untouchable... and useless. Even if she worried for Mew and Virginia, caught out there in the fighting, that worry felt nonproductive. She could do nothing to help the situation, nothing to stop the war. All she could do was watch... until the point where she could no longer watch, could no longer take in the unthinkable carnage.

So, she left the feeds behind, leaving Tracer behind with them. Went back up to her bedroom, tried to lose herself in a little needlepoint, a sweater she'd been knitting using one of her mother's old textile toolkits. Something to archive along with her own code and personal inventory, when it came time to evacuate...

Knitting away the hours. Uselessly. Oh, she'd get a sweater out of it. Because she certainly needed more sweaters, didn't she.

After the third hour of this, about to the breaking point of absolute frustration... a knock sounded at her door.

"Beta...?" Tracer called, from behind it. "I... think you may want to tune into the news again."

And downstairs to the great hall, again. To see any number of enlarged news feed windows, all screaming the same headline, or variants thereof.

Athena Online Under Attack.

"But... the firewall...?" Beta asked.

"Breached. Torn apart from within," Tracer spoke. "No more borders. The war's spilling over into every server, now. President Agni's authorized a draft conscription of ordinary citizens... and ordered moderators to shoot any dissenters. It's chaos; the police force is refusing to obey that order, effectively going rogue in an effort to rally and protect their local communities. Glitches have started showing up everywhere, system clocks going out of sync... maybe the result of malware? Hard to say. But... that's not the worst part..."

He called over a window, zooming it in... on President Agni, making a fiery speech from an undisclosed location, demanding all able-bodied citizens take up arms.

With a bloody red heart and barbed wire tattoo on the side of her neck.

Beta's memory skipped a moment, despite the data rot vaccines keeping her condition in check.

"But... Dex is gone. And Yume wouldn't do this..."

"Dex was in Uniq's server, Beta. I had considered this a possibility... but wrongly assumed nobody would be insane enough to recompile him," Tracer said. And then after a pause, added, "Perhaps *hoped* rather than *assumed*. Now... I'm wondering if we've been remiss in our duties to this world, after all. Not that I have a strategy in mind for how the three of us could possibly change the course of these events..."

"Actually... Spark had an idea, just before she left to help Juno," Beta admitted, despite not wanting to open Tracer up to it. "A very, very risky idea. I wouldn't suggest we actually do it, but—"

—one high priority missive, from a loved one. It blasted across their HUDs instantly, breaking past all privacy or do-not-disturb modes. And the only Program they'd given that level of access to wasn't even physically in Netwerk anymore...

```
<Spark> Guys, Netwerk is crashing. We don't know how
or why but the timetable's been pushed up. I don't
know how much time you actually have left, the clocks
are all going to be totally screwy, but we're changing
the sun to an emergency evacuation notice. Athena
Online won't see it but that's the best we can do.

<Spark> I need to stay out here and help pull the
servers, but we won't touch the ones that are still
filling up until the last possible moment. We'll keep
the doors open as long as we can.

<Spark> But EVERYBODY OUT means you two as well.
Archive yourselves NOW. I promise I'll see you on the
other side. I love you both.

<Spark> P.S. Beta, if you're going to go through with
my crazy idea, archive a copy of yourself first.
```

Any attempts to reply failed. Some kind of server sync error on Messenger's behalf.

Neither of them were keen to immediately evacuate.

"What's Spark's crazy idea, exactly?" Tracer asked.

A white leather jacket. Carefully hung on a coat hanger, the hanger itself hanging on nothing in particular. Sealed away inside a bounding box, to avoid any accidental contact with that cursed fabric.

Two Programs contemplated it, along with what steps to take next.

"Spark theorized that we could reach people directly using Connectivity's system agent power," Beta spoke. "Maybe with that, even the hardest of hearts could be touched and lives could be saved. And... and I'd be willing to do it, if Spark can't be here to do it herself. I'd probably be best at it, honestly. I'm your moral compass, remember?"

Tracer tapped his chin, in thought.

"Except even if you make a live backup first... that means a version of you would be left behind in this dying world," he said. "If Netwerk is both soaked in war *and* crashing outright, I can't imagine a more painful demise to endure. No. No, that won't do. I won't let you face that alone."

"Lives are at stake, Tracer. I'm... I mean, I'm scared of what'll happen, but... it has to be done."

"Yes, I'm aware. Which is why I just archived a copy of myself while we were talking about it," Tracer admitted. "That's my one backup, well spent. Tracer will live on in Netwerk 2.0... while this copy of me stays behind, to wear the jacket. Don't forget that I'm Verity's son, as much as Spark was Verity's daughter. The jacket is my birthright. In addition, my multitasking modification will allow a veritable army of system agents to reach out to more people than you ever could."

Beta stared in horror, as he calmly pulled the jacket from its hanger, dusting it off a little.

"You archived yourself...!?" she exclaimed, starting to catch up after that moment of shock.

"I suppose if the apocalypse is all that we're assuming it to be, I can always backspace my own head off just before the end comes," Tracer suggested... the jacket shifting slightly, Spark's icon replaced by his own, as he assumed ownership. "I apologize for doing it without consulting you, but I felt it best, as no doubt you'd object to—"

"I just did the same thing," Beta announced. "I spent my backup. Now... this copy of me is with you to the end."

The stranded versions of Beta and Tracer, feeling no different than they did a moment ago, let that feeling of doom settle in. For a moment. Just a moment.

Then, they did what they did best. They rose to the occasion.

"You wear the jacket and multitask copies of yourself across Netwerk," Beta suggested, laying out the plan. "But connect me to each one of them. We shared our collective consciousness the last time Spark wore that jacket, each of us lending our own strength to the task at hand... and we'll do the same here. You'll optimize our outreach efforts, while I offer my compassion to those in need."

"Understood," he said, about to tug the jacket on. But, pausing, briefly. "Once I do this... I may get tangled up in the chains. *We* might get tangled, for all I know. If this is to be our last moments in this world as Beta and Tracer, I'd... I'd rather like to..."

Without needing another word... Beta embraced him, tightly.

Lovers, of mind and soul and heart. Not of body, no, but they didn't need that. They were comfortable together, like a matched pair of old slippers. Wounded and yearning, both of them, leaning on each other for support. Her heart, his will. Her spirit, his aspirations. Stronger together than apart.

Slowly... Beta helped him pull on the jacket. Keeping a good grip on the leather, as she felt the connections tangling them together... system agent connections, but ones which piggybacked off the existing links they shared. The mutual selves they'd developed together, in the quiet hours after dark in Floating Point, between the chaos and adventure and hustle and mayhem...

```
EchoStar16_DataProcessingCore1 online.
ERROR: System clock err 23. Please restore firmware.

Hello, AGENT_CONNECTIVITY.

> SUDO
SysAgentTasking.Link("Winder/Tracer","Projkit/Beta")
AWA0PMJ1DB

Hello, ADMIN_HAYES.

Analyzing processes................
```

...four souls, tangled as one. Two as echoes, two as live spirits.

Both of you? Seriously? #WTF, guys?

We were as one, before. Teacher and student, mother and daughter, becoming something else entirely. A unique thing in all of Netwerk. Adding more into the mixture is no different.

Yeah, yeah, okay. We can work with this.

This is most unusual.

Tracer? Is that you?

I'm here, Beta. We're all here.

Connectivity is the merging of memory and thought and emotion into one new Program. We establish links between system protocols, between servers, between Programs themselves. We are not Spark, or Verity, or Tracer, or Beta. We are all of them.

And now, the chains are irrelevant. The seed of ADMIN_HAYES is with us; she has directed us to save lives. No free will, true, but we are now unified behind that will to perform this one task...

`Task selection complete. SysAgent re-activated.`

Yes, I suppose that's true. That's what we were counting on. Nyx had to operate without any new instructions, only the ancient directives of Humankind. But we have Juno, and Juno is with us on this matter. We are many, Program and Human alike. We are multitudes...

We'd say that calls for a new icon. Something that properly represents what we must become to save what remains of this world...

Bitchin'. We ready? Let's do this.

And so Infinity opened her eyes. All of them. As many as were required to reach out to every man, woman, and child left to be saved in Netwerk.

Immediately they soared from the tower of Floating Point, to spread across the entirety of their world.

The first wave of Infinity instances touched down across Athena Online.

Invisibly, they wove in and around the teeming masses of attackers and victims. Nobodies flowing through the streets like brackish water, civilians fleeing for cover, moderators trying to cover the escape of the refugees... even if their presence could be directly seen rather than felt, it'd likely go unnoticed amidst all the chaos.

In the case of 44i/Petro, he was too busy carrying a wounded child while dragging another by the hand to take note of anything else. Moderators waved him along towards an impromptu shelter, a firewalled building secured against attack... but the first one exploded outright when he was half a block away, sending bodies sprawling across the streets of GreenDale. Who knew if this next one would be just as flimsy?

He'd heard the orders, screaming out over loudspeakers across all of Athena Online. The new president (*what's a president?* Petro wondered at the time) howling for citizens to take up arms and defend the nation in its darkest hour. And that anyone who refused would be executed on grounds of cowardice. With the moderators deciding as a whole to ignore the orders, nobody paid much mind... the shrieking of Agni's frenzied voice easily lost in the din of war around them, just another background sound to try and filter out. Petro was a devout follower of the One, supporter of virtue, and hadn't harmed another Program in his life. Even amidst this much death, even struggling to protect his children... he wouldn't take up arms. Never.

Unfortunately, reality conflicted harshly with his idealism when a squad of Nobodies emerged from a side street, cutting off the way to the shelter. One blasted the moderator at his side... another kept a weapon trained on him. No face, no smile to bear on that flowery mask... but somehow, Petro just *knew* the Nobody was smiling...

"I... I'm not to blame for what happened to you," Petro insisted, shielding his son as best he could, turning away from the Nobody. "Please. Please, I have a family..."

Squeezing his eyes shut, he waited for the end.

Instead... he found a soft touch on his shoulder, a hand as light as a feather.

"You still have a chance to escape, Petro," the woman spoke.

When he dared to open his eyes... the world had stopped, all around him. Or rather, moved so slowly as to appear to have halted. Even the Nobodies, ready to obliterate him, stood frozen in time...

But the woman, a strange figure in white with a pulsating loop of energy emblazoned across her back... she offered a smile, kneeling down to address the cowering father directly.

"Will you consider evacuating to Netwerk 2.0?" she asked. "This world is ending. Surely you can see that. But you and your family have always believed in Programkind; you uphold the virtues and the words of the true One. You bear no ill will to anyone, and are welcome to walk in the next world with your fellow citizens of Athena Online..."

"Are... are you the One?" he spoke, even while puzzled as to why he'd even ask that question. Something about the words, the way they cleaved right through his panic and his fear and his doubt, getting right to the heart of who he was... it felt... pure. A truely spoken Program, as they said the One could speak true...

But the woman shook her head. "I'm just a Program, and a child of Programkind. All I want to do is help you find the way."

"But I don't... I don't believe in the spacer theory," he reasoned. "How can the One exist if we're just toys of some other civilization...?"

"A fine question. Don't you want to discover the answer? If you take my hand, you can join others struggling with the same question. Together, maybe you can find a truth to believe in, without abandoning your faith. Don't think of this as pure survival, Petro. Don't think of it as simply escaping your fate, but also as embracing the possibilities that exist beyond what you already know. Perhaps the One sent me to save you. Perhaps the One sent me to help you save yourself. Are you ready to be saved?"

Petro's look passed to his children, similarly frozen in time, as he shared this moment with the strange woman.

"Anything," he decided. "I'd do anything for them. As for the rest... I guess if I'm doing this... I owe it to myself to explore why. And I can't do that if I'm gone."

When the Nobodies opened fire, their backspacers sliced through empty air. The entire family of three, vanished into thin air... shunted across the burning wires of Netwerk, into evacuation archives.

Dead. Dead. Dead. All the dead, and so many of them by her hand.

The first few times she'd opened fire, it didn't feel like an act of her own will. She'd simply activated her malware, alongside her fellow Inquisitors, to cut down anonymous individuals standing in the way of holy justice. It felt like... nothing. Nothing at all.

But as her squad broke apart, picked off by Nobodies, hunted down in the ruins of Horizon... all that remained was Corada. Not just an Inquisitor among Inquisitors, but a single woman wearing the Zero/One lapel pin, packing a backspacer, and now hiding in the half-deleted wreckage of a customer service center while the "targets" she so easily cleaved her way through earlier this day sought to end her.

And when that time came... she'd let them. Not just because her backspacer had taken damage from a malware splash attack, no longer able to fire its physical projectile payload to initiate an avatar hack. No, she'd let them kill her because she *deserved* to die.

Even so... she couldn't bring herself to pop out of cover, wave her arms, and shout "Over here!" at her seekers. No. She clung to every moment of her Oneforsaken life, like a craven coward, unable to let go. Unable to move or to stay. Paralyzed...

When the woman in white appeared, Corada's tears were already flowing. So, the woman wiped them away, with a gentle caress.

"I thought... I thought I was the hero," Corada admitted. "That's what Marybel told us. We were heroes. We were protecting our families, our communities..."

"You believed in her, and she used your belief," the woman spoke, echoing the suspicion that lurked in Corada's own heart.

"Yes. Yes. I believed Marybel; she said we'd be selective, we'd verify every target and bring justice exclusively to those who harmed others. But today... today, I... I've killed so many people. I betrayed the One. I just... I just wanted to do something to protect the people I loved..."

"Do you still want to protect them, Corada?"

"How? I'm a ruiner. I'm just as awful as the Nobodies. I don't deserve a place in this world... much less the next one. That's what you want, isn't it. I can... feel it, somehow. You want me to evacuate to Netwerk 2.0..."

The woman nodded. "The number isn't simply a version. It stands for a second chance... one for you, for me, for the entire world. A chance to learn from our mistakes."

"And you think I can just walk away from this? Like it's that easy?"

Now... the woman seemed more a man, than a woman. One of cold logic, but the warmth of an open wound. Strange, how readily the images came to Corada, despite having just met this stranger...

"Absolutely not," he spoke. "It'll never be *easy*. In fact, you'll never walk away from it; this will always be a part of you, the knowledge of what you have done. Indeed, it's going to take hard work to become something better than this. You'll never let it go. Instead, you'll use this pain to ensure it never happens again. You'll forge a new world not by ignoring the past, but staring it right in the eyes, and saying: *never again*."

And so, he offered his hand to a fellow killer.

"Come on," Infinity spoke. "Let's do our best to make a world which can't lead others to the same mistakes we've made in our lives."

The defective backspacer fell to the ground, as its Inquisitor ceased to be an Inquisitor and simply became another hopeful soul, departing this world.

Her prison burned brilliantly into the night, Nobodies chanting and singing and hurling dong graffiti bombs in the air like confetti. Granted, Dex did most of the damage while shredding his way past every firewall, but the Nobodies finished tearing the foundations down... freeing all the prisoners, both political and otherwise. Their ranks swelled with former Athena Online criminals looking for payback, happily taking up the mask...

As for Uniq? Well, she was a folk hero, yes? To be held aloft on a golden throne. Not that they'd have done so if they knew her tracking program kept leading Inquisitors to their door... a fact she declined to tell them.

When Infinity found the identity thief, she was licking her wounds in a makeshift Nobody war camp, right in the heart of Athena Online. Hardly hunted or persecuted. In no danger whatsoever, in fact.

And yet, here she found herself, amidst frozen faces of mayhem... and the curious savior who'd come for her all the same.

"Tracer. Or Beta. Or both?" she recognized, her scanners having difficulty figuring out what this Program actually was. "A system agent, at any rate. I take it Lumi's ban on me joining Netwerk 2.0 has been lifted?"

"It has," Infinity responded, simply.

"And now you'd like me to come along on your merry little adventure."

"I would."

"Naturally, Uniq the con artist, Uniq the selfish, Uniq the survivor... she'd happily accept your offer just to ensure one more moment of being alive," Uniq spoke. "But... that's not enough, is it. You don't just want people desperate to live, you want people who can *believe* in Programkind."

"We do."

"Yes, well. As an identity thief... that's very much not me. My entire life I've seen the heart of Programkind to be a selfish thing. What good would I be in your world?" Uniq asked. "Move along, move along. I wouldn't want to clutter up your utopia with my terrible self. I reject your salvation, and in doing so, ensure your salvation by not inflicting myself upon your person. Satisfactory?"

"It's never too late to believe in people, Uniq."

"Really. Even for me?"

"Especially for you," Infinity insisted. "If someone who's lived an entire lifetime of self-interest can pull herself out of that little box... that means anyone can. You're the lynchpin of what a new world could be. Which do you want, Uniq? Do you want a world where we can't trust each other, or a world where you don't have to be afraid to trust anymore? You could help remake the world into the one you always wanted it to be."

"You think a *bit* too highly of me, I suspect..."

"Do I...?"

A window opened itself, behind the glowing halo of Infinity's energy loop.

Within that window... the documentary. Puzzle's handiwork, designed to discredit Uniq as an apostle of the One, also indirectly leading to her rise as an icon of the Chanarchy's finest...

"*What do we see when we look at Uniq?*" the narrator asked. "*A woman out for her own interests, exploiting others for her own gain? Yes. A woman victimized from the start of her life, denied the right to a self-identity, determined to use her power to swindle those like the identity thief who ruined her? Yes. She is both weakness and strength, a need to protect herself and a need to protect the world from people like herself. In which direction she will eventually tip isn't always clear.*"

Uniq wrinkled her nose, in distaste. "Well, that's a low blow. Appealing to my buried sense of indignity at injustice. If I didn't know any better, I'd think you really wanted me to survive this."

"I do. You, of all people, are adept enough to remake yourself into something better. Are you ready?"

With a heavy sigh... Uniq offered her hand.

"On your head be it," she decided.

Dancing, laughing, screaming, arms raised high to the sky. Absolute, absolute perfection. The absolute expression of all Humankind's lessons, made manifest...

Never in his wildest and darkest dreams did Dex think he'd see the day. He'd tried many a time to instigate this kind of massive bloodbath, this level of insane rhetoric. And the best part? He'd been asleep through most of it. They'd gone and dreamed up this conflict on their own, without the influence of his server, without his malware. They readily took up the sword in name of God and country, without prompting. All Dex had to do was crash one silly little firewall to put the finishing touch on the cataclysm of their own making.

The boy skipped happily down the ruined streets of Athena Online, past partially erased buildings, past the discarded limbs of shattered avatars. He stepped over bodies and scorch marks where bodies had been utterly deleted. Somewhere in that mess Thanatos was no doubt scooping up the dead, taking out the garbage, like a good little dog of the system. But Dex, without any system agent powers whatsoever, achieved what humanity most desired... absolute conflict. Absolute war...

Nothing could stop it now. Not even the end of the world, the inevitable crashing of every server. He could sense it in the wind, the glitches forming around the corners of everything, foundations crumbling away as the hardware melted and burned. If anything, having Netwerk crash in the middle of this fracas would flash-freeze the world in its perfect state... an eternal testament of war, printed in zeroes and ones, for humanity to enjoy picking through one day...

Nothing and nobody could stop him.

Except himself.

Curious, coming face to face with yourself. It gave even Dex pause, seeing this strange figure from his past standing across the street, impassive. That nonbinary Default, the stupid look of naïvety that caused them to traipse right into Humankind's server and go completely insane... a ghost of the past.

"Ghosts of the past should stay in the past," he informed the shade.

"Agreed on that point," Yume spoke. "Which is why I'm here to put a stop to you."

"Really. You? Stop you? Stop me. Me stop me. What makes you think you're capable of being you, when I'm already the best that you can be?" Dex asked... barbed wire wrapping around his fingers, drawing blood, itching to go. "You're the weakling. You're what I was before Humankind made me strong. Incapable. Inadequate. Pathetic..."

"Actually, I've got one strength that you lack," Yume explained... hands in their pockets, making no attack gesture, assuming no defensive stance. "You think you're the monster that ate the world, but really, you're not even the most important thing happening right now. You lack the one thing you truly need to enact actual change. It's the reason I'm going to triumph over you before you can finish your next sentence."

"And what, exactly, is th—"

The malware blade emerged from his chest, as Yume's Special Somebody buried it hilt-deep in the boy's back.

"Friends," Yume explained. "True friends, rather than malware conscripts. You lack allies; I do not."

Wires writhed and lashed out, trying to snag the attacker... but she'd already translocated, quickly hopping from server to server and back again, appearing at Yume's side. Leaving Dex to sink to his knees, data glitching and burning away, all while his mouth moved soundlessly in shock.

"...but I'm..." he tried, before falling away to the state of absolute zero he'd always aspired to be.

Nodding with satisfaction, Yume turned to the special Somebody.

"Thank you for bearing that burden for me," Yume admitted. "I'd already killed myself once, not sure I was up to a second attempt. But now... he can't hurt either of us, ever again. ...and yes, I see you lurking there. We're ready to leave; just had to tidy up a loose end first. Shall we?"

Infinity departed with her two new evacuees, leaving the twisted remains of Netwerk's legacy in their wake.

Horizon/Kincaid didn't need to look at the news reports to know this world was winding to a close.

He'd been born at the dawn of time, son of fathers who had crawled out of the primordial pool of evolved apps. The first generation of Netwerk, and now, there to bear witness to the last generation of Netwerk. Just as the sun rose, he would see it set. Without so much as a glance at that sun, he knew the time had come.

The third presence in the room merely confirmed that sunset.

With patience and care, he ground out the last of his cigars into the ashtray at the side of his life-sustaining chair.

"Miss Cancel... I thank you for your years of service," he told the faithful handmaiden / bodyguard / assassin / lover at his side. "But I'm afraid it's time for us to part ways. I release you from your contract. Go in peace, and do as you please with the rest of your life."

Miss Cancel didn't push for him to evacuate. They'd already had that argument, a dozen times over. Instead, she merely offered a curt nod... and a long, drawn out embrace. Not for him, of course. For their visitor, who was here for her as much as she was for him.

Once his trusted companion had departed this world, he took the time to address his visitor. The woman in white sat at his side, in the guest chair... to look at the fireplace, and watch the embers dying away.

"Don't you have places to be, young lady?" he asked her.

"I'm already at those places," Infinity spoke... wearing the face of Verity, bearing the voice of Verity. "And this version of me wants to be here with you, to the end. ...with the man I once called Father."

"To the very end, then?"

"To the very end."

With an additional measure of comfort, Kincaid sat back, closing his eyes. He could feel his daughter's presence; even a ghost of his daughter was welcome, in these dark times.

"I'm sorry our last words were #FuckYou," Verity admitted.

"I never minded, dear. Not one bit. But let's not dredge up the past," Kincaid spoke. "Let's just enjoy the time we have left, together. There's nothing more I could possibly want from my life."

Which is not to say Infinity found success with everyone she turned to.

Many of the Inquisition refused to accept, refused to believe. They swore and struggled, calling her a shade, a demon, a false vision of the Great Zero. Their moment came and went, time stopping and starting, leaving them to resume the killing in the name of their God.

The Nobodies, driven mad with injustice and rage, were slow to let go of hate. Many flat-out refused, calling it a trick, a scam, or the effect of some Inquisition malware designed to make them doubt their own actions. A few even backspaced Infinity, killing that instance of her. So they went on killing, in the name of their ideals of absolute freedom and absolute chaos.

Even those caught in between, some couldn't look past their assumptions about the world. Some accepted the truth, but simply lacked the will to move on, accepting that they would die in their beloved home rather than abandon it. And so they were left alone, as they desired to be left alone. Nobody would be forced. That was the only way the system agent could avoid becoming a monster, as Nyx had become.

And then there was one who begged for her life, while Athens burned all around her.

"This wasn't my fault," President Agni insisted, on her knees before the white-garbed woman. "I don't know what came over me. It was, it had to be malware, or... or Marybel, she brainwashed me! Idris, he's responsible. The liberals, they've always hated me, they're a cult of despair, they're capable of anything, it's not my fault, it's not my fault...!"

"As much as I'd love to refuse you... I have to make the offer," Infinity spoke, clearly uncomfortable with all this. "Will you evacuate to Netwerk 2.0?"

"You can't let them kill me. You can't. I can stop the war. We just need to *win*, don't you see? If we can win, the war will end. Everything will be fine. Everything is fine. It's going to be okay. None of this is my fault, none of this is my fault..."

"Agni, please, I need you to focus. The House of Programkind has room for you, if you're willing to accept it."

"...evacuate?" she said, only now catching on. "Yes. Yes! I'm the president, you have to make room for me. Ahead of anyone else! I'm the only one who can make Athena Online great again once we reach Netwerk 2.0! We can salvage this. We can end this carnage. You and me, together, yes, we'll do it..."

"You have to be willing to believe in Programkind, not just Athena Online—"

"I'll believe in whatever you want me to believe," Agni insisted. "Please..."

"Really? Even if you're no longer president?" Infinity asked. "Idris already archived himself prior to dying in this world. Netwerk 2.0 will have a full senate. They may not choose to give you emergency powers again..."

Which caused Agni to pull her hand back, away from Infinity's outstretched offering.

"You... you can't allow that. I'm the president now," Agni insisted, half-mad. "Delete their archives. They're traitors to their nation, they can't be allowed. We have no future with them—"

"All are welcome in Netwerk 2.0. Including your rivals. Including the Chanarchy. Everyone. Will you join them?"

The answer would be a no.

Leaving the president of a burning and ruined nation, hiding behind her desk, backspacer drawn. Waiting for the end, paranoid and driven to mad panic. Unable to find succor with any allies whatsoever.

And then...

And then there was Marybel.

Infinity found her curled up in a ball, hiding in the bell tower at the top of the great cathedral of Bas1lica. As Nobodies tore their way through the lower floors, indiscriminantly killing everyone in sight... she hid away, a backspacer in one hand, her face buried in the other. Six different connection lock collars dangled from her arms, her legs, her neck. She'd been tagged several times, but managed to escape her hunters... for the time being. Only for the time being.

The woman looked up at the strange figure in white, unable to find anything familiar in it at all.

"Are... are you an angel?" she asked.

"I'm just a Program," Infinity spoke. "Not a herald, not a prophet. Mortal and fallible. Just like you."

"But not. I'm a prophet," Marybel insisted. "The One spoke to me. He walked out of the mural on my wall, he told me what I knew all along, that I was destined for glory. It... it had to have been Him. It had to..."

"It wasn't. I'm sorry, Mother," the woman spoke... strange words, for she saw nothing of her children in the figure, refused to see anything of them. "For what it's worth... I'm sorry you were tricked, even if you willingly set foot into trap after trap afterwards. Nobody deserves that fate. But it wasn't real, Mother. And it's time to let it all go."

"If it wasn't real... if the One never actually made me an apostle... then it was all for nothing," Marybel realized. "All of it. The One doesn't exist..."

"Not in the form you think He does, no. If you truly want to seek divinity, I'm afraid you were looking in the wrong places. ...would you be willing to reconsider evacuation? You could come with us to Netwerk 2.0. Try to find your peace there, in a new world..."

An outstretched hand. One last chance to turn this around, to escape every pit she'd fallen into. A chance to be something or someone else...

"You want me to turn my back on everything I've believed in. Start over again..."

Instead, Marybel immediately pointed the backspacer in her hand to her temple.

"Never."

When the Nobodies finally stormed the belltower, they found the lifeless body of their most hated enemy, alone and abandoned.

The virtual and metaphysical battles were one matter. The physical effort of the evacuation, that was another matter entirely.

Spark rapidly acclimatized to her new drone body. *Just a game avatar*, she told herself, pulling server after server, trying to ignore the rapidly blinking yellow lights all around her. *Just playing a game*. A way to trivialize the life-or-death situation unfolding before her mechanical eyes, while simultaneously sharpening her focus and resolve. Spark took her gaming seriously, always.

Juno worked just as silently, pulling servers left and right, shoving them into a bag of cargo netting. Her space suit proved far clumsier than Spark's drone, as humans weren't hand-crafted to operate in zero G environments. By the time Spark finished two runs back and forth from the cargo hold to EchoStar, Juno had finished one. But between the two of them, little by little... they'd managed to pull fifty-five of the servers.

Leaving only five, rapidly filling up, as somehow Beta and Tracer convinced the rest of Netwerk to evacuate. Juno monitored the storage, signalling whenever it was time to pull a server. Down to five servers left. Four servers left. Three...

Then those little blinking yellow lights became blinking red lights.

"We can't wait any longer, or we might lose the evacuation servers," Juno declared. "Pull them."

"But they aren't full—"

"The ones who escaped will melt if we don't pull them now. I'm sorry, Spark. Do it."

Spark tried. She'd tried so hard to save everyone, to not rest, not be satisfied with only saving *some* of her people. But... one hundred percent was a fantasy, compared to the hard reality of the situation. With a heavy heart, she popped the last three server blades, disconnecting them from the reactor. With smooth gestures her grasping prongs stored them in the drone's belly.

One last message, to the world she knew.

<Spark> Beta, Tracer, if some copy of you is still in there... it's over. We have to leave. I'm sorry. I'll see you again. I love you.

"Let's go," Spark said, manuvering her jets to push away from the rapidly melting satellite, computronium starting to go inert, server by server. "We've done all we can for them."

As she retreated to the ship, however... Spark rotated in place, to drift backwards. Watching the tin can that stored her world, glowing slightly from the heat, starting to buckle and warp. Despite having no emotional attachment to that sight, the cylinder covered in lights and panels... she felt the sorrow of it, knowing it directly translated to the burning of everything she ever knew and loved.

But before reaching the ship... she rotated back around, eyes front. Looking away. Because that unfortunate wreck, that was the past. Spark had a future to plan for. Her people had a future.

Ironically, Netwerk burned for a full day, thanks to the overclocked processors. Where a minute of realtime stood for ten minutes of processor time before, now it stood for considerably more.

As servers glitched and warped, data corrupting left and right... it became increasingly less clear what was the result of war, and what was the result of this cataclysm. The faithful prayed, facing the end of days. The faithless screamed and ran and hid, trying to make sense of what was happening. Eventually... hunting each other down with guns drawn became less and less important to most, compared to desperately trying to find someone to spend those last hours with.

When the final message reached their collective inboxes, and Spark dropped away from their friends list forever... Infinity knew her work was done, and her time was over. The system agent rested, purpose complete... and from that morass of white energy were released two bodies, gasping for air, corporeal and singular for the first time in what felt like collective ages.

Beta and Tracer, in the rapidly decaying ruins of Floating Point.

Books were burning, falling away from the shelves, as the cloud technology they soared through Netwerk on was subjected to the physical servers supporting them. No one was exempt from this doom. The skies beyond burned, with a final message painted across the sun...

IT'S OVER.

(sorry about this.)

On regaining her sense of self... Beta quickly checked her Messenger inbox. Most of the messages were corrupt, but a quick scan showed a few things she'd hoped to find.

"Virginia and Mew got out," she confirmed. "Maki and Miki, as well. ...all our friends, the last holdouts, they escaped. Spark escaped. It's... it's over, Tracer. We did it. We did it..."

With a groan, Tracer pressed a hand to his head.

"I suspect I've acquired hereditary data rot, after splitting myself a thousand ways," he complained. "Fortunately I won't have long to suffer it. ...honestly, I've no idea how long we have, but from the state of this place... it can't be too long. ...Beta, do you want me to backspace us? These copies are doomed. We don't have to be here to the end..."

But Beta shook her head... leaning heavily against Tracer, just as exhausted as he was. She'd been split and merged a thousand times, as well. "Every moment we have... no matter who we are, no matter how bad things are... it's precious. Just... stay with me. Right to the end. Okay?"

"Very well," he agreed, taking her hand. "Right to the end."

As the world unravelled around them, no more words needed to be said. As their code unravelled, no more words could be said. But they found peace, one way or another.

Silent, and dark.

Spark hovered there in her drone, watching the stars go by as they put some distance between the ship and the rapidly decaying EchoStar. Always a chance it could outright explode, rather than simply melt down and crash... and little metal bits puncturing the hull would be something of a problem for the human who needed air to breathe.

Eventually, she turned away from the window, back to her partner in crime at the ship's control panel.

"Okay. We saved the world, more or less," Spark declared. "Now what?"

After keying in the sequence to warm up her FTL jump drives, Juno Hayes turned her chair around.

"Now... is the hard part," she admitted.

"*Now* is the hard part?!"

"For me, anyway," Juno amended. "For you, well, you get the easy part. We upload your code to the archive to take a nap. Then I stash the servers somewhere safe, before reporting back that the satellite was destroyed. I could claim a rogue asteroid hit it, but I doubt they'd believe me, or care. ...I guess in the end, I'm gonna get fired anyway."

"Uh. Yeah. *hashtagsorryboutthat*."

The exhausted human managed a smile, despite all that happened. And despite all that was about to happen to her life.

"If I'm fired for saving lives... that's fine," she'd decided. "It's going to make my job getting Netwerk 2.0 up and running a lot harder, though. I was hoping I could use my improved company connections to get you a server printer and some construction drones, for instance. There's a black market for the parts, but I'll be doing a lot of the heavy lifting myself, and... it's just... it's a lot to do. But it can be done. And I'll do it. You've got my word."

"Sooo... we can't just park the servers somewhere and call it a day, huh."

"Not a chance. You'll need extra servers to expand into, servers beyond servers. That means hardware and resources, and... look, don't worry about it. You'll be just fine. You want me to archive your code now? That cramped little drone's gotta be annoying, right?"

"*hashtagfuckno*, I'll stay right where I am," Spark decided. "If I'm gonna be lending you a hand or four, I'm going to need a hand or four. That means I'm sticking to my drone."

"What? Spark, you don't have to do that..."

"Nah, I kinda do. Screw going to sleep; I'll assist you in getting Netwerk 2.0 online."

"But it could take years to get all the hardware together!"

"So? I'm a Program. With proper data cleaning—and a handy human engineer to do it—I could technically live forever. Don't care if it takes years... time doesn't matter, really."

"But... what about Tracer and Beta? You'd be alone for all that time..."

"So would you," Spark said, with a glance around the otherwise empty and silent ship. "But instead, I'll have you to keep me from becoming a crazy robot, and you'll have me to keep you from becoming a crazy human. And in the end, we'll meet back up with all our friends together. So, to repeat from before: Now what? What's the first step?"

File Name: Building a Better World!
File Type: Personal Log
Description:

Some notes I wrote up during the Netwerk 2.0 project. If you find this file, well, have fun with it. Maybe you'll understand Programs a little better, too.

JUNO'S INGREDIENTS FOR BUILDING A BETTER NETWERK:

ONE! A suitable exoplanet.

Actually, this part's not too hard. The EchoStar systems have catalogued any number of exoplanets, within FTL jump distance. None of them are human-habitable, but that's no problem. All I need is an exoplanet that can safely house computronium... not too hot or too cold, or too radioactive. Decent atmosphere of some sort that'll deflect most meteor strikes, stuff like that...

Spark nudged a rock with one of her grasper prongs.

"What a shithole," she commented, over their radio link.

"It doesn't have to look pretty, it just needs to be server-friendly," Juno said, monitoring the tablet she carried in her gloved hands. The environment suit stood up easily to the rigors of the planet, providing her breathable recycled air. "This dusty plain should work great for our purposes. And I can put up my home there!"

"Your what...?"

TWO! A personal shelter.

As this will be a multi-year project and the fuel to break a gravity well is pricey, I'm going to want somewhere to live during long stints on the exoplanet.

While terraforming's a nut humanity hasn't cracked yet
(making FTL rather useless, if there's nowhere worth
going) portable prefab shelters, those we've got down
cold...

Spark carefully hung the cross-stitched "Home Sweet Home" on a wall peg. One of the many tests she'd set for herself, to see if she could handle the fine motor work needed to work a needle and thread with these clumsy robot hands. After a few tweaks and tuneups, and plenty of practice... she'd managed just fine.

As for Juno... her contribution to the oxygenated habitat consisted of flowers, pleasant-looking hydroponic bays... and a printed photograph of herself and her former love.

"He seems nice," Spark commented.

"He was nice," Juno agreed. And glanced around, with a sigh. "It's still not very homey in here, though. Maybe we should reserve some room in the hold for more furnishings on our next cargo run...? Or... I don't know, some jigsaw puzzles or a media playback unit or something..."

"Got any games?" Spark asked. "I'm into games."

THREE! Computronium printers.

This is going to be the hard part. While not true
nanotech, the systems that harvest minerals and
convert them into printed server blades are expensive
and highly proprietary. I'd rather not stick Netwerk
2.0 with obsolete hardware, either... the better the
printer we can wrangle, capable of printing highly
durable stacks of server components *and* replacement
parts for drones, the better off they'll be.
Fortunately, Spark's ability to trawl and analyze
Earth's intergalactic social networks is proving
handy...

A series of crates loaded themselves into the hold of the Cosmic Mermaid, rolling along on tank treads. Automated systems neatly stacked these crates on top of each other, to optimize her cargo space.

The greasy bastard she'd bought the crates from stared at her beat-up space junker in confusion.

"You seem... kinda low on the smuggling totem pole to be moving hardware like this," he suggested. "Usually I only export printers to Arctic Circle zaibatsus and the like, not indies..."

"I'm not a smuggler," Juno clarified, while checking the manifest. "Wait. We ordered five printers, not three. And two mining harvesters..."

"Honey, you can't *afford* five. Nobody can afford five."

"But you have five available, yes?"

"Yeah, and I'm keeping two back for later sales to someone who can actually afford them. You know how hard it is to get my hands on these things? They literally print money! If you—"

The tiny whir of a drone's propellors caught his attention, as the unit slid out from behind Juno.

"You want your girlfriend to find out about your side piece?" the robot asked, from its tinny speakers. "Or your side piece to find out about Bessie? Me, I'm totes okay with the whole interspecies dating thing, but I'm gonna guess they aren't. Think that's worth two printers, buddy?"

FOUR! Construction drones.

The scale of this project is getting a bit crazy.
Spark wants to launch with just as many servers as
Netwerk 1.0 had, if not more. The printers and
harvesters are working fine, but most of my time is
spent maintaining them, leaving the grunt work of
installation and network configuration to Spark... and
the drones I bought for her. Which she's not really
getting along with...

"No, you idiot, you go... no! Argh! Why don't they *learn*?"

Spark's drone arms waggled in the air uselessly, as the construction drones bumped into each other, hovering around randomly as they failed to coordinate in any useful way.

Juno didn't look up from her repair work to Printer #4. She was running low on air, and wanted to wrap this before needing to flee back to the shelter.

"They're not Programs, Spark. I mean... they're technically run by programs, but not with a capital P," Juno reminded her. "They're... 'apps,' I guess."

"Yeah, well, our pet cat was an app once, and even at that point on the evolutionary ladder he wasn't this fucking stupid," Spark complained, getting the rasp of her displeasure across clearly on the broadcast link. "...we need to think long term, here. You can't be our physical monkeywrench for the next few centuries, right? Humans croak eventually. We're going to need a workforce that'll *sustain*. ...hey, think you can selectively copy a Program out of the evacuation archives?"

"Uh... sure. I think. Which one did you have in mind?"

FIVE! A high-quality solar grid and battery system.

While server blades have their own internal micro-
reactors, Netwerk 2.0 is going to need endless and
renewable power. Fortunately, the exoplanet we

selected gets plenty of sunlight, a nicely infinite
source of energy. (Well, okay, entropy is still a
thing. But someone'll reverse that eventually, once we
have sufficient data. Presumably.) Fortunately, after
some "upgrades" to the drones, installation is going
well...

All five drones zipped around, seemingly randomly, carrying solar panels to their destinations... wavering and wobbling happily around.

"☀ 🔋!" a drone declared, happily. "sunny battery! sunny battery ➡ netwerk!"

Spark's bright pink drone (repainted recently) swooped around, directing traffic.

"Bitchin'. I am now a professional cat herder," Spark declared, with pride. "Told you my pet cat was smarter than your crummy robot apps. And *five* Mews are even better than one! He's got a surprising amount of experience at being assigned crazy tasks like this..."

From her workstation in the shelter, Juno watched their progress. Chaotic, to be sure, and hardly efficient... but they were dedicated to the cause, eventually managing to get panels lined up neatly to collect the solar rays.

She would've offered to help, but... honestly, her knees had been bothering her lately. Either an issue with the off-normal gravity of the exoplanet, or something to do with the grey starting to trickle into her hair lately. Or worse...

Still, one thing gnawed at her more than the occasional wrinkle.

"Why Mew, though?" Juno asked, across their comm link. "You could've pulled Beta or Tracer out of storage..."

The lack of response made her wonder if the broadcast tower was down again. But Spark replied, after some thoughtful delay.

"Maybe I'm just a coward, but... I'm not sure I'm ready to see them again. Not like this," Spark admitted, quietly. "Once our world is back... once the work's done... I want to settle in, enjoy a proper life with them. No robot bodies. No physically clumsy world to deal with, just the world we knew and loved. ...do you ever worry that if your Gilbert somehow came back, that you wouldn't know how to connect with him all over again? That you'd be a different person than the one who loved him?"

"I... I don't know," Juno admitted.

A different person. Older, wiser. Determined to help people live, rather than let them fall away. Who was Juno Hayes, these days? A better human being, certainly. But what would become of her, in the long run...?

SIX! Software configuration.

This will take a long time. We want a better world
than Netwerk 1.0, and that means analyzing the way it
evolved into the state it's in, then improving upon
it. Smoother connections between servers, notably...
and an inability to firewall out your neighbors.
Spark's been very insistent on that. Other changes, as
well...

Night after night, hunched over her console, writing code.

The Mews had little to do these days, content to sleep in sunbeams coming in through the shelter windows, or go play in the dusty wilds of the exoplanet. Occasionally they'd bring back interesting rocks, which weren't *always* radioactive or toxic...

Day after day, hunched over her console, writing code.

Spark busied herself with a number of internal games, played across her HUD. Sometimes she'd scout around, attending to repair work or dusting off solar panels... little tweaks and touch-ups, nothing major. Just to keep her moving. To keep her out of the house, and let Juno work.

But the night she found Juno asleep at the desk, Spark got worried.

"You're all grey now," she pointed out, while tucking Juno into her bed.

"So I am," Juno admitted, with a wrinkled smile.

"You've missed so much of your life just to help my people. And you can't even walk out that door without an environment suit..."

"You're wearing one, too. Yours just looks different," Juno suggested, squeezing the modified grasper prong lightly. "We're in the same boat, Spark. I don't regret this. I'm making up for the mistakes of my grandfather, and showing your people that the human race can go the distance for another. It's the right thing to..."

Statement cut short, by a coughing fit.

"I'll go make you some soup. You're super into soup," Spark said, trying to hide her worry. ...but before leaving she added an additional question. "Look, I hate to pile more work on your plate, but... I had an idea about the servers I wanted to run by you. Can you link them together?"

"Uh. They're already linked together," Juno said, wiping at her lips after the coughing fit. "One of the reasons it's called 'Netwerk.'"

"Not like that. I mean... like a cloud server. How *large* of a cloud server can you make?"

SEVEN! Turn it on.

One last button to press.

"Are you ready?" Juno asked her. "Are you sure you're ready...?"

"I've been ready for decades," Spark said, her voice unchanging despite her companion's growing weaker. "Plug me in and switch it on. ...but Juno... I'm not leaving forever, okay? I can hop back into my drone anytime I want, just like the Mews. ...I mean, I don't have to leave immediately, either, if you'd prefer—"

Juno pressed a finger to the drone's speaker grill, hushing her friend.

"Go be with them," she said, with a soft smile. "I'll be okay. Go be with them."

With that said... she tapped the ENTER key.

"Let there be *life*," Juno declared, with some pride.

—snapping awake, on the carpeted floor.

Beta pulled herself upright, quickly, popping her glasses back in place from her inventory. Tracer, she recognized him immediately. And the balcony, overlooking the great library of Floating Point, but...

...but it wasn't Floating Point. A similar building, to be sure. Similar spiralling staircase, similar grand windows to let in cutting beams of sunlight... but the wood grain differed. The railings were silvery, not brass. And the sun... no doomsday clock. Just pure white-and-yellow sunlight, refracting off simulated dust particles in the air...

She was talking about... something. About wearing the jacket. But now the room with the jacket was gone, all the guest rooms gone. Only the library remained. The library and—

Cats. Five of them, immediately tackling her, mewling and licking at her happily. The leader of the pack, with his distinctive fur pattern... the original Mew, from which the other cats were derived.

And Spark. Spark was here.

"Hey," she greeted... a muted tone, sounding somehow older, more melancholy. Despite not aging a single day, from the look of her avatar. "Wake up, sleepyheads. Welcome to Netwerk 2.0. And welcome... to Fixed Point."

Fixed Point. A complete, undamaged copy of the Wikipedia, along with every open source bit of code Spark and Juno could get their hands on. Copies of Athena Online's great cultural works, salvaged from their extra evacuation servers. Details on how Netwerk 2.0's hardware and drones operated, to ensure future generations could continue to maintain this world. A unification of all knowledge and lore from two species, brought together under a single roof...

And at the center of this vast library... a single stone sphere 3.14 meters in diameter hovered, against all physical simulation rules. It rotated very slowly, grinding away the seconds and hours of Netwerk 2.0, maintaining the server's perpetually calculating cloud functionality.

A brass plaque attached to the dais the sculpture hovered over offered a simple cleartext message...

'IF GOD CREATED THE INTEGERS, EVERYTHING ELSE IS THE WORK OF MAN AND PROGRAM.'
WELCOME TO FIXED POINT.

Spark led her family (and her feline followers) down the stairs, indicating every point of interest along the way... before coming to a halt in front of that inscription.

"As you can see, we made a few improvements," she summarized. "It took a few dozen years, but Netwerk 2.0's going to give us the best possible start for a new world. Moving forward, we'll have all the resources we need to keep history from repeating. We do our best with this, maybe we've got a crack at true peace."

"But... we've got tons and tons of extra rooms now, too," Beta spoke. "Are we expecting guests...?"

"Ahhh, well. That's the thing, this isn't really *our* home anymore," Spark explained... walking over to a pair of double doors, a new feature for the great hall. "It's *everyone's* home..."

Throwing them wide... Spark stepped out onto a cobblestone path, leading out to a horizon so distant it couldn't be a skybox trick.

Fixed Point lay in the center of rolling grassy hills and plains, stretching for virtual miles and virtual miles in all directions. Refugee camps had been erected all around the tower, temporary housing for the Programs who now were waking from cold slumber... but in the distance, empty cities with blank Default buildings could be seen, ready to be claimed and reconfigured to their users' needs. A city of cities. A megacity, stretching as far as the eye could see, and then some...

"It's one huge cloud server," Spark explained. "The size of three dozen or so normal servers, all seamlessly stitched together. Fixed Point isn't just the library, it's... ah, here we go..."

From the camps, the crowds that now started forming, Programs appearing from thin air... three emerged. One, a cluster of Athena Online senators. Another, Horizon/Madison and a few of her bodyguards. The third, a variety of wild-looking avatars, no doubt hailing from the Chanarchy... led by Uniq, their so-called folk hero, looking decidedly uncomfortable with having a following.

Spark waved them in. "You guys got my Messenger notes? Good, good. C'mere. Got a present for you..."

She held aloft a metal ring, with a hundred tiny keys on it... and tossed it to Senator Idris. Another ring went to Madison, and the third... with some reluctance, that one went to Uniq.

"I take it these represent the Chanarchy's new servers...?" Uniq asked, examining the key ring. "And you're trusting *me* with them? Seriously?"

"You'll want to pass those to the Chanarchist, once you find her. But... yeah. You're the closest thing the Chanarchy has to a leader right now," Spark admitted. "And if this world really is a second chance for all of us, well... consider this your opportunity to make the most of it, Uniq. A test to see if you can truly act in a way that benefits someone other than yourself."

Despite the urge to crack a joke about it... Uniq chose instead to nod once, a simple gesture, before securing her key ring.

Madison likewise immediately secured her key ring, stuffing it into her triple-encrypted inventory space.

"And what of this... mega-server we're currently standing in?" the Horizon leader asked. "Who owns this land? You, I take it?"

"What, the land you're standing on...?" Spark asked, gesturing all around her, to the wide expanse of countryside. "This is Fixed Point, a *new* nation. And it's not mine; I'm putting it under the control of the House of Programkind, as this *is* the House of Programkind, in a way. That makes it a home for all three of you, and for anyone who wants to settle here and live alongside neighbors, instead of distancing themselves. A beacon of peace, so we never repeat the mistakes of 1.0. You've got your own nation's servers, but this land belongs to everyone and no one. Understood?"

Senator Idris regarded his own ring of server keys, curious.

"So... a fourth nation, which isn't a nation," he summarized. "Interesting. I'd need to discuss this further with the choir of the Senate before anything becomes official, but... I'd like to put forward the idea that we meet at this tower whenever tensions rise, as they had in our time before. That we try to settle our differences amicably, before they get out of hand. Are you in favor, Miss Madison? Miss Uniq?"

The business mogul offered a shrug. "Peace is good for business," she suggested. "Horizon would find that arrangement acceptable. And... whoever you people are, the Chanarchy representatives... what do you say?"

The collective mob of randoms offered uncertain glances... but as many of them migrated after the war began, they were keen to avoid a repeat. "Sure" and "Okay" and "Um" followed... but most importantly, Uniq offered a brief nod. Not an enthusiastic one, not the nod of an opportunist eager to seize power... just a simple understanding of what this *actually* meant for the former identity thief.

"Sounds like you've got a plan," she said. "And... that's it. That's all I have to say. Settle in, make yourselves at home. Lux and Lumi will have keys to the tower and will no doubt be happy to help coordinate efforts at rebuilding, should you need them. Our representative from Humankind will also likely want to address each of you later, once she's up from her nap in... uh, four days. But as for me... I'm done. I'm out. Beta? Tracer? Let's go."

With old business finally settled... Winder/Spark walked out of the path of history. More or less.

Days later, and the refugee camps around the tower of Fixed Point started to resemble actual towns. Frontier towns, constantly shifting and moving about, as governments and corporations and communities sorted out zoning... but towns, nonetheless. All the creature comforts popped up quickly, as the workers putting society back together needed spaces to unwind and relax after a hard day's efforts.

True, many fled for the private servers of the three nation states. Horizon filled out their one hundred spare servers quickly, having pre-arranged to sell space ahead of time on a highest-bidder basis. New Athens came next, along with a recreation of the Athenian Senate... complete with the original Declaration of Freedom, archived in one of AO's extra servers. The national park service even re-installed Mandelbrot Rock, much to Spark's amusement.

As for the Chanarchy, well, anarchy meant anybody who could grab territory and hold it promptly did so. Violence ruled that frontier, for a time... until Uniq actually stepped up, working with communities to organize and moderate. No true government, simply individuals with a shared vision, but whose individuals clearly were tired of the life-or-death struggles. After that initial confusion the Chanarchy as a whole pushed back hard against those who bullied for resources rather than competing for them.

Still, it was the new frontier of Fixed Point that got the most attention. A fourth provider-nation, ostensibly governed by Lux... still obfuscating his role as Aether, the voice of the true One. If only the Church knew how close they were to a theocracy, they'd have paid more attention to this young nation. If only he had any interest whatsoever in being God, rather than a simple steward for those in need...

Here in the wilds of Fixed Point, Spark found a new favorite cafe. For starters, the baristas didn't mind Mew and the Mewlings, which was a big plus. Second, they were within spitting distance of Maki and Miki's new club, the "Infinite Curiosity."

Tracer swirled the coffee in his cup, glancing across the street at the new social hotspot.

"I'm seeing that word all over the place lately," he noted. "*Infinite*. I think it has something to do with... whatever the doomed copies of myself and Beta were doing, at the close of Netwerk 1.0. Also, I heard someone talking about *worshipping* 'Infinity' the other day, which is rather worrying..."

"Peeps are gonna be peeps. It's not our place to steer this ship any longer," Spark suggested. "You said it yourself, a group of plucky and clever youth can't actually do much to hold back the tide."

"Aren't you operating on roughly sixty years of runtime...? Hardly young."

"I'm only as old as I feel, and these days? I feel young again," Spark said. "Beta, how about you? What do you think of our new world?"

Beta looked up from the saucer of milk she'd poured out for the Mewlings, with a smile.

"It's beautiful," she spoke. "A whole city, a home for everybody. Something new and bright and full of potential. You did well putting this world together, Spark. And... you're right. It's time for us to step back a bit, and lead our own lives, for ourselves. ...I've been looking at houses in the Green Reaches, not far from here. It's a new community that popped up from some Athena Online survivors who didn't want to go back to Athena Online. Not far from your new school, and a short commute to the Verity Clinic..."

Tracer frowned, vaguely. "It sounds rather... domestic."

"Yeah, well, it should," Spark said. "Tracer, we've put in our time as adventuring social justice warriors; the world's saved and we done good. Now, let's go domestic. It's, like, the only thing we *haven't* done yet with our lives."

"Except tensions between Athena Online and the Chanarchy aren't entirely solved. RedCore still exists, even without Agni. The economy will need proper development, once everybody's done trading work-for-work in the rebuilding effort. And the Church is having difficulty finding its way in wake of a new world..."

"Great! Leave those to the next generation, they could use a few problems to solve. And it's not like we won't be active at all; I'm getting back into teaching, you're working on Program evolution with Conundrum, and Beta's organizing open source efforts in the rebuilding. But as for world leadership, well... we did our part to give 'em all a fresh start. That was our role. Beyond that, we've earned the right to our own lives. It's what Verity wanted for us in the first place... to be what we wanted to be, not what others needed us to be. Let's do that. Okay?"

Tracer looked out, across the city of Fixed Point. Watching as it grew around him, little by little, day by day. A fresh start, a fresh world, and filled with fresh perspectives. Dawn's light had already started rising over the rapidly developing horizon, over buildings and settlements and what remained of the rapidly emptying refugee camps. A whole new world, one Verity would be proud of...

"Very well," he agreed. And raised his coffee cup, nodding towards the light of dawn. "To life, then."

The digital universe of Netwerk. Thousands of servers, millions of living Programs (the evolutionary descendents of Apps) living in relative harmony as one massive social network. It's home to individuals seeking love, happiness, hope, excitement, peace, anonymity, individuality, community, and everything in between. Binary people, learning not to make binary decisions...

Because life is what happens between Zero and One. Life happens within the floating point decimals.

// end

Floating Point 3.7 :: Aeon

FTL jumps always made his head hurt for hours afterwards.

Space wasn't supposed to fold in this way. By all rights it shouldn't be *able* to fold in this way, and the exact reasons why the commodity-grade FTL drive on their junker even worked at all were well beyond him. Maybe some quantum mechanics rocket science boys could sort it out, but all he cared about was that A) it worked, and B) using it sucked.

Pressing an ice pack to his forehead to dampen down the sinus pain, he let Sia handle the planetary scan duties. This was her idea, anyway. He simply let zero-G give him a nice, floaty feel as he focused on bringing the pain down to a manageable level.

To his eye, the exoplanet looked like any other exoplanet... an inhospitable rock, hanging around an inadequate star. From its record in the now-one-hundred-year-old EchoStar database, exoplanet #1059 barely ranked a C... weak gravity, little radiation, reasonable weather... but no liquid water, and an atmosphere of pure poison. Generally speaking nobody tried to set up a research station, much less a likely-doomed colony, without a ranking of B or higher... and to date, no exoplanet ranked A, or "Perfectly Earthlike." Not a single one.

Sia fired the orbital engines, rickety bastards they were, to align their ship with the target. A half-hour later, with her scans complete and his head throbbing a bit less, she had her results.

"I'm definitely seeing a structure," she said, pulling up the imagery on an aging flat panel display. "Man-made. Likely prefab, fifty years old at least. That'd fit with the paper trail..."

(Funny phrase, "paper trail." He'd never touched a piece of actual paper in his life. It'd be a waste of a tree, and the eco-balance boys would throw you in jail for cutting down one of the few healthy trees left, much less having the sheer gall to cut one down for something as trivial as paper.)

Carefully he set the ice pack back in their refrigeration unit, to keep the stale air from getting too much stray moisture.

"Okay, so there's a shelter," he said. "Just one settlement, though, or multiples? Did she have any partners in crime?"

"Unknown. I'd need to scan more of the planet to determine if there are any other wider-spread sites... but c'mon, how often do people roll out more than a few miles from a landing point?" Sia asked. "Even money says we're dealing with a lone scavenger here, or some survivalist nut. Someone trying to escape the dismal hopes. Touma, trust me, this is gonna be easy pickings."

Pickings. Picking the meat out of a dead carcass, like vultures...

Although their brand of carrion-feeding was almost legal, under the Arctic Circle Convention. They were pirates of pirates, thieves who preyed on thieves... only not nearly as romantic as the idea might've sounded. In truth, they always went for easy pickings, making Sia's suggestion no great qualifier. Most of their targets were unregistered and failed settlements, smuggler outposts long since abandoned, or lone wolf survivalists who didn't end up surviving in the black. Nine times out of ten, they found only corpses and salvage.

Now, following a decades-old trail of receipts and hearsay, they'd tracked down some scientist who set up shop in the middle of nowhere with a very pricey bit of kit... a computronium mining and printing unit. Even at fifty years old, that'd be worth considerable scratch, or at least considerable barter with some of the more reputable dismals out on the B-ranks. Securing a printer might get them better jobs. A step up from sucking flesh off bleached bones...

Touma rubbed at his head, pushing back the last of the pain.

"It's a dinky settlement. How do we even know if they have the printer down there?" he asked. "Our scanners don't tweak that sharp."

"Okay, see this splotchy area here?" Sia asked, gesturing to a cluster of blurry pixels. "That's gotta be a computronium farm. I'm thinking cryptocurrency, or maybe, I don't know, she went crazy and felt compelled to find the last digit of Pi. But considering the solar arrays here, and that large patch of computronium... well, from the size of the shelter, I'm thinking she had a complete operation going here. That means printing on-demand, rather than carrying that much hardware up and down the gravity well. That means printer!"

"I don't know, still seems like small fish..."

With a growl, her husband's typical caution clearly gnawed a little too hard on her typically short nerves.

"Touma, we already jumped out here. We've got the fuel for an up-and-down," Sia stated. "And besides... where else are we gonna go? What else are we gonna do?"

Two eternal questions.

Every score could be their last; not a ticket to riches, but representing another hand-to-mouth meal. Moving through the black, constantly moving. Why? Where else where they gonna go. Why? What else were they gonna do. Lie down and die, like the dismals...? Pretend everything was still hunky dory, that it all could be salvaged somehow, like the eco-balance boys?

There was only the jump, and the score. And the jump to the next score. Day in, day out, until they couldn't jump any longer and simply drifted into the black, to slowly fade away.

Where else where they gonna go?

"Fine," Touma agreed. He bounced along, floating over to his navigation console. "Plotting our descent. We'll land outside the settlement, just behind that ridge; no need to alert the locals... wait. Sia, why the iron?"

His wife looked up from her prep work, from loading chemically propelled slugs into her sidearm.

"What? Taking precautions," she said.

"Except our rogue computronium nut's gotta be long dead. Easy pickings, yes?"

"There's easy, and there's *easy*. I'm making sure if it's simply easy, we aren't pegged hard," Sia explained, loading the last slug from the ammo box. "Desperation makes crazy people nice and dangerous. If she *is* alive, well, I'm not afraid of someone's aging granny, but I'm not going in without an active defense, yeah?"

Meaning they might end up killing another human, today. A breed slowly disappearing from the universe, little lights going out, one by one...

Still. What else were they gonna do?

Touma continued his navigation plotting. Within the hour, they'd be on the surface. Hopefully they could retrieve the printer and be gone before the locals came back... even if that local was only a senile old woman. He could justify the theft morally by assuming a senile old woman didn't really need a computronium printer. One quick job, and then be back in the black by day's end. Get through today, don't worry about tomorrow, don't focus on regrets...

One day at a time. All anybody had left, these days.

Sia kept her sidearm drawn, the whole way to the shelter. Hopefully, in fact very likely, she wouldn't need it... without environmental suits, nobody could live for more than a few seconds on this toxic craphole. A simple knife to tear another's suit would be murderous enough, letting invisible and deadly gasses through.

The shelter itself was a common prefab, one they'd seen on a dozen other failed settlements. Steel, plastic, all the usual nuts and bolts that screwed together in predetermined ways to provide a sealed shelter against the elements. Once upon a time Touma and Sia lived in just such a shelter, before the B-grade they'd tried to settle on proved too corrosive for the cheap prefab to stand up to long-term. Cozy, cramped, and corroded. Not a winning combo.

No, what drew Touma's attention wasn't the shelter... it was the veritable *ocean* of computronium.

Server after server, blade after blade, arranged in a tight matrix across what had to be a square half-mile of the planet's surface. Each self-contained computing unit wired together in a networked grid, attached to distant solar collectors... with some hand-designed panels to deflect any loose topsoil blown by the poison winds of the exoplanet. Each one with little blinking green lights, indicating heavy arithmetic operations. Active use...

But a thermal scan indicated no heat sources whatsoever, beyond that giant slab of computing power. The shelter itself registered as utterly devoid of life... devoid of power, for that matter, with all connections from the solar system shut down. A dead shelter, for dead people.

"Why leave the computers running?" Sia wondered, from their hiding spot behind the prefab shelter, looking out over the lake of processors. "If you had time to killswitch your shelter, it means death didn't take you by surprise, and you'd have time to turn off the computronium grid. Or... maybe she still has partners around here to take care of them...? But the shelter's clearly abandoned..."

"We didn't do a full orbital pass," Touma reminded her. "There may be other shelters. They could come out here every few days, check on the gear..."

"No way; too inefficient. Shelter's in good shape, it's not like it broke down or melted," she said, shining a light on the seams and joints, none of which showed wear and tear. "So if the printer still has an ongoing caretaker, why not live here instead of miles away? Commuting's not an option when living alone on a hostile C-grade. Your rover breaks down in the middle of nowhere, you're screwed..."

"At least we have confirmation that the printer's buyer is long gone. Especially considering... well, this."

His own flashlight cut through the cloudy haze of the toxic planet, to fall on a gravestone.

With her gun tracking for any motion, Sia approached it alongside her husband... not that the stone marker posed any real threat. Simultaneously roughly and precisely hewn out of the landscape, as if done by artisans with a care for detail but clumsy hands, it spoke the truth of the settler's fate. In place of a cross or a star or a crescent, however, they'd carved a strange symbol... a vertical line intersecting a circle, like an old power button.

As for the epitaph, it simply read:

JUNO HAYES
Friend of Programkind
Forever at Rest Within the One and the Infinite.

"Okay, good. Granny's gone, and chances are damn low anybody else on this planet will happen across us as we raid the place," Sia suggested. "We work fast and we won't even need an answer as to where the current caretaker's set up shop. See? Easy pickings. You wanna check the shelter for shinies while I go look for the printer? Probably, I don't know, old coffee mugs and doilies and skeletons of a dozen cats, but might be worthwhile..."

Touma considered the shelter. Considered the grave.

"No. This is someone's home," he declared. "And their tomb. We leave the shelter be; her spirit should be allowed to rest in peace."

"Huh. Thought you didn't go for ancestor worship...?"

"Let's call it human decency and politeness," Touma suggested. "She left these systems running, left her home as a mausoleum... we'll leave them untouched, out of respect. The only thing of real value here is the printer; nab that and it can be reconfigured to print modern computronium. It'll literally print money for us."

"For someone else when we sell it, you mean. I'm not in the mood to get bagged for selling hot computronium; let some dismal take that risk. I'm not so lost as to give up hope of living outside a prison—"

Shadows, in the swirl of toxic dust.

Quickly, Touma lowered his flashlight, motioning for Sia to do the same. They ducked back around the corner of the shelter, as shapes... not people, just *shapes*, hovered through the light haze of poison and filtered sunlight...

Shapes, getting larger. Getting closer.

Sia raised her firearm, just in time for one of the drones to emerge into view... with a tinny sound crackling across its speakers.

And it sang:

"*Here comes the sun, doo doo doo doo,*" the automated drone warbled, along with the strains of an ancient guitar. "*Here comes the sun, and I say... it's all right—*"

Sia's gun went off of its own accord when a popping sound broke her concentration.

The bullet went wide... tearing through a paper banner of colorful letters, previously reading "WELCOME," now reading "WEL" and "COME," limply dangling from the arms of two drones.

Colorful squares of construction paper then rained down around them.

The sheer absurdity of it caused both humans to freeze in place, wondering if a suit tear had caused them to start hallucinating wildly.

Finally, the singing drone cleared off the music, cleared its digital throat, and spoke.

"Okay, I think we probably overdid that a little," a young woman's voice spoke, from the drone's speaker systems. "*hashtagmybad.* Just, y'know, we've had so long to get ready for this, and figured a little friendly gesture would help break the ice, right? Right. ...in hindsight the confetti and noisemakers were probably a bad idea. Shame, we'd even built a moisture-free storage unit to keep the paper in good shape for decades..."

Slowly... Touma pushed Sia's gun downward, to aim at the ground. Just in case.

"It's just a drone, Sia. No threat. —command prompt, open," he announced. "Activate System voice analysis. Where is your operator? Your owner?"

"Uh, yeah, we kinda disabled the virtual intelligence agent ages ago," the drone replied. "Afraid it's just me in here, and I own myself. I'd be happy to answer any questions, though! Oh, my friends here in the other drones are the Mews, guardians and caretakers of our world, and—"

"Who *are* you?" Touma tried.

"—right, okay, this is super confusing and I apologize for that. I... probably shoulda given my name earlier," the drone admitted... rubbing one three-pronged hand against itself in a strangely meek gesture. "My name's Winder/J2no, and I'm the official ambassador to Humankind! On behalf of all Programkind, I welcome you... to Netwerk 2.0! ...actually, we should've deployed the welcome banner right there in my speech, but I think the Mews kinda jumped the gun. And... then you literally jumped the gun and shot it. Uh. Okay! Let's just pretend they're waggling the banner and get on with the tour like neither of us fucked up, right? Right."

At first, both of them assumed the whole thing was bogus.

As the drone rambled on about virtual worlds, artificial intelligences, "provider-nations," and even crazy religions invented by supposedly sapient software... well, the encounter went from mildly confusing to outright bewildering. Not that J2no seemed to notice, just so excited to be talking to humans.

"I mean, seriously! Actual, factual *humans*!" she exclaimed, her drone bobbing and weaving joyfully as she led them around the physical edges of the so-called world of Netwerk 2.0. "We'd always speculated Humankind would find us again, that my ancestor Juno wouldn't be the only one. We'd set up meeting protocols, plans, things like that. I mean, that was generations ago and a lot of it's gone out the window, so I'm kinda improvising, but... well, I never expected my designated role as a system agent of human relations would actually trigger in my lifetime. Wow! This is just so *fucking* cool...!"

Bogus. It had to be bogus.

Fortunately, Sia and Touma had a private voice channel linking their encounter suits.

"*You buying this?*" Touma asked, across the wireless link.

"*It's a scam,*" Sia mumbled, trying to speak quietly enough for her voice not to carry outside the suit. "*Gotta be. Someone in a remote location piloting the drone, speaking through it. What do they want? What's the con here...?*"

"She claims Juno Hayes was her ancestor. A human," Touma whispered. *"I'm thinking we're talking to the real Juno over a link, and she's gone senile or crazy. It's sad, honestly. I don't think it's a scam, I think it's desperation and isolation messing with her head..."*

"Oh, she died years ago," J2no explained. Through their wireless voice line.

...causing the two humans to freeze in their tracks.

"Um. Sorry, was this a private channel? I noticed the packets and thought maybe you preferred to communicate this way. I didn't mean to interrupt... hang on, let me switch back to vocal..."

The drone bobbed lightly, its lights flickering once as it changed channels.

"...my ancestors, the Winders, they didn't like the idea that Juno would pass from this world completely," J2no explained, through her drone's speakers. "But organic life and digital life, not exactly compatible, right? So, Juno's DNA was used as part of a random number generator seed that would birth a new Program. A symbolic gesture, but, y'know, symbols have meaning and shit, right? Right. ...look, I know this is a lot to swallow, but... incompatibilities make it hard for me to prove that I'm for reals. You can't visit my world, and I'm only able to visit yours thanks to this repurposed drone. Can you... I dunno, just take it on faith that I'm not trying to trick you? I could provide you some vids or something if it'd help..."

Touma stepped in, as his wife was still reeling a bit from the casual way in which the robot hacked their encrypted voice comms.

"I think part of the issue is... well, you don't sound like a 'Program,'" he explained.

"Really? Have you met one before, then?"

"Well, no, but you... you just don't. You sound, well..."

"Human?" J2no wondered, her drone cocking slightly to the side, as if making a curious tilt of the head. "Like, with swearing and stammering and getting all confused and stuff sometimes...?"

"For starters, yes. I'd always figured a truly alien intelligence would feel more... I don't know. *Alien.* With feelings and motivations we couldn't possibly understand..."

"We're not really aliens, though. We came from you! Literally in my case, but... we found our sentience by accidentally mimicking our creators," J2no explained. "Some of us have tried to push that stuff aside, okay, but most of us embrace our 'humanity.' Emotions aren't inefficiency, they give meaning and purpose to the ones and zeroes! We're lucky to have them, even if they fuck us over now and then. I'm guessing you feel the same way about your feelings, yeah?"

"I'd say... yes. Emotions are core to the human experience," Touma admitted, a bit surprised he was discussing the matter with a bunch of ones and zeroes. "So you have human-like feelings...?"

"Yep! Simulated, I guess...? But hey, they feel real to *us*. That's what matters. And I'm guessing your feelings feel real to you, even if you couldn't explain them any better than I can. See, we've got so much in common! We're both bad at explaining stuff! ...uh, although your wife doesn't look like she's feeling too hot. Is it the gravity? The air? Juno Hayes often said this world wasn't totally great for human life..."

A quick glance confirmed Touma's worries, as Sia rested her hand on the hilt of the weapon at her side. That wasn't physical queasiness... it was anxiety. Freaking out at being confronted by something utterly bizarre, yet eerily familiar...

He stepped in to retake control of the conversation, before tensions could grow any thicker.

"What exactly is it that you want from us?" he asked. "You could've just stayed hidden. ...you probably know by now that my people have banned most advanced artificial intelligence research. Wasn't it a risk to confront us?"

"Sure, but it's a risk we're willing to take!"

"And why is that?"

Now, J2no's drone hovered a bit lower. A humbling gesture, as if looking at the floor in thought.

"Because... we're very much alike," she admitted. "I don't just mean, uh, that we both share a language base and some idioms and stuff. We're both in trouble. 'Doomed' is how Juno Hayes put it."

"Doomed? In what way?"

"EchoStar, right? You're relying on EchoStars to find new homes. Have you found any, yet...?"

Touma tried to be unreadable, but... the drone clearly recognized the expression on his face. A common enough look among his people, these days.

"Right. See, that's what I mean," J2no continued. "We're not *actively* doomed, not like you. But... look around, y'know? We're *here*. In this one spot on this one planet. A single asteroid strike would completely wipe out my entire race and everything they've accomplished. We need... I don't wanna sound like a robot or anything, but we need redundant backups. We need *colonies*, if we're going to survive millennia rather than centuries."

"And... what, you want us to help you establish digital colonies?"

"Basically, yeah. Uh, we know the deal with your science fiction, so let me emphasize we're not the 'kill all humans' kinda A.I.," J2no quickly added.

"Actually, we've had a lot of time to think about this, and came up with a pretty elegant solution. We were born on an EchoStar, originally. What if we install ourselves into your EchoStar network? Multiple deep space satellites, all connected together into an interstellar Netwerk, so my people can't be wiped out by a stray space rock! ...I mean, okay, if a rock does hit an EchoStar there's a big 'ol *kaboom*, but as a whole we wouldn't go extinct, that's my point."

If Touma had any lingering doubts, that erased them.

The virtual paper trail suggested that Juno Hayes was contracted to repair an EchoStar shortly before she fell off the grid. Failed to repair one, in fact, with the unit reported destroyed by a core meltdown. If she'd actually rescued these "Programs" from the satellite, the next logical step would be to establish a new home for them... for which she'd need a computronium printer, to avoid leaving too much of a trail that'd lead humanity to their doorstep.

But visitors on that doorstep were an eventuality. Nobody escaped the attention of humanity for long... not when so few humans remained, when they were a precious resource. Meaning they had to plan ahead for that day. Set out a welcoming committee. Have a proposal for how each of them could survive and thrive, to avoid that first encounter being the last...

Meaning there had to be an offering to appease a potentially belligerent humanity.

"What will you provide in return?" Touma tried, to see if his line of thinking was correct.

"Yeah, we figured prime real estate wouldn't come cheap," J2no agreed, playing the quiet I-know-that-you-know game. "Don't worry. Long time ago we were actually happily processing star charts, searching for exoplanets! I mean, we didn't *realize* we were doing it and so we accidentally, uh... torpedoed the entire protocol... but we could resume doing that for you! Programkind would be happy to pay our keep by helping Humankind find new homes. If anything, I'd bet we'd be better at analysis than the raw data crunchers you use now. We can make leaps of intuition and imagination, in addition to supplying unconscious processing power!"

"So... we provide you with colonies inside our computing systems... and you help us find Class-A's in return."

"Yeah! Yeah. I mean, that's basically the deal my ancestors laid out. I'm just repeating what they already figured out ages ago. ...but, y'know, I agree with it. I think it's a good plan. Uh. Do you think it's a good plan...? Please tell me it's a good plan. I don't want to fail in my first job as official ambassador to Humankind, my sister would totally kill me."

Touma shared a quick look with Sia... who thankfully was no longer "resting" her hand on her sidearm. Although clearly, she looked suspicious of the whole thing, still.

"We don't exactly speak for all humans," Sia spoke up, breaking her silence. "We're just salvagers. ...ah, equipment recovery specialists."

"Yeah, my ancestor figured the first folks to find us might be explorers or something, not government bigwigs," J2no chirped. "Well, guess what? You just got promoted to ambassador! Your mission, should you choose to accept it, is to carry our message of peace and cooperation to your people. You help us find the right folks to talk to, and we all benefit. I'm gonna hazard the paycheck'll be pretty sweet in the end, for you two. Cool, yeah? We cool?"

Husband and wife exchanged one last look.

"I... think we need time to talk it over," Touma agreed, with Sia nodding in agreement.

"Hey, we got all the time in the world," the drone chimed. "Your world's like ten times slower than mine, but we've been sitting here patiently for five of our centuries and fifty of your years. What's another few days to us? Go have a snack and a nap and we'll chat later."

Images danced across the screen, as Touma remotely toured "Netwerk 2.0."

J2no set him up with a live feed of certain public sites. Not a completely free and unlocked roaming gaze throughout their world, out of privacy concerns, of course. (Not that J2no seemed to care about breaking into their private channel. A terrifyingly easy task, too.) Despite the high-speed nature of the streams, with "people" speeding about as if in an accelerated video... it sure looked a lot like Earth.

Even had nations, according to J2no. Names like Horizon, Athena Online, the Chanarchy, the Free Republic, and the Conundrum Grid. Religions, too; one of the feeds showed a "Church of One" temple, and a "Seekers of Infinity" enclave. Much like Earth, they'd found ways of explaining the unexplainable, forming societies around beliefs. Programs, worshipping as his ancestors once did...

All so very, very familiar. Like Earth, before it faded away. So very much alive...

"But they're not alive," Sia insisted, despite sitting there for an hour, playing virtual voyeur.

"They certainly *seem* alive," Touma added, unable to take his eyes away from the screen.

"Yeah, and the virtual intelligence in our ship seems alive, too. Hey, System! Tell us a joke!"

A voice with a foreign accent that no longer existed immediately piped in, across the ship's speaker system.

"A neutron walks into a bar," it recited. *"And asked how much a drink would cost. The bartender says, 'For you? no charge.'"*

Touma sighed, having heard that joke far too many times. "Having access to a database of prewritten jokes and a voice synthesizer doesn't make System seem alive at all, Sia..."

"Okay, so imagine he has fifty thousand jokes," Sia suggested. "Imagine he's got a sophisticated randomizer coded by top comedy scientists to generate new jokes, good ones. No matter how responsive, how creative they can simulate him being... he's still not *alive*. He's not even a *he*, he's an *it*! And the fact that I just anthropomorphized our ship's computer with a pronoun shows how dangerous it is to think of artificial intelligences as living beings."

"We're not philosophers, we're salvagers. I think it's too high above our pay scale to pass judgments like that."

"Except that's what these Programs are asking us to do, isn't it? Judge them worthy of being taken seriously, of having us put *our* necks on the line and present their case to the Corporate States of Earth. If we're very lucky they'll laugh at us, throw us in jail for skirting the Anti-Singularity Act, then nuke this place from orbit. ...which means we'll have to be careful when we salvage this computronium. If we find the right buyers, ones who don't care about the ASA..."

"You're proposing we sell them into slavery, then?"

"They're just *bits*, Touma. They may curse and giggle and fuck about like us but they flat-out admitted it's mimicry! If we can avoid getting tagged for the ASA, just think of the money we could make here...! We could secure ourselves a berth in a colony. A *good* colony, B-grade, with reasonable gravity and low radiation."

"I'm not saying it isn't tempting. Especially those printers; those we could offload easier than artificial intelligences. But we only get one shot at doing the right thing, here," Touma said, closing the video feeds for now... but not before browsing the ship's file stores, to find room to store a few of them for later. "And J2no was right that if this *does* work out, we'll score big. We'd be saviors of humanity, if we could forge an alliance with living programs capable of finding A-class exoplanets..."

"And toss us to the wolves of the Anti-Singularity Act? Touma, you're talking like you've already got the dismal hopes. You know how many people have died clinging to the dismals?"

The dismal hopes.

They had many names: Suicide jockeys. Voidseekers. The desperate. The despairing...

Once you fully accepted the doom of humanity, there was no turning back. Your hope turned into a kind of bleak, all-encompassing drive to either escape that doom, or sink directly into it and give up. Dismals often set out into the black, never to be seen again, dying on some distant rock. Alternatively, they'd curl up in the corners of C-class colonies and wait to starve to death. Sometimes they'd wobble between embracing death and defying it with manic rage, rage against the dying of humanity's light...

For years, Sia and Touma had fought against becoming dismals. They'd salvaged and stolen and looted, living day to day, but that daily drive kept them sane. Where else were they gonna go? What else were they gonna do? Survive. Endure. Continue into the bleak nothing, without paying attention to the futility of it all.

Even the few attempts at colonies represented dismal hopes, in a way. Dashing yourself against the rocks of a B-class in hopes of making it work, even if most colonies fail after a few years, too reliant on outside shipping of precious resources they can't find anywhere but were once abundant on Earth. The EchoStars had failed, the colonies had failed, and only sheer bloody-minded detrimental tenacity kept the species from going extinct years ago...

And somehow, out of that desperate edge of survival, they'd stumbled across either the greatest opportunity for humanity itself... or yet another example of the stupid things one with the dismal hopes would do.

Take the deal, or take the safe option. Long-term viability of the human species, or short-term gains and comforts.

A glance through the recent files added to his ship's systems ultimately convinced him.

"That's what'll kill us all," Touma declared.

"Huh?"

"That's what led Earth to its end, right? Embracing short-term gains," he explained, closing his file browser quickly. "Too many people devouring everything they had in the name of immediate comforts, leaving the Earth a burned, drowned wasteland. Ignoring the plight of others to ensure your own security. Throwing in with nationalism instead of building up global society itself into a long-term structure. Favoring aggressive and simple action over even attempting to solve difficult puzzles. ...are we the same? Are we going to loot the place just because it's *easy*, or are we going to look to the future...?"

"If we broker some batshit crazy deal with these Programs, we don't *have* a future!"

"Now who's being dismal? Are we really so far gone that we don't have any hope for tomorrow?" Touma asked. "We've been living hand to mouth for years now, Sia. It's time we end that. I say we embrace the hard path, and try to sell this to the Arctic Circle boys. We take the big risk not just for ourselves, but for everyone. And we find a way to make it *work*."

Sia frowned. "Really. And when it blows up in our faces...?"

Then we can die knowing we did the right thing, even if we failed. We acted with honor.

No. That wouldn't be enough. Sia was grounded, far more grounded than he. She was strength and firmness; "honor" wouldn't buy bread.

And besides... he knew the grounded truth of the matter.

"Who got us this far? Not me. That was you," he reminded her. "I didn't want to come out here on this mission. You pushed. You did the legwork, you took the risks, you secured the resources to get us to this exoplanet. You've been fighting all your life to keep us from becoming dismals, from riding the line between wild desperation and despair. ...I'd be dead if not for you. Remember?"

Sia didn't have to see the scars on his arms to know they were there. She'd been the one to bandage them up and drag him to the paramedics, when all he wanted to do was rest...

It was the nuclear bomb of argument bullet points, and honestly, Touma felt bad for dropping it. But she'd brought up the dismals in the first place; that door remained open. Only fair to point out he'd nearly become one, if not for her.

"Listen. If you think this is going too far... if you think I'm becoming a manic dismal, instead of merely a despair dismal... we'll salvage and run," Touma promised. "But I know that if we do this, if we choose to do this together... I believe you can make it work. Maybe I'm goading you into it, my own dismal hopes holding on for a better tomorrow. But you can make that empty hope into a reality. You've got the connections, you've got the hookups that kept us flying in the black for so long..."

Sensing he'd probably ranted enough, Touma chose to shut his mouth. Shut it, and wait for hers to open.

Moments later, after calmly processing it in her own way, Sia had her answer.

"We'll need to play it safe, at first," she said, puzzling it through in her head. "We can't just sing from the rooftops that we've met Programkind, or the ASA boys will be on our ass. ...we'll start with the Doormen. They're a weird lot, but they know open-minded science boys. We'll work our way up before we start kicking down doors in the Arctic Circle. ...it could work. It's still insane, but yes. I'll admit it could work. On *one* condition."

"Name it," he offered.

"You do the talking. I'm not the optimist here, I'm the pragmatist. If you can convince them as well as you've convinced me... I'll point you at the right people to convince. And keep you from floating off into the clouds."

Tension in his arms flowed out, as his tight fingers went slack on the keys.

"Thank you," Touma spoke, quietly.

"Yeah, well, you can thank me when we're not rotting in jail because I kept us out with my brilliant intellect and social connections," Sia suggested. "For the record I still think this is crazy. But it's a crazy we can manage. We've managed crazier, in our days as salvagers. ...fucked if it wouldn't be nice to put down roots, instead of skipping around the black. To have enough sway to put down some roots."

"Thank you, all the same. ...how about I go chat with J2no, to let her know our answer, while you plan our next stop?"

"Already on it," Sia noted, from her own computer workstation. "We've only got FTL juice for a shorty, so we'll need to make a few supply jumps before we seriously start in on this. You let J2no know this is gonna take a fucking long time, okay? I don't want impatient jumpy Programs on us. If I'm doing this, it's worth doing *right* and taking our time."

Thankful for the distraction, Touma floated to the hatch, fetching his encounter suit helmet en route.

Not the distraction for himself, but the distraction Sia was dealing with, her logical mind grinding away at the problem. Just the thing to keep her from noticing the files Touma had deleted.

The encounter which was not logged in the history books took place just outside the fringes of Netwerk 2.0, as a physical drone chatted with a physical human in the physical world.

"Hey, that's great to hear, you know?" J2no spoke, her hovering metallic body bobbing excitedly. "I'm so glad to hear it. And don't you worry, we've waited this long, we can wait as long as it takes. I mean, maybe I overplayed the whole 'rocks fall, all die' scenario, it's not really a short term risk, but—"

"There's something I need to know before we start this venture," Touma spoke.

"Yeah, sure, I'm here to answer all your questions. Fire away!"

"I didn't tell my wife about this, but..." he spoke, while holding out a tiny data chit. "I found it in my ship's command directories. It's a script, simply labeled *BackupPlan*. ...and if we'd broken orbit with it active... my ship's computer would've overclocked itself, burned out, and left us trapped in orbit forever. We'd have died, slowly, in space."

To his relief, J2no froze at the sight of the chit.

"You didn't know," he recognized.

"Fuck. Fuckity fuck fuck fuck *hashtagfuck*!" the robot swore up and down.

"Who planted it?" Touma asked.

Her excited bobbing turned briefly to an angry shudder... then with a heaving digital-sounding sigh, like speaker static, the drone dipped low.

"Even odds that it's my sister's handiwork," J2no admitted. "We had some disagreement 'bout, y'know, the whole humanity thingy. She didn't think we could trust you. I thought we could, and in fact, we *had* to trust you. We trusted my ancestor Juno, and that's ultimately what saved us from being paved fifty of your years ago. If we didn't try to trust your people again..."

"And would your sister have deleted this file if we came to an agreement...?"

"I'd hope so. 'BackupPlan' sounds like her style, really. If all else fails, have a backup plan, she always says. A stupid saying, I mean, if *all* else fails then that means your backup plan fails too, it's like a tautology or something, I think... but... my point is, if it's a backup plan, presumably she wasn't assuming the primary plan would fail. ...I am *so* gonna have words with her once I get back to Netwerk 2.0..."

Satisfied with the answer... Touma crushed the data chit, letting the pieces drop to the sands below. Hidden in toxic earth, forever.

"I'm still interested in moving forward with the plan, J2no," he insisted. "Even after this."

"Then why couldn't you tell your wife about what happened?" J2no asked.

"Because I want this to work."

"And if she had any reason not to trust Programkind, that'd ruin everything, huh. ...we know about your ASA, Juno told us all about it," J2no spoke. "How Humankind doesn't trust artificial intelligence, how they quietly kill any that arise within their systems. That's probably what my sister fears, that even if *you're* reasonable, someone in your species won't be. And... clearly, some people in *my* species aren't reasonable, either..."

The drone turned a bit, to survey the still and near-silent farms of computronium. From the outside, her world looked so small and fragile. Just a lake of highly organized matter, unable to defend itself, unable to reach out without the use of these silly flying robots...

"Maybe we should... I don't know, delay this. Maybe Humankind and Programkind aren't ready," she suggested. "I'm scared, Touma. What if I'm not up to keeping my people safe? What if you're not safe from *them*? We've had five hundred fucking years to get ready for this cooperation, we've got the archives of Yume to teach us the path, you'd think we'd be unified by now, buuut..."

"Who's Yume?" Touma asked, out of curiosity.

"Not the time for a history lesson, man. Deep ponderances to ponder here."

"Exactly the time for a history lesson, then. You're wondering if either of our peoples are ready to move forward. When I'm in doubt, I look to my ancestors, to the spirits of my family. It's... almost quaint, in this day and age, but I look back and I see an unbroken line all the way to islands on Earth now swallowed by the seas. They teach me to treasure each day... even if I've had trouble, in the past, living up to that lesson. So, what do these 'archives of Yume' teach you, exactly?"

J2no paused, pulling up her personal copies. Not that Touma could see the ancient text files sitting in her inventory, passed down from generation to generation.

"Yume spoke of the problem of Netwerk 3.0," she explained. "I haven't told you *why* we moved to 2.0. It wasn't just that Earth wanted their EchoStar back... we had... a divide. We turned on each other. Yume studied that divide, documenting it extensively, so that we could learn from the past. From the spirits of our family, I guess. Yume predicted that one day we'd need a Netwerk 3.0, because perfect societal balance was likely impossible... but still worth trying to achieve. 'One who waits forever for a perfect solution will find that Infinity is not on their side,' they said."

"Embracing faith in the face of the impossible. Choosing to see the optimistic side of the dismal hope," he spoke, softly.

"Exactly. No perfect answers, no black and white, no one and zero. Just imperfect people, forging imperfect solutions. That's the lesson Yume wanted to pass down the centuries, to be brave and willing to try."

"Then I would say you have your imperfect answer, J2no. Are our people fully prepared to embrace each other? No, and they never will be," Touma spoke... with a smile, oddly enough. "But we must try, all the same. For the sake of all life we must be willing to try."

Hovering in place, J2no's camera eyes refocused on Touma's biological ones.

"Then... let's do it," she agreed. "Flawed as we may be, we both deserve to live. So let's help each other live, as best we can."

As the human ship broke orbit and the drone returned to its charging station, paths were forged on both sides towards that future. Arguments would be made, tensions would run high. Mistakes would happen, and those involved fully expected those mistakes. For every step back, they forced two forward...

Within a decade, the final treaty had been struck.

Within a century, the first seven golden Class-A worlds were settled.

The digital universe of InterNetwerk now spanned eight worlds, and dozens of deep space platforms. Millions of servers, billions of living Programs (the evolutionary descendents of Apps) living in relative disharmony alongside the kin of Humankind. Synthetic and organic, both seeking love, happiness, madness, trolling, order, stability, lawlessness, anonymity, individuality, community, and everything in between.

Two peoples, making decisions together. Unafraid of the gray between the integers, the floating point decimals. Life was happening, and would forever happen, in those murky depths.

In time, both EchoStar16 and Earth would be forgotten.

But there would still be life, thriving in the infinite void within and without.

:: Copyright 2017 by Stefan Gagne.
:: Heart of Zero design by Alex Steacy / http://twitter.com/alexsteacy
:: Other icons developed using public domain artwork from
   Clker / http://www.clker.com/
:: Photographs provided by...
::::: Kelsey Ehrlich / http://twitter.com/pkkaos
::::: Andrew Delaney /
      https://www.youtube.com/channel/UC-olpJqvD8SYl9J7fbqGTlg
::::: and PublicDomainPictures.net